KNIGHT GAMBIT

By

Harry Armstrong

Copyright C Harry Armstrong 2024

The right of Harry Armstrong to be identified as the author of this book has been asserted in accordance with the Copyright, Design and Patents Act 1988. While some real institutions are referred to provide context, the narrative is counter-factual. All characters and events described in this book are fictional; and any resemblance to actual persons, living or dead, is purely coincidental.

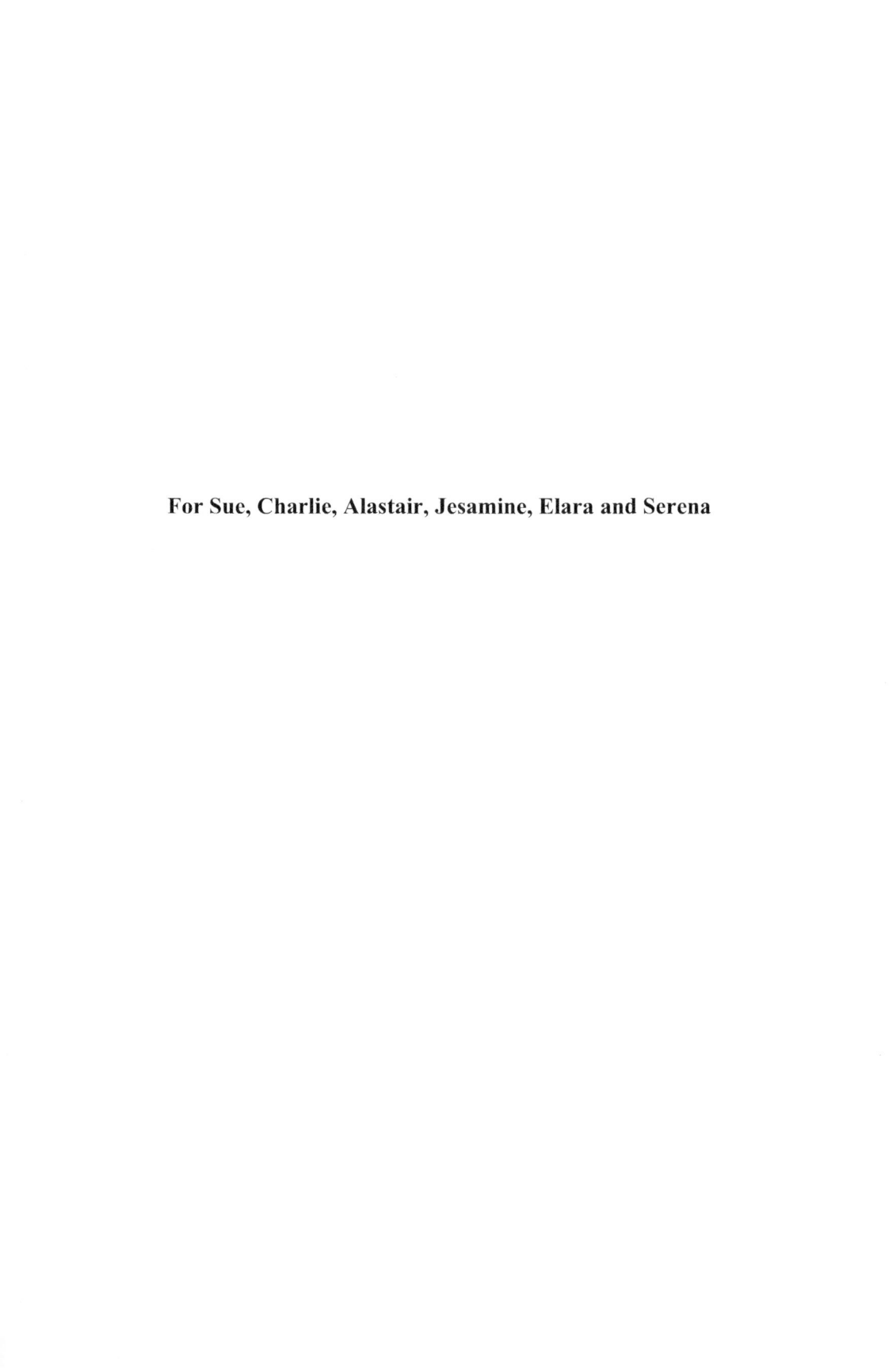

For Sue, Charlie, Alastair, Jesamine, Elara and Serena

CONTENTS

prologue	1
Chapter 1	5
Chapter 2	10
Chapter 3	15
Chapter 4	22
Chapter 5	26
Chapter 6	32
Chapter 7	37
Chapter 8	41
Chapter 9	44
Chapter 10	52
Chapter 11	59
Chapter 12	66
Chapter 13	70
Chapter 14	75
Chapter 15	78
Chapter 16	81
Chapter 17	85
Chapter 18	91
Chapter 19	100
Chapter 20	108
Chapter 21	114
Chapter 22	122
Chapter 23	125
Chapter 24	129
Chapter 25	134
Chapter 26	142
Chapter 27	147
Chapter 28	152
Chapter 29	159
Chapter 30	163
Chapter 31	173
Chapter 32	182
Chapter 33	188
Chapter 34	203
Chapter 35	209
Chapter 36	214
Chapter 37	218
Chapter 38	222

Chapter 39	228
Chapter 40	234
Chapter 41	239
Chapter 42	243
Chapter 43	247
Chapter 44	254
Chapter 45	261
Chapter 46	269
Chapter 47	277
Chapter 48	281
Chapter 49	286
Chapter 50	298
Chapter 51	302
Chapter 52	307
Chapter 53	316
Chapter 54	323
Chapter 55	328
Chapter 56	333
Chapter 57	340
Chapter 58	347
Chapter 59	355
Chapter 60	360
Chapter 61	367
Chapter 62	372
Chapter 63	379
Chapter 64	388
Chapter 65	393
Chapter 66	399
Chapter 67	404
Chapter 68	409
Chapter 69	415
Chapter 70	424
Chapter 71	429
Chapter 72	436
Chapter 73	445
Epilogue	451

PROLOGUE

00.01 Hours 4th November 2014

53 degrees 40 minutes North, 5 degrees 34 minutes West

Ray Simpson, Drilling Director of the gas exploration rig *Ocean Enterprise II,* looked at his watch, noticed with some satisfaction that, at a minute past midnight, his eight-hour shift had just ended, and looked around for his deputy, Jan Lundquist, who would now take over for the next shift. Given Lundquist's reliability, he would have been surprised if there were no sign of him and, true to form, he saw the large, rather shaggy outline materialising from the ground level of the accommodation block on the rig, ready to supervise the next eight hours of relentless drilling in the never-ending hope of finding new sources of gas in commercially exploitable quantities.

Simpson and Lundquist had a good working relationship but were both rather taciturn by nature and so gave each other the merest of nods of acknowledgment. After 52 days of failing to find any sign of the gas deposits, which the company's geologists had said ought to lie below them, this was sufficient to let Lundquist know that nothing of interest had materialised in Simpson's eight hours of supervision of the drilling. In these circumstances, the only matter of interest for Lundquist was the weather, and this he could very well see for himself. Though blustery it was, for once, quite a fine, clear night. There would, no doubt, have been a rather starry sky for them to see were it not for the extremely powerful arc lights which surrounded the drilling well head, making visibility as good as, or better than, in the middle of a summer's day.

Simpson extracted his flash drive from the hand-held computer, which was used by each shift supervisor to record any events pertaining to the drilling and handed the computer to Lundquist.

"I'll see you tomorrow" was the extent of his greeting. Lundquist merely nodded again, and Simpson set off for his own accommodation unit, leaving the team of eight men operating the drill head to carry on under his deputy. They would finish their shifts at various two-hour intervals to provide a total 24/7 overlapping continuity of operations except for major maintenance or damage.

At forty-seven, Simpson was a well-respected veteran on exploration rigs, but despite this, or perhaps because of it, he found the current assignment extremely frustrating. This was not entirely due to the failure of his team to discover any signs of gas deposits – he had often had that experience in the Gulf of Mexico, in the Far East, and in the North Sea. Rather, it was the failure given the very confident geological assessments that had been prepared before operations began. Earlier surveys over a considerable period had led the company, EnergiCorp, to be considerably more confident than usual that the rock strata they had plotted and analysed and modelled, using some of the most highly sophisticated computer programs anywhere in the world, contained within them large quantities of trapped gas that, once found, could be recovered, probably quite easily given the shallowness of the Irish Sea and its relatively protected nature. Though Simpson, as the man responsible on site, had been slavishly following very well-established methods of coverage of the seabed, he couldn't entirely shake off the feeling that, given what the computers said, the fact that the supposed reserves had not been found was somehow a failure on his part. His progress, or rather lack of it, was reported back to the head office every day, where more modelling and remodelling of what rock and other strata he had found were rapidly carried out and, where appropriate, new instructions forwarded to him, but all yet to no avail. He knew there was some time still to go before the company would call it a day, at least another month or two, but it was not getting any easier.

Simpson strode slowly back from the drilling area, across a metal bridge linking it to the accommodation area and headed for his unit on the second of six floors. The deck level floor housed several general facilities, including the canteen, and the senior drilling operatives were on the first floor up to give the quickest access to the drilling head if anything went wrong. With space at such a premium, the accommodation for most of the workforce was meagre. Still, Simpson, as Drilling Director, had a study-cum-living room in which he could, where necessary, conduct small meetings, a separate bedroom, and a very definite perk of the job, his own, albeit very tiny, bathroom.

Once in his unit, he removed his hard hat and then, slowly and methodically, stripped off all his equipment, protective clothing, and thermal underwear, positioning it all in the spaces designed for each, and had a shower. He made some tea, filled in a brief written log, more a habit from his early days than was necessary now, set his alarm, and climbed into his bed. As always, he started to read, but the books he chose lasted him a very long time as he rapidly drifted off to sleep. It vaguely crossed his mind that he perhaps needed a session with the geologists in their comfortable computer-filled office in a large company building just opposite Reading railway station. What he could infer from the drilling operations counted for very little in comparison with the analytic techniques available to the geological team, but years of experience, and not a little geological knowledge of his own, acquired both formally and informally over the years had, on occasion, provided some useful input and a significant steer to the continually evolving process of mapping the earth's structure under the sea bed. He might just suggest it tomorrow.

He had been asleep for a little under two hours when a knock on his door woke him. It was from a very deep state of unconsciousness, but a lifetime in his line of work trained one to be instantly alert to anything even slightly unusual – and this was unusual. He shouted a loud 'yes' as he swung out of bed and saw that it was a young Canadian, Chris Hallon, and a member of the three-man support group that backed up the drill head team with everything from spare parts and standard maintenance checks to refreshments. Hallon stood in the doorway, his body tense and his face animated.

"Jan thinks you should come down, boss," he said.

"I guess that's straight away," replied Simpson, more to himself than to Hallon, as he started to get back into his rig suit.

"Oh, yes, boss, definitely, straight away."

PART ONE

CHAPTER 1

Four hours earlier, and eleven hundred and sixty-five miles due East, Richard Warburton, second attaché at Her Britannic Majesty's Embassy in Moscow, had walked out of the large private dining room of the Four Seasons Hotel, a short distance from Red Square, and settled into a seat in the comfortable bar/lounge area. He and Simpson did not know each other and, indeed, neither would ever have any clue that the other existed, but their respective experiences this night would come to be inextricably linked, with consequences far beyond anything that either could ever have envisaged.

Because he was rather vaguely named as a second attaché at the Embassy, it was normal for people to assume that Warburton was, in reality some sort of intelligence officer, gathering, if not the military or atomic secrets of the Cold War period, then at least political or perhaps even economic intelligence on Russia, its politicians, its resources, policies and more. Warburton did not perhaps always do quite as much as he could to dispel this idea, but the truth was rather more prosaic. He was, in fact, a relatively low-level administrator and factotum at the Embassy, spending most of his time promoting trade and other business interests of British businessmen and women in Russia. No-one at the Embassy was entirely immune to the expectation that they would keep their eyes and ears open and report back anything that might be of more specific interest to the British Government. Still, in nearly three years Warburton had not come across anything more than a smattering of previously unknown business interests or connections of a few Russian industrialists with whom he had come into contact in the normal course of his work.

Warburton would be the first to admit that he had a rather bland appearance - average height, short brown hair, a slightly too round face he always thought, but not without some character. What he did not realise was that he also had that indefinable air, not arrogant, not even objectionable but for some of his colleagues, quite irritating that was only produced by a British upper-middle-class upbringing and a good public-school education in his case Stowe School. Thirty years before, most of the personnel in the Foreign Office would have displayed the same. Now, he was a member of an endangered species, and maybe the foreign nationals he spent his time dealing with didn't even notice - it was such an English thing. But it was part of what made him tick, and smoothed his way through life, not a very dynamic or inspiring figure, but effective in what he did. His superiors in the Foreign Office well recognised this, and he got considerable satisfaction from being an efficient cog in an important wheel. Where he might go from here, he did not know, and it was not a great concern to him.

Now, as Warburton entered the lounge of the hotel, he felt nothing but relief that another extremely long official dinner for business leaders from both the UK and Russia, with a few members of the Embassy staff to oil the wheels, in all senses, had finally come to an end. The food and wine had been excellent, in fact some of the best he had experienced since coming to Moscow, but inevitably the speeches were too many, too long, especially when most had to be translated, were utterly bland and punctuated with round after round of toasts in Vodka which, however good it was, dulled the wine and, apart from the caviar, most of the food as well.

The event had finally wound to its end, with bonhomie and protestations of undying devotion to all and sundry in relation to the new business links forged earlier in the week, the guests had gone, and Warburton was free to head back to his flat in the northwest district of the city. His wife, Melissa, might well still be awake, as she was not a natural sleeper, but he had mentioned the usual warning that, with these types of events, there was no knowing when he would be back. Having facilitated at least a hundred such events to date, if not two hundred, his wife knew the score and would not wait up especially, not least because she would have a full day of translation work the next day. She was an excellent translator, enjoyed the work and was well paid, but at some level they both knew that it was also to assuage her sadness at being separated for long periods of time from their two sons, both at an expensive boarding school in England, courtesy of the British taxpayer, but only infrequently with their parents and less and less influenced by them as they respectively approached and embarked on their teenage years.

Warburton suddenly realised how tired he felt and decided it would be good to have what he would regard as a proper digestif before getting a taxi home. He took a seat, caught a waiter's eye, and decided to order a small single malt, no water, no ice. He remembered from previous occasions that the hotel had a very extensive selection of such whiskies and, by the time the waiter arrived, was anticipating a respectful inquiry as to which malt he would like. Not a great connoisseur, however, Warburton mentioned the first one that came into his head, settled back into his seat, and observed the room.

The scene was one with which he was all too familiar. Perhaps a dozen or more people, all in suits, though most these days without ties, mainly in twos and threes, having late-night drinks, a few waiters going to and fro, a little light music in the background. Comfortable, with some elegance, just a little soporific if on one's own. It would be a short period of relaxation for him before heading off into the night. The waiter brought his drink, along with a selection of nuts, which he certainly didn't want, and he gently sipped the Scotch.

He was close to finishing it when a tall, well-proportioned, and undoubtedly attractive woman, aged maybe late twenties, walked into the lounge. She would have made quite a striking entrance at any time, but this was substantially enhanced by the way she was dressed, in a short and quite tight skirt, knee-length leather high-heeled boots, and a light-coloured blouse which, in the circumstances, could not be quite as unbuttoned as it was by accident. The ensemble was, if not particularly elegant, certainly expensive, and finished off with a matching bracelet and earrings which, for all Warburton could tell, might just be very expensive as well.

Having taken in the new arrival, he looked away quickly, partly because he did not want to be seen gawking at such an obviously sexy sight but also because he did not want to risk eye contact with someone whom he instantly knew as everyone else in the room instantly knew, was a high-class prostitute, probably Russian but quite possibly from one of the Republics of the former Soviet Union, and a far from unusual presence in an expensive, centrally located hotel late in the evening. In fact, few such hotels did not have at least a small number of such working girls, as they tended to be referred to by the businessmen who made up most of the hotels' clientèle. They were rarely alone for more than a minute or two, though quite often, their contact with a potential customer went no further than a shared drink or two, either because the latter got cold feet or, more likely because he had the price whispered in his ear. Warburton's knowledge of such matters was entirely second if not third hand. Still, stories were rife of the large sums that were sought and extracted for an hour or so of uninhibited sex in an otherwise rather lonely hotel room.

Curiosity led him to take a couple of surreptitious glances in the woman's direction while appearing to be focused on downing his Scotch. He was aware that she had spotted him, a man alone late into the evening and, therefore a potential customer, but he kept his gaze averted. Very soon, as expected, she locked onto someone else, achieved by the simple expedient of setting herself down opposite one of the few other men on his own in the room. More drinks were ordered, cigarettes lit up, and some sort of conversation started, all apparently - but only apparently – unnoticed by anyone else in the lounge.

Matching his continuing curiosity to see how things would develop was Warburton's relief that the woman had not approached him. It had only ever happened to him once before, and he had not really known how to deal with the situation. He couldn't respond to her request for a light, as he didn't smoke, but he didn't feel he could ask the woman, whose intent was quite manifest from the start, to leave him alone. They'd had a drink, but then, politely as he could, he had said he must be going, left far too much money on the table, and departed. His new companion had merely smiled a good night with no fuss or commotion, and he felt he had been rather silly in not handling the encounter more maturely. But he'd made sure that he never encouraged such an occurrence again.

Sneaking another look, he saw that the woman was clearly making headway with her potential customer. Another round of drinks had been ordered, and their conversation was becoming slightly more animated and slightly more intimate as well. She had a very natural smile and must have known how good her shoulder-length hair looked as she, oh so accidentally, swished it around her neck and very beautiful features. Warburton rather wanted to see what the outcome would be, but he didn't want another drink, and he felt it really was time to go. He got the bill, signed for his drink, and got up to leave. As he did so, he saw the woman and the man she had approached both stand up as well and start to head for the lifts. So, she had been successful, and her new acquaintance was no doubt in for a very good time if his wallet could stand it. As Warburton headed for the revolving doors to the street, his path took him quite close to the couple as they headed at right angles to him, she now holding her new partner's arm in a very casual manner.

As they passed, at no more than ten feet or so, Warburton was now able, in the deliberately rather dim lighting of the lounge, to see her more clearly, and he had the strangest feeling that he had seen her before. He felt himself staring at her, which, fortunately, she did not notice, and he thought that it must have been on another occasion in this, or perhaps another hotel, as she plied her late-night trade. But as he passed through the revolving doors, he told himself that that wasn't right. Something told him that she had looked different and that his recognition of her wasn't from observing a previous pick-up of the sort he had just watched.

As a porter summoned a taxi for him from a line of cars waiting off to the side of the forecourt, he racked his brains, but nothing came to mind. Oh well, maybe it was a case of false deja vu, which he had read about in a magazine – the brain registering something that the eye sees but then momentarily disconnecting from the sighting. The brain then registers it again and notes that it has seen the sight before but erroneously believes it is in its memory rather than from a millisecond before. The person has a clear sense of having had the experience sometime before, but it all stems from an unnoticed perception just a moment before. Maybe that is all it was, he thought, though why his brain should, even for a millisecond, lose sight of such an attractive woman, however bleak her intentions, was beyond him. He got into the taxi and headed home. His mind started to drift to his agenda for the next day: a few meetings, some paperwork, not undemanding but not particularly onerous either, another dinner in the evening but a much smaller affair than tonight's, for only eight of them, altogether more agreeable. The taxi reached his home, he paid off the driver, and headed for his front door. As he got out his key, it suddenly hit him.

"Oh my God," he said to himself, in what any observer would think of as a highly theatrical style, but it was what came out. "Oh my God," he repeated. He had just remembered where he had previously seen the Four Seasons hotel's lady of the night.

CHAPTER 2

Graham Seymour, formally known as the First Lord of the Treasury, but colloquially known throughout the world as Prime Minister, of the United Kingdom of England, Scotland, Wales and Northern Ireland, sat alone at the centre of the large coffin-shaped table in the Cabinet Room of 10 Downing Street. A tall, sturdily built man, with a rather grave, patrician countenance, accentuated by a strong aquiline nose and greying temples, he often worked there, liking the sense of space in the room, until, that is, it got filled up with cabinet ministers, for which purpose it was far too small. He always spent some time there, as now, before a cabinet meeting to clear his mind, review the agenda, try to pin down exactly what he wanted to achieve in the ninety minutes or so that they would all be present. How necessary this was he increasingly doubted. Very rarely was anything, still less anything important, decided at a Cabinet Meeting. Most were nothing more nor less than an opportunity for the PM, the Cabinet Secretary and various ministers to summarise progress on various issues, bring everyone else up to date and occasionally put a rubber stamp on the resolution of some interdepartmental tension.

Real policy conflicts or serious political divisions abounded, but were debated elsewhere in all but the most exceptional circumstances, sometimes in ministerial meetings but more usually in staff meetings, between advisers and, of course, in the media. Not for the first time, Seymour reflected that 'Cabinet Government' was no longer remotely appropriate a term for how the affairs of the nation were managed, though he had not as yet come up with an alternative term to describe the much more dispersed and rather chaotic process that had replaced it.

Due to start in a few minutes, the cabinet meeting would not be very different from any of the previous ones during this Parliament; Seymour considered himself well prepared with time to spare. So, again not for the first time, his thoughts drifted to the underlying depression he felt, not so much about the current position of the government which he headed. However, it wouldn't take much to go down that road – with moderate and more right-wing Conservatives increasingly at each other's throats and the Party, despite little effective opposition, doing rather poorly in the opinion polls. Rather it was a deeper, at once a more profound and more personal depression he felt. He was in theory, and probably in practice, the most powerful individual in the country, and yet he was struck again and again by how little he could influence the key issues of the day. His government had pursued significant reforms in education, welfare provision and the health service to name only some. While the jury was still out on all of them as to whether they would be successful, he took some satisfaction from how they were so far developing. And his Chancellor's steering of the economy back from the brink of disaster arising from the global financial crisis and the previous government's reckless economic policies was a major success, even if the economic benefits still needed time to filter through to the population. But, important as all this was, it did little to assuage his feeling of total impotence in the light of much graver issues, and three in particular with which he seemed to wrestle in his mind, day in day out, without any progress or even a glimmer of insight as to how matters might ever be addressed.

The issue that most directly affected his political future was energy – not so much, as previously, energy prices, which had eased - the result of China's slowdown, US fracking and, above all else, Saudi Arabia turning the oil taps on. Stock markets had responded less positively than expected, even though they would have responded badly to a big rise in energy prices; and Seymour hadn't any time for what he regarded as their ludicrous antics. He knew that the fall in energy prices was giving a very welcome boost to the economy. No, the problem, which was perhaps what the stock market was both anticipating and forewarning, was security of supply. Coal-fired power stations were now extinct; renewables were growing fast, but from a tiny base and, in any event were still too expensive. Nuclear could and should have been a core contributor to the UK's energy supply, but the development of the necessary power stations had been on hold for far too long. The contribution of existing nuclear stations was declining and it would be many years before new ones, now at last sanctioned and underpinned by astronomically high price guarantees, would make any difference to fuel supply. Gas was supposed to be the great salvation, and to some extent was; but, with North Sea gas supplies dwindling and Russian gas embargoed in retaliation for its seizure of the Crimea, the UK was increasingly in thrall to LNG, Liquid Natural Gas, shipped in from the Middle East in huge tankers.

But this supply would never be enough to solve the problem and, worse still, was now falling. The importance of these tankers had not been lost on Islamic terrorists based in Syria and Libya. The ships were not particularly vulnerable, hard to board, well defended and fairly indestructible; but, after several failed attacks, two had been successful, in that terrorists had captured the crews. They had achieved this by approaching each tanker in six small boats, each aimed at different parts of the tanker. They then fired small rockets up and over the railings of the tankers, with a rope and rope ladders attached. The rather minimal crews on board had been quite unable to deal with all the dispersed attacks simultaneously, and that had been enough for some of the terrorist units to swarm aboard. Well-armed, it was then easy for them to take control. It was what they did next that caused international outrage and severely disrupted the flow of LNG. The videos they released of what they did to the crews - no simple beheadings here but agonisingly slow deaths by fire, crucifixion or chain saw - had appalled the world, but very quickly extinguished the supply of men to crew such ships. There had been rapid deployment of equipment and tactics to defend the tankers, but to date this had had little impact on the supply of able seamen ready and willing to risk such terrible deaths. And so this supply of energy was not going to be the UK's salvation any time soon. With winter approaching, the forecasts clearly pointed to at least reduced power on the Grid, maybe intermittent energy supply failures, and longer term black-outs not far behind if the temperature was even a little lower than normal.

The one potentially bright spot in this depressing scenario was the prospect of developing shale gas supplies in the UK, and a number of fields had been identified. But the opposition from both local interests and the green lobby had been well organised, incessant and, based on numerous rather dubious scare tactics, highly successful. Even this might have been overcome until those opposed to shale had invoked the courts, whose judges, based on both UK and European law, had determined that few if any such schemes could go ahead for a period that stretched into the indefinite future. As if that wasn't enough, the government was also committed to reducing its dependence on gas as part of its international obligations towards reducing and ultimately offsetting climate change. The result was that, despite lower fuel prices and a return to reasonable economic growth, the population, not least the old and the poor, faced the real prospect of losing their lighting and heating, leaving many cold and some at risk of deteriorating health or worse. This, Seymour knew was an intolerable situation, and failure to keep the lights on would almost certainly lose him the next election.

The second big problem - and an additional frustration - was the knowledge that the UK's flight from coal, oil and gas didn't, to any significant degree, make much difference to another great issue of the times - climate change All the UK's efforts were fairly pointless, given the minimal contribution that the country made to overall global warning. But to have any clout at interminable international conferences, asking others, most noticeably the US and China, to rein in their pollution, you had to show that you were doing you bit. So, the UK had soldiered on, to the point where it could no longer be sure of maintaining energy supplies. The world was probably still going to a fiery hell at a rate of knots, and the UK with it; but it might be quite cold and dark on the way, and there seemed to be nothing that he or his government could now do about it.

And, just to make matters worse, the third problem was that the UK he cared so much about was likely to disintegrate. The Scots had voted in a referendum to stay as part of the UK, but the majority was so slim, far smaller than any opinion polls had predicted that, contrary to what he and many others had forecast, it had not remotely put the issue to bed for a generation. Rather it had stoked up the notion that independence for Scotland was now all but inevitable at some point fairly soon; and the only question was how long he could seriously delay another referendum which would almost certainly lead, after four hundred years, to a separate Scotland. In the wake of this, Catholic and Nationalist elements in Northern Ireland were now campaigning for their own referendum, seeking to break off from the UK and join the rest of Ireland, with the real prospect that the UK would be reduced to England and Wales; and who knew what the Welsh might start to contemplate then. There was the very real prospect that he would go down in history as the Prime minister who oversaw the collapse of the UK as a geographical entity, the impoverishment of its people, and its slide into global climate catastrophe. Not quite the agenda he had come into politics to promote.

It was a relief from such black thoughts when the Cabinet Secretary came into the room, followed fairly rapidly by a succession of cabinet members, each offering a polite 'good morning, Prime Minister' as they headed for their allotted positions at the table. None of the 'big three topics', as Seymour liked to think of them, would be discussed today. Given their insoluble nature it was probably just as well; and the matters that were on the agenda would at least be a welcome distraction for a while. He did, however, need to keep his wits about him. It was never far from his thoughts, nor that of the many political pundits in the Press and elsewhere amongst the commentariat, that he had become Prime Minister in miserable circumstances and, in the subsequent general election, had seen a substantial reduction in his party's parliamentary majority. His predecessor as Prime Minister, Alan Gerrard, had been murdered by a dissident IRA group, in revenge for what turned out to have been the ordering of the cold-blooded murder of five IRA members by Gerrard thirty years earlier, when he had been the minister responsible for domestic security, and for reasons that had more to do with his own career prospects than with any genuine threat to the UK.

Seymour, as Foreign Secretary at the time, and the most senior minister after Gerrard had, in the grief-stricken aura of the time, taken over the helm without opposition, but that was then and this was now. The party had lost ground under his leadership, had a majority of only twelve, and was currently, due to the austerity measures they had felt it was essential to implement, quite unpopular. The party would have to decide within the next twelve months or so who was to lead them into the next election and, while Seymour currently had the inside track, the tensions in the Party and the depressing results from opinion polls for well over a year now could easily lead to a leadership challenge within that time frame. Any such plotting would occur a long way away from the Cabinet Room, and yet a challenger would need to demonstrate in that arena that he had the standing, the authority, the manner even, to carry cabinet colleagues with him in; and that was something that Seymour knew he would have to look out for. And, if necessary, squash.

CHAPTER 3

Warburton quickly scanned the new emails he had received since the day before. Nothing looked pressing. He had got into his functional and comfortable but unprepossessing office earlier than usual, at a little after 8 am and, as soon as Hampton's secretary was in, fixed to see him as soon as possible, which was 9.30 am. James Hampton was the Deputy Ambassador in Moscow and, in essence the chief operating officer under the Ambassador. While the Ambassador dealt with all important policy matters, handled relations with the Russian government and acted as the UK's representative to the country, Hampton effectively ran the Embassy, its staff and all its operations. He had been a very successful and rapidly rising career diplomat in the Foreign Office, was still only in his late thirties, and was clearly destined for his first ambassadorial role fairly soon, even if in a relatively minor posting. He was, therefore, at least one or two grades above Warburton, but the hierarchical structure of the embassy was both rather flexible and fairly flat. Hampton knew Warburton reasonably well, and there was no great problem of protocol about Warburton going straight to him if a topic justified it.

Warburton was pleased that he could see Hampton so quickly but knew that the Deputy Ambassador was busy. Initial pleasantries would be very brief and he would need to be clear, succinct and to the point when he saw him. This would not be too difficult, however, given that he had been rehearsing what he would say for several hours the previous night; and, beyond that, had worked out what answers he would give to the most obvious questions that Hampton would have for him. He didn't feel wonderful after such a disturbed night, but a hefty shot of caffeine once he had got to the office and, more, much more than that, the excitement he felt at what he had discovered both served to make sure he was alert and functioning on all cylinders.

His own secretary arrived, and he explained that he had fixed an urgent appointment with Hampton, but gave no clue as to its purpose, and then tried for an hour or more to work through a normal routine, mainly of emails, diary work with his secretary and a couple of calls to other members of the embassy staff. Eventually time crawled to 9.30 am and he headed for Hampton's rather palatial office. Hampton's secretary waved him through with a smile, and only as he entered Hampton's room did the full import of what he was about to divulge hit him. Quite unexpectedly, his throat went rather dry, and a rather hoarse 'good morning' made him sound like he was going down with a cold or 'flu. Whether Hampton noticed this or not he couldn't tell, but showed no sign of doing so as he offered Warburton a seat across the desk from him.

Pleasantries were, indeed, brief. Hampton, a clearly rather handsome man, with powerful, craggy features, a rather intense look, and an athletic figure, reflecting a very successful sporting career at Cambridge University, merely welcomed Warburton in, though in a very friendly manner, and said that he understood that Warburton wanted to see him rather urgently. How could he help? Warburton launched into his prepared little speech.

"You remember the conference, reception, and dinner we held last June to promote British technology in environmentally sound municipal waste disposal. It was based on using microscopic bugs to break the waste down into ethanol which could be converted into aviation fuel – so, no land fill costs and a saleable energy bi-product – and we reckoned that there might be a significant number of Russian cities that might want to buy our technology?" He paused, less for an answer but just for acknowledgment that Hampton did remember the occasion. Hampton, whatever he might have been expecting, had not remotely thought that environmental waste disposal was the topic of the day; and it briefly flitted through his mind that Warburton might have slightly lost his marbles

"I remember, yes" he said, in a rather neutral manner, and let Warburton proceed.

"Well, then you will remember the Russian leading their delegation, their energy minister, Gudanov, Yuri I think." Hampton merely nodded. Warburton headed on. "He brought his wife and his daughter to the reception and closing dinner."

"I remember them too" said Hampton. "his wife was rather shy and mousy, probably didn't have much English, but the daughter was something to behold – not at all what any of us were expecting after a conference on waste disposal." He smiled, almost laughed.

"Exactly" said Warburton. "I can't remember the daughter's name, but I saw her late last night, in the Four Seasons hotel. She's a hooker. A very high class and, no doubt, very expensive hooker. I watched her pick some guy up last night and head off to his hotel room." For reasons he couldn't quite fathom, it seemed easier to refer to her as a hooker rather than a prostitute. The American term somehow seemed softer, more user-friendly than the British term, which sounded both nasty and prudish simultaneously.

Hampton had been paying reasonable attention to what Warburton had been saying, but now his manner evinced a new alertness which had certainly not been present before.

"Are you sure?" he asked.

"No question about it" replied Warburton. "I didn't recognise her at first, though I had a vague idea that I had seen her somewhere before. Then it hit me as I was heading home. She had her hair up at the reception and all down around her shoulders last night; and she was dressed quite differently – in fact very differently" he added with a knowing look, "but I was quite close to her as I left; and there is no doubt in my mind. She's not the sort you forget. It was only the very different circumstances that threw me to start with. It's her, no question."

"Do you think her father, or her mother for that matter, knows about this night time career?" asked Hampton. It was one of the many questions that Warburton has anticipated.

"I'll bet any money they don't" he said quite forcefully. "Gudanov is a rising star in Kremlin politics. He is urbane, well-educated and quite well-connected. He's ambitious too; and there is no reason why he couldn't fairly soon make it into the core of the very inner circle around the President. But having a daughter on the game, in the centre of Moscow, presumably quite often having sex with men who, in many cases will be foreigners, would be one hell of an embarrassment to him, and her; and even if he could ride it out, there is no shortage of other aspiring young politicians who would be more than happy to play that type of card and see Gudanov out of the race. Suppose foreign nationals are involved, and most of the clientèle at the Four Seasons are foreign. In that case, even if there is no great security issue about a minister of energy, he isn't going to go any further with that scandal hanging round his neck. So, if he knew about it he would have stopped her, I'm sure."

"I guess you're right" conceded Hampton. "I wonder what induced her to play such a dangerous game" he mused.

"I'm sure the money is huge" replied Warburton. "There's some very big bucks floating around a hotel like the Four Seasons any time of the year; but maybe there is an element or rebellion in it? You know, some of these Russians can still be quite medievally oppressive when it comes to bringing up their children; and it just doesn't wash, now that the kids have seen the decadent West."

"Ah, well, that's for her to know, not us" said Hampton. "Have you thought about how we might best use this information? I can't see that blackmailing the woman, threatening to reveal her little secret can gain us much." While Warburton had also anticipated this question, he was, for once, disappointed in Hampton. He clearly hadn't seen the potential of the situation though, to be fair, unlike Warburton, he had only had a couple of minutes to digest the news.

"No, no, that's not what occurred to me" he said, now getting quite animated. I thought we should let Gudanov know about it, and then we have some leverage against him, not letting the secret out as long as we have whatever suitable co-operation, or information that we might want. It might not be much now, but could be a lot more substantial later."

Two rather contradictory thoughts flashed through Hampton's mind. The first was that Warburton was more of a strategic thinker than he had ever previously given him credit for. He liked Warburton, and had a good opinion of him, but very much as a solid, dependable type who would never attain the higher reaches of the diplomatic service. Maybe, just maybe, he would have to revise that opinion. But the second was a fairly obvious objection to what Warburton had proposed, which he now voiced.

"I see where you are heading," he said "but the moment we notify Gudanov, he is going to pull his daughter off the street, or out of the hotels anyway, and lock her away somewhere, I don't know, send her off to Siberia perhaps, but he will get her out of the way; and then it's just a rumour hatched by the wicked West which he can deny for as long as it takes. We won't able to pressurise him."

Warburton registered that his first fit of disappointment at Hampton's initial reaction had been a little premature. The man was clearly thinking the matter through, but Warburton had thought such a problem through many hours before.

"Point taken," he muttered rather formally. "But what I had in mind was rather different. Last night was clearly not a one-off thing. She will be looking for clients again, maybe in other hotels, but I guess she will turn up again at the Four Seasons fairly soon. It's an obvious place to latch on to some big money. We should get ready for that, set someone up – a sort of reverse honey trap – as one of her customers, but in a room we will have bugged with audio-visual. Then we get her on tape, the more steamy the better, and let Gudanov have a copy. That should hook him don't you think?"

"You don't mean you......" Hampton blurted out, just beginning to imagine the prospect of the British Press get holding of the fact that Embassy staff were having sex romps with Russian prostitutes courtesy of the British taxpayer.

"Oh no, not at all" said Warburton, to Hampton's great relief. "Not quite my scene," he added with a deprecatory smile. "No, I thought we might recruit someone, specifically an American with CIA links of some sort - given the stand-off between Russia and the US at the moment over the Ukraine, and Syria, that is really going to up the stakes. It probably doesn't really matter much who, as long as we have the sound and the pictures." Somehow the former sounded vaguely more disgusting than the latter to Hampton, but he let it pass. He was too busy thinking about Warburton's proposal, while further ramping up his assessment of the man.

"I see" he said slowly, partly to give himself time to reflect. But he was never one to be slow on the uptake; and had already more or less formulated a way forward. "Yes, interesting. Leave it with me for twenty-four hours, to mull it over, and maybe I should talk to Six about this. It's more their end of the business."

"That did occur to me" Warburton inserted into his thinking. In fact, it was one of the bigger issues that had kept him awake so long the previous night. He really didn't want the Secret Service, otherwise known as MI6, intruding into this particular little game, partly for personal reasons, but for professional ones as well; and he now played that card. "But might I suggest that you don't mention it to them at all?" Hampton raised a querying eyebrow, but Warburton ploughed on quickly, before Hampton had time to speak. "If Six know about it, they will take it over, and then it will get more widely known. I'm sure they have all sorts of ways of keeping things secure, but the fact is that if they know about it then, sooner or later, news will spread. I'm not saying they have a mole or anything dramatic like that, but things have a way of leaking into the ether, and if that happens over this, then the Russians will just pull out Gudanov's daughter, which will be the end of the matter. If we keep this to ourselves, then there is no reason why anyone else should know. We will need a couple of techies to bug the room, but they needn't know why or what we come up with. That would just leave the 'plant', but if he has the prospect of rampant sex with a beautiful woman, all paid for, as long as it is kept secret, then I don't think we will have too much of a security problem there. I can run the operational side, and you would know all the information that might be helpful to us. Plus..." and this he had thought was the clincher, "we are more likely to get co-operation from Gudanov if he knows that it is a little private enterprise on the side by a couple of British diplomats than if he knows the UK's secret service is stitching him up."

He paused. He had made his pitch. It was now up to Hampton, to decide on the logic of what he had said, but also reflect on the bait being offered him - a private line into Kremlin thinking that he alone would control and have access to. For some while, Hampton said nothing. He looked briefly at Warburton but then his eyes seemed fixed on a point some way off into the middle distance. He folded his arms, breathed a big breath, and slowly exhaled. And then he nodded, partly to Warburton but also to himself. "Okay" he said quietly. "Let's do it that way. But it will raise some practical problems. We'll need resources to spot Gudanov's daughter again, for which I'll need a good reason; and I'll need to organise the techies, as you call them, to bug a room, which will be even harder to explain. So, let me think about how to fix these, though you might spend a little of today reflecting on the same two issues. And you will need to find your American." There was no mistaking that Hampton was leaving that aspect firmly in Warburton's lap. "Let's meet again at 9.00 am tomorrow and see what we have each come up with".

"I'll do that" said Warburton "and thanks, for supporting the idea I mean. I thought you might just shoot it down as too cavalier, or just not how we should...... approach.....such matters."

It was an indication of how little experience of such a world Warburton had that he had struggled to find the right word, or euphemism, for what was, despite its very patriotic motivation, illegal blackmail on foreign territory, which could probably wreck a family and quite possibly a promising career.

CHAPTER 4

Warburton arrived at Hampton's office on the stroke of 9:00 am. Neither had had the best of nights as they grappled with the implications of what they had tentatively agreed the day before, and Hampton had some strong coffee on the go. He eschewed any sort of welcome or small talk.

"Well, why don't you go first? What have you come up with?" Perhaps surprisingly, the question of who Warburton might get to act as the trap for Gudanov's daughter turned out to be relatively easy, assuming that the man he had in mind would agree. Still, he had a fairly comfortable feeling that he would. Harvey Green was a larger-than-life Texan whom Warburton had encountered while organising a trade fair in St. Petersburg a year or so previously. At first sight, Green was a caricature of a Texan - a large presence, with a slow drawl and, on occasion even a Stetson. He looked the archetypal red neck oilman but, in fact, ran a highly successful computer software company, which he had set up after some years working for a large US computer company, where he had an awesome reputation for being able to solve any and all IT problems no matter how difficult. He had never been an actual employee of the CIA. However, he had good contacts there, having carried out several highly confidential IT projects for them, of which they could deny any knowledge. His commitment and intelligence were demonstrated by the fact that, when he started trading with Eastern Europe and Russia, he quickly learned passable Russian. Not needing an interpreter in business negotiations endeared him to his Russian counterparts; and as he was fond of pointing out, he stood a much better chance of cutting out the bullshit. Needless to say, this aspect of his work meant that the CIA kept in close touch with him.

Warburton revealed his thinking to Hampton. "As the willing customer for Gudanov's daughter's services, I will put the proposition to Harvey Green, the IT guy you met at the US Embassy last Christmas. Not CIA, but close to. He's married, but she's his third wife and he told me that they are separated to all intents and purposes; and he's the sort of man who'd go for it. Anything in a skirt I'm told. He's mega rich, so he wouldn't bother about being paid, but I've no doubt he would seek a *quid pro quo* – there is some risk to his business interests in Russia if it ever came out that he was involved – so, I reckon he'd want at least, say, one sizeable contract from us, and maybe back-up or support in getting other contracts in Russia. I guess we could do that?"

"Sure. He sounds just right" said Hampton. "I'll let you set it up".

"Fine. I don't know much about the details but, given he is in computers, and it wouldn't be difficult to confirm his CIA links, there should be no problem conveying to Gudanov that Green is somehow involved in sensitive freelance work in the security field for the CIA. Then his daughter's behaviour will appear damaging not just from an ethical and political point of view but from a security stance. He really won't have any choice."

"Okay. Good. How about on the technical side?"

"Well, as I said yesterday, the guys from the department won't know the purpose of the surveillance, they won't come into contact with Green or Gudanov's daughter, and they needn't see the digital output afterwards. So, all we need is a valid excuse for bugging a hotel room, which I assume you can come up with, though we will need to check the room thoroughly to ensure that the Russians haven't already bugged it as part of their general surveillance activities. If it is, we will just have to abort and find another room."

"I can easily suggest that we are worried about some bribery problem," said Hampton, "and need to bug a hotel room that might be used for a pay-off. It doesn't happen often, but it's not unknown. I don't think the technical boys will be at all suspicious."

"That sounds fine. But none of this covers what seems to me to be the biggest problem: setting the woman up – let's call her Trixie for the moment because I don't know her real name - with Harvey. I imagine that she will work a number of the expensive hotels, and not necessarily with any regular pattern. So, we would have to wait until she returns to the Four Seasons; and we have to co-ordinate that with bugging the room. I initially thought we could just book Green into a room for a couple of weeks or so, wire the room, and wait for Green to meet her in the bar; but that won't work. Given his work and his life-style, I very much doubt he will agree to move into a hotel for a week or two, even one as opulent as the Four Seasons; and he certainly won't want to sit around in the foyer night after night until Trixie turns up. So, it's not straightforward, but I have had an idea as to how it might work." Hampton was silent, quite gripped by the discussion.

"We will need someone else who will recognise Trixie - not me I hasten to add because she would recognise me - to spend each evening moving round the foyer or bar areas of the top five or six hotels until he spots her, and then hook up with her. That shouldn't be too difficult if he moves fast. He then texts me - one letter will do - and I call Green. He checks in to the Four Seasons and then goes and joins the pair, wherever they are, as if he is a friend or colleague of whoever has hooked up with her. The look-out then bows out - gets a call, sees his boss come into the hotel, whatever - and Green gets to take Trixie back to his room at the Four Seasons. He pays her what even for her is a lot of money, and fixes to see her again the following night, by which time we will have the room bugged. I think that should work. If the Russians have bugged it, we would just have to try again, but the chances are that we will be okay. It's not the Cold War anymore. Then we are ready to negotiate with Gudanov." He couldn't help ending with a slightly too self-satisfied smile.

"My, you have been thinking this through, haven't you" said Hampton with mock amazement. "Not sure you have been in the right post here at the Embassy". He laughed to lighten the thought but, if the truth were known, both men silently thought that perhaps that was right. "But there is still one problem" added Hampton. "Who can we get to monitor the main hotels, and how will he recognise dear Trixie? I can't assign embassy personnel, and even if I could it would undermine the idea of keeping this operation very private. He'd need a photo of her, which I guess you didn't take."

"I think I can solve most of that" replied Warburton. "I can recruit someone from a private agency, who wouldn't even know that I am from the Embassy. They could do the monitoring and deal only with me. The problem is how to get the funding to pay them. It wouldn't be cheap unless we are lucky and find her very quickly." Hampton nodded abstractly, musing on the problem as he gently stroked his lip with one hand.

"I think that can be fixed. You probably don't know, but we have commissioned that sort of thing before – surveillance activity - not often but when necessary, and business related not politics these days. So, it could easily be financed again. And if it is not too large, I could authorise it without going to Henry." It was the first time in either of their two conversations that any reference had been made to Sir Henry Arnison, the Ambassador, who would have to explain if the plan being hatched went pear-shaped for any reason. But Hampton recognised that Arnison would be much better off not knowing, If problems arose, he would have to carry the can himself, but he'd make sure that, once they got going, the whole thing would be deniable. "But how do we show them who we want them to locate?"

"I'm sure there will be a photo of her from the reception" said Warburton. "There are always loads of them taken. She looked a lot different when I saw her at the hotel, but I reckon I can get them to digitally alter the photo to get it roughly how she looked."

Hampton was even more impressed, but all he said was "That sounds okay."

"So, we are agreed?" replied Warburton, trying to sound as relaxed as possible but, underneath, almost quivering with excitement at the prospect of organising such a sting. Referring to an 'agreement' between his superior and Warburton was, he thought nicely judged to show that he, Warburton, was taking just as much responsibility as Hampton, though, if it all went pear-shaped, he had no doubt where all the responsibility would suddenly lie.

"I think we are" said Hampton. "I'll set about fixing the funds, while you identify an agency that can provide someone to carry out the surveillance. Let's reconvene, say, the day after tomorrow?" Warburton nodded assent. "We need a name for this little project, don't we? Operation Trixie might be just a little too obvious. We need something completely unrelated to any aspect of the plan." He mulled the matter over for a while but Warburton intervened before he could come up with anything.

"Better not" he said "From now on, I suggest this project just doesn't exist. There will never be anything on paper, in a computer; and no-one but you, me and Green will ever know what is going on apart, that is, from Gudanov, when the time comes. I think we should leave it that way." Hampton smiled his assent.

CHAPTER 5

The murmurs of 'Morning Prime Minister' were somewhat less fulsome than Seymour might have wished as he entered the small conference room on the ground floor of No 10, but that, he appreciated, was because everyone present knew that this was going to be a tricky meeting by any standard. Stephen Marlowe, his Minister for Energy and Climate Change, had been pressing for such a meeting for nearly two weeks. Seymour had known it must happen but wanted to be fully briefed, not just indirectly by officials in the Energy Department before he chaired the meeting. So, he had had is Policy Unit in No.10 on the case and was now ready to talk. Or at least as ready as he would ever be, given the rather dire information his team had delivered.

The message, in short, and stripped of all its 'maybe's and 'however's, its scenarios and contingencies, was that energy supplies in the United Kingdom were now only just meeting demand, with the safety margin of stored oil and gas to deal with peaks of demand now below the 1% minimum deemed necessary. With economic growth now finally beginning to emerge – the beginnings of the boom that alone would bring Seymour another five years in office – even that narrow margin would disappear. The result, it seemed, unless they were very lucky with the weather, would first be 'brown-outs' with reduced supply, not black outs but potentially quite disruptive to many electrical systems, and then full-blown black-outs, returning the country towards the days of the three-day week in the 1970s, when homes and factories suffered up to two or even two days a week without any electricity at all. At that point, it didn't matter who was in power or the causes. The government of the day, his government, would take the rap, and he would be out of office for at least five years. With an election lost and at age 58, it would be all over for him, no doubt a seat in the House of Lords if he wanted it, but the end of power, the end of any ability to see through either the rest of the recovery or the various policies which had brought him into politics and which were, he believed, beginning to deliver real benefits to the country. Plus, if he was honest with himself, the end of the trappings of power which, like anyone normal, he publicly eschewed but adored. No, it was not going to be a good meeting.

While being quite well informed about the background, he had, in earlier meetings with his own staff, echoed the simplicity of Her Majesty the Queen when, in the depths of the recent, massive global recession she had asked a bunch of economists the elementary question – how had it happened and why did no-one foresee it? He couldn't remember what answer Her Majesty had received. Still, the ones which he had received on asking similar questions about the emerging energy crisis were as depressing as they were straightforward. The looming shortage had been entirely predictable; and had been predicted for some time now. And the lack of action to avert the problem had been entirely a failure of policy, by previous governments of both left and right, their strings jerked hither and thither by various single-policy interest groups with media clout and, thereby, electoral clout as each of the two main parties struggled to pull together a majority for an election victory. The beneficence of North Sea oil and gas was waning fast; and efforts to stimulate more secondary and tertiary production from ever less commercial fields had been largely thwarted by the anti- carbon lobby.

Nuclear power had been simply a 'no go' area on safety grounds for over two decades, despite its evidently 'green' characteristics, with the ironic result that the UK now imported some of its energy from the French nuclear power industry. A neat solution if one wanted the power but not the nuclear power sites, except that it left the UK at the mercy of overseas fuel prices, overseas energy policy and, worst of all, overseas energy availability. Salvation from shale gas had been very effectively killed, for some time at least, by green activists who condemned it as still a carbon-based energy source and local activists who didn't want shale mining, however far underground it might be, anywhere near their property. So, renewables – wind, solar, tidal – were the answer, except that wind and tidal were also increasingly being blocked by local activists; and none of these sources was as yet significant, reliable or cost-effective, at which point Seymour's frustration sounded like an old record even to himself.

The meeting, apart from Seymour and Marlowe, involved two of his No. 10 unit; four members of the Energy Department, including the Permanent Secretary, his Energy Deputy and two more specialist members; representatives from the Department of Business and from the Treasury; the Minister's SPAD, or Special Political Adviser, and an Oxford University academic who had spent many years in research on energy issues and was now a part-time external adviser to the Energy

Department. Only twelve people but, Seymour thought, if this lot can't come up with an answer, then who can?

The first twenty minutes of the meeting was taken up with a Powerpoint presentation of the problem by one of the departmental specialists. Most if not all of it was familiar to everyone present, but it served to get their minds away from the many other issues that all of them had to contend with, and focus their collective mind on the single issue for which this meeting had been called – how to increase energy supply. Various demand scenarios were presented and weighed against the various sources likely to be available. Seymour noted that the problem was, in some ways, the reverse of the climate change issue. There, we could all carry on quite happily for a while, but if more action wasn't taken soon, a severe long-term problem would be on us and it would be too late to do anything about it. In contrast, on the energy front, the long-term position looked fine. Decisions had now been taken that would crank up the UK's mothballed nuclear power programme; renewables would eventually become significant; shale gas was making a big difference in the US and would eventually do so elsewhere in the world; and everyone was getting into energy-efficient cars, houses, consumer products and more, not to mention the booming recycling industry. The problem was that none of this was happening soon enough or fast enough, and the next few decades could be very difficult. Seymour's electorally determined time horizon was precisely three years and two months; what he wanted to know, without appearing too short-term or too political, was the likelihood of shortages emerging in that time period.

At the end of the presentations, the meeting deferred to the PM. The presentation had covered a lot of ground, some moderately complex, but it had been presented very clearly to an informed, non-specialist audience. Seymour had had a classical education, with little maths and still less science, but was a focused, shrewd and intelligent man. He had one big question arising from the presentation, but he first wanted to check that they were all on the same page.

"Thanks" he said. "So, in brief, am I right that, on your central or most likely scenario, we are likely to face intermittent shortages at periods of high electricity demand within a year, and potentially more prolonged ones within two years; but if worse weather and/or faster growth than assumed in your central case occurs, these shortages will start to emerge somewhat earlier?"

"That's a very fair summary, yes, Prime Minister" replied the departmental official. "By the same token, better weather or slower growth of the economy would push the problem back in time, though by no more than a year or so."

So there it was, thought Seymour, in black and white, or rather in multi-coloured charts. His government was trying to do everything it could to boost the economy's growth; the weather had been atrocious in the last couple of winters. So it wasn't just a case of him being unduly pessimistic when he inferred that the crisis was more than likely already upon him, effective as from now. His big question was fairly obvious.

"So what is the Department's latest thinking on dealing with this issue?" This triggered an extended debate about 'demand management' which essentially meant trying to get some industries to operate for at least part of the time at less normal hours, to smooth away the spikes in demand for electricity – but the impact of this did not seem likely to be huge; or arranging to import more electricity from the French, but here the problem was that the UK only needed the electricity at peak demand times, whereas the French nuclear power stations pumped out a regular so-called base-load of electricity, that couldn't be varied much if at all without huge cost. A third option was to import ever more LNG from the Middle East, but this was the reverse of what was currently happening; and was unlikely to be feasible until a 'solution' - which meant nothing short of the defeat of Isis in the Middle East - was found to the terrorist threat to supply.

The fourth and final option, that offered the most attractive prospect, one on which Seymour had had an introductory briefing, but which he now needed to know more about, was Russian gas. With the completion of a European-Russian pipeline network, there was now the prospect of making a long-term deal with Gazprom. .This Russian gas behemoth would allow the UK to take whatever extra gas supplies it needed, when needed, and currently at a very reasonable price. The only problem was that the UK was fully signed up for an international boycott of Russian gas until President Kirov backed away from the threat he currently and very openly constituted to the Ukraine. Russia had so far ignored the Western nations' sanctions regime, but there were distinct signs that

Russia's rapidly deteriorating economic situation would bring President Kirov to the negotiating table over the Ukraine, and the common threat of Isis in Syria was, in the ever bizarre world of international diplomacy, starting to help relations between the two countries So Seymour wanted to explore salvation from this unlikely source.

"If the West can come to an understanding with Kirov, what are the prospects of a Russian deal?" he asked. Marlowe took this question himself.

"The gas is there, and the pipeline infrastructure is now in place. If – and it is a big 'if' – Gazprom can get its extraction and distribution operations working properly then there is abundant supply which they will be anxious to sell. So there could be a reasonable meeting of minds on long-term prices. But there would need to be an end, or at least an easing of sanctions, plus, Gazprom is notoriously inefficient. As far as we know, it was operating way below capacity before the current crisis - both extraction and distribution problems - and, in any event, can't do much without political approval from the top, which means all sorts of other considerations can and will come into play. It may be Gazprom and our utility companies sitting at the table, but it will, in reality, be the two governments negotiating."

"What time scale would be involved?" asked Seymour

"Most of the basic groundwork was done before the Ukraine crisis, and I'd guess we'd be ready to move from official level to ministerial level in about two months after the ending of sanctions. But a lot could go wrong; the Gazprom people will no doubt go for some fairly tough - which means protracted - negotiating. We would push ahead as fast as we could, but we can't even start the process while the sanctions are still in place."

There was a pause in the conversation while everyone reflected on this silent but very familiar elephant in the room. Seymour seemed distracted, unaware that everyone else was waiting for a lead from him. When he finally spoke, his words comprised an extraordinary combination of very simple, indeed utterly obvious logic on the one hand and a leader's far-sighted rallying cry on the other.

"Well then, we need to get the sanctions lifted." He turned to one of his aides. "Peter, fix me another meeting to brief me on the sanctions regime and suggestions for how the UK can initiate a process to dismantle it. Within a week. Thank you, gentlemen." And with that he got up and left a rather startled and, to some extent, bemused collection of energy experts to wonder if this was brilliance or denial on the part of the Prime Minister.

CHAPTER 6

Warburton's latest conversation with Hampton had been on a Wednesday. The next couple of days were as busy as any Warburton had known since arriving in Moscow. His usual work load was not that heavy, but it all had to be kept moving along while, at the same time, his real focus - and quite a lot of his time - was geared to the clandestine operation he had dreamed up. He first called Harvey Green and spoke to his P.A. Warburton was sufficiently motivated by the project that he hoped, and indeed had somehow rather presumed, that he could talk to Green very soon, but found out that he was currently in London and quite busy. Ultimately, the best he could do was to arrange to meet him in London for dinner on Saturday evening. He only secured this by telling the P.A. that he had a very attractive deal to offer, but one he could only discuss face-to-face with Green. This intrigued Green, and the P.A. returned to Warburton with the offer of dinner.

Next, he fixed to meet Dave Hutton, head of the Embassy's IT department, at 9 am the next morning, getting a suitably prompt response as soon as Warburton dropped Hampton's name into the conversation. He then dug out the files on the reception that Gudanov had attended with his family, to see what Trixie's real name was. To his slight dismay, he found she had been listed merely as 'Miss Gudanov', along with his wife, 'Mrs. Gudanov'. So, Warburton thought, she will have to remain Trixie for the moment, but it had the advantage of keeping the whole thing more impersonal than it might otherwise have been. It helped him avoid contemplating just what an unpleasant operation he had somehow come up with.

Later that day he dropped in on Claire Weston, the Embassy's head of PR and publicity, and asked for any photos they might have in their archive of the reception or dinner after the waste disposal technology dinner. He did not explain this somewhat odd request, and adopted a slightly more official - not to say officious - tone than was his usual style; and Claire, quickly picking up on this, did not ask why he wanted them, or even what he might be looking for. She told him to leave the matter with her and she'd get back to him, probably later that day but in any event by the next morning. Other duties then intervened, and it was not until the early evening that he could turn his mind to the slightly more problematic issue of recruiting someone to intercept Trixie, either at the

Four Seasons or one of the small number of other five star hotels in central Moscow.

Google quickly produced several private investigation agencies based in Moscow, but Warburton was very cautious. He assumed that many of them would be fairly fly-by-night operations, if not more dubious than that. He wanted to make sure that he got hold of a substantial, up-market enterprise, one which he hoped he could rely on to be effective and discreet, even if this cost somewhat more. So, he made a list of six that, in some way or other, looked from their Google listing to be more substantial and then went onto each of their websites. On this basis, he whittled his list down to three, noted their addresses, and then went home for what he regarded as a well-earned dinner. He chatted, as ever, to his wife about his day, but made no mention of his new project. He knew instinctively that she would not approve.

Promptly at 9 am the next day, he entered Dave Hutton's office in the IT section of the Embassy or, to be more accurate, he joined Hutton in his area within the large open plan area which housed, if not all the Embassy's IT, then certainly all the facilities to which the Embassy was prepared to admit. After initial pleasantries, Warburton indicated that they would need more privacy, and they made their way to a so-called 'quiet' room - one of several small, glass sided areas sectioned off for meetings, perhaps, Warburton thought, more appropriately called 'noisy' rooms, but kept the thought to himself. Once inside, he briefly went through a prepared speech, trying to make it sound less prepared than it was. He explained that a senior Washington official would soon be coming to Moscow and would need to have an off-the record meeting with a Russian - someone of influence but could not say more about him. They would meet one evening in the official's hotel room; and Washington wanted a full record of the discussion. This would mean getting the room bugged for sound and vision earlier in the day having, to be on the safe side, first checked that the Russians had not bugged the room. The subject matter was highly secret, so the recordings made needed to be retained in the bugging devices, not transmitted anywhere else; and Warburton would attend the next day with IT to take the recordings away with him. He hoped that that would all be fairly straight forward for Hutton's team.

As Hampton had indicated, this was not a particularly unusual request, and Hutton merely nodded. "When would this be?" he asked.

"I'm not sure until I hear from Washington" replied Warburton " I would guess in a week or two. But I may not be able to give you much notice. If I get in touch one morning, could you set it all up by the early evening?"

"Not a problem" said Hutton. "I'll have the equipment ready, and someone alerted to be ready to move. The de-bugging check and actual installation can be done in an hour or two at most."

"Excellent" said Warburton. "But Hampton wants a complete black-out on this. Can you do the work yourself? The fewer who know the better."

"Okay" replied Hutton "If that's what he wants. It will take longer, but I can still get it done during the day." This was all said very casually, but Warburton could tell that this last request had stirred some concern in Hutton's mind. He was not surprised when Hutton added " But I'd like to get an authorisation from Hampton. I assume that's no problem?"

Warburton would have preferred not to have to deal with this but, Hutton having raised the matter, there was no way it could be avoided.

"No, no problem" he said, as casually as possible. "I'll get Hampton to have a word with you or email you. The main thing is to keep this as restricted as possible." He stood up, not wanting anything else to disrupt what he had set up, thanked Hutton and left. He then headed for Claire Weston's office. She welcomed him in, and if she was curious or suspicious, she showed no sign of it. She produced a file in which she had over forty photos, a few from the dinner but mostly from the reception at which Warburton had first seen Gudanov's daughter. He quickly scanned through them, noted that several had her in them, quite demurely standing next to her father, and gathered the photos back into the file.

"Just the job" he rather purred. "I'm most grateful. Will you want them back, or are these copies?"

"You can have them - we have others if we need them". Just the slightest emphasis on 'we', with its implied question of what 'he' needed them for, was her only concession to the questions she would like to have asked Warburton. Instead, she just asked, "Anything we can help with?"

"No, no thanks. Just some follow-up work Hampton's given me." That was as far as he would explain, and Hampton's name conveniently ended any further interrogation. He departed with another round of thanks, leaving a slightly bemused head of Publicity behind, but not sufficiently curious to try any follow-up herself.

More regular work, mainly previously arranged meetings, now intervened; between which he managed to fix a Saturday flight to London He could, of course, have got his secretary to do this, but he felt more comfortable arranging all this himself. It was, after all, the weekend. So, it was not until the middle of the afternoon that Warburton managed to get out of the Embassy, waved down a taxi and headed for the first of the three investigation agencies on his list. He was surprised to find that it was housed in a very smart, modern office block and, if appearance wasn't deceptive, seemed very much the sort of operation he'd be interested in engaging. But, remaining cautious, he went on to the other two he had identified. One was in a much less salubrious street and, while it looked quite respectable, did not appeal in the way that the first place had done. The third, which he had trouble locating, was, of all places, in a shopping mall, over a rather large women's clothing store. It didn't have quite the cache, or exude the style of the first one he had seen, but some instinct told him that this one might operate just a little further below the radar than the first, and he decided he would try it first. If he had any reservations, he would return to the one with the rather palatial offices.

The firm had a Russian name, but also advertised itself in English by the somewhat opaque name of 'Infotel Services'. Having discharged the waiting taxi, he entered and was greeted by a pleasant young receptionist. Warburton said that he wished to speak to Sergei Kriskin, whom he had identified from the website as the firm's Managing Director, now it possible, or later if that was more convenient. The receptionist was very apologetic that Mr. Kriskin was not in the office at present, but readily fixed for Warburton to meet him the next morning. She asked if she might tell Mr. Kriskin about the meeting. Warburton was about to avoid this but thought it might be worth laying down a marker or two.

"I am thinking of engaging your firm for a task, but it is, I suspect, an unusual one, which requires maximum discretion, and I need to assure myself that Mr. Kriskin can provide what I need." Whether the receptionist had heard this type of introduction in the past or not, she showed no surprise, nor asked for any further clarification. "Thank you" she said, confirmed the time and said that she would look forward to seeing him again tomorrow. Only as he left did Warburton realise how very good her English was.

Once again, regular commitments intervened, but he managed to secure a clear hour later that afternoon, told his P.A. he'd like to be undisturbed, and concentrated on the photo file he had picked up from Claire Weston. It didn't take him long to identify one with a fairly clear shot of Trixie's face, which he was confident he could use for the identification purposes of the investigation service he was planning to hire. But he was also confident that it could be improved - enhanced digitally to make it look more like she was the night he had seen her at the Four Seasons. But, more significant, he had no doubt, was that she would be dressed for work, dressed in a manner that no-one could possibly miss was a signal that she was selling sex.

CHAPTER 7

The Embassy had a regular photographic staff, with its time split fairly evenly between innocuous work relating to the Embassy's trade and diplomatic work on the one hand and more clandestine surveillance work on the other. Warburton called in on them just before 6 pm that evening, sought out Clive Morrison, the deputy rather than head of the department, purely because he knew him much better, courtesy of a shared addiction to early morning tennis, and produced his selected photo. After checking that Clive did not have to leave his office any time soon, Warburton got to the point.

"This is a photo of someone that Hampton wants to be monitored - I think there is a suspicion that she is some sort of go-between in certain matters that he is not happy about. Largely precautionary at this stage but we need a good photo of her. I've traced her, seen her, and she has altered her appearance somewhat. So, could you do a digital photo-fit around the photo, based on what I can describe to you how she looks now?"

"Shouldn't be a problem," replied Morrison. "Let me just set up my computer, get the right program and we can do it now, if that's convenient?" Warburton was more delighted than he showed that this part of the project could move forward fast, and said that would be fine. He let Morrison set things up and then, standing just behind him started to give some guide to how he had seen her.

"The main thing is that she now wears her hair down. It's long, well over her shoulders, with slight curls, making her look much more blonde than in the photo." Morrison played around for a few minutes, came up with some modifications based on Warburton's description, and fairly soon had got to what Warburton thought was a very good likeness.

"Next, she was wearing a lot more make-up, more lipstick certainly but mainly, much more black - is it mascara - around the eyes, with very prominent eyelashes. That's a big difference from this photo." Morrison duly obliged and, almost spookily, he thought, an image of the woman he had seen at the Four Seasons emerged in front of him. He had, rather recklessly he admitted, thought of trying to get some young woman to dress up in high boots and a short miniskirt, take a photo of her and then put Trixie's head into the photo, so that the private investigator would have the whole picture, so to speak; but he'd had to admit that he wasn't at all sure how he would go about setting this up - he didn't know any young women well enough at the embassy to even think of suggesting such a thing - and was, sadder and wiser as a result, relieved that the image he had was quite good enough for the purpose intended. He got several copies from Morrison, thanked him for his good job, and headed home.

The next morning, Friday, he set off once again to the office of Infotel Services, was welcomed by the same receptionist, and shown without any wait into Sergei Kriskin's office. Kriskin, if appearances were anything to go by, was clearly a no-nonsense character, tall, broad-shouldered, a large, square head, with hair cut very short, altogether a rather powerful looking figure, and almost certainly, thought Warburton, ex-military. He therefore found it slightly disconcerting when Kriskin, speaking fluent English, invited him to take a chair in a quiet voice and undoubtedly very polite manner. He thought, I am a potential client, so might expect such treatment, but Kriskin's style nonetheless was quite at odds with his appearance.

"How can I assist you?" asked Kriskin, again quietly, with almost excess politeness but no other preliminaries.

Despite Kriskin's manner, Warburton felt that he was someone by whom it might be quite easy to be intimidated, and decided that he had to make sure he stayed fully in control of the conversation- and perhaps negotiation - to come.

"What I need has two elements" he said. "The actual work itself is very straightforward. I need someone to spend some late nights in the reception areas of several expensive hotels here in Moscow, looking out for a particular person whose photograph I have. On seeing her, he needs to text a number, then engage the woman in conversation until a colleague of mine arrives, and create the opportunity for the two of them to meet. Then your man finds a good excuse to leave them alone together. That's all."

"Do you have any particular pretext for my employee 'engaging' as you put it the woman you are seeking?" replied Kriskin.

"He won't need one. She is a high-class prostitute, so he will just need to show some interest in ...... engaging her.

"That sounds straightforward," said Kriskin. "Hardly" - and in a moment his whole bearing had become more steel-like, more intensely focused on Warburton - "enough to need a private investigation firm to take on?"

"That is where the second part comes in" said Warburton. "I need complete discretion, or rather, complete secrecy. Only one person in your firm must know of this contract, preferably no-one apart from yourself; you will not know the names of anyone involved, me, the woman in question, or the person I want her to meet. From me to you, payment will be direct in cash, a half before, a half on completion. There will be no paperwork. I have come to you because I imagine that you are used to high levels of such discretion in your line of business, but I can only proceed if I have assurances to that effect from you."

Warburton deliberately fixed Kriskin eyeball to eyeball, hoping to emphasise how serious he was about these conditions, but Kriskin just stared back at him, his face impassive, indeed immobile; and it was Warburton who looked away first. Nonetheless, Warburton felt he had gotten his message across in the silence that followed. If Kriskin just agreed, and the fee was not too outlandish, he would go with Infotel Services. Any quibbling, questioning, or hint that Kriskin would do anything other than just accept a simple operation and ask no questions, he would walk away. There was quite a long pause and then Kriskin's answer quite surprised Warburton.

"Would you want a fixed fee or a fee per hour?" he said, in a very matter of fact way. Warburton had not even considered this point, but recognised, despite the seemingly inconsequential nature of the question that he and Kriskin were very much in business.

"What would each be?" he said, trying now to focus on which might be more cost-effective.

"Let us say one thousand US dollars a night until your lady is found". Kriskin's formidable presence would have deterred many a stronger willed person than Warburton from seeking to negotiate this figure downwards; but his manner in saying it also left no doubt that it was a first and final offer. In any event Warburton, who had thought in terms of around ten thousand dollars for this part of the operation, reckoned they should find Trixie in less than ten days, though on what basis he really couldn't have said, and so was quite happy with the fee. His one private satisfaction, in readily agreeing on the figure, was that Kriskin might think he should have asked for more, maybe a lot more, but he showed no sign of this thought, and Kriskin merely nodded, more to himself than to Warburton. They had a deal.

"I'll return on Wednesday of next week, with a photo and an initial three thousand dollars on account if that is satisfactory?" Kriskin merely nodded again. "I'd like to brief whoever will undertake the task" Warburton added. "Very well" agreed Kriskin. "I will arrange that for Monday, let us say at 5pm?"

"I'll be here." said Warburton. "Thank you." He got up, they shook hands and left. He had the photo, someone to 'engage' Trixie, and the surveillance set up. All he needed now was Harvey Green.

CHAPTER 8

Seymour headed for the Cabinet Room, walking fast, grim-faced. He was, in fact, furious, and had been for the best part of three days, but tried, with only partial success to keep his anger under control. The Cabinet would be very supportive, but he knew he was on the ropes – the fact that such an overtly party-political issue would be discussed in Cabinet spoke volumes for how serious the situation was. He would be expected to come up with something and, with only minutes left before the meeting, he as yet had no idea what it might be. So, he would need to buy time – indicate that a strategy would be forthcoming but one which needed some thought first. Hardly a great rallying cry, and he would lose some points in the inevitable leadership stakes that would emerge fairly soon; but that was the best he could do at short notice.

He launched straight in once the Cabinet had taken their seats and gone silent. There would be no serious focus on anything else until he had dealt with what was on all their minds.

"As you know, three days ago, a major electricity sub-station in Essex failed, having seen its gas supply temporarily interrupted - I won't go into the details of what happened right now - but, as a result, over three-quarters of a million homes were without power for around fourteen hours. Not the greatest such disaster ever, certainly much less damaging than the bout of floods that hit the North of England last year; but no doubt very annoying for those concerned and, in some cases, a lot worse. But the statement by the Leader of the Opposition later that evening, alleging that this is....." he paused to look at a brief note on the table in front of him, purely to indicate that he was distancing himself completely from what he was about to say, ".... the direct and predictable result of energy privatisation, of excessive profits and pay-outs to shareholders by the main energy companies at the expense of proper levels of investment to expand and upgrade our generating stations....." he paused again to hammer home his disregard for such views, "has struck a very damaging chord with both the media and, it seems the electorate. In fact, it is one of the relatively rare cases where the impact of an individual announcement can be tracked directly onto opinion polls. As of this morning, it has resulted in a three-point jump, giving the Opposition a lead of over eleven percent.

"The statement is, of course, economic nonsense. The problem arises because of dwindling oil and gas supplies and years of opposition to new investment in nuclear power stations. Williams knows this of course, but the real reasons aren't going to cut any ice with either the Press or social media. The BBC won't help us. I will have a painful time at Prime Minister's Questions tomorrow, and we will be branded as the party of reckless, greedy business, caring nothing for the ordinary voter, which should never have let the utilities out of public ownership. Williams has promised to reverse this if he is elected. That would, as we all know, be an irrelevance, at worst a disaster, but it is a potential albatross around our necks to the next election. I don't think Labour would do it, but either way, it would be too late by then, and all our good work on restoring the economy and the country's finances will be lost." He paused, hoping that this rather polemical speech would satisfy the fury he knew they were all feeling, and put them all on the same side, rather than all challenging him to solve the problem. Before he could continue, the Chancellor, David Flemming, intervened.

"I should add that I have the CEOs of the six main energy companies coming to see me tomorrow to discuss the situation. They will no doubt be looking for tax breaks to ease the situation, but they need to understand that there is little the Government can do on that front." Never a man for many words, he fell silent. But no-one there missed the furious look on the face of Valerie Bell, the Business Secretary, who regarded contact with senior industrialists as a matter for her but who, not for the first time, saw herself outflanked by the Chancellor. Do what she might, the Chancellor had the clout to make things happen, and she didn't; and any CEO worth his salt knew that. Fewer noticed a similar look of anger pass across Stephen Marlowe's face. Energy was his province. It wasn't at all clear what reason the Chancellor could have for intervening, but the matter was pure politics, and Flemming was, after Seymour – perhaps even more than Seymour - the prime orchestrator of the Party's political strategy. So Marlowe, like, Valerie Bell, would just have to put up with the intrusion. Noting the tensions in the room, and not wanting to get side-tracked, Seymour took up the running. "We clearly need a powerful response to this shameful and fraudulent announcement." He had thought hard about whether to be so damning in his wording, given that most, if not all, of the people in the room would have, at least in passing and perhaps more than that, wondered why the

Conservatives had not been more forceful in addressing the UK's growing energy problem previously. But that was then and this was now. They were in power, and they had to carry the responsibility. The privilege of opposition was that one could promise the stars, without any risk of being able to implement anything until it was too late for the electorate. So, complete condemnation was the order of the day. "The Policy Unit is working on this, as a matter of the highest priority; and I will keep you all fully informed as to our response through the usual channels"

"Can you let us know your initial thinking?" asked Bell, so thoroughly annoyed with the Chancellor that she had ceased to care if she was putting the PM on the spot or not. Unfortunately, it was the one question that Seymour had wanted to avoid.

"We're looking at some options, in particular ways to smooth industry usage, and give top priority to households; but I'd obviously want the Unit to discuss options thoroughly with your Department and with Energy before we start to move on this." It was a fairly vacuous reply, but still a deft deflection of what could have been an unsettling moment, which was not lost on anyone in the room. All Bell could do was nod an acceptance of the suggestion, though how much input, if any, her own department's people would be allowed was far from clear. Seymour took the opportunity to move on to the regular business of the day, but his mind was not properly focused on it. None of this, he reflected, was remotely his fault. Under his predecessor he had been Foreign Secretary, about as far from domestic energy supply issues as you could get, and he'd been in opposition for thirteen years before that; but the way things were shaping up, he was going to have a grim few years, with everyone at his heels, and the strong likelihood of electoral defeat at the end of it. However, he had no solutions, and it didn't look like anyone else in his government or amongst its advisers had one either.

CHAPTER 9

Warburton flew to London on the Saturday morning, took the Heathrow Express to Paddington, and took a taxi to the Reform Club in Pall Mall, where he had kept up his membership when he moved to Russia, for just such flying visits to London. He had a late lunch in the dining room, historically named the Coffee Room, did some emails and paperwork in his room, and at 7.30 pm set out to meet Harvey Green.

Green's P.A. had booked them into The Ivy. To do this at short notice for a Saturday evening indicated just how much clout, or more likely, money, Green had at his disposal. Green was already seated at a table when Warburton arrived - quite soberly dressed for him though without a tie; and after initial hellos, Warburton decided he'd be a little gauche and ask how Green had managed the booking. The answer, sadly, was more prosaic than Warburton had imagined.

"I often eat here when I'm in London, which is quite often these days, mainly with clients, usually lunch but sometimes dinner. So, as a regular, good customer, including buying some of their very good, which is to say very pricy, wines, they always fit me in. Glad you could make it over here," he added, neatly bringing the conversation back to more immediate concerns.

But Warburton was not in a mood to be rushed and, over two courses of extremely delicious food, he politely quizzed Green on his business, what he was mainly into now, how it was going, where he mainly worked and so on; and Green reciprocated, catching up on what Warburton was doing in Moscow. Only as they turned to the cheese board did Green wrap this up.

"Well now" he said we must get to business. As you no doubt intended, I was rather intrigued by what you said to my secretary. Some business from the British Embassy in Moscow is bound to interest me, and if it can only be discussed face-to-face, I am even more interested. So, fill me in." He leaned back a little, an encouraging smile on his lips, ignoring the cheese on his plate.

"Well, this will surprise you, but I don't think it will disappoint. It isn't big bucks, is nothing to do with IT, and is for me, not the Embassy - that's critical - though it will, I can assure you, give you an inside track on at least a couple of IT projects for the Embassy during the coming year or so." If Green was startled by this he covered it up well, but immediately intervened.

"Before we go any further, I have a question - yes or no - no funny in between stuff. Is the job legal? Because, if it isn't, and there's no big bucks involved, then there's too much at stake for me. I'm not interested, and I don't want to know any more."

"Curiously enough, I don't think it is illegal," was Warburton's enigmatic reply, "but I'm going to be very up front with you. It could seriously annoy the Russian authorities if it ever came to light. But I don't think it will, and when it is all over, you'll be able to dine out on the story worldwide." He calculated that that would be enough of a hook to get him to the next base. He wasn't wrong.

"Okay" said Green, actually putting his hands up a little in mock defence. "I guess I don't particularly want to piss off the Russians, but it's not a deal breaker. Fill me in."

Warburton metaphorically but also in reality, took a deep breath. "I would like you to meet - I'll arrange the meeting - a very beautiful high-class hooker late one evening in a hotel in Moscow, as soon as can be arranged, and then spend an hour or two with her in a hotel room, have sex with her, pay her a lot of money and arrange to see her the next night as well. Then have another good romp with her the following night, the more debauched the better and, after she has gone, have a good night's sleep. That's it. I'll reimburse you all your expenses, including the no doubt extravagant cost of the two evenings and, as I say, there will, completely unrelated of course, subsequently be some good business for your company from the Embassy."

Warburton suspected that Harvey Green was not a man who was often non-plussed or lost for words, so it was some gratification to see that he was both on this occasion. Green just stared at him, not moving. Then he began slowly moving his head from side to side - not in a negative way but as a sign of complete bewilderment. Finally, he allowed himself a low laugh, a puzzled expression, perhaps more one of bemusement.

"I see why this needed to be face-to-face," he said, giving himself more time to respond. "You will have to tell me two things, and they had better be convincing. What the hell is this all about, and what's the catch. If you say there isn't one, it's on to coffee, and I'm out of here."

"The catch is that the second night there will be total surveillance of you in the hotel room – hidden video cameras and bugs all round the place. But apart from me and another person, no-one else will ever see the display. What is going on is a little blackmail. Her father is a high-ranking Russian official, and armed with the video of your night together, we will have some leverage over him. That's it. A sordid little tale, no big deal, but potentially very useful."

Green now openly laughed. "So, I'm to get some business favours for appearing in a real-life porno movie? I've had some jobs offered me in the past, politically sensitive, a number clearly illegal, and some very, very corrupt. But this beats 'em all. I'd have to be very careful which friends I dined out on with this. Jesus, what a proposal." He paused, thought for a while. "Why me? Surely the Embassy has some enthusiastic young studs who'd leap at the prospect. Or why not you? If she's as hot as you say, you could combine a little business with pleasure. Am I missing something here?"

No, you're not missing anything. This has to be kept as far away from the Embassy as possible, and I couldn't do it because she knows me. Anyway, I'm a happily married man. You're not tied down in that respect; you're American, which helps, and your job means that the suggestion that you do some work for the CIA will be very believable. So, you're the right man for the job."

So who is the Russian official - the father? How high up are we yanking their chain? I don't want to risk ending up in a Russian gutter with some bullets in my head."

"Not the highest. But a good source of information - mainly economic – and definitely someone high enough to be useful. A daughter selling sex to an American with CIA connections would finish him if it came out. And that's why this little film will……recruit him. He is the only person who will see the video, he won't know you at all, and would have no way of finding out even if he wanted to. And all you will be doing is what countless foreign businessmen in Moscow, and every other city in the world come to that, do, which is pay for some sex while away from home. So you, I do assure you, will not be the focus of his attention."

Green decided he would like some cheese after all. As he munched his way through he looked up at Warburton once or twice, with that same shake of the head, as if to say that it was all a little too preposterous to believe, but with an increasingly mischievous smile on his face. His next comment really shook Warburton.

"Did you know that I've got a new partner? Cheryl and I aren't actually divorced, but we separated nearly a year ago - I guess you must have known that. I'm spending time now with a delightful young woman who works for Google's charitable division, dolling out some of their profits for good causes. I'm not sure what she'd make of all this."

Warburton was very taken aback. He actually stopped breathing for a moment. It was an obstacle that just hadn't occurred to him, but he saw straight away that he should have done. A simple enough thing to have checked. He inwardly cursed himself - a totally wasted trip and, as yet, he hadn't thought about a back-up.

"Oh" he said, with real surprise. "No, I didn't know that. I wouldn't have come to you if I'd known. I thought you were 'free', and wouldn't mind a rampant night with no strings. I should have checked."

"Now, don't go all British on me" said Green, with understated irritation. Jayne and I have a rather... let's say, transatlantic relationship. I've no idea if she gets in the sack with anyone else in the States while I'm away - probably not, but you never know. And I doubt she thinks I don't when I'm over here in Europe for weeks on end. I guess she'd be mad if I started up a relationship over here, definitely a bit of a betrayal that. But shacking up for the night with a hooker, she'd be surprised if I didn't. So that's not a problem. No, I just need to think through what could go wrong and the consequences."

Warburton was monumentally relieved. He hadn't hooked his fish yet, but his error in not checking out Green's private situation had not ruined the project. In fact, he thought, if he had checked it out and found out about 'Jayne' from Google, he wouldn't have approached Green. So maybe it was all for the best.

"There really is nothing can go wrong" said Warburton. "I know that sounds a little complacent, but what can go wrong? The night happens. No-one else knows there is a video or any recordings. Your job is done as soon as she leaves. Her father will never have a copy - he'll just see it with promises that it will be destroyed in front of him if he does what we want. There can't be any comeback on you. Not even our side will know anything of your role. If it won't bugger up your private life, just do the West a favour and go for it. Lie back, as they say, and think of America."

At this, Green laughed so loud that a couple at a nearby table stopped to look. "Sorry" he mouthed at them, returning to his last piece of cheese. The waiter arrived before either said anything else. They ordered coffee, both aware that the decisive moment had come.

"Okay" said Green "You're on. Sounds a lot of fun and, like you say, I'll dine out on it for years afterwards. How do I meet this charming young lady?"

Warburton wanted to cheer, or at least stand up and yell something, but the surroundings, even if he hadn't been far too restrained actually to do it, militated against. Instead, he just said "Thanks" and explained how he planned to hook Green up with Trixie. Green confirmed that he would be back in Moscow fairly soon, and could be ready around 9 pm for a few nights in his hotel room, awaiting a call from Warburton to head for whichever hotel was Trixie's hunting ground for the night, meet up with Warburton's go-between, assuming he had got Trixie's attention, and start to get acquainted. The rest would be easy.

"When does this all start?" asked Green.

"As soon as you are available back in Moscow."

"Let's say a week on Monday then. I'll be back by then and have caught up with one or two things."

"Monday week it is, and then on stand-by from then on until we strike lucky. It shouldn't be many nights."

"Just out of interest" asked Green "how much exactly is a 'lot of money' in this situation?"

"I'll find out" replied Warburton, but my guess is about a thousand dollars a night, maybe more. We will err on the generous side, because we want to ensure she returns for round two. So maybe we will make it two thousand. It will be money well spent." They arranged contact details for when they were back in Moscow, drank their coffees, and went out into the night so that Green could have a cigar. Both felt that it had been a rather enjoyable and successful evening.

Warburton flew back to Moscow on the Sunday, spent a pleasant evening with his wife and, during the course of Monday, arranged for Hampton to authorise the release of the funds he needed, for Kriskin and for Green. As Warburton had anticipated, it took the rest of the day and Tuesday to get this through the relevant bureaucracy. The accounts section were undoubtedly curious that Warburton - not one of the spooks based at the Embassy - wanted cash, and in US dollars - clearly something clandestine - but theirs' was not to reason why, merely check that the payment had been properly authorised. On Wednesday morning, as he had arranged, he returned to Kriskin's office, with the doctored photo and three thousand dollars.

Warburton handed the photo over to Kriskin. "This is the woman I want you to meet up with" he said. "As you can see, she is very attractive and very, how should I say, very 'noticeable' which should help." Kriskin remained impassive as he inspected the photo.

"As you say, very noticeable. Do you have the advance?" Warburton took an envelope from his inside pocket and laid it on the table in front of him. Kriskin did not pick up the envelope, but merely nodded, and asked "when would you like the surveillance to begin?"

"Next Monday. I hope that is convenient." Warburton replied. "My other arrangements will all be ready by then, and week-days are probably better than the week-end for her line of business. But I would like to talk to whoever is going to carry out the work."

"I shall carry this job out myself" said Kriskin. He noticed Warburton's slightly questioning look. "Your request intrigues me" he added, by way of explanation. It is somewhat different from even the more.....curious..... cases I get offered, and the chance to meet such a beautiful woman is a small bonus."

Warburton was slightly alarmed at this, and thought to dispute the matter. The last thing he wanted was an oversexed Russian deciding that he might sacrifice the dollars - or even keep the dollars - and spend the night with Trixie himself. But enough of this sentiment must, even in an instant, have shown in his face because, before he could say anything, Kriskin added "Do not worry, I shall not engage in any, shall we say, private enterprise of my own, tempting as I'm sure it will be. This is strictly business. You will get what you want, and I shall profit satisfactorily from the commission. In fact, your task will be safer with me than with some of my employees." For the first time, there was just a trace of a smile.

"So, I will call round the main hotels next Monday evening, I think around 9.30 pm. Let me have the number I should text when I contact the target." Using this word to describe Gudanov's daughter was not quite what Warburton would have chosen, and it once again gave him a few qualms about what he was setting up; but there was nothing to be done about it. He gave Kriskin his mobile number and told him to just text 11111. If he had already set his phone to Warburton's contact number, Kriskin could text the code without having to take his phone out of his pocket.

"I'll be back the day after we are successful with the rest of your money" said Warburton.

"Perhaps another three thousand if we get to the end of next week?" suggested Kriskin, though it clearly was not just a suggestion. "On further account."

"That's fine" said Warburton. "Don't worry, I'm not going to jeopardise this project any more than you are Mr. Kriskin".

"I'm sure that's correct" - a definite smile this time. "I look forward to seeing you in due course." Warburton got up and left. As he did so, he felt both alarm and heady excitement. The game was in play, and all for Queen and country.

The next day he fixed a brief meeting with Hampton to bring him up to date, ask him to authorise Hutton to carry out the IT side – face-to-face to avoid any email trail - and to let him know that the operation would start the following Monday. Hampton got Warburton to go over the details, but showed no obvious signs of having re-thought the project, and offered neither comment nor criticism of anything that Warburton had set up. He was particularly pleased that apart from Green and themselves, no-one else - inside or outside the embassy - knew what the project was for. And Harvey would have every incentive, in the form of future contracts, to keep the whole thing secret for the foreseeable future. The operation might or might not succeed in its aim, but it was hard to see that it could go wrong in any way, and if it did in some unexpected way, it was very deniable, perhaps not to the Ambassador, but to anyone outside or, more importantly, anyone back in Whitehall.

On Friday, he went to see Hutton at IT, and confirmed that he would need to be ready any day from the following Tuesday. Hutton said that was fine; he had all the equipment he needed all ready to go. He just needed the signal from Warburton, the hotel room number, and a key to it, which Warburton said he would deliver himself. Back in his office, he walked himself through the whole thing a couple of times, the first to make sure all was in place, the second, asking himself what could disrupt the plan, and how to respond. The three potential problems he encountered were if the room was already bugged; if the link up to Green didn't work; or if Trixie wasn't available for the second night. But the first and third would just mean some delay. As far as Warburton could see, only the link-up was critical. If that went pear-shaped, there'd be no second chance. But there was nothing Warburton could do about that. Some things were just inherently risky.

Warburton had a very enjoyable weekend. His wife had fixed a chance to see her two boys for some days back in England in a couple of weeks' time, which always cheered her. They did some shopping together, saw friends for dinner one night and a film the following night. It was all very relaxing, but Warburton could barely conceal how much adrenalin was pumping round his body as he contemplated what the following week might bring, and what it might just possibly do for his career.

CHAPTER 10

Prime Minister's Question Time had been as bad as Seymour had feared and predicted. Wisely avoiding a lengthy question designed only to get many adverse facts into the debate at the start, the Leader of the Opposition, Colin Williams, delivered an incisive but carefully thought-out question. "Does the Prime Minister take any responsibility for the devastating loss of power to schools, hospitals and nearly a million people this week in East Anglia?"

The question was fairly close to what Seymour and his team had anticipated, but this made it none the easier to deal with. He would look foolish or even deceitful if, as Prime Minister, he denied any responsibility but would be attacked mercilessly if he acknowledged some responsibility. So he would have to use the time-honoured route of largely ignoring the question and going onto the attack. But with widespread, and not unreasonable, concern, in the Press, amongst the population and, indeed, in Parliament, this would appear to be exactly what it was, namely an attempt to duck the question. None of the three options offered any salvation.

"We on this side of the House know full well where responsibility lies, in the shameful underinvestment and disregard for nuclear power shown by the previous government, a disaster which we, as ever, are now having to clear up". Seymour had planned to go on, but the braying of support from his back-benchers, combined with the howls of protest from the Opposition ones created such a cacophony of noise as to render all further speechifying useless. He sat down and waited for the next question from Williams.

"So, you accept do you, that seven years of this Conservative government, during which its friends and supporters in the privatised energy companies have together made over 50 billion pounds profit have been unable to keep peoples' light and heat on, schools running and hospital operations maintained? What shambolic sort of government is that, Prime Minister?" This time the braying of support and the howls of anguish were reversed, but no-one could miss how the Opposition fervour was gaining ground, and the Government's support was sounding more synthetic.

Seymour was a seasoned warrior at PMQs; and he knew there were answers to this - that seven years was very little time to turn round the number of power stations in the country, that nuclear had been repeatedly opposed by the Opposition and its local councils, and that much of the £50 billion of profit had been reinvested into power generation and the upgrading of electricity transmission and distribution. But none of that, he could see, would count for much in the febrile atmosphere that now surrounded him.

"We are retrieving the woeful situation we were bequeathed just as fast as we can go " he said but, too late, realised that this was a catastrophic error. Not only was it not remotely any sort of rallying cry to his backbench troops but, fairly explicitly, admitted that it *was* the government's responsibility if the situation was not being restored quickly. He might have retrieved the situation slightly had he had the opportunity or requisite deftness of touch, but neither materialised. Even before he had finished the sentence, the opposition was shouting him down, with cries of 'disgraceful', 'time to go' 'failed the nation' and such like. But much worse was the silence from his own side. Suddenly Seymour literally stood alone, with the opposition baying for his blood, and the journalists up in the Press Gallery already drafting their articles on the day the Prime Minister was torn to shreds, maybe finished as leader of his party.

Seymour briefly reflected that, at least that was the bad, no, the absolutely terrible, bit over, as PMQs would now move on to other matters, safer ground. But it was not to be. Williams stood up in what was clearly a rehearsed move - quite unique in the history of PMQs - and waited for what was a gratifyingly long time until his party had finally quietened. He had the rapt attention of both sides of the House, and then said "No further questions. None needed for such an ineffective rabble." Again his backbenchers roared their disapproval of the government, and, in a highly orchestrated plan, no other opposition MP stood to ask a question. Seymour was to be left dangling in the wind of disapproval.

A few Conservative back benchers shouted 'shame' at such a ploy, but the majority were again silent. Two of them attempted to ask unrelated questions, to try to steer the occasion away from the train wreck it had become for Seymour. However, the counter-ploy was entirely obvious and just led to much derisory laughter from the opposition benches. The government benches quickly fell silent. It had been game, set and match to Williams, and even now Seymour's humiliation wasn't over. With no further questions, he couldn't just sit there, stranded and impotent in the face of Williams's onslaught. So, instead, with as much dignity as he could muster, he set off out of the Chamber - only a few yards but it seemed a few miles to Seymour as the opposition back benchers started chanting 'resign', 'resign', until long after he had left. As he headed for his car to take him back to Downing Street, the thought that rattled round his brain was one going through those of several others in Parliament who had just witnessed PMQs - could he survive such a defeat? Would his party tolerate that?

As soon as he was back in the Cabinet Room he summoned his Principle Private Secretary, an up-and-coming fast track civil servant called Anthony Morgan, and asked him to get hold of Andrew Palmer straight away, no matter where he was or what he was doing. Palmer's title was Seymour's Press Secretary, but that did not remotely indicate what he did for Seymour or how he did it. He had been Press Secretary to Seymour's predecessor, Alan Gerrard and, unlike previous Press Secretaries, had decided to take on the Press, and use every trick in the book to manipulate it towards more favourable coverage of the government. This included not just selecting to whom he gave advance warning of breaking news, whom he allowed exclusive interviews with ministers or officials, and whom he temporarily or permanently excluded from access. These had been used before, though Palmer took such practices to new, vertigo-inducing high levels. His unprecedented influence came from a highly disciplined network of what could only be called 'informers', whom he was prepared to pay, bribe, threaten or blackmail to keep them on side. They in turn provided mountains of information to Palmer about the journalists he was dealing with, back benchers and, most importantly, about Ministers. While the party whips ensured, as best they could, party discipline, Palmer had acted as Gerrard's enforcer - even Seymour had been scared of him, simply because Palmer had found out that, over twenty years ago, when Seymour was an energetic young entrepreneur, running his own management consultancy business, he had in two consecutive years under-declared his income.

The sums weren't large, were probably, as Seymour had claimed at the time due to oversight at a very busy time - indeed he could point to some other errors at the time that were in favour of the taxman, and it had all been readily settled with a fine of 10% of the overdue tax. But Seymour knew, just as well as Palmer, that if it became known that the then Foreign Secretary, now the Prime Minister, had once 'fiddled his taxes' as it would be portrayed, he'd be finished. It was not surprising that, on taking office, he had asked Palmer to stay on in the same role and now, two years on, he was, without doubt, the second most powerful man in the land, maybe more than that. He could make or break anyone's career, even the Prime Minister's. The oddity was that he had had a rather chequered career himself; two divorces, one illegitimate child, and a period of heavy drinking, during which he could very quickly misbehave, becoming unreasonably angry, rude or dismissive. But he had now got this fully under control, had a new partner, while maintaining such a swashbuckling, larger-than-life presence that he somehow got away with 'Andrew being Andrew'. He was very definitely not someone to cross and, in any event was neither a politician nor a conventional civil servant - the standard fodder for the Press's curiously tuned ethical standards - so that no one, to date at least, had tried to bring him down a peg or undermine him as he went about his business of promoting the position, the image and the power of the Prime Minister.

Palmer, anticipating that it would be a bad day for Seymour, had been in the Press Gallery for PMQs, had made it back to his office in No. 10 shortly after Seymour got back, and joined him in the Cabinet Room a few minutes later.

"Well, that was a fucking disaster" he said, but this was so obvious to both of them that he rather mumbled it to himself.

"I know, I know" said Seymour, slightly despairingly. "I just didn't have enough ammunition. As you have often been won't to say, Andrew, what's done is done. The question is how to get back on the front foot, somehow grasp the situation so that everyone understands who really is to blame."

Palmer had been happy to transfer his allegiance from Gerrard to Seymour, partly because he loved doing what he did, and knew that he was very good at it. But also he had considerable respect for Seymour, an honest politician he thought, a decent man and with very sound ideas as to how to promote and maintain the economy and the nation's security. He clearly had leadership skills, which greatly impressed Palmer but, best of all, knew that Seymour had a very keen appreciation of Palmer's rather dark arts and knew how to recognise and police the dubious boundary between Seymour's political and policy role on the one hand versus deployment of Palmer's tactical expertise on the other. They worked well together.

Palmer nonetheless was slightly dismayed at Seymour's current state of mind. He had clearly been winded by the knocks that he took in the House, and now seemed deflated and out of ideas. Understandable perhaps, but this was the sort of situation that called for resolve, resilience, and innovative thinking; it would be a lot harder if Palmer had to generate all that on his own. Still, not the best time to air these thoughts.

"Graham, you are never going to win any sort of media battle about who really is to blame for the power cuts. It's too complicated, tugs at no powerful heartstrings, and it is just a lousy news story compared to the line Williams is pushing. We need to appeal to the Party, the Press and the People and to do that, we have to shift the story away - I don't mean away from energy policy - that would just seem defeatist and Williams would never let us get away with it. No, I mean we have to shift the energy story away, to somewhere else, to something pro-active, dynamic, innovative, something you can lead and shout about and, above all something *interesting* for the media to get stuck into."

He paused and, for a moment, neither spoke. Seymour at once realised that Palmer would not have spoken this way unless he had something in mind; and it had been sufficiently upbeat a statement that, shrugging off at least some of despondency he had felt after PMQs, he wanted to respond, with at least the start of some idea of how to achieve what Palmer had described. And, with an acumen that had served him well in his political career, he realised that, however much Palmer might already have some ideas of how to move forward, he would want Seymour to engage, start to contribute again - in short, pick himself up off the floor and get fighting, move forward again.

"Well" he said cautiously, "this debacle will all be forgotten if we can demonstrate that we have a plan to solve the problem, and then actually solve it at least a couple of years before the election. If, in that period, there have been no problems, Williams harping back to what is happening now will have no traction. I've talked to Energy who, of course were great on analysis but had no more idea than me how to solve the problem. But, if there is a way forward, and soon it will be Russian gas. If we can find a way to end the international boycott and sign a major, long-term supply contract with Gazprom, we'll be fine. That will shift the story and solve the underlying problem. I don't see how we can do that in any sort of fast timetable, but I have scheduled a meeting to explore this."

Seymour would never know if this was the line of thought that Palmer had himself already set off along - Palmer would not dream of undermining this Phoenix-like stirring from the ashes by Seymour from his recent humiliation - but it was clear from Palmer's reaction that he saw this as something to work on, a possible way forward if they could orchestrate it properly.

"That has the right sort of feel" he mused, "certainly some possibilities there. The boycott takes us into the problem of Ukraine, European sensitivities, some fairly messy international politics, no doubt plenty of hurdles, but they could also be distractions from present problems, with scope for some British leadership, British initiative. Hmm. At some point we will have to involve Energy, Defence and the Foreign Office but, for the moment, why don't I fix up to talk to one or two of our Special Advisers with more detailed knowledge of where we stand, what the options are, and then we might just be ahead of the game at the meeting. And, yes, I know it's urgent. I'll get back to you in a couple of days at most. Okay?"

Seymour nodded agreement. "The Russians have come up with an initiative that might be worth looking at, though I'm not hopeful. Their Foreign Minister, Demitov, called our Ambassador in Moscow - Arnison - I think you know him - a couple of weeks ago, suggested that there be a referendum in Eastern Ukraine on its future, and would we support that? Of course, with so many Russians having settled there, they know the result, which is why the Ukraine would never buy it, nor Europe. He mentioned Gazprom and possible future long-term contracts - seemed almost to be trying to bribe us away from the boycott with the promise of cheap gas for ever - but Arnison was pretty negative. Not much else he could be. So, as I say, I'm not optimistic, but you might want to see if there are any options there."

"Okay" said Palmer. "That sounds like a good place to start. There's always a way forward if you just look hard enough, think outside the box. Two days, and I'll let you know my progress." Seymour realised all over again why he valued this rather abrasive man, how right it had been to take him on from the previous Prime Minister's office. From the very black pit he had felt he was in after the PMQs, he now felt at least a glimmering of hope. He had no more idea how to solve the problem than before, but the fact that Palmer was on the case and seemed to think there might be some mileage in the Russian dimension quite cheered him up. Where it would lead he didn't know, but at least he could leave it with Palmer for a couple of days and focus on the many other affairs of State.

CHAPTER 11

Harvey Green duly flew into Moscow on Monday and booked into a suite in the Four Seasons hotel. Warburton met him briefly to give him a photograph of Trixie, as they still had to call her, and a description of his supposed business colleague Sergei Krishkin. He then phoned Krishkin, told him that his new arrival would be one Harvey Green from the US; and then agreed a code for his texts, five ones for the Four Seasons, five twos for the Metropole, and so on. For his part, Kriskin was ready to move at around 9.30 pm; and Hutton was on standby with his equipment. Warburton then quite literally did not know what to do with himself. There was nothing more to be done but await a text from Kriskin, sometime in the next few days. There was nothing to stop Warburton from getting on with his daytime job, but he could barely focus enough to remember what that was. Part of him, he had to admit, was loving the excitement, but he did have qualms about the amount of adrenalin pumping round his cardiovascular system; and he reminded himself on more than one occasion that he was not the fittest of men, despite the early morning tennis. But the simple fact was that, if all went well he, a middle-ranking career diplomat, would hold one of the strongest cards that could be played in the dangerous game of international politics; and against, arguably, the most threatening player in the world, certainly in Europe. No wonder I can't concentrate on trade fairs for the moment, he thought.

Kriskin decided that he might as well arrive a little early at the Four Seasons hotel, which he was familiar with but had not visited for months. So, at ten minutes past nine that Monday evening he walked into the rather splendid, wall-to-wall marble reception area and on into the bar and lounge area. It became immediately apparent that all the Englishman's plans – he still didn't know his name – to cover all the five or six top hotels had been a monumental waste of time, for there on a bar stool at the bar, without any question or doubt, sat the woman in question – unmistakeable from her picture and rather more stunning-looking in real life than in the photo. She wore a tight-fitting white blouse, over which her shoulder-length hair cascaded, a short, figure-hugging black skirt, and black calf length boots. A clearly very expensive small bag hung from her shoulder. A match for even all this was her face, with its large, oval shaped eyes, high cheek bones and a wide mouth, all delightfully symmetrical and quite radiant. But both his admiration for this quite startlingly attractive woman, and his professional sense of satisfaction - that he should be able to complete this rather well paid contract without much difficulty - were heavily offset by one factor that, stupidly, neither he nor the nameless Englishman had contemplated, namely that she was already deep in conversation over bar cocktails with another man.

Kriskin, both by temperament and from years of experience of encountering the unexpected, was not unduly put out by this turn of events. But he instantly realised that, if he let those events take their due course, he could expect, probably fairly soon, to see the couple head off to the set of lifts across the foyer. The target might, just might, return to the lounge for a second customer of the night; but all his instincts told him that she would, on re-appearing, leave the hotel, possibly for another hotel or, more likely, for home, with a substantial amount of cash in her shoulder bag. He might follow her, but he knew, again from experience that secure tailing of someone needed a team, of at least six and preferably more; and if she did head home, then he would have to start all over again the next night. So, while standing by a pillar apparently consulting his mobile, he decided on another way forward – not entirely riskless but, all considered, a better bet, based on his quiet conviction that the man now ordering a second round of drinks was not Russian. He could not say immediately why or how he knew this, but he knew that he did – perhaps the suit, the slight air of deference, the slightly flabby face, though there were of course many flabby Russians, but maybe not so many in the New Seasons hotel. In any event, he was sure he was not Russian, probably American or British, possibly Dutch or even possibly German; that offered him his way forward.

Kriskin walked up to the couple and, in English, in deferential words but a slightly ominously official tone said "Excuse me sir for interrupting, but are you a guest of the hotel?" The man looked round at Kriskin, surprise rather than alarm in his eyes, but then made what both he and Kriskin recognised as a small but catastrophic mistake.

"yes….." he said but then, just a half second too late realised that this might not be leading anywhere good and added "I mean, no, I'm just having a drink here." Seeking to regain some advantage, he said, "Who are you, may I ask?" Kriskin took out his private detective's license holder and showed it to the man but, as it was in Russian, all he saw was the same face as was now looking quite sternly at him.

"I'm with the hotel's security staff, sir. Could you explain how you know this young lady?" He slowly and very politely moved his hand in the direction of the woman next to him, who had, throughout this brief interchange sat quite still with a very slightly bemused look on her face.

"We just got talking in the bar" said the man whose very slight accent indicated that, despite his faultless English, he was indeed, Dutch or maybe Scandinavian. "There's nothing wrong in that."

"No, indeed" replied Kriskin, "but you have had your conversation and I would suggest, with all respect, that you now return to your own hotel."

"I think that is for me to decide" said the man, just starting to feel vaguely belligerent, though he knew he was on somewhat thin ice.

"Unfortunately not," replied Kriskin. "We both know the situation here; and I am speaking on behalf of the hotel management when I say again that it is time for you to leave." This was coupled with an unmistakeably stony look which only the foolhardy would not regard as threatening. If its recipient had any notion of resisting, it lasted less than a second, not least because it now dawned on him that he would have to leave and then, hopefully unnoticed by this intimidating, not to say positively menacing security bastard, slip back into his room. With as disrespectful a shake of the head as he could manage, he got up and, as a parting shot to Kriskin said to his lovely but now erstwhile companion

"I'm sorry about this. I hope we can meet up another time"; and headed for the main door.

Throughout all this, the lady in question had said nothing and, indeed, had barely moved, the slightly bemused smile still adorning her beautiful face. But now she came to life.

"What was all that about?" she said in Russian. "You are no more hotel security than I am".

Kriskin now kept to deferential words but added an equally deferential tone.

"I do apologise. The explanation is very simple. I am due to be joined by a business colleague from America. He is absolutely vital to my business interests; and I have promised him a good time while he is in Moscow. Make suitable introductions. It was very clear to me that you are not just in a position to help me but would, if I may say so, be a perfect evening companion for him. I want the best for him; and you are, quite simply, the best. I couldn't let my slightly late arrival interfere with that."

He didn't know quite how she would respond, but was pleased to see that she made no quick response, indeed she made no response at all except to smile slightly more than before, a smile that, Kriskin felt quietly acknowledged and accepted the rather exalted status he had bestowed on her.

"Shall we go and sit over in the lounge, and may I get you another drink?" asked Kriskin. She merely nodded, he presumed to both proposals, and they headed for the padded luxury of three sofas around a large square glass-topped table. Kriskin caught a waiter's eye on the way, indicated the same again for his companion, and a malt whisky for himself. Also, walking slightly behind his new companion, he texted five ones to the pre-set number on his phone. As they settled themselves he asked

"May I know your name?"

"Irina" she replied' "and may I know what it was that you produced to indicate that you were from hotel security?" Kriskin noted that, in one short question, she had revealed that along with the face and the body he was recruiting came a sharp and alert mind.

"Just my company ID. I knew he wouldn't be able to read it."

"May I see it?" was the worrying reply.

"I'd rather keep my name out of our conversation" he countered and, to his relief, she merely nodded her acceptance.

"Your friend is American? What is his business in Moscow?" she asked, without much interest backing the question.

"Computers" replied Kriskin, repeating what Warburton had told him, but added no more information. "Are you from Moscow?" he asked, seeking to move the conversation away from their shortly-to-arrive guest, but she merely nodded, no keener to discuss herself than Kriskin was to discuss Green. So they sipped their drinks, the silence, rather to Kriskin's surprise of no great embarrassment to either of them, whereupon, decidedly faster than he had anticipated, Harvey Green strode into the reception area, Warburton having got Kriskin's text and tipped off Green that he was set to go.

Green had deliberately ditched the caricature American style of dress he usually adopted. Instead he was in a very well-fitted dark blue suit, white shirt and sober tie, not a hair out of place, with what was clearly, to the initiated or uninitiated, a very expensive gold Rolex watch. "Hi" he said in an expansive though not unduly loud voice. "Sorry I've been running a bit late. Good to see you. How are things?" No-one would have guessed that they had never met before.

"Fine" replied Kriskin, getting up and shaking Green's hand. "Sit down, have a drink, this is a friend of mine, Irina." She had remained seated and said nothing, but gave Green a pleasant smile.

"A pleasure to meet you" said Green, taking in that she was a stunningly beautiful woman and metaphorically pinching himself that he was being paid to have sex with her. Not to be added to his life-long list of amazing anecdotes – no-one would believe a word of it.

Kriskin and Green engaged in some desultory chat about Green's flight, Kriskin's business – all very non-specific - and non-existent plans to meet up; and then Kriskin got up. "I must be going" he said. "I'll fix the bill on my way out. See you tomorrow at 10. Have a good evening", this departing word delivered with no trace of irony; and he was gone.

"Nice guy" said Green. "Only known him since last year, but we've done some good business; and he has been very hospitable to me." Irina smiled, but was clearly not up for much conversation, so he added "Would you like to come up to my room?"

"That would be good, yes" she said. Green stood up, she followed suit, he set off for the lifts and she took his arm. Green couldn't actually spot anyone watching, but he did not doubt that his exit from the reception area with this woman on his arm would not go unnoticed. But, unlike Kriskin's mythical hotel security, no-one was interested in querying Green's intentions.

They rode up to Green's floor in silence, but with Irina's arm still linked to Green's and entered his room. "Would you like another drink?" he asked. She shook her head.

"May I use your bathroom?" she asked

"Of course" Green replied. While she was there he put on the television, and was idly watching CNN when she re-appeared, dressed in one of the hotel's opulent bathrobes. She smiled at him again, placed a packet of condoms on the bedside table, and lay down on the king-size bed.

Green was very much an Alpha male, very used to being in charge, of himself, his situation, and those around him but, in that moment, realised that he was very much in the hands of a professional – this was her game, her territory – and, while he was obviously the beneficiary, it was very clear that she made the rules. He switched off the TV, turned down the lights, undressed, and lay beside her. His hands were very soon inside the bathrobe, caressing an otherwise naked body. Soon after that he donned the condom and was shortly after inside her, discovering all over again just how delightful uncomplicated sex was. Irina he found was welcoming and co-operative but dispassionate – this was his night, not hers – and, all too soon, he had consummated the sexual part of the evening.

As he sat there afterwards, with Irina comfortable at his side, three thoughts flashed through his mind, almost simultaneously. He very much wanted a cigarette, but would have to get dressed and go down to the ground floor for that; he wondered at the fact that Irina had at no point raised the question of how much the evening's entertainment was to cost him – but perhaps she knew that any sum acceptable to her would be relatively small change for an obviously very prosperous American businessman; and, most important of all, he still had to ensure that the whole point of the evening – a return match the following night – was arranged. He got up and poured a drink from the minibar, at which point Irina went back to the bathroom. When she returned, she was fully dressed, picked up her bag, and stood by the bed. Green took this as his clear signal, went to her, gave her a small kiss on the cheek, dropped the envelope that Warburton had given him with $2,000 in it into her bag, and asked, would she like to meet up again tomorrow evening? If she had doubts about the amount he had just deposited, the suggestion that she come back clearly doused them. "Certainly" she said.

"Why don't you come here around ten o'clock tomorrow evening?" Green suggested.

"Ten *o'clock*" she echoed in a voice that implied she was unfamiliar with the phrase. "Yes but we meet in the bar. I have no key to operate the elevator."

"Fine" said Green. "I will see you in the bar, at ten *o'clock,*" mimicking her pronunciation; "and I very much look forward to it – a special evening perhaps". At this, for the first time, she actually laughed.

"A special evening it will be" she said and, with that she was gone, Green noting that she certainly knew that one didn't need a key to go down, only up, in the lift. He would have gone for his cigarette before calling Warburton, but thought he should give Irina time to leave first, so called Warburton straight away.

"Richard, Hi, it's me, emission accomplished" he laughed. Warburton was tired – it was late and he had been in a state of considerable tension for quite a while – and so was not disposed to find Green's childish humour very funny.

"Good" he said, in a perfunctory manner. "Meet me tomorrow for breakfast, in the hotel restaurant, at 9 am, and we can sort out the next step".

"Okay" said Green "but don't you want to know any of the finer details?"

"Tell me tomorrow" said Warburton "I should go now" and hung up. Green got dressed and headed off for his cigarette.

CHAPTER 12

Two days after saying that he would look into the Russian gas deal, Palmer was back with Seymour, this time in his study. It was 7 pm; Seymour was clearly tired, but was anxious to hear what Palmer had, if anything, come up with. He poured them both generous gin and tonics. After some brief, and fairly desultory discussion of one or two contemporary little problems to be sorted out, Seymour asked for an update - had there been any progress - on the energy problem. In the two days since Palmer had rather cheered him up, he had once again tended to despondency on the matter, but was keen to hear anything favourable, however slight.

"Well, yes, I think there has been" said Palmer, in what for him was a surprisingly good mood. "I've spent much of the last two days getting very fully briefed on the situation. At first sight, it's not good. With the Crimea gone, the Ukraine is determined to hold onto its Eastern province, and the Europeans are all being good Europeans - almost like it is a test of their resolve. Russia is undoubtedly suffering from the sanctions, and freezing some of their oligarch's fortunes in London has really annoyed them. Still, it isn't going to lead to Russia backing down, for some time at least, if at all - too much face to lose - which implies a long time before the boycott is lifted. But..." he paused for a little dramatic effect "there is maybe one chink in all this which we might exploit, and which could really open things up for us".

Despite the large gin, now very tense, Seymour waited for Palmer to continue.

"As you said, the Russians have suggested a referendum in Eastern Ukraine, whether to stay part of the Ukraine or secede to become part of Russia. It's clear that during the cold war, and in fact even after it ended, there has been a steady stream of Russians locating in Eastern Ukraine; they now constitute a majority of the population. So they know how the referendum will go and, for the same reason, the Ukrainian government has been dead set against any such move, largely backed by Europe - mainly the French."

Seymour took a long sip of his drink and looked slightly irritable. He had told Palmer all this himself when last they had met. "I know the situation, Andrew, but I don't see how it helps us."

"Well" responded Palmer, we haven't been that much involved to date - broadly just gone along with Europe's position." He paused again to have a long sip of his drink.

"However, there might just be a way to unlock the situation. The UK government's position on Northern Ireland has always been that it is up to the people of Northern Ireland whether they want to stay part of the United Kingdom or secede to become part of a unified Ireland and, as you know, following the Scottish referendum on independence, there is now unavoidable pressure to have a similar referendum in Northern Ireland. And the unifiers want it soon, while the rise in the Catholic population gives them a real chance of success, but before demography - the young seem more inclined to stay with the UK - works against them. So, it would be quite consistent with this policy for the UK government to be prepared to accede to Russia's proposal."

"I see where you're going with this" interjected Seymour, as he poured them another round of large gin and tonics, "but the UK changing its position won't be enough to get the thing agreed internationally."

"I thought the same" said Palmer, in a reflective tone, "but the guys I have been consulting have been keeping their ears to the ground, and they are not so sure. For one, they're certain the US, if primed properly, would agree, because they are very anxious to work with Russia over Syria -, since Kirov has de-escalated the situation, they have already started to, in a small way - but the Ukrainian problem and the sanctions keep blowing that co-operation off course. The US doesn't really give a damn about the Eastern Ukraine, especially not if it's now mainly Russians, so they'd be very likely to follow a UK lead. And, crucially, that means NATO is out of the picture. That's critical because the only real military threat to Russia in the region is NATO, not the EU.

The Ukraine would know that the game is up and will never win this particular battle. And then......" another sip of gin, but really a theatrical pause ...."the whole thing tips over. Germany has had a special dispensation within the boycott because it is so dependent on Russian gas, provided it keeps to a steadily reducing cap, but is just as keen as us to re-gain full access to Russian energy, especially since they closed all their nuclear plants after the Japanese meltdown. The advice I've had is that they'd almost certainly come into line, and they'd bring the other northern Europeans, the Dutch, the Danes, the Scandinavians with them.

France would probably object, but it would have no real cards to play, and even if it got Spanish and Italian support, they are all basket-case economies at the moment and simply wouldn't have the clout to offset the US, the UK, Germany and the others. So we could precipitate the election, Russia would win, Eastern Ukraine could join Crimea, we could all claim to be good democrats, and the sanction would be lifted. I reckon four months from now we could be piping Russian gas by the bucket load into our power stations. We'd have solved the fuel crisis, shored up supplies for the indefinite future, and shown what an effective and committed Conservative government can do for the British economy and its people." This last was delivered with an increasingly flourishing bravura, no doubt fuelled by the gin but not entirely inappropriate to the plan he had delivered for Seymour to consider.

Seymour prided himself and was well known for being very insightful when receiving policy advice. Time and again, he would go straight to the heart of any problems in such advice and, while it often seemed at the time very negative, it was widely recognised that it saved time, focused discussion, and tended to ensure either sound rejection or a much better-supported proposal than would otherwise have been pursued. So Palmer was quite prepared for objections from Seymour, and ready to take them away and address them if he could. He was therefore surprised, as quite possibly Seymour was himself when he said

"Andrew, that sounds brilliant." He held up his glass in mock salute. "You can be very impressive when you have a mind to. We'll need to think it through as thoroughly as possible, but I can't at this stage see any obvious pitfalls. Except for annoying the French, which is no big deal, given how bloody useless they're being over our negotiations with the EU. Could you get a team from the Policy Unit together and game it - full works, everyone represented, especially the French - and let's check that it works as well as it sounds? If that's okay I'll get the Foreign Office in, make sure they know where we stand. They can prepare their counterparts in the US, and then I'll talk direct to the President." He downed the rest of his drink, and decide he felt better than he had done for quite some time.

"I'll get it going right away" said Palmer, who finished his own drink, stood up and started to head out. But Seymour called him back.

"Can you also fix a further briefing on Gazprom, where we are, where we would be on doing a deal if the sanctions are off. and one further thing - let's keep this very buttoned up - nothing to the Foreign Secretary until we know it will work. They're bound to see it undermining the 'international community' they always bleat about. We need this to be a *fait accompli* before they get wind of it. Same at Energy."

"All duly noted Prime Minister" replied Palmer with mock formality. "And once we are up and running, I'll start work on getting some good Press coverage. Williams will have a job attacking democratic choice, even if it is in a faraway land of which we know nothing." He smiled at Seymour as he left. "I'm beginning to enjoy this" he said.

CHAPTER 13

When Green entered the hotel restaurant the next morning, he found Warburton already there, with a young-looking colleague, whom he introduced merely as 'our technical expert'. Over a quick breakfast, Green briefly summarised his meeting up with Kriskin and the beautiful Irina – clearly highly experienced in her chosen field – the payment of two thousand dollars for less than half an hour's labours and, most important, that they had a date that evening at 10 pm. He then led them up to his room, with the 'technical expert' carrying an oversized briefcase. In the lift on the way up the 'techie said "I'll need about an hour". Best not to talk in the room until I have checked it out. Stay around if you want, but you don't need to if you have other things to do."

"Okay" replied Warburton. "We will go and get a coffee. Come and join us in the coffee shop when you are finished," and they left Dave Hutton to get on with his magic. He joined them 50 minutes later, looking distinctly pleased with himself.

"First, the room isn't bugged, so need to change rooms, or even, I had thought, possibly, your hotel. Second, I have rigged up completely invisible monitoring devices, one in the ceiling, which should pick up more-or-less everything, and two on the walls, which cover every part of the room. What's recorded is transmitted to this little box I've screwed into the skirting board, next to an ordinary electric socket – no-one will even notice, still less wonder what it is. Everything will end up on what is in effect, a flash drive inside the box. You will be able to see and hear everything that goes on. It's all sound or motion-triggered, and I'm confident the quality will be as good as a TV show. When do you want me to collect the equipment and recover the recordings?"

"The meeting I told you about" said Warburton, is scheduled for this evening; so if all goes according to plan, tomorrow will be fine. Let's all meet here at 9 am again, I'll confirm and Harvey can let you in." Hutton nodded his agreement and was gone. "I'd better get back to the office" said Warburton. "I don't know if you have any business here in Moscow to follow up but, if not, have a day's sightseeing." He was about to add something about keeping his energy levels up for the evening, but again eschewed the schoolboy humour of it; and bid Green goodbye.

Warburton had worried that he would not be able to concentrate on anything at work, but the success of his plan so far, the evening's assignation, and Hutton's confidence concerning the monitoring devices he had installed, all left him feeling quite confident rather than anxious. He went about his day's duties in a rather merry mood, though he took considerable care not to let this be apparent to anyone else. Green, meanwhile, had in fact taken the opportunity of his trip to Moscow to fix up a couple of business meetings, one over a very long and leisurely lunch, so that both had a surprising sense of normality about the day as it ticked by to an evening that was not likely to be quite so normal.

Green was already well installed in the reception area by the hotel bar, and on his second Bourbon, when Irina walked in, dressed in quite different clothes yet essentially the same uniform, encompassing a short skirt, tight blouse, high heels and long flowing hairstyle. Green greeted her in his most charming manner, gave her a restrained kiss on the cheek; and asked if she wanted a drink before heading to his room. This she declined, Green swallowed the rest of his and, in an exact repeat of the night before, they headed for the lifts, arm in arm.

Once in his room, Green sat on the bed and motioned Irina to join him.

"I'd like to tell you something, and ask you something, if I may" he said. "They are connected."

Irina looked slightly wide-eyed but smiled and nodded her assent.

"First then, I have travelled the world over for my business, and you are one of the most beautiful women I have ever met. You have no doubt been told that before, but I wanted you to know that I think that and am very lucky to have your company." Yet another demure smile but he ploughed on, before she could respond, always supposing that she was so minded. "Second, I think I would have expected someone as attractive as you to have captivated a charming, intelligent and very prosperous Russian business man, who could provide you with anything and everything you ever wanted, beyond most people's wildest imaginings, without what I suspect must be the quite tedious business of ….spending time with many different men. I don't mean to pry, but we are, however briefly, together; I find this a puzzle. If you'd rather not discuss it, just say. I'm a good listener either way".

"I do not mind" she replied. "I have had the same thoughts from time to time. But that other life....? You have everything except your freedom. For such men, you are – I think it is an adornment? You must fit in. You have things, but no money of your own. You cannot just go where you want with your friends. You are like in a prison. Yes, it is a very comfortable prison, but prison all the same. My life is fine. It is mine to choose. Who I 'spend time' with is my choice. I have a job in the day which I enjoy. I have my friends. Any evening I wish, I can spend with them. I save a lot of money for the future – my money. Why would I give all that up?"

Later, looking back, Green would identify this as the moment when he saw Irina not just as a magnificent fuck, but as someone he rather liked and admired – the self-knowledge, the self-confidence and the control she exercised on her life – things that went beyond just a beautiful face and a magnetically attractive body. At the time, however, he just said "I can understand that. I shouldn't have really asked". And then he kissed her again, put an arm around her; and began to undo her clothing.

The sexual activity of the next twenty minutes was, as had somehow been agreed between them the night before, 'quite special'. They jointly wrestled with her clothing, and she then alternated between being a very passive and then very active participant As she sat astride him, he recalled that it was all being filmed but, to his surprise, he found this quite erotic. Later, locked round her body, with his hands on her breasts, he rocked to a climax and wondered, in that moment, whether she might as well. But that was not for him to know, still less to ask as, more exhausted than he had imagined, he fell back onto the bed, with his arms around her now still body. He remembered that this was all being monitored and noted that he didn't care. It was terrific sex with a woman he couldn't remotely say he knew but for whom he began to realise he had some feeling beyond the merely erotic.

They lay together for some time, before she slowly wriggled free, went to the bathroom and, on returning, started to get dressed. Green put on a dressing gown and watched her with one thought in his mind – was it part of his deal with Warburton that he did not see her again? That had no doubt been assumed, by both of them, but was that part of the deal? He wasn't sure, but he wanted to keep the option open.

"I have to leave Moscow tomorrow, but can I have a number to contact you, next time I'm here? I can't tell you how much I'd like to see you again".

"Give me your business card" she said and, when he fished one out of his jacket pocket, she wrote a mobile phone number on it. "I will look forward to your call" she said with another winning smile. Green again discreetly dropped an envelope with another two thousand dollars in her bag and kissed her cheek goodbye. She left, and Green felt with more force than before, that he would miss her.

The next morning, while exciting for Warburton, was very much an anti-climax for Green. They met up with Hutton over breakfast, headed for Green's room and waited while Hutton removed his bugs. Warburton took charge of the small receiver box, insistent that he should take charge of the material recorded without Hutton seeing it – a simple case of the security level involved he explained –. Still, Hutton showed no interest in the content whatsoever. He unclipped the back, took out the flash drive, handed it to Warburton, and headed off back to the embassy. "Will you be staying in Moscow?" he asked Green, who said that he would have liked to, but needed to return to the US. Warburton confirmed that Green's PA had been contacted, to arrange for reimbursement of all his travel and hotel costs; that he had already made sure that Green's company would get invitations to tender for all upcoming IT projects at the embassy, and that he, Warburton, would personally guarantee Green got at least one, and would aim for a minimum of two, provided Green didn't go off the spectrum in terms of estimated costs. With that they parted.

"One day, Richard, you must tell me whether this was all worth it" said Green.

"It may be a while" replied Warburton; "in the meantime, it goes without saying that not a word of this must go anywhere, to anyone – not even the CIA" he joked.

"You've got it" replied Green. "Nice working with you. I'll await invitations to tender" and headed off back to his more normal life.

Warburton hurried back to his office and plugged Hutton's electronic device into his computer after having already cleared the morning of any meetings. He instantly saw Green and Irina entering his hotel room;

everything that ensued was very clear definition and sounded good enough to pick up all of their admittedly limited conversation. As he watched, Warburton was aware of several conflicting emotions.

At one level, he was watching a man and a woman have sex – not exactly a unique event in the history of mankind. But at another, it was erotic – if he put it on the internet, it would undoubtedly count as soft porn. Yet he also felt – and not actually to his surprise – a real sense of distaste, less the sex itself, more the intrusion – such acts were, and should remain, private. He was quite deliberately flouting that injunction, for a greater good he had to remind himself. But dominating all these thoughts, in fact, rapidly sweeping them from his mind, was the fact that he was undoubtedly seeing the daughter of Yuri Gudanov, a significant player in the Kremlin, freely engaging in sex for money with an American with known connections – and Warburton would have no problem beefing up those supposed connections – to the CIA. He also registered, first that she had, in answer to a question from Green, given some explanation for why she was following her particular career and, more importantly – a real unlooked-for bonus this – had responded positively to a suggestion from Green that they meet up again when he was next back in Moscow.

This had not been part of his planning, and he would have to think through the implications but, at first sight, it could only make the planned leverage over Gudanov all the stronger. And on top of all this, apart from Kriskin and Green, neither of whom would talk he was sure, he, Warburton, and James Hampton were the only people to know, to have this potential hold over a member of, if not the innermost circle of the Kremlin, then certainly someone not far off it; and potentially well placed to become part of it in the not too distant future. This, he acknowledged to himself, was so far beyond the limits of his pleasant but relatively mediocre career to date, that he felt elated in a way that he could not remember feeling in a very long time. Hampton would no doubt be waiting for a report on their little project, and Warburton's anticipation of his next meeting with Hanson, to recount developments was about as good as his life got.

CHAPTER 14

Seymour's anticipation was more anxious. He had to wait until the beginning of the following week for further developments. Palmer called in to see him at Number 10, at 7 pm on Sunday, shortly after Seymour returned from a weekend at Chequers, the Prime Minister of the day's country retreat. Seymour seemed somewhat refreshed by the experience, more sanguine than ever since his disastrous PMQs, and with more of his usual energy, even bravado. Palmer noticed this immediately and was rather pleased. Seymour would need all such qualities if he was to push through what Palmer had in mind. With drinks poured, Seymour opened first.

"Well, what news? Will the Russian ruse work, Andrew?"

"There are obstacles but, yes, I think it will" was his moderately optimistic reply. "I've spent the last few days going over every permutation of the diplomatic initiative, and I'd say it will succeed. We will temporarily lose a few friends, but not ones we need to bother too much; and they'll come back as soon as something else makes it worthwhile. The key, as we discussed, is the Americans. We haven't been in touch yet, of course, but we have talked it through with some very clued-up observers of US foreign policy - you need very good eyesight for that - and they're fairly confident the US will play ball. The Germans might be more difficult than I originally thought, but you will just have to strong-arm Genscher. He really needs us on the immigration problem anyway, so isn't going to ruffle you on the Ukraine. It'll be okay."

"That's all good news" said Seymour, "but it all sounds as if there is a 'but' coming".

"Not on getting the embargo lifted, not that we can see, anyway" replied Palmer, but in a rather muted manner that did nothing to allay Seymour's suspicion.

"The issue is Gazprom. I have got the team to pull out all the stops on the gas side of things, total due diligence. All we had before and everything we have had since by way of updates. That includes open and secret sources in Russia, satellite surveillance, consulted some former employees now in the UK, everything we can lay our hands on. I'll get you a full briefing, but the bottom line is that decline in the Russian economy has hit Gazprom's investment program hard. They are managing to pump the oil and gas that they can sell domestically, but that is way below capacity, and way below what they would need to pump if they could start full-scale selling abroad again. We don't know, but are rather pessimistic about, whether they could gear up again in any reasonable time frame. And we wouldn't by any means be the only buyer to re-enter the fray if the embargo is lifted, so if they have major problems in either drilling or distribution, we might not get anything like what we want out of the project." He paused to let that sink in, before continuing. Seymour recognised that there was more to come, and remained silent.

"I gather that the heart of the problem is that the whole system - any such system - needs regular, heavy maintenance. If that slows or stops, which is fairly much what has happened in Russia, then the equipment, the pipelines, everything starts to deteriorate at an ever increasing speed, and so the cost of getting it all back working again, starts to rise exponentially. Our people aren't certain that that is what has happened - they just don't have enough bang up to date information. Gazprom may have kept things ticking over enough that they could, maybe with some new loans, fairly quickly recover their former output; Kirov will be keen to see that happen. But there is a real risk that it will take Gazprom years to recover. If so, we might lose Eastern Ukraine and gain little or nothing in return." Both men sat in silent for several minutes. Palmer could have gone on, but both of them knew that it was for Seymour to stake out the next move, determine the focus of debate and, in this way, steer the direction of discussion from this point on. Eventually, he broke the silence.

"That's admirably clear, and a real bitch. But there is no point in embarking on the diplomatic front unless and until we know that it will fairly quickly give us the gas we need. *Can* we find out more, and more accurately, Gazprom's situation?"

"The honest answer is that I don't know," said Palmer "but I am treating that as a top priority. We are somewhat restricted in that we do not want to bring any of our usual sources – the Foreign Office or MI6 into this for the moment; and we just can't talk to the CIA if our own people don't know; but I'll see what we can come up with. When an appropriate moment presents itself, it might be sensible to re-iterate our position on Northern Ireland – it's up to them – so it's no surprise to anyone when we use that line for the Ukraine".

"Okay, leave that with me," said Seymour. "Get back to me as soon as you have anything more." They finished their drinks and headed off to all the myriad other things that would keep them busy in the coming hours and days.

CHAPTER 15

In what proved to be a very irritating delay, Hampton was away from the embassy that day; and Warburton could not get in to see him until early evening. However, this gave him ample time to call in on Kriskin and give him the balance of the funds he had agreed to pay. Kriskin would have been interested to know more about the operation's purpose, but his was a profession where one did not ask unless it was essential to do so, and he confined himself to saying that if he could be of further assistance in the future then to be sure to contact him.

Once he was back at the embassy, Hampton was as keen to find out what had transpired as Warburton was to tell him and show him. As Hampton watched the video, he showed none of the various emotions that Warburton had experienced that morning. Instead, he watched it, over half an hour, in studied silence and with a degree of concentration that he might have reserved for a particularly complex internal memo. Whether this was because he was contemplating how they would proceed, or whether it was just to cover a degree of embarrassment watching it in Warburton's presence, Warburton could not tell – perhaps both.

As the video ended, he rubbed his forehead with one hand, either thinking hard or wishing to give that impression. "If we can talk up Harvey Green's links to the CIA" he said in a very measured manner" then I think we have Gudanov, I think we do. Well done," he added, a throwaway line, but not lost on Warburton. "So, where do we go from here?"

"Well, I can certainly monster up Green's connections to the CIA – no problem. So, how best to use this? I have been giving that some thought" said Warburton "ever since it was clear that our ploy has worked. We could, of course, go to Gudanov with this the next time there is an opportunity for a discreet word with him; but I wouldn't recommend this. We don't, at present, have any concrete idea of how he could help us, even if he falls over backwards to co-operate. While I can't see him wriggling out of this, we don't want to give him any opportunity to find a way out before we actually press him for assistance. But waiting until we want to play this card is problematic too, because you and I may not know or hear of situations in our relations with Russia where this leverage would be useful. So, I think the best way forward would be to get word of what we have to those best placed to determine when and how to use it."

Hampton interrupted him at this point. "Do you mean the Ambassador or the Foreign Office? I thought we agreed that that might not be the wisest move and, in any event, they will go apoplectic if they find out what we have done without consulting them."

"I think we have to say something to the Ambassador" said Warburton, "but if you agree, I think it should be in very vague terms – unsolicited information sent to us which might give us a degree of leverage over a high-ranking Russian, best if he doesn't know, and we would seek advice from London on what to do. Then we take this to Number 10." He noticed Hanson's eyebrows rise a little at this. "If you think about it, they should be delighted that we have a new element of influence in our relations with Russia; so they should be quite pleased with us. At the same time, we will have saved both the Ambassador and the Foreign Office any possibility of embarrassment of being involved if any of this should ever come out. If the PM wants to pull them in, or MI6, then fine, but that will be his decision and his responsibility, not ours. To put it all another way, if you were the PM, how would you want us to play it?"

Hampton was silent as he thought about this, but recognised very quickly, as Warburton had done earlier in the day, that this was the only sensible way forward. They could destroy the video if Number 10 wanted nothing to do with it. If, more likely, they valued this extra card - and quite a card it was - then they could hold it until ready to play it. He didn't know whether they would let Warburton play it or find some other conduit for approaching Gudanov he didn't know of, but hoped for Warburton's sake that it was the former. Warburton would take it like a sledgehammer blow if his idea and, to date his execution of it, were later to be re-assigned.

"I agree" he said. "You realise that the game may then be taken out of our hands?"

"I know, I know," replied Warburton "but there is nothing we can do about that. We can't go ahead on our own - we wouldn't know what to ask for from Gudanov in return for the video, so I think my suggestion is the only possible one".

How would you envisage getting this information to Number 10" asked Hampton.

"I've thought about that too" said Warburton. There's a SPAD there who I worked with when we were both in the Foreign Office. He works more on Treasury matters now but would know who to speak to. I could easily fix a trip back to the UK, contact him informally – we have remained in touch socially – and take it from there".

Warburton and Hampton, both knowing that they were at a rather crucial point, in Gudanov's life, in their own careers, and quite possibly in Anglo-Russian relations, looked each other straight in the eye. They held each other's gaze for several seconds. Then Hampton nodded. "Okay. Let's do it that way" he said. "I'll talk to Henry, make it clear that he doesn't need or want to know more than I tell him. I suppose he may want to be kept informed, but I think he will be very happy to pass the buck on to Number 10." He paused, looking just a little lost in thought for a moment then he added "Did you know that the phrase 'the die is cast' supposedly used by Julius Caesar as he crossed the Rubicon, is often interpreted as meaning 'the matter is now set'; but in fact 'the die' probably refers to what we would call a dice; and so the phrase would mean that the matter is now in the hands of chance – what will the dice come up with – and hence the exact opposite of the traditional meeting. But, paradoxically, as far as we are concerned, I think it might mean both – we are now set on a course, but what the outcome will be is very much up to the vagaries of chance – I often think that history is just the set of accidents that, of all the possible ones, are the ones that actually occur. I wonder if Caesar had both meanings in mind."

This minor monologue was a side of Hampton that Warburton had not seen before, but he understood that it might be appropriate to mark the moment with more than a simple 'okay' from Hampton. "Your view of History sounds right" he responded. "If I had left the Four Seasons hotel five minutes earlier, none of this would be in play. Anyway, I hope we are as successful as Caesar was in his subsequent march on Rome."

"Yes indeed," Hampton replied very soberly. And let us hope our colleagues do not stab us in the back."

CHAPTER 16

In the following few days after his latest meeting with Seymour, Palmer pursued every unofficial line of inquiry he could about Gazprom. He contacted journalists who worked on global trade magazines concerned with oil and gas. He met up with industrialists in the oil and gas industry who had widespread knowledge and a variety of perspectives on Russia's capabilities in the field. He spoke to contacts in the EU's energy divisions; and through some of these contacts, he met several energy trading companies' directors or employees. He visited two energy research think-tanks, one university-based, the other funded by the Saudi Arabians, both having amassed much long-term research and more immediate information on Russian energy and Gazprom in particular. Finally, he talked at length with Damien Holt, the economics professor from Oxford who specialised in energy economics, had been an unofficial adviser on energy matters to the PM for some time, and who had been at the earlier meeting Seymour had called with the Department of Energy.

Holt had turned out to be a mine of information on Gazprom and had steered Palmer to several articles, some academic but mainly journalistic – though quite well informed – on what Palmer increasingly understood was the highly complex but fundamentally weak, if not disastrous, state of Russia's energy industry. In other circumstances, Palmer would have had an aide to note everything and then write up a succinct but comprehensive report. But all his instincts told him that, in this case, he had better do his own leg work, utilise diffused sources of information, keep his interest in Gazprom very much to himself and prepare his own summary for Seymour. This whole process took him nearly three weeks, but by the end, he knew what he had to tell Seymour. The good news and the bad news. He asked if they could, once again, meet the next Sunday evening, after Seymour had got back from Chequers but, to his surprise, Seymour's private secretary said that Seymour would be very pleased if Palmer could join him for lunch at Chequers that Sunday; and they could talk then. This was only the second time Palmer had been invited there, despite being about as close politically to Seymour as anyone in Whitehall. He took it as a clear sign that the issue was just about as important to Seymour as possible.

Palmer duly arrived the next Sunday at shortly after noon, was checked in by the Chequers security staff and shown into a large drawing room. Seymour arrived shortly after, and a staff member of the famous house poured them pre-lunch drinks. Palmer did, for a moment, wonder whether they were awaiting other lunch guests, but soon realised that their conversation – what Seymour wanted to hear from him – was for no-one but them. It would be lunch for just two.

With the staff member still in the room, Seymour spoke disarmingly about the house, its origins, architecture and how it had come to be the PM's country residence but, almost as soon as they were alone, he fired the predictable question at Palmer. "What have you been able to come up with?" No mention by name of the subject matter was forthcoming or required.

"I have carried out some very extensive research" said Palmer, "and put it all in a three -page report for you, which I will leave with you, unless you want to read it now. The situation has its complexities, but the bottom line is this. If the embargo goes, the Russians will put very substantial effort and money into gearing up their gas production and distribution for export. But there are physical and financial limits to how far or fast they could go. The good news is that they could, quite quickly increase production by enough to meet the UK's requirements – probably within a few months at most – but there would be huge competing demands from other countries, most notably from Germany but also from almost all other European countries. We might be able to get some special treatment, get to the head of the queue so to speak, because of the role we would have played in getting the embargo lifted; but there is no guarantee of that; and a number of experts, analysts and so on think this would be unlikely to be a major factor. Kirov would be too busy playing for future advantage; and we don't have much to offer. Therefore, the prospect is that we would be able to achieve only a small increase in gas imports over the next three or four years, which is the critical period for us."

"Fuck" was Seymour's inelegant but expressive response. But he had not risen to the position of Prime Minister without possessing and displaying certain talents, one of which was to respond rapidly and innovatively to situations as they arose. "What if we spoke to them first, said that we were thinking of backing a plebiscite in Eastern Ukraine, getting other nations behind us, to resolve the issue and get the embargo lifted, but the *quid pro quo* would be a subsequent long term gas contract big enough to meet the UK's needs? I'm not sure how we would keep them to it – maybe we couldn't – but it's worth exploring isn't it?"

Palmer had, in fact, toyed with suggesting this idea to Seymour but, now the PM had introduced himself, he was happy to run with the idea as if a brand new one.

"We could certainly offer that informally and quite of the record – no problem about that – but, as you say, it's hard to see how we could keep Kirov to it once he had got his plebiscite win; and if he walked away from it, there is no way that we could denounce him - we'd lose every ounce of international respectability – and he'd know that. Still let's not dismiss it out of hand. I'll talk to Holt – you remember the guy from Oxford – he's very well informed, got good antennae – maybe he will think of something."

"Okay" said Seymour. "Do that. You might want to show him some figures I've dug out from the Treasury – with some difficulty. They are essentially forecasts of our public sector finances and the economy as a whole if we continue as we are – it really is rather like the boom we got from North Sea oil but in reverse – not a pretty picture at all. Plus, how it looks if only we can get access to plentiful supplies of relatively inexpensive gas. You've only got to look at how the US economy has boomed, despite a mad President, as it has developed its internal gas supplies to see how significant the effect can be; and these figures show that in spades. Show them to Holt – though I guess he will be familiar with them, or figures like them – to emphasise how critical it is to come up with some solution; and Russia looks to be the only answer."

Palmer said that he would, and the rest of lunch was taken up with going over the figures; and Seymour re-iterating time and again how everything else he wanted to achieve in health education, defence, social care, and beyond, depended on the public debt figures, hence government expenditure and the tax burden, and economic growth more generally. Most of it was argument that Palmer had heard many times before, was well aware of and quite understood. In other circumstances he would have sought to cut the discussion short. But over a pleasant and leisurely lunch at Chequers, he was as happy to absorb himself in the story, the figures, the politics as Seymour was to rehearse them. And while he didn't, as yet, remotely have any answer, it was curiously energising to hear Seymour expound on the problem and gratifying that Seymour was prepared to rely so heavily on him – an unelected official – for this most crucial of all issues. So, as he left to head back to London, he didn't know how to defeat the enemy, but felt that he was certainly getting armed up; and he liked nothing better than a battle in the shadows. He allowed the thought to pass through is mind that if he couldn't do this, then no-one could.

CHAPTER 17

Hampton saw the ambassador, Sir Henry Arnison, the next day. Rather to Hampton's dismay, Arnison wanted to know all about the 'leverage' Hampton vaguely described: what it was, how it came about and against whom specifically. Hampton reluctantly offered up all these pieces of information except one – he stuck to the line he had discussed the day before with Warburton that the video had been sent in anonymously. Whether Arnison really believed this or not, he didn't question it. However, on the critical issue – how best to proceed – he was very much in step with Hampton and Warburton. "We can't take this back to the Foreign Office – they will be bound to drop it like a hot potato. Might just as well pack the whole thing in now. Number 10 might say the same, but I suspect they will think through the potential, the risks, the trade-offs. Naylor probably won't even show it to Addington – he's been a disastrous wimp ever since they made him Permanent Secretary – and even if it did get to Addington, he's such a risk-averse Foreign Secretary he'd just sit on it 'till it died. No, much better to get it to the PM if you can – he does at least have the balls to follow it up if he is so minded." And that was all Hampton needed. He reported as much to Warburton, who set about implementing the next stage of their little project.

Warburton's commitments at the Embassy prevented him from getting back to London on a weekday for at least two weeks, which he couldn't remotely contemplate; and so he rang his sometime friend, John Lawrence, now a special adviser on things financial in number 10 – though everyone recognised his main role to be one of finding out what the Treasury was doing and report back to the PM. Warburton said he would like to meet up fairly urgently, and John was free that Saturday. Intrigued, and free, John agreed to meet Warburton for lunch at a Thai restaurant near Borough Market that they had frequented some time before and both liked. Warburton made one copy of the video, which he put in his safe, pocketed the original – though he doubted he'd be showing it to anyone this trip; and flew into London Friday night, had a good night's rest and was at the restaurant at 12.30 pm feeling, he had to admit, more excited, more *alive,* than he had for some time. Lawrence arrived at almost the same time, quite tall, of sparse build and with a rather calm and self-possessed air, somewhat older than the typical

SPAD, who were often extraordinarily junior for such important roles; but clearly delighted to meet up again with Warburton. They ordered food and drink and then John opened up with "we obviously have much to catch up on, and we must, but I can't sit here concentrating on any of that until I know what brings you here, and to me. So, let's 'cut to the chase' as they say in bad US movies and tell me what's going on. I am, as you may imagine, quite gripped."

Warburton could not have been more relieved. He had wanted to get straight on to his matter in hand, but felt that it might be slightly rude not even to inquire about John's activities since last they met; and, not least, his life in Number 10. So, Lawrence's steer was most welcome. "Well, okay, straight to it, and catch up later. The embassy in Moscow has come into possession of some compromising material relating to a senior Kremlin politician. It could be quite useful, if not straight away, then perhaps in the future. Neither the Ambassador nor his deputy believe that the Foreign Office would wish to get involved – too undiplomatic, too risky perhaps, just not cricket" he joked. In practice there is really only one person who can decide if this should be taken forward in any way and, if so how; and that's the PM. But we cannot go through any sort of formal channel. We don't have any obvious way of approaching him informally and, of course, in complete secrecy – unless you, given your role inside Number 10, could suggest a way or even, perhaps, help us?" He ended this very deliberately in question mode.

Warburton presumed that Lawrence would need to mull this over a little, perhaps ask for more detail about the 'compromising material' or how it came about – he would clearly understand that Warburton was not going to reveal the name of the Kremlin person involved – so was truly amazed when Lawrence just said "no problem. I'll alert Robert King – that's the PM's foreign affairs SPAD – we know each other well; he can mention it to the PM in outline terms; and see if he wants to pursue it further. If so, he can authorise a confidential meeting for you – it might be with Robert, with the PM, or with someone else the PM pulls in on this. Where it goes from there is anyone's guess, but you will have brought it to the PM's attention; and from then on it is, as it must be, up to him."

To say that Warburton was delighted would certainly be an understatement. He was, quite literally, euphoric. He had come armed with several arguments in support of what he wanted to ask; none of them was necessary. "That is, quite simply, terrific" he said. "A confidential meeting with whoever the PM thinks appropriate would be ideal. I'm very grateful." But even better was to come.

"How long are you in London?" asked Lawrence.

"I fly back tomorrow night" said Warburton.

"Could you delay until Monday night?" was Lawrence's unanticipated reply.

"I guess so" surmised Warburton, rapidly running through what he would have to cancel to do so. "Why?"

"Well" said Lawrence "if I can talk to Robert later today, maybe get you two to meet tomorrow if he is free, then he could maybe run the idea past the PM on Monday morning and, if he wants to authorise a meeting, we could get it set up for before you fly back to Moscow. Otherwise, I presume there is going to be some delay before you can get over again?"

Warburton, who had presumed precisely that timetable, could scarcely believe his good fortune. He would cancel any and everything on Monday to meet Lawrence's suggested timetable, and rapidly confirmed that that would be quite perfect. With that, Lawrence got out his phone, rang Robert King and, three minutes later had confirmed that the three of them would meet at 11 am the next morning, Sunday, for coffee and a 'chat'. Having fixed the meeting, Warburton did wonder if Lawrence would now want to know more about his 'project', but Lawrence clearly understood 'need-to-know' rules and asked nothing more about it. They moved on to lighter matters, each recounting what they had been getting up to since last they met; and generally having a very pleasant lunch together. All that spoilt it for Warburton was the exhilaration pulsating through his body, at the prospect of the meeting on Sunday and, with luck on Monday; and the resulting inability to really concentrate much on anything that either Lawrence or he himself was saying.

That night he thought again, in fact over and over again, as to how much, if pressed, he should reveal before getting any closer to the PM himself; but never got further than his initial conclusion that he would just have to play that by ear. It might become a game of poker – how much did they want to pursue it versus how much did he want to; and he wasn't at all sure he was any good at such games; but there was little, in fact nothing, he could sensibly plan in advance; and so he left it all to the next day.

The next morning, he arrived promptly at 11 am at a coffee bar in Bond Street, where Lawrence introduced him to Robert King, a much younger man than Lawrence, with a rather debonair manner – almost certainly Oxbridge thought Warburton – but an engaging and, Warburton soon found, quite a likeable personality. And Warburton wanted to engage, because all his plans now rested on his being able to persuade this man, sat sipping a Latte in front of him, that he Warburton, could deliver something not far short of an intelligence coup to the government of the day.

Unsurprisingly, King wanted to know a lot more details than Lawrence had. He didn't need to spell out that, if he was going to pass on the information to the PM – summarised to a degree as yet undetermined – he would need to be very sure of what he was doing. Warburton suddenly realised, in a way that he had just not seen before, that he would have to tell the whole story. The PM would have to know that it was action by officials at the Embassy in Moscow that had generated the compromising material on Gudanov. If he went ahead without knowing that, and it came out later, it would be a disaster for everyone involved, not least Warburton himself. So Warburton related the whole sequence of events – the trade meeting where he first met the Gudanovs, his subsequent sighting of his daughter Irina working the hotels, his plan to use this, his recruitment of Kriskin and Green, how he got the video and why he had come to King, via his old friend Lawrence rather than go to Foreign Office officials in Whitehall. He concluded, "We undoubtedly have leverage over Gudanov. His promising career would not survive it being known that his daughter was offering sex to a CIA-linked man for money. The questions are when and how best to exploit this advantage, which must be for the PM to determine." He hoped it wasn't too obvious that he had left out the rather more basic question of whether to use this situation at all.

Without asking, King began jotting down some notes. This was rather understandable, but Warburton instinctively felt nervous about it, because he realised that apart from the video, there was currently no evidence of what had happened. The video was only on two flash drives. But the sense that the project was beginning to escape from him was, he saw, inevitable; and he would just have to live with it. But worse was to come.

"Certainly very interesting," mused King. "Can you let me have a copy of the video; and I will see whether or how to take the matter forward." This was very far from the response that Warburton had been hoping for. Lawrence sensed this; and perhaps was starting to feel that he had sounded too positive to Warburton earlier.

"Couldn't you maybe look at it today, consult with whoever tomorrow morning, and, if it runs, Richard would still be in town to discuss it further?"

"That's not going to work" replied King in a sufficiently blunt tone to warrant no argument. "This is pretty unusual what you have here. I'm going to need to think it through somewhat, and if I put it to the PM, he is going to want to know everything there is to know about this guy Gudanov. Plus he will want some pointers as to how, if at all we could use this leverage, as you call it. So, I'm sorry, but nothing is going to happen at all fast," added with a degree of finality that punctured any remaining hopes Warburton might have had of his project maintaining the momentum it, or rather he, had generated. Added to the obvious futility of questioning King's response, he also had to admit that what King had said made obvious sense.

And so he found himself just saying that he hoped it would be of major importance – from his perspective at the Moscow Embassy he really thought it would be – and asked to be kept very much in the loop if and when things developed, He added, though with much less optimism than he had had before, that if and when it was necessary to approach Gudanov, he felt he was very well placed to do so, having met him on more than one occasion, and being as well clued up on the activities of his daughter as anyone. King nodded, but made no further sign or comment indicating assent which, Warburton thought, was as much as he would get out of King.

Warburton handed over the flash drive he had brought to London to King and, shortly afterwards, the meeting broke up. After King left, Lawrence immediately said that he was sorry that things had not gone better, but there would have been no way forward that didn't go via King; and so at least they had cut out any intermediate steps to get to him. Warburton readily accepted this; and was quite fulsome in thanking Lawrence for his assistance. They would just have to see what King came up with.

CHAPTER 18

King had very deliberately played his cards very close to his chest, offering no assurances that anything would ensue; and no real indication of what it would be if it did. Behind this façade, two thoughts had been uppermost in his mind: that he was rather pleased to have become involved in a situation that was both unusual – at least for him – and potentially quite pregnant with possibilities, but also that he had no real idea how the video he now had in his possession might be used; and he couldn't think of taking it to the PM unless, as he had said to Warburton, a whole lot of background work was done first, on Gudanov, on his position and prospects, and on the set of political relationships with Russia that would form the context within which any action would occur.

He headed home and watched the video on his computer. It was compelling, but he couldn't immediately see himself showing it to the PM. Well, that hurdle would have to wait. The bigger one was how exactly to proceed. He assumed that he would conduct as much background research as possible and then write a position paper. He was used to presenting material, followed by options and usually a proposal. But all that was usually geared to policy – sometimes broad, sometimes more specific, but, always policy. This was quite different, much more the intelligence services' remit; maybe that was where he should head with this. But then, ingrained instinct told him that that would not be wise unless and until the PM had sanctioned it. And it was so off track to consult the Foreign Office or anyone outside No. 10 without the PM's say that it never seriously crossed his mind. So, the only solution was to seek advice from No. 10; and as soon as that was clear to him, the person was obvious, Andrew Palmer. He was not part of any established hierarchy, even within No. 10 let alone Whitehall more generally; and he had not only the ear of the PM like no-one else, but was well known for reading Seymour's mind, knowing his thoughts on issues, even before Seymour himself did. Palmer would know what to make of Warburton's video.

Monday morning, as Warburton was settling down to work late, after an evening flight back to Moscow the night before, King got one of the staff team in No. 10 to dig up any and everything she could on Yuri Gudanov, Russia's Energy Minister, but insisting on no contact with anyone else; and arranged to meet Palmer that afternoon. They met in one of the large sitting rooms which No. 10 houses, on two deep sofas, facing each other across a low table with tea and biscuits delivered, all very English, and about as far away from the content of their discussion to come as possible. Palmer, whose natural tendency was to be overly critical, was nonetheless quite respectful of King's talents as a SPAD – he would no doubt have had him moved on if he wasn't – and without preamble invited him to kick off.

King had decided there was no point in trying, as he might normally have done, to give a quick one or two sentence summary of what he intended to cover. Instead he said that he had a strange, but potentially important story to tell, from first to last, if Andrew would just bear with him. Palmer merely nodded and, with a small wave of his hand, invited King to tell his story. Certainly, one of King's talents was an ability to summarise fluently and succinctly but without missing out anything important; and these talents he now deployed to good effect. He summarised the trade meeting at which Warburton, Gudanov and Gudanov's wife and daughter had been present; described Warburton seeing the daughter again, working as a high-class prostitute in an expensive central Moscow hotel; and Warburton and Hampton's subsequent sting operation designed to get highly compromising video evidence of Gudanov's daughter with an American who had CIA connections. This was now in King's possession and, could, in principle, be used against Gudanov. The questions – and these King presumed would have to be ones for the PM – were whether to use the material and, if so, when – now or kept for some time in the future - and if now, to what end. King relayed that he had already started research on Gudanov, but felt that a decision on the best next step was above his pay grade; hence his request for the meeting with Palmer.

Palmer was a long way past the point in his somewhat zigzag career when something surprised him. Perhaps more significant, Warburton's perception that what he had seen that night in a Moscow hotel could be used, and his preparedness to do so, were entirely at one with how Palmer saw the political landscape and how he liked to operate within it. But, as he listened, his most immediate and most important thought was that in what he was hearing might just lie an answer to the gas supply conundrum with which he had been wrestling. Suppose the UK had the ability to put serious pressure on Russia's Energy Minister. Could that not be deployed to ensure that the UK would get the lion's share of the new supplies coming on- line if the embargo was lifted? None of this did he mention, of course. King was a SPAD, a good one but only that, someone to research and advise but not normally to be involved in major decisions, and certainly not in ones as sensitive as this. Plus, as so often was the case, there would be innumerable aspects to be considered, steps to be worked out, pitfalls to be examined, but 'the line' as Palmer saw it was there, of that he had no doubt.

When King had finished his tale, Palmer responded immediately. "Robert, that's all very clear; and you were right to bring this to me. I will raise it with Graham, but it must not go anywhere else at all – you will appreciate that. It's political dynamite, even if we don't do anything with it. Imagine what a field day the Press would have if it ever got out. It could finish Graham. I make it eight people who know already, nine when I tell the PM; and that's too many. So, let me have the flash drive, and the research on Gudanov when it is ready, but do not involve anyone else in that – just google, newspaper reports and so on. Okay? Otherwise, there will be no further action or discussion until I get back to you. All clear?"

King said it was, pleased that Palmer had said he would return to him. He handed over the flash drive, finished his tea and headed off to his rather small and unprepossessing office at the back of No. 10, an inevitable sense of anti-climax, albeit he would still be involved in researching Gudanov. Palmer, on the other hand, could scarcely contain his excitement. He didn't know if it would work but, for the first time, he felt he had something to take back to Seymour. But he would do nothing precipitate. He'd wait for King to come back to him, see what that produced, meanwhile getting himself more informed about as many aspects of Russian energy supplies and the UK's relationship to them; and as much of the diplomatic war over Ukraine as he could find time to explore.

Forty-eight hours later, King delivered a three page report to Palmer. While it was a model of clarity and succinctness, King had to admit that he had come up with relatively little of interest. Gudanov had been born in St. Petersberg. He was 49 years old, so had been only ten when the Soviet Union collapsed, too young to remember much, still less to have had any sort of role in it. He studied Engineering at Moscow University as a student and then, having learnt English, took a graduate degree in Economics in London. He then returned to Russia, had a first job as an engineer with a pipeline construction company and then, aged twenty-seven moved to Gazprom. After six years there he moved into a junior research/adviser position with the Russian Civil Service and then, three years after that moved into a similar but more explicitly political post. From there he had several promotions, becoming Energy Minister three years ago.

As far as it was possible to tell, he seemed to have been promoted purely on merit, by no means a universal characteristic of Russia's current political elite. He did not appear to be associated with any particular faction within the Kremlin, though that might be careful news management, and it was assumed that he must be supported by Kirov, to have been appointed to a significant position at a relatively early age. One or two commentaries hinted or suggested that he might be towards the reforming wing of the Kremlin on economic matters, which implied opposition to the rampant corruption that pulsated through much of modern Russia's government. Still, if this was wrong, Gudanov would be far from the first apparently honest politician in Russia to end up in prison, whether justifiably or not. Of his parents, his upbringing or his family there was nothing.

Palmer thanked King, agreeing that there wasn't much to go on; but Palmer had nonetheless noted one key point that might be highly relevant to emerging plans. Gudanov did not appear to have a powerful set of political allies to support him and back his rise through the political establishment, people who might happily cover up or ignore any scandal related to him if they thought he was a useful ally in the ever changing world of political warfare that characterised the oligarchic regime now dominating Russia's politics and economics. If so, then a scandal would surely finish him or, more important, Gudanov would be bound to *think* that a scandal would finish him, if he had no obvious backers, or people with whom he had been scratching reciprocal backs in recent years. Indeed, there might well be those who would prefer to get a more compromised, and therefore more malleable, colleague into the key position in the energy industry; and so would be happy to use any excuse to dethrone Gudanov. A family link via sex and money to the CIA could be, for them, most welcome and, if so, Gudanov would know it.

Over the next two days, Palmer viewed the video; and reviewed what he had learnt from King and his own researches, gearing himself up to approach Seymour. There would be absolutely no paper on this – a purely verbal presentation – and that might allow ideas to emerge. But Palmer had a persistent feeling niggling away at him, that he wasn't really ready to talk to Seymour, that he just wasn't on top of the subject in the way Seymour would expect him to be; and over the year he had learnt never to ignore these instincts. He needed to consult someone knowledgeable on the context, even if it meant one more person knowing what was going on, but there was no question of going anywhere else in Whitehall. The only realistic option in No. 10 was Seymour's Chief of Staff, Phillip Plowden. But their relationship was uneasy. Plowden very much resented the undefined roving brief that Palmer, notionally the PM's Press and Media Adviser, had, but in practice Seymour's deputy; and Palmer resented what he saw as the overly bureaucratic approach that Plowden brought to the issues with which Seymour had to grapple. He had little doubt that Plowden would be instantly negative towards Warburton's plans, whereas Palmer wanted to give them every opportunity to materialise; and maybe boost the economy and get Seymour re-elected.

The answer to his conundrum was, he suddenly realised, obvious. Professor Damien Holt, whom he had been planning to consult further anyway, was the man to talk to. Holt was quite at home in the corridors of Whitehall, but by no stretch of the imagination was he *of* Whitehall. He was very knowledgeable on global energy matters; and quite prepared to think innovatively and challenge orthodox thinking. Indeed, Palmer had early on been very impressed by a lecture Holt had given, later written up in an academic article, in which he told a distinguished group of ministers and civil servants working in the energy sector that the UK's policy of massively eliminating carbon emissions by 2030 was, simply, absurd. The necessary measures would hit the UK economy hard, and, at best, reduce global emissions by about 2%, making virtually no difference to climate change trends at all. If, instead, the money invested in carbon reduction was invested in developing the *technologies* of alternative energy sources, carbon reduction processes and carbon saving, these could be applied throughout the world, would have a much bigger effect and, what was more, give a boost to the UK economy. The logic, Palmer thought – as did most others listening to the lecture – was impeccable. It had not the slightest impact, because to have any sort of voice at the international conferences and meetings on climate change, a country had to show that it was doing its bit; and politicians of all hues had to show that they were greener than green, such were the pressure groups involved. But Palmer had been impressed that Holt had been quite prepared to spell out what he saw as the idiotic nature of government policy; and somehow managed to do it without finding himself frozen out of the debate. So, yes, Holt would be just the sort of person to advise on whether Palmer was holding a loaded gun or not and, if he was, how best to deploy it. That would give him what he needed to take the matter to Seymour; and the confidence to propose whatever seemed to him to be the best way forward.

Palmer decided that he did not want to meet Holt in London. He recognised that he might be being over cautious. Still, anyone in Whitehall or the Press, seeing Palmer and Holt alone together, might rapidly surmise or manufacture some intrigue, which Palmer could do without. With some mirth, he reflected that such conspiracy theories were virtually always so much more than any possible reality. In contrast, this time they would almost certainly be very much less.

So, he arranged to have lunch with Holt in a pleasant Brasserie in North Oxford, quite some distance from Holt's college, but which greatly reduced the chance of bumping into any of Holt's colleagues. They asked for a table in the back section, which rarely filled up at lunchtime, ordered food and wine and got down to business.

"You know as well as anyone" said Palmer how vulnerable the UK economy is to inadequate supplies of energy, with the North Sea nearly exhausted, renewables only slowly coming on line, nuclear heavily delayed and fracking in limbo; and how much this is hitting, and will continue to hit, our economic growth. You will have seen the forecasts – in fact you probably did some of them – so you know that we just have to secure imported energy supplies, in practice gas, soon and for at least the medium term. There are ways we can stagger on for the moment, but the key is large-scale, long term contracts for Russian gas, which we can't access due to the embargo. The PM is thinking of developing an international initiative over Ukraine – I don't need to go into the details of that now – which could lead to an end to the embargo. The problem is that our analysis suggests Russia's gas production and distribution facilities are in such poor condition that it would be some time before they could get up to full production. In the meantime, numerous countries would be competing for limited production increases; and the PM is concerned that the UK might not appear near the top of Russia's priority list. I guess my first question is, do you think that analysis is correct?"

Holt, who had not only a very logical and informed mind but one that moved very fast, replied straight away. "It's rather worse than that" he said. "If Russia again becomes a major gas exporter, President Kirov will, undoubtedly use that position for political leverage. His two main, and related bugbears are the US, who are now self-sufficient in energy and so cannot be influenced at all in this way; and NATO – how to weaken it any way he can. In Europe, which is where his gas supplies will hold sway, the biggest supporter, by a long way, of both the US and NATO is the UK. So, either we will be bottom of his list or, Kirov will hold out some sort of deal to us – lots of gas in return for cutting back NATO's role, presence in Europe etc. – a deal that no UK Prime Minister could remotely countenance. So, the answer to your question is that a policy to end the embargo will have little beneficial effect on the UK's economic position for several years, I would say."

"So, worse than I thought" said Palmer, "which leads me to my second question. Do you know Yuri Gudanov?"

"Russia's Energy Minister?" replied Holt. "We were once both at a conference in Budapest, but I never met him. He hasn't been a particularly major figure internationally, despite his position. Why do you ask?"

"For reasons that will become obvious, this cannot, absolutely must not, go any further. The UK has obtained material which would, if made public, severely, indeed I would say totally compromise his position, and any prospect of career progression. I needn't go into what this material is, or how we got it, but it would be a scandal of, if not epic proportions, nonetheless, quite enough to sink Gudanov for good. So, my third question is whether you think, in principle, that this could be deployed to ensure favourable treatment for the UK post- embargo?"

Holt's reaction was not at all what Palmer had expected. Holt just stared at him, saying nothing. When he did speak, it was just to re-iterate what Palmer had said "You have compromising material on Gudanov?"

"That's right" said Palmer. "Do you think that could be used?" Holt now sat, his hands crossed across his stomach, gazing slightly abstractly at the plate of food in front of him, but made no reply. It vaguely crossed Palmer's mind to ask if Holt was okay. It would be natural to reflect a little on the startling suggestion Palmer had given him; but Holt seemed a long way away. So, Palmer tried prompting him. "Any thoughts?" he asked. Finally Holt spoke.

"If you have compromising material on Gudanov, then two things. First, in answer to your question, it might get Gudanov on side, but it wouldn't get Kirov; and Kirov is not going to jump through any hoops he doesn't want to just to save Gudanov's skin. So, no, I don't think that what you have on Gudanov is going to solve the problem." He paused, still sufficiently distracted in his manner not to notice how much disappointment this reply had caused Palmer.

"And the second thing?" asked Palmer.

"Given what you say, there might just be another route."

"Tell me more" said Palmer. Holt then spoke, without barely any hesitation, and with not a single interruption from Palmer for about twenty minutes. What Holt told him was at once clear and logical but absolutely extraordinary, at least to Palmer's ears; and there wasn't a lot that he found extraordinary these days. It made absolute sense while almost taking Palmer's breath away in its audacity. It covered history that he had not known, analysis he had never come across before, and conclusions that seemed to answer all his – and Seymour's – prayers while being quite different from what he had been pursuing.

Holt concluded quietly "So that's how it could be done." By then Palmer had made his decisions.

"Could you spend a day just thinking through anything that might go wrong; and then, subject to that, I need you to spell this out to the PM. Just you, me and him. Is that okay?"

"Absolutely" said Holt, still it seemed, more wrapped up in the logic of what he had presented than the potentially monumental economic and political implications of his conclusions. "Happy to do that." He let Palmer know he was readily available over the next few days, and Palmer said he'd get back to him as soon as possible. Together they went back over what Holt had said, while finishing their meal and, slightly light-headed, Palmer made his way back to Oxford railway station, caught a train to London and headed back to No. 10.

CHAPTER 19

The next day, Palmer alerted Seymour that he just might have an answer on the UK's gas problem, that he'd like to see Seymour along with Professor Damien Holt, but no-one else, and recommended that the meeting be entirely secret. Seymour responded with another invitation to Chequers, to Palmer and Holt, the next Saturday lunchtime. After pre-lunch drinks had been poured, Palmer said, "Graham, I have brought Damien along to spell out what he said to me a few days ago. It is not a short story, and it won't be clear where it is going at first, but I can assure you it's well worth the journey."

"I guess that's a polite way of telling me to shut up and listen" said Seymour with a smile.

"Something like that, yes" replied Palmer.

"Then over to you, Professor," said Seymour, with an inviting wave of his hand. "I am, as they say, all ears."

"Thank you" said Holt. "It will be useful if I start with a rhetorical question. How much of the UK's gas consumption comes from Russia? There are two answers to this, quite different and yet both correct. How could that be? The answer is that one is physical, the other economic. Let me explain. Currently, something like 45% of the UK's gas consumption comes from imported gas, some of it shipped in as liquid natural gas but most from the European pipeline network that straddles Europe. Around a third of all the gas that goes into that network originates in Russia. The gas in the system is indivisible; so, thinking in terms of all the gas molecules in the system, one third of our imported gas is from Russia. So, the first answer to the question is one third of 45%, or about 15%." He paused to see if there were any questions.

"So we are in breach of the sanctions?" asked Seymour. "Surely not?"

"Not at all" replied Holt. "That leads us to the economic basis. "no-one delivers gas into the system unless they have a contract with someone else ready to take an equivalent amount out and ready to pay for it. The system has hundreds and hundreds of such contracts. Apart from two minor so-called 'legacy' contracts – hangovers from past times – the UK has no contracts with Russia. So any gas that Russia pumps into the system is accounted for by the buyers – gas importers in other countries, independent gas traders and so on - with whom Russia has contracts; and who are taking an exactly similar amount out of the system. In that sense, none of Russia's gas comes to the UK. That's the second answer. So, just to be clear, if Russia engineered a huge new contract with, say, Poland, pumping much more gas into the system, which Poland extracted from the system. The physical intake of gas by the UK from Russia would go up, because more than a third of all the gas supplied into the system would be from Russia; but the economic answer for the UK would still be zero; and it is, of course, the latter metric that is the basis of the embargo." This time, he did not pause, wishing to head straight on to the core of the analysis.

"Now, purely hypothetically, it would be possible for Russia and the UK to agree that Russia would supply so many million cubic litres of gas to, say, a Dutch gas intermediary. Meanwhile, the UK contracted to buy the same amount from the Dutch firm. If the price was even infinitesimally higher per cubic litre, the Dutch firm would make a very substantial profit, so would have every incentive to do these deals. Now the gas would go into the system from Russia; and would come out of the system in the UK, in practice a breach of the embargo, but without the UK having any contract with Russia, so technically not a breach. This, of course, could never work in practice. However secret the deal, it would rapidly become clear to traders in the business that something odd was going on; and it would be only a matter of time before the true position became public. And there is no doubt that it would be regarded internationally as a flagrant breach of the embargo."

At this point, Seymour decided that he had to chip in. "I see that, but, if so, how does this take us forward?"

Holt almost, not quite but almost, continued as if there had been no question from Seymour. "So, let us imagine a more complex version. Suppose the deal is that Russia supplies varying amounts of gas, for varying contract periods, to a number, say half a dozen independent traders, who in turn do some deals between themselves, again for varying amounts, and then those with the rights to the gas then enter into a set of contracts with a number of UK gas importers. These would bear no discernible relation to the original Russian contracts. There would just be several contracts among the many hundreds of such contracts. If you knew what was going on you could quite easily discern that the net result of all the contracts was just a major shipment of gas from Russia to the UK, but if you didn't know that then it would be just about impossible to identify what was actually happening. It would be rather like trying to identify where the other end of a single piece of spaghetti was in a large plateful of spaghetti."

"And you are saying" interjected Seymour "that we could use that strategy to get the gas we need?"

"Well, we are not quite there yet" said Holt. "This idea emerged from a quite informal discussion I had with some people in the Department of Energy recently. There was some division of views about putting it higher up, but one group worked on the idea for a while, tried to flesh it out somewhat. They even arranged for a Danish gas trader who had very good relations with some of the top people at Gazprom to, very quietly, sound them out. There was no traceable link between us and the Dane, but he came back to say that he had gotten a quite positive response. The more gungho people at the Department said that was exactly what they had expected because, they argued, Gazprom is just as anxious to pump more gas as we are to import it."

"So, what happened?" asked Seymour. "I never heard anything about any such scheme, did you Andrew?"

"Not at all" said Palmer. "So, what did happen?"

Holt resumed where he had left off. "The idea died. It never went anywhere outside the department. The reason was that the more cautious elements there identified what they saw as a flaw; and a fatal one at that. It wasn't quite right when I said that no-one could know what the true position was. Two players would know, namely us and the Russians. We would never reveal what was happening, but the Russians might given enough incentive. If, for example – the one that was used then – the Russians wanted us to pressurise NATO to pull back from the Baltic countries, or maybe have the UK withdraw its forces from there, they could threaten to expose our sanction-busting activity. If they did that, we would become an international pariah – there might even be calls for sanctions against us. So, we would be under immense pressure to concede what the Russian wanted. I guess that nowadays it might well involve the situation in the Ukraine".

"But, just a minute" interjected Seymour. "If they did that, they would be exposing that they were part of the deception, so they'd shoot themselves in the foot as well".

"I initially thought that" replied Holt, "but it's not right. We would certainly be shunned internationally; but Russia has always said that the embargo is either illegal or a conspiracy by the West against them, or both; and have made no bones about the fact that they would be prepared to thwart it any way they could. If it all came out, they would say that the West had it coming to them, two fingers to any international outcry; and internally Kirov would be even more of a national hero than he is at the moment, valiantly defending his country against an unreasonably hostile West. So, if they threatened to reveal all, it wouldn't, in the limit, be a bluff. The result was, as I said, that the idea died."

"Well, forgive me for saying it" responded Seymour, with perhaps less irritation in his voice than he actually felt, but given all that, why are we here?"

Holt turned to Palmer. "I think this is maybe where you take over" he said with a faint smile. Seymour rather ostentatiously turned to Palmer, eyebrow slightly raised, waiting for some explanation.

"I think Damien's analysis is one hundred percent correct," he said, "but the situation has changed in one important respect. You know who Yuri Gudanov is?" he asked Seymour.

"Sure" said Seymour. Their Energy Minister. I've never met him, don't know much about him, why?"

"Our embassy in Moscow has got hold of some highly compromising material on him. If it ever went public, it would finish his otherwise very promising career. The upper corridors of the Kremlin are a political snake pit; and he just wouldn't survive. So, the question arises, might we do the sort of deal that Damien has described, with Gudanov – if he didn't want to play ball we could use what we have on him to change his mind, but I guess that he might well want to use a secret deal with us to get Russia's gas industry back towards normality. The key thing is that we would hold a card that would prevent him from revealing – to anyone – the nature of the deal with us. We could make it quite clear that if it came out at all, in any way, then we could, and would, release what we have on him."

Seymour finally saw where all of the meeting had been going, and was, if not stunned, then certainly, for the moment, speechless. The three just sat there, vaguely looking at each other. Palmer and Holt knew that the ball was in Seymour's court, and so did he, but needed time to process what he had heard.

"What is this material that you have on Gudanov" he said, eventually.

"Someone at the embassy recognised a high-class prostitute at a very expensive hotel as Gudanov's daughter; and now has very clear video evidence of her trading sex for money with an American businessman who does contract work for the CIA. No-one will draw any distinction between that and *being* CIA. Gudanov would, of course say that he didn't know; and that is probably true. But the scope for his daughter to pick up things from him and, inadvertently or otherwise – maybe for more money – pass it on to the CIA would unquestionably finish him, and he'd know that. And before you ask the obvious question, the video resulted from a very efficiently conducted sting operation, the details of which are best left unsaid."

"Where is this video now?" asked Seymour.

"I have it in my possession" replied Palmer. "I suggest you forego watching it. It is very graphic, clearly identifies both of them and would be quite a popular piece on the internet. Indeed, Gudanov might play ball with us just to stop his daughter's misdemeanours going viral, never mind his own career."

"Supposing you're right" said Seymour. "Suppose we have enough to skewer Gudanov. How would the whole thing play out?"

"We would first have to get him on board, for the gas deal and with him getting a clear understanding of the consequences if it ever becomes public. I suggest we use the embassy guy for that. He knows the whole score, knows Gudanov, if only slightly, and it stops us having to bring anyone new into the plan. Assuming that that all works, we would work out a schedule of contracts, identify a number of traders who would be offered lucrative buy-sell deals; and then present the schedule of initial supply contracts to Gudanov. Like all Russia's energy ministers, he is a non-executive director of Gazprom, but with more clout if he chooses to exercise it than any mere CEO. We would have to leave it to him how he got the contracts implemented, but I don't think it would need a heavy hand – any direct instruction from him might raise a few suspicions – just making sure that our designated traders got in touch with the operational guys in Gazprom. Their strong desire to get whatever contracts they can should be enough. Similarly, at this end, our traders would contact UK gas importers offering attractive long term, very competitively priced contracts. None of them need know the overall position; and with everyone making very comfortable profits, no-one is going to risk rocking the boat even if they do have any suspicions that it's not all exactly kosha. We will need to do some surreptitious research on who exactly to recruit to do the deal, but Damien says that, while we need to take it carefully, that won't be much of a problem."

"What would be the endgame?" asked Seymour. "We couldn't do this indefinitely".

"A point I should have covered" said Palmer. "I propose that we would go for, at most, three-year contracts. If it is all carried out on a large enough scale, perhaps not all at once but building up, then we would have secured the UK's energy supply needs, see lower energy prices coming through, giving scope to raise taxation on fuel while still getting lower prices than before, all of which in turn allows lower income tax, more spending, from infrastructure to social care and so on. None of these effects would be huge, but together they would give us a sufficiently respectable economic performance – certainly much better than it has been or looks like being at the moment – and, crucially, no black-outs – and then, Graham, you go to the country. The contracts fall away, but you then have another five years, eight from now, by which time the renewables – solar, wind, tidal – and the first of the next generation of nuclear stations will be coming through. We may even have been able to turn the tide on fracking. We can really hook into a viable future, energy wise, if – if – we can get through the next three years and get re-elected."

"I guess I buy that" said Seymour. "Damien, any other observations?"

"It's audacious" he mused, "but I think it will work. I can see only one risk – if Gudanov moves on, gets promoted, and a new energy minister comes in. We can ensure that Gudanov won't tell him what's happening; he might not become aware, but it is one hell of a risk. So, I think we should accept that, if Gudanov goes, then we would need to cancel the contracts – there's a price attached to that but, in the larger scheme of things, I don't think that's a big problem. We would stay safe, but if it happened soon in the three year period Andrew envisages, the strategy would have failed."

"I take the point" said Seymour "but it would seem better to try, and hope it survives through, than not try at all."

Another silence befell the three men. There was a perhaps unconscious but no doubt mutual understanding that there really wasn't much more, if anything to say. The situation, and the proposal were both clear enough. There was just a decision to be made, although Seymour's final comment began to suggest that, perhaps, the decision had already been made.

"I need to sleep on this" said Seymour quietly. "But there is no point in letting a decision drag on. We can't consult anyone else; and we aren't going to get any more useful information. So, both of you, stay the night – the staff will get you all the overnight gear you need – and I'll let you know by lunchtime tomorrow."

Palmer and Holt nodded assent and, as their meal ended, Holt went off to phone his wife, to let her know that they wouldn't be home that night. Being required by the Prime Minister of the United Kingdom to stay the night at Chequers was a sufficiently grand reason to assuage what might otherwise have been a distinctly chilly reaction.

Despite the numerous distractions which Chequers had to offer – including extensive grounds, a billiards room and a croquet lawn – and an interesting set of guests for dinner, including two cabinet ministers and their wives, America's ambassador to the UK and two senior businessmen, both Palmer and Holt found that the time dragged somewhat; a feeling that was no less prevalent the next morning. And then Sunday lunch was with Seymour's family – his wife and two daughters – which precluded any discussion of the topic of their previous day's lunch. But, finally, over coffee, the day being pleasantly warm and dry, Seymour led Palmer and Holt out to a small patio. Without preamble Seymour said "Okay, let's do it. As I understand it, neither the Russian private detective nor the US guy really know the score. So, tell King and Lawrence that we are not pursuing the idea, at least not now. That means that the only people in the know going forward are our two embassy guys in Moscow and us three. Let's keep it that way."

"I understand the importance of that" replied Holt "but we must include at least one more. There is no way that an embassy official can set up the raft of contracts needed. That will require an experienced gas supply man who can negotiate on an equal footing with whoever Gudanov puts us in touch with." He was about to go on, but Seymour interrupted him.

"Do you know anyone who could do that for us; someone completely trustworthy?" he asked.

"I don't, no" said Holt "but I have some contacts, people in companies who I have advised from time to time; and I think I could dig out a name without raising any suspicions. I'd just be asking for someone who could fill me in on some details – nuts and bolts so to speak – of gas supply issues in Europe, to assist me for a new article.

"Sounds good" said Seymour. "See who you can find, preferably more than one, let Andrew know who they are and he can discreetly check them out. When you have a name, let me know. I want to say that, apart from the relevant experience and expertise, we need someone trustworthy, but the stakes are too high to rely on trust. How about we offer half a million dollars at the start, half a million on completion, and another million dollars in five years if the matter has remained completely secret. Would that be sufficient?"

"I don't know" responded Holt. "Maybe double that? A total of four million dollars should do it, if you can squirrel that amount away from the public's finances without anyone noticing."

"I can fix that" said Seymour. Don't ask me how – I can do it. So, over to you Damien. Andrew, let me know if and when we have someone, and then we will need to contact the embassy guy – what was his name?"

"Richard Warburton" replied Palmer.

"Yes, Andrew, contact him, ask how he plans to get to Gudanov without alerting the world, check it sounds okay, and then I think we will be ready to press the button. If it doesn't work, I will be out of office anyway. The only question is whether I will be facing some sort of prosecution. I'll take that risk to take the UK into sunnier uplands than at present; and my government with it." All three men engaged in a conspiratorial smile, but all three knew just how high the stakes were.

CHAPTER 20

It took Holt only nine days to identify three potential recruits to the project, without raising any suspicions about his interest in them. He passed the names to Palmer, who asked an old friend now in the banking world to contact an agency which would very discreetly find out all there was to find out about the three men. Three weeks after their last meeting with Seymour, Palmer had a name, Martin Fielding.

Fielding had a British father and a Finnish mother, spoke both languages and Russian fluently, had originally had a career in pipeline construction but then moved on to gas industry economics, and now ran a consultancy advising gas companies – producers, distributors and purchasers – on gas supply contracts. He had a reputation in the industry for knowing his business thoroughly and being a tough adviser behind the negotiating scenes. If he would take on what Seymour wanted then, Palmer reasoned, he would be ideal. He surmised that it almost certainly depended on how much he wanted up to four million dollars.

Fielding spent a lot of time in Rotterdam, but had an office in London. Holt contacted him and asked if they might meet when next Fielding was there. Fielding had read some of Holt's written work, said he was happy to meet; and they fixed to meet on his next trip to London, which was in only three days' time. Palmer had said he wanted to be there as well; and Holt, who had been comfortable with what might have been termed the design stage of the project, but was increasingly feeling uncomfortable in the development stage, was happy to agree. They met in Fielding's office, part of one of the numerous glass towers now towering over Canary Wharf. Fielding was, in every way, an imposing figure, well over six feet tall, muscular, a powerful, tanned face with short silver hair, and with an air that suggested he was very comfortable in his surroundings. Holt introduced himself and Palmer; if Fielding recognised him, he did not indicate it. They all shook hands, coffee was ordered and Fielding asked how he might help.

Palmer and Holt had agreed that most of the discussion would probably have to come from Palmer, but that Holt, having made the appointment, would have to kick off, which he did.

"What we wish to discuss, for reasons that will become clear, has to be totally confidential. Could I have your assurance that, whatever may or may not transpire from this meeting, you will treat it, for all time, as such? I assume this is not unusual concerning gas contracting issues?"

Fielding merely nodded and, as Holt did not go on added "of course, I'm happy to give you that assurance."

"Thank you" replied Holt. "At one level, the proposal we bring is very simple – to arrange for us a series of interlinked gas supply contracts that will run over the next three years or so. We understand that you are well placed and, in fact, very experienced in this type of work?"

Fielding, who, to anyone who knew him well would have seemed, if not a little tense then certainly rather quizzical, now eased considerably. "That is very much the type of work I carry out so, in principle, that is not a problem. But you said that was 'at one level'. Can you explain the 'other', I infer, more complicated level?" This seemed to Palmer to reflect the rather direct approach which his researches had identified and which, Palmer further reflected, he rather liked.

"The contracts will be many and various, between a number of players in the European gas supply and distribution system, with no obvious link between them, but the source of all the gas will be Gazprom; and the final destination for all of it will be UK gas importers."

So there it was, thought Palmer, in a sentence, a single sentence – the project, the risk, the potential benefit to the UK economy, the political ramifications, Seymour's career, even his place in history, and Palmer's career as well in all probability, all there in this one proposition, to a total stranger; and Palmer would only be able to include it in his memoirs if the whole thing went pear-shaped. He was not the sort to over-dramatise, but it did feel like quite a pivotal moment in his life.

"Ah, I see" said Fielding. "Yes, that does complicate things somewhat. I take it, therefore, that this is an unofficial UK government initiative?" Palmer decided that this was the moment for him to step in.

"There would be no link to the UK government or any agency that comes under its authority. There would simply be the set of contracts, for which you would be rewarded very generously, but from a Swiss bank account with no link to the UK. And no-one besides us three, and one other person based in Moscow, would have any sight or knowledge of the overall structure of the contracts."

"Who is the fourth person?" asked Fielding.

"Someone based in Moscow who would seek and hopefully secure Gazprom agreement to the plan" replied Palmer, but he would have no bearing on the contract structure nor knowledge of your role in setting it up, of that I can assure you."

"Roughly how many firms would be involved?" asked Fielding. Palmer decided that he did not want to appear too dominant in the discussion; and turned to Holt.

"We would need to discuss that with you, but I would say between six and ten."

Fielding nodded again, indicating that this estimate did not surprise him. After a pause he added "I presume that you have made some realistic estimates of the probability that the overall structure would become public.?"

"We have" said Holt. "Our view - which you are in a very good position to verify or reject – is that, while the overall structure would be clear to anyone who knew of its existence, for anyone who didn't know, it would be very improbable indeed that, out of the hundreds and hundreds of contracts operative in the European gas pipeline system, these particular ones could be extracted and stitched together to reveal their overall impact. If, on looking at what we propose, you did not agree, then we would re-design it or, if no structure looked sound to you, then we would have to drop the plan completely." There was no doubting that this statement was welcome news to Fielding; it knocked out at least one reservation he had.

"What is the prospect of my ending up being prosecuted, would you say, if this breach of the embargo did come to light?"

Palmer stepped in again. "I will be absolutely straight with you; and the answer is that no-one really knows. The embargo is an international agreement, to which the signatory governments are bound, but it is completely untested whether such an agreement could ever end up being employed with the force of law in a court as against a private operator. My guess – it is only a guess but I am fairly confident about it – is that it would be the UK government, despite a lack of any supporting evidence that would, as the clear beneficiary, be regarded as having broken the embargo; and any action, sanctions, fines or whatever that were imposed would be against the UK government. But I cannot guarantee that."

"Fair enough" said Fielding. "I thank you for your candour on the point. It naturally leads to my next question, which is what remuneration you had in mind."

Palmer was widely regarded, by friend and foe alike, as someone who could size people up quickly, and know best how to get them to respond the way he wanted. With journalists, other media types, politicians, civil servants and, less frequently, businessmen, he had an instinct for when to bully, when to charm, when to negotiate; when to use persuasion, when to confront, when if necessary to threaten. As he now contemplated Fielding's predictable question, he made an instant decision, not to make an offer that he might be persuaded to raise – he reckoned that that would only exacerbate any negative feelings Fielding had about the proposal. Rather, Palmer needed to feed, to endorse ant positive feelings, and so he decided to go all in, offer the maximum, make it clear there and now that it was the maximum, non-negotiable; and if Fielding didn't like it, then they would just have to look elsewhere. But some gut instinct told him that this would not be necessary.

"We would pay you one million dollars at the start, another million dollars on completion of all the contracts – that's in addition to any commissions you may be able to extract – and then another two million dollars in five years' time, *if* the whole process has remained completely unidentified. Any publicity, whatever the cause, would negate this final payment. That's the deal. I have no leeway to negotiate. I hope it is sufficient, but if not, we must go our separate ways."

"I think that is acceptable" said Fielding "and I do not seek to negotiate for more. But I do have a question which has a bearing on what my remuneration is likely to be. If someone does discover the truth of this arrangement, and seeks to capitalise on it, are you, in principle, prepared to buy off such a whistle blower?"

Although Palmer had not contemplated this possibility, he responded immediately, as if it had been fully thought through. "Yes, no question" he said. "We very much hope to avoid this, but what is at stake dwarfs any ransom that someone might demand from us. So, we would be prepared to pay a significant sum. But if a potential whistle blower looked to be too greedy, then we might apply a little stick as well as carrot. You needn't concern yourself with what that stick might be" he added casually but, in a second, the atmosphere had changed dramatically.

The next few seconds did not pass quickly for Palmer or Holt, but Fielding eventually broke the slightly stunned silence. "Very well" he said, "I'll do it. How detailed is your planning to date?"

Holt once again took up the threads of the conversation. "The first step will be to get Gazprom to agree the principle. That you can leave to us. Then, we envisage two tiers of gas traders being involved, one facing Gazprom, the other facing UK gas importers. First, your role would be to get the UK-facing tier to offer a series of provisional contracts to UK gas importers that they will not want to refuse – long term guaranteed contracts at up to 10% below current gas prices. Once agreed, these traders would contract with the Gazprom facing tier, some directly others via other UK tier traders, to purchase the gas they need to meet their UK contracts. Then, your second role would be to set up the contracts with Gazprom that these traders need to meet these new supply contracts. With all the provisional contracts in place, they would then be finalised, not all at once but staggered over some months."

"And then what?" asked Fielding.

"We reckon that the first benefits to the UK could come through in months. The full effect would be a 15 to 20% reduction in the price of what would then be well above one third of all the UK's gas requirements. continuing for at least three years plus, no less important, absolute security of energy supplies against foreseeable demand fluctuations. The boost to the UK economy, through lower energy prices, or through substantially higher tax revenue without raising energy prices, or, most likely, some combination of the two, will be invaluable to economic growth, employment and wider economic well-being in the UK. Plus, while it is no part of our brief, the boost to the Russian economy will also be significant. Very much a win-win situation. But that's the bigger picture. The first step is to review the plan I outlined, see if you think it will work, or maybe it needs adjusting. We will give the go-ahead to our man in Moscow only if and when you are satisfied that it will work."

"That all sounds doable" replied Fielding. "You will probably be aware that it would by no means be the first time that such operations have been carried out though, as far as I know, never on this scale or over such a sustained period. So, yes, let's do it. When might I expect the first payment?"

"As soon as we have Gazprom approval" said Palmer. "That might take a few weeks, but I hope not more. If you have, or can set up, an untraceable bank account in Switzerland or wherever you want, and let me know the details, I will arrange it. We envisage the contracts all being in place over, say six months at the most, preferably less, but not so fast as to draw unwanted attention to them. does that sound okay to you?" Fielding confirmed that it did. After that, there seemed nothing much else to say and so, with a few minor pleasantries, Palmer and Holt took their leave.

"You have just witnessed" said Palmer, "the first steps in saving the UK economy, and Seymour's prime ministership, or the biggest political scandal since Watergate. I sincerely hope that it is the first."

CHAPTER 21

The next day, Palmer got directly in touch with Warburton at the embassy in Moscow. To Warburton's almost uncontrollable delight, he said that the PM had approved use of the 'information', as he tactfully called it, on Gudanov; and had authorised Warburton as the contact with Gudanov. What they would ask of Gudanov was not entirely straightforward, so Warburton would need to come to London to be briefed on the project. The whole matter remained, of course, entirely secret and unofficial. So he would like to see Warburton in London the following weekend, a trip that would be entirely personal as far as the embassy was concerned. Once Warburton booked a hotel room, he should notify Palmer and they could meet there. Palmer did not indicate what the 'not entirely straight-forward' element to be put to Gudanov might comprise.

With Holt at his side, Palmer duly met up with Warburton the following Saturday morning. Holt spelt out the details of gas supply and trading in Europe, the scope to get round the current embargo, the need for Gudanov to set up the Gazprom end of the contracts envisaged, the need for total and eternal secrecy on Gudanov's part and, most important of all, the consequences of his failing to meet the last of these requirements. Once Warburton had absorbed all the energy-related details, discussion turned to the crucial aspect – how to approach Gudanov without alerting anyone to what was happening and how far to go, specifically whether Warburton should show Gudanov the video, or just leave it with him. Warburton said they should leave setting up a meeting to him, he'd need time to find a way but had little doubt he could do it. On whether to show the video, they agreed that the plan would be just to leave a flash drive copy with Gudanov, but have a computer available so that it could be provided if he insisted on seeing it there and then.

It was Holt that offered one further piece of advice. "Keep the video back until the last minute" he suggested. "We know that the Russians will be very keen to conclude such a deal, however clandestine, and I think Gudanov will love it. He will get a huge amount of kudos from this in the Kremlin. Get him fixated on that for a while let him really feel the potential, before somewhat raining on his parade. He will hate the blackmail, so we want him to fully know the offer's benefits before he contemplates throwing a fit."

"A good thought" said Palmer, something, he speculated, that he might well have come up with himself. Holt might, at times, be a bit of a maverick thinker, but he clearly could be very incisive as well. He looked intently at Warburton "Rather a lot riding on this" he said, meaning, as Warburton immediately understood, riding on him. Success will not go unnoticed." Five low-key words, but Warburton knew perfectly well what they meant – certainly a promotion and, quite possibly a gong of some sort. Well, he might not be a star of the Foreign Office, but what Palmer wanted him to do was precisely the sort of thing he was very good at, and he felt entirely confident that he could achieve it.

Warburton flew back to Moscow that evening, his mind racing through how he would move in on Gudanov. By the time he landed he felt fairly sure he had the answer, subject to Hampton's approval, to whom he would report all on Monday morning. He spent a pleasant Sunday with his wife, marred only by the fact that he couldn't mention anything about what he was doing, or planning, but she did not seem to notice anything untoward.

The next day, over a cup of coffee in Hampton's office, he related all that had happened, which mightily impressed his boss. He then explained his thinking on how to contact Gudanov without raising any alarm bells. Several well-established engineering businesses with operations in Russia, past, current or prospective, had been requesting some help from the embassy. The embargo prevented the UK buying Russian oil or gas but did not prevent overseas firms from entering contracts to repair or extend the Russian gas pipeline system.

Fewer such contracts had gone to British firms than they would have liked; and so they had wanted the embassy to organise a meeting – maybe a small conference, or a reception – at which they could network with key Russians in the energy sector. There had been agreement in principle to this, but not much had yet happened. Warburton's plan was simply to bring this forward, as soon as possible, and seek to have Gudanov attend, maybe only briefly, say a few words, but, from a Russian perspective, give it some form of official blessing. As this would either lead to some good contracts or enable the Russians to put more pressure on other potential suppliers, most notably from Germany, there was a good chance that he would see it as potentially significant gain for minimal input from him.

Once in the embassy, it would be for Warburton to engineer a brief private meeting with Gudanov. Warburton felt that he could hold out a sufficiently enticing possibility to snare Gudanov and, once alone with him, could complete the deal. The plan wasn't without risk, but neither he nor Hampton could see any other way forward, certainly not one with a greater chance of succeeding; and so they agreed the plan. Warburton immediately returned to his office to set the process in motion, drawing up a list of invitees, setting a date, notifying the staff who would lay on the reception. Warburton had no problems with any of this, but recognised that it was, undoubtedly, the easy bit.

Working at maximum speed, it took Warburton just under three weeks to set up a two hour conference plus reception at the embassy and agree with Gudanov's office that he would attend at the end of the conference, make a short speech and join the reception for half an hour or so. The event itself went smoothly enough, with around thirty UK businessmen and a number of Russian energy specialists of one sort or another listening to updates on Russian energy supply conditions, associated technological problems, financial issues and the like. Right on cue, Gudanov arrived, with a secretary and two associates, role unspecified but clearly running security for the minister. Gudanov made a short but powerful speech, politely but firmly rejecting the validity or the usefulness of the international embargo; and emphasising the importance of Russian energy to the world as and when this little problem was resolved. He was fulsomely applauded, and then led, by the Ambassador to a very luxuriously provisioned reception. Warburton's moment had arrived.

As soon as Gudanov had been supplied with a drink, and was talking to a small group of other attendees, Warburton edged up to his side, as discretely as he was able and, when he had the opportunity, said , sufficiently quietly in the general hubbub to avoid being overheard "Minister I wonder if I might have a private word with you? I would be speaking, confidentially, on behalf of the UK government and on a matter which might be of mutual benefit."

Warburton had no way of knowing whether this was the sort of contact with which a Russian minister would be very familiar, or whether it was, for Gudanov, quite unprecedented However, he looked not the slightest bit surprised, and merely said "Certainly. Do you mean now?"

"Yes" replied Warburton. "Perhaps we could go into the Blue Salon over there" – he pointed to large double doors leading off the reception area. "Do please follow me." Gudanov's secretary was some way away, and Gudanov moved towards him; but Warburton intervened. "I think you might prefer it if we kept the meeting to ourselves, so you can judge how much you would wish to share with your staff?" He felt that the implication, if Gudanov resisted this, that he really didn't have such discretion, might help secure the desired outcome, which it did. Gudanov just nodded and set off with Warburton towards the Blue Salon. Gudanov's security detail was no doubt instructed to be discreet in a foreign embassy setting. Still, there was little that was discreet about the way that the pair immediately trailed behind Gudanov towards the next door room.

Warburton had prepared for this. As they reached the door, he turned to Gudanov. "Might I suggest that your security people way here, in front of the door? There is no other access to this room, so they can guarantee your safety, as they should, but we will be able to speak more freely. On behalf of the Ambassador, I can assure you that there will not be the slightest problem."

Gudanov seemed, again, unperturbed, though he did pause a little longer this time, before speaking very quickly and quietly into the ear of one of his bodyguards. He and his colleague nodded and took up a casual, but blocking stance in front of the doors, as Warburton and Gudanov went in. Speed, Warburton knew, was now of the essence, but he would only get one chance for glory. He was, therefore, so fully prepared, that he no longer felt, as he had done days earlier, a near panic attack at the thought of what he was about to attempt.

The two men sat in comfortable armchairs, and Warburton pitched straight in. "Minister, we clearly do not have much time together, so I will be both brief and direct if you permit." He did not pause for acceptance. "As you are no doubt fully aware, the UK, as North Sea oil and gas run down, attaches a very high priority to securing its future energy needs. We do not doubt that that involves Russian gas. And we, for our part, believe that Russia is keen to recommence exporting gas. We therefore have a convergence of interests, but the embargo on Russian energy exports currently blocks that. Her Majesty's government has authorised me to ask whether you would be amenable to recommencing Russian gas to the UK somewhat ahead of the ending of the embargo. This would, of course, have to be confidential; we have developed a mechanism by which this could be achieved. I can elaborate, but the first question is whether such a plan would be acceptable to you."

There was, predictably, quite a long pause. Then Gudanov smiled. "Mr. Warburton, you probably expected me to be rather surprised by your proposal, so let me surprise you in return. I have already had more than one discussion with my senior staff as to whether such a scheme might be proposed to the British Government. But we have been very uncertain as to whether it was feasible, how your government might react, and how such a proposal might be advanced. What you have said appears to answer all three of our questions."

"Well, yes, I am surprised" said Warburton, and by heavens he thought, did he mean it. Unbelievable. "We seem to be on exactly the same wave-length."

"We do indeed" Gudanov responded. "As time is short, perhaps you could quickly outline how you envisage such an arrangement being put into operation?"

"Certainly" said Warburton, and as briefly as possible explained the contractual network they proposed using to conceal the overall source and destination of the gas supplied. He ended by spelling out what they would need from Gudanov, a main contact person in Gazprom who could oversee that end of the contracts and who would fully recognise that his career, if not his liberty, depended on keeping the arrangement secret. Once Warburton had that name, Gudanov could effectively bow out of the process. Gudanov thought only for a moment, and then indicated that he could fix that, and would get a name to Warburton shortly. At no point had Gudanov actually confirmed that he agreed to the plan, but there was no doubting that he had done so, fully and unreservedly. Now, thought Warburton, for the rather tricky part.

"Before we go" he said "there is one other thing and, again, I will be direct. The one concern that my government has is that, depending on how various international situations develop, there could come a time when your knowledge of this operation could, if it became public, cause grave embarrassment to it – sufficiently grave that it could not countenance such a revelation – which would put it irretrievably in your debt. In normal circumstances, we do not envisage that you would wish to reveal the operation any more than we would. However, there could be circumstances in which disclosure – of a successful operation to circumvent an embargo which your president is on record as regarding as illegal – would be of no great concern to Russia, if there were other advantages, but which would be fatally damaging to the reputation of the UK. "

"I see the point" said Gudanov, but I'd be happy to assure you that under no circumstances would I reveal our agreement."

"If I may say so, I did anticipate that" said Warburton, "and my personal view is that that is sufficient. I have argued as much in London. However, my lords and masters back home view the stakes as too high to rely only on assurances, however strong the commitment behind them is. They are only prepared to proceed if there are cast iron guarantees of the confidentiality we have discussed."

"I am more than happy to provide such guarantees" replied Gudanov, "if you can explain to me what they might be." At this point, Warburton produced the flash drive from his pocket.

"It genuinely pains me to pursue this, and please accept that I am only the messenger, but this flash drive, which I will give you, is their guarantee. I would urge you not to view it, but recognise that that implies a degree of trust on your part which I cannot reasonably expect. But I will tell you what is on it. It contains a video, which came into our possession, of you daughter, Irina, carrying out activities as a sex worker in a lavish hotel in Moscow with an American businessman who has worked intermittently but over a long period for the CIA. She is, of course an adult who may pursue whatever activities she wishes, though this is, technically, illegal in Russia, but my superiors believe that, certainly in the UK, this would be incompatible with a ministerial career for her father. I should immediately assure you that they have absolutely no intention of using this to embarrass you, given the mutually beneficial arrangement we have just discussed; but would understandably feel less well disposed if the secrecy on which we have agreed had been flouted.

As I said, I think this step is uncalled for, but if we all act according to plan, the video becomes irrelevant. I'm just sorry that you have needed to know more than you might wish about your daughter's late- night activities."

In the days before the reception, Warburton had had several discussions with Hampton as to what Gudanov's reaction to the information about his daughter might be, and how to respond. This included, at one extreme, absolute fury, withdrawal from what they anticipated would be prior agreement to the gas supply proposal, and a stormy exit from his meeting with Warburton. At the other, total, humiliating shock, and an immediate perception that he had no choice in the matter. In between were various degrees of, and combinations of, anger, denial, argument and reluctant acceptance. They had agreed that, no matter what, the crucial issue was to terminate the meeting without an outright rejection. This would give time for Gudanov to view the video, allow the enormity of his situation to sink in, and time for him to realise that, as long as he kept the project secret, there was nothing to worry about. He could even get to understand that, if he kept to their agreement and its secrecy, Britain had no further hold over him – if they released the video, he could immediately release details of the gas contracts, and they would not risk that. So, all in all, not such a great problem, if only he took the time to think it through. With these thoughts vaguely in his mind, Warburton awaited Gudanov's response.

Despite all this preparatory thinking, Warburton was, nonetheless, surprised by Gudanov's reaction, which was to fix Warburton with a penetrating, and increasingly, Warburton thought, intimidating stare; and say absolutely nothing. Gudanov must, Warburton thought, have been somewhat shaken; and his look might have an element of shock in it, but not enough to reduce the somewhat menacing element. Warburton stared back, but was no match for Gudanov in this respect. Eventually, Warburton found himself breaking the ominous silence. "May I ask, did you know of your daughter's activities?"

"I know my daughter very well, Mr Warburton; and I therefore know that whatever is on this device is fake. It is therefore irrelevant." At no point did his gaze move a fraction from Warburton's eyes.

Warburton saw his opportunity and went for it. "I must let you get back to the reception, minister" he said. "Please review the material, and get it checked by whichever technical people you trust. You will see that there is no possibility of it being faked. But I agree with you that we should regard it as irrelevant. In the meantime, I very much hope we can proceed with our gas agreement. You have my card, with my personal phone number on it. All I need is the contact details for an appropriate person in Gazprom and we can get to work." With that he stood up, hoping he could get Gudanov out of the room without further discussion.

Gudanov rose, but initially did not move towards the door. "How many copies of whatever you have on this device are there?"

"The original is in the Prime minister's office in London" replied Warburton. There is a copy for safety purposes on our back-up computers in a remote location. Both are heavily encrypted. Therefore, this material cannot be released unless the Prime minister authorised it. You are welcome, indeed, I would say well advised to destroy the copy you have. Shall we join the others?"

After what seemed like an eternity to Warburton, but was no more than a couple of seconds, Gudanov followed him to the door without any further acknowledgement of Warburton. Once there he paused. "You have a way with words, Mr. Warburton, with soft words, but we both know the true nature of this transaction. You must hope that I am never in a position to repay you for what is fraud or a despicable intrusion into my family's life." With that parting shot, he met up with his security guards, and re-joined the reception.

CHAPTER 22

Warburton met up with Hampton as soon as he could to tell him what had happened. Hampton congratulated him, and Warburton was reasonably pleased with how it had gone. His one regret was that he had not made clear, or even hinted, that the leverage they now had over Gudanov was not only to buy his silence but his co-operation in the gas supply operation. However, Gudanov could, no doubt, work that out for himself; if he didn't, this additional point could be made to him later, so overall, this was not a fatal error. Warburton then called Palmer. Despite the heavy security on both the embassy's phones and No. 10's, he spoke obliquely, saying only that he had the meeting as arranged, it was too soon to say how successful it had been, but that he now awaited what he hoped would be a positive response, together with the appropriate contact details which they had requested.

To Warburton's surprise, only three days later did he receive a request from an official in Gudanov's office to meet up that evening in the bar of a rather expensive restaurant in central Moscow. Warburton readily agreed, hoping this would be the first step towards implementing Holt's scheme. The official was late at the restaurant, so Warburton ordered himself a gin and tonic. A few minutes later, a man Warburton did not recognise walked up to him and gave Warburton an envelope.

Warburton was about to offer him a drink but, before he could do so, the man turned and left the restaurant without having spoken a word to Warburton. The obvious message, that Gudanov was as angry as hell about the situation, barely registered on Warburton as he discretely opened the envelope. Inside was a business card, with the name Mikhail Sokolov, Contracts Manager, Gazprom, on it, with an email and phone number. It was not clear if he was *a* contracts manager or *the* contracts manager, but Warburton didn't care which. Gudanov had given him the name he wanted; and would have been sure to choose someone whose discretion he could trust. In short, he, Warburton, minor official in Her Majesty's embassy in Moscow, had done it. He had dreamed up, and pulled off what must surely be one of the biggest coups in intelligence history since the end of the Cold War. The leverage he had secured, together with Holt's gas supply plan, were, he felt sure, going to be the key factors, if forever unknown to the wider world, in the UK's economic renaissance. Not bad, he thought to himself, not bad at all.

As he sipped the rest of his drink, he reflected that much was still to be done. But once he had passed on Sokolov's details to Martin Fielding, there was little, in fact nothing more for him to do, except get updates from Fielding on his progress, for reporting back to Palmer. Probably just as well, though he thought. He had found Gudanov's last words to him distinctly chilling and, much as he had delighted in pursuing the project – his project – he was aware that it wasn't anywhere near his comfort zone. He knew that Hampton had been impressed with him and seen qualities in him that he hadn't seen before or anticipated; and this, he confidently expected, would help boost his career. But he was self-aware enough to know that, wherever his career went, it was unlikely to involve much, if any, clandestine intelligence work; this did not unduly sadden him.

The next day he contacted Fielding in Rotterdam. They agreed that nothing of their business should be discussed on the phone or by email; and arranged to meet in Leningrad the coming Friday evening. Warburton invited his wife to join him on the trip, saying that after a brief early evening business meeting on the Friday, they could go out to dinner; and then have the whole week-end sightseeing. She was delighted; and Warburton felt that life could not get much better than this.

The meeting with Fielding was even briefer than Warburton had anticipated. He passed over Sokolov's business card, got Fielding briefly to rehearse the logistics and sequencing they had agreed previously; and secured Fielding's secret bank account details, saying that he would aim to have the first tranche of money transferred the following week. With that all done, he parted company with Fielding, said a metaphorical and slightly sentimental farewell to his conspiratorial life, and headed back to his hotel to meet his wife for dinner.

PART TWO

CHAPTER 23

Four Months Later

Andrew Palmer's life was not one given to great moments of cheer or elation. He nearly always got his way in the corridors of Whitehall, but often only after great stress and strain, with someone's – though fortunately rarely his – blood on the carpet, and with little time to reflect on any particular victory before the next crisis was upon him. But such was the life of a trouble-shooter, for he had no illusions that he was anything more than that - a senior one, a successful one, undoubtedly good at his job, but just a trouble-shooter, the pressures of which were unrelenting and, in the long-run, not good for his mental or physical health.

That said, in the last four months he had felt an underlying satisfaction, even a degree of *bonhomie* quite outside his usual experience in recent years; and all because Holt's plan, dear Professor Holt's deft scheme for circumventing the embargo on Russian energy, had been implemented without any problem. Exactly as planned, Fielding had rounded up some gas contractors he knew, established provisional deals with UK gas importers, hooked the contractors up with others in a myriad, varying set of contracts, and then tied them all back eventually to Gazprom via the good offices of Mikhail Sokolov.

It was far too soon to see any real benefit to the UK economy. But his SPAD with the Treasury brief, John Lawrence, reported that the data was showing significantly lower gas prices, the Treasury was feeding this into its large-scale econometric model of the economy, and this was predicting a small but significant pick-up in economic growth – and hence lower unemployment – lower inflation and scope for easing the pressure on the public sector's finances. One did not need to know much about politics to know that this would, in time, translate into better poll ratings for the PM, and at just the time he would need such an impact. No matter what nasty or, more likely, absurd problems or conflicts came his way to deal with, on a day-by-day basis, this underlying improvement in his master's fortunes, kept hm happier than he had been for quite some while.

Richard Warburton was, in his own somewhat quieter way, also rather content. He had been promoted to Assistant Secretary grade at the embassy; and was in the process of taking over a more policy-oriented role promoting the UK's business interest in Russia. It was too soon for him to know if he would be good at this or not, but he enjoyed the enhanced responsibility; and felt that he could give it as good a shot as anyone else in the embassy. He had not yet received any Honour; and the system was such that no-one would give him the slightest hint as to whether he had been recommended for one, in case the Honours committee, which received thousands of recommendations each year, declined to put him forward. But he was now at a level where an OBE would not be unusual; and he was confident that the Ambassador, advised by Hampton, would be pulling all the stops out to secure him such recognition. His wife was very pleased for him; and his only regret was that he could never tell her what had led to his promotion or, if it happened, to an OBE.

One consequence of his enhanced status was that he had now had much less to do with the day-to-day organising of embassy events. But his past experience and his overarching new role meant that he stayed in close touch with those now doing his old job, seeking to ensure that everything maintained or enhanced the embassy's reputation, while avoiding any degree of micro-management. One of the joys of this was that he could attend conferences, seminars and receptions and, because he was not organising them, relax and quite enjoy them, listen to lectures, network with both public officials and private sector businessmen, and enjoy the always very lavish food and drink that was supplied.

He had not seen or heard anything about Gudanov since their meeting four months previously; but noted that he was due to speak at a half-day conference one Saturday morning. The theme was the attempts by the Russian government to open up the vast, rather depressed eastern parts of the country, which both needed foreign investment and created what would no doubt be portrayed as very good opportunities for western firms to make good returns on that investment. Warburton had absolutely no wish to meet Gudanov again, still less for Gudanov to see him. Still, he couldn't resist going along to the conference briefly, slipping in at the very back when Gudanov was due to speak, just to see how he looked, not that this would give him any clue to how Gudanov was handling the new pressures that he had reluctantly come under.

Having explained to his wife that, as it was a Saturday, he would not be gone long, he headed to the conference centre where the meeting was being held. His timing was just about perfect, as Gudanov was introduced about one minute after he arrived, with no risk that Gudanov would spot him amongst the quite large crowd, over one hundred, in attendance. Gudanov's speech was, in Warburton's view as good as he would have predicted, giving a lot of useful information and, while clearly extolling the virtues of the business opportunities out East, did not at all appear to oversell the proposition or ignore the obstacles and risk involved. Altogether, a very polished performance, he thought.

Warburton was ready to beat a quick exit if Gudanov were to join the coffee break that followed his speech but, with some relief, he saw that after a few pleasantries with the organisers, Gudanov headed off to his government limousine, his security people by his side. Warburton thought he might just grab a quick coffee before heading home and joining the small queue that had formed, found himself behind someone he was sure he vaguely recognised. This was clearly reciprocated, and the mild embarrassment was dissipated when the other man held out his hand. "Colin Brewer" he said "we met a year or so ago at the embassy."

"Of course" replied Warburton and supplied his name too. "You're with a software engineering firm if I remember rightly?"

"That's right" Brewer replied "I've taken over as Finance Director since then. My CEO is here, and gung-ho for opportunities from here to Vladivostok, so I need to be here to keep his feet on the financial ground." He then asked Warburton what he was up to these days at the embassy, and a mildly pleasant conversation ensued over their cups of coffee.

"What did you make of Gudanov's speech?" asked Warburton.

"Rather good" said Brewer. "I've known him for quite a while, and I always thought he would go quite a long way. He's got a good mind; and seems to be able to play Kremlin politics rather well. He certainly gives out the aura to us cynical businessmen that he is someone we can trust; and there aren't many of whom that can be said out here."

"True enough" echoed Warburton. "How do you know him?"

"Oh, we go back a long way. We were in the same year at LSE, a graduate degree in economics. He was rather westernised in his thinking, though quite a serious type. We got on rather well and have stayed in touch over the years, not often, but I try to see him if I'm in Moscow."

Warburton didn't really think about it, but couldn't resist asking "what do you make of his daughter, Irina?"

Brewer looked slightly bemused. "Someone must have slipped up in their briefing note to you – Gudanov doesn't have a daughter."

CHAPTER 24

Warburton's registered the shock physically before his mind even began to absorb the implications of what he had been told. His whole body tensed up, and an awful pain began to build up in the pit of his stomach. He desperately tried to fight off these symptoms and re-engage his brain. "It wasn't a briefing" he said. "I met her" which wasn't strictly true, but he was past such subtleties. "Maybe she was his step-daughter?"

"I don't think so" replied Brewer. "He has two sons – I've stayed with them; and seen family photographs. And Sonia, his wife was very much his young bride-to-be when we he was at the LSE." Maybe you just misunderstood."

Warburton was now beginning to feel short of breath, with a slight pain in his chest; he knew that he had to get away from this conversation above anything else. "Probably, yes. It's no great matter. Anyway, I must be going – I promised my wife I wouldn't be long here. I'll hope to see you at another of these sessions soon." He wasn't sure that he wasn't rather mumbling by now, but Brewer didn't seem to notice anything untoward. With that, he got up, shook hands and left, now feeling slightly sick, and as if he was stumbling on the way, but desperate to make it to the lavatories. Once there, he locked himself in a cubicle and sat down. He was now beginning to sweat, his breaths were getting shorter and shorter, and the pains in his chest and stomach more noticeable. "Oh shit" he said to himself as it occurred to him that he might be having a heart attack. If so, he absolutely mustn't stay where he was, completely unnoticed. He started to stand up, but then whatever irregularities were going on his body became too much. He blacked out and slumped to the floor, the fall slowed only by his falling partly onto the lavatory seat..

While he lay there, unconscious, several people came to use the facilities, and then went, completely unaware of the medical emergency going on behind one of the cubicle doors. Fortunately for Warburton, with his head now no higher than the rest of his body, he started to regain consciousness after a couple of minutes, and, as luck would have it, as he tried to lift himself back onto the lavatory seat he let out a light groan, which someone from the conference using the lavatories heard. He just managed to see Warburton's leg under the door before Warburton managed to get back upright, realised that all might not be well, and asked "are you alright?"

"I think I may need help" was Warburton's very English reply.

"Can you unlock the door?" replied the potential good Samaritan. Warburton did so but in doing fell forwards again. It was enough, however, for the other man to ease open the door, against Warburton's weight and sit him back on the lavatory seat. He got out his mobile, but there was no signal. "Sit here" he said, I'll get help, and went to find a signal and rustle up an ambulance.

Warburton's next thought was 'please don't die'. He was now functioning enough to know that he must get his breathing back into shape, so for several minutes, he concentrated on taking light but smooth long breaths; little by little, this eased things. The pain in his chest eased, though not the one in his stomach. He felt a little less dizzy and wouldn't actually be sick after all. But, as these minor improvements kicked in, so did his mental functions began to click into action again. How could he have mistaken the woman in the Four Seasons hotel so badly? He had been sure it was Gudanov's daughter. And then the real pile driver hit him. Of course he hadn't been 'mistaken'. Gudanov had *introduced* her as his daughter at the waste processing conference; he had clearly acknowledged he had a daughter at the meeting when Warburton told him of the video he had in his possession. Why would he do that if he she wasn't his daughter?

Before he could wrestle any further with this, two paramedics appeared. They immediately hooked him up to a machine and started testing his cardiovascular system. They asked him several questions and, a few minutes later, said that although his heart rate was high and a little irregular, he did not appear to have had any stroke or heart attack. It looked more like an acute panic attack, but nothing would be left to chance. They asked for next of kin to be notified, led him carefully out of the lavatory area, put him in a wheelchair; and soon he was on a short journey in an ambulance to a hospital just beyond the main ring road.

He desperately wanted to think about what had happened, but the paramedics who accompanied him now had a long checklist of questions to ask him about his medical history; and then, having got through to his wife, passed the phone to him. He assured her that he was going to be alright, just a panic attack – unpleasant, even scary, but not life threatening. They were going to check him out, and she should come to the hospital as soon as she could.

While all this was happening, his mind, like a computer operating in parallel mode, was churning away; and as soon as he had a moment, it registered, loud and clear, that Gudanov had obviously set him up. Irina, or whatever here real name was, must be exactly what she seemed to be – a high class prostitute working a few expensive hotels in central Moscow. Gudanov, or someone working for him, must have recruited her, no doubt for an attractive sum of money, to pose as his daughter – no great problem if she pretended to have little or no English - and then simply asked her to co-ordinate her routine with the various trade fairs, conferences and receptions that the British Embassy organised at those same hotels from time to time. He'd have no difficulty getting such a schedule, from one of the many Russian secretaries or clerical staff who worked at the embassy – the meetings were hardly top secret. Then it was just a case of waiting until some idiot from the embassy – the idiot now lying in a bed in a Russian hospital - noticed her, and she was, of course, highly noticeable, and let their imagination run away with them. No wonder Kriskin had found it so easy to trace her. Warburton thought he was looking for her, but in reality, she was looking for him.

He was just about to ask himself the big question, why would Gudanov do all this when Valerie, his wife arrived. She looked quite shaken but soon sensed that Warburton was unlikely to be seriously ill. Their conversation, about what had happened, but not remotely why, was interrupted several times as different medics came to do different tests on Warburton. Eventually a more senior doctor came round, having looked at all the results and declared that they would keep him in for another three, hours, to monitor him; but that if all was satisfactory, he'd be free to go home, but should start a course of blood thinners, just as a precaution.

Valerie was a great comfort, sympathetic but down to earth; and was ready to put what had happened down to 'overwork' though neither Warburton nor many of his colleagues would think that was a very likely diagnosis. After a while she asked him if he wanted to have a nap before they got ready to go home, a proposal to which Warburton readily agreed, and he lay back with his eyes closed. But sleep was far from his mind. Why had Gudanov done it? And then, all of a sudden, he knew. The realisation jolted him so much he half sat up, which slightly alarmed Valerie, but he just tried to smile, not very successfully, and lay back again. He had remembered what Holt had said – that the gas supply operation had been tested out earlier, and an informal – and very secret - approach had been made to Gazprom.

The favourable response would, of course, have ultimately come from Gudanov. And, somehow, the reason why the UK then pulled out – that they couldn't trust him not to use his knowledge of the deal if the stakes were high enough – must have got to him too. But he wanted the deal; and so he needed a way to assure the UK that that would never happen, a way to give it, as it would think, some leverage over him; but leverage which, if it ever did come out, would be patently absurd. What had some Moscow prostitute got to do with him? His daughter? He didn't have one. Warburton, supposedly a safe pair of hands at the embassy, had walked right into the trap. How Gudanov managed not to laugh at him as he waffled on about not wanting to use the video he had no idea.

And then, as he lay there, pretending to be asleep, with his wife by the bedside, did the full enormity of what had happened hit him. He had given the Russians precisely the hold over the UK that officials in the UK had feared. At a time of Russia's choosing, he had completely undermined any position that the Prime Minister might wish to take if it was not to Russia's liking. The panic that had hit him at the conference began to re-assert itself; and he could no longer lie there prone. As he sat up, Valerie gave him some water and a soothing hand; and a few minutes later a medic asked if he would like a sedative. This he readily consumed, and tried, at least as far as Valerie and any visiting medics were concerned, to go back to sleep.

'What have I done, what have I done' he kept thinking. 'This is just terrible'. For a moment he suddenly thought he saw a glimmer of hope - he had photos from the trade meeting where Gudanov *had introduced Irina as his daughter*; but instantly saw that this offered no salvation. Gudanov would probably be delighted if Warburton produced the photos, revealing just how stupid the British Embassy officials were, how easily they had been tricked in their pursuit of gas supplies and how thoroughly he, Gudanov, had driven a coach and horses through the illegal embargo imposed on his innocent country. And then to Warburton's utter despair, he realised that he hadn't, even now, begun to register the desolation that now lay before him. He would have to resign, before they fired him, that was clear. And with the loss of his job in the Foreign Office, he would lose the Foreign Office funding of his sons' schooling back in the UK.

He certainly would not be able to afford the school fees, so after several years in the private school system, they would be jettisoned into a local comprehensive. That would hit them hard, but, more than that, it would devastate Valerie. And what was he going to say to Valerie? She would have massively disapproved of his project if it had been successful. Now it was a catastrophic failure, with such dire consequences, he wondered if she could ever accept it – or accept him anymore. He would lose his job, his livelihood, his children's education and quite possibly, his marriage. At which point he started to sob. At first it was just a watering of his eyes, and Valerie did not notice. But then, uncontrollably, he cried. She held him, and assured him that it was just the shock, the delayed reaction to a very disturbing turn of events, to let the emotions flow, and to know that he was in good hands and would, without any question, be safe. The thought went through Warburton's mind 'I don't want to be safe, I want to be dead'.

CHAPTER 25

Warburton was eventually discharged from the hospital and driven home by Valerie. He had to fight hard not to panic again as he tried to face up to the fact that he would have to say something to Valerie, Hampton and, inevitably, to Palmer. The first might well cost him his marriage. The second would be no less appalling, because Hampton would recognise that his own career, always likely to be much more illustrious than Warburton's, was also at an end, and all because of Warburton's naivete. Explaining to Palmer that he had fatally undermined the PM was an equally terrifying prospect.

Once home, he sat in a daze of despair. Against Valerie's advice he poured himself a large scotch and soda, which relaxed him a little, but did nothing to restore his spirits. Eventually, in the late afternoon, he accepted that he had to talk to Valerie, explain what would happen and, as best he could, why. He sat her down and said he had to talk to her. Valerie, who had been careful not to press him on what might have befallen him – why he might have suddenly had a panic attack, when he had never had one before – waited for him to say something.

"Val, I've done something terrible, made a catastrophic mistake at work. I'll tell you what I can – it's secret intelligence work – but the main thing is, it is so bad I will lose my job, in fact I will have to resign before they fire me. I do not know what I will do; and I don't think we can keep the boys at St. Paul's. I'm so terribly, terribly sorry." With great effort he just managed to stop himself from crying again.

Valerie took his hand. "We'll get through it" she said. "Do you want to tell me what happened?"

"I ran a project, not one I'm proud of, to gain influence with a Russian minister. It tuns out that he was running rings round me and, as a result, I may have fatally compromised the British government's relations with Russia in the future. It's so bad I can barely take it in. I only found out this morning, how I had been duped; and that's what triggered the panic attack. No-one else knows at the moment, but on Monday I will have to report back – Hampton approved the project so he will lose his job as well – and then I'll be sent back to London to debrief people there. It will be absolutely humiliating."

"Won't there be any sympathy for your position?" asked Valerie, "if you were carrying out a project on the embassy's instructions. Anyone can get things wrong. Maybe you will get pushed back down to the rank you had before, but isn't drumming you out of the Foreign Office excessive?"

"The problem" said Warburton, "is that it was all my idea; and then Hampton and I pushed it forward without anyone else being involved. We only let Henry in on it in the vaguest of ways, precisely so he could deny knowledge of it if everything went pear-shaped. So now James and I will be hung out to dry. I'm so sorry" was all he could lamely add.

"Well, let's see" said Valerie. "They may not be as drastic as you think; and whatever you have done, even if you do have to move on, I don't think they will stop the boys' fees until the end of the year; and that gives us time to see what else we can do. We have some savings, and if we have to, I'm sure we can downsize enough to see them through to university. Maybe it is going to be really bad, but we can be resilient enough to cope."

The sense of relief Warburton felt was quite overwhelming. Not just that his wife would be there to support him, but that she wasn't, at least not for the moment, going to pry into quite what he had done. And that support might just be enough for him to face the next set of consequences he would face. They had supper and he went to bed, in a bad state no doubt, but in a considerably better one than he had remotely thought possible earlier in the day.

The next day, Sunday, was undoubtedly the worst Sunday of his life, as he started to face up to what he had to do - talk to Hampton, commiserate over the ashes of their careers, and then head off to London to see Palmer. It would be brutal, but he felt, if not more resilient, perhaps more accepting of what was to come. He had a good education and a good CV. He'd get another job, the nightmare would, one day, pass. But that Sunday was a small harbinger of just how gut-wrenching the process might be.

On the Monday morning, he went to see Hampton. Past caring about any protocol, he ignored Hampton's secretary and her concerns that no meeting had been arranged and headed into his office. His manner was such that Hampton knew the news was not good. In a few deft sentences,

Warburton explained that Gudanov had no daughter, that the whole thing was a set-up, to re-assure the Brits that Gudanov would never reveal the gas deal; but what they thought they had on Gudanov was, in fact, completely worthless. Holt's plan was going well – abundant new gas supplies were flowing from Russia to the UK; but, having circumvented the sanctions against Russia, in a way that Gudanov could reveal at any time, the PM was at the mercy of the Kremlin whenever they chose to exercise their leverage. Warburton had prepared his letter of resignation. He did not mention that Hampton had approved the project; but left him to consider his own position.

Hampton was, predictably, shocked to the core. He asked how Warburton had found out the truth; and checked that there could be no doubt as to its validity; but all the while his mind was racing. After a short pause in the conversation, he said "If you go, I will have to go too. I approved the project – you wouldn't, you couldn't, have gone ahead without my approval and assistance. The money, the technical support. But let's just slow down a little. In the first place, no-one here knows anything about this, except for a vague and deniable conversation with Henry. Second, if the Ambassador inexplicably loses two of his complement simultaneously, it would do the one thing Henry will be determined to avoid: provide clear public acknowledgement that something has gone horribly wrong. And third, while the problem is about as serious as it can be, it is not an immediate problem. Gudanov's card - or Kirov's I should say, because it will be his to play – can only be used once; and so it will only be in a situation of particular importance to Russia. That might be quite soon, but it might not. Either way, we have at least a little time. I don't at the moment see how we can use that time, but let's not panic. We need to talk to London - maybe, just possibly, it is deniable? All thought up by European traders for whom sanctions busting is a very profitable business. I don't know if that will run, but, as I say, let's just take time to think this through. Go and see Palmer, but don't say anything to anyone else and, for God's sake, don't resign."

The distracting thought that went through Warburton's mind was that he could see, much more clearly than ever before, why Hampton had been on a more stellar career trajectory than himself. Warburton might be over his panic attack, but his whole response over the weekend had essentially been one of complete defeat. If Hampton had felt any panic, which was doubtful, he had got over it in minutes; and was thinking as clearly and strategically as the situation demanded. Warburton was impressed; and he was also mightily relieved. He had dreaded facing Valerie; and dreaded facing Hampton; but he had now done both and was still at least afloat, however leaky the craft. Palmer would be an altogether different prospect, someone nearly everyone was terrified of, and with good reason; but maybe, just maybe, there would be some way to mitigate the damage he had caused. It seemed unlikely, but in his present state of mind he was prepared to clutch onto any ray of hope, however distant it might be.

Warburton had not registered that, while these thoughts were floating around in his mind, Hampton had been silent, clearly thinking hard. When he spoke he had a further surprise for Warburton. "No" he said "that's not right. Not yet, anyway. The only reason we have to think that the whole thing has gone pear-shaped is what this guy Brewer said to you. He is probably right, if he has known Gudanov since university days, but let's not scuttle the ship without some sort of corroboration. Maybe Gudanov had a troublesome daughter whom he fell out with and never saw until much later. 'Never darken my doors' stuff. Christ, she definitely is a prostitute so, if she *is* Gudanov's daughter, she was presumably quite wild when young. Then a big, but recent, reconciliation – all lovey-dovey again, 'come to one of my receptions' and so on. It's not that likely, I know, but let's at least check it out."

"We certainly could" said Warburton. "On the video, Green asks for her number; and she gives it to him, on one of his business cards. So, we could get the number, meet her and see what she says."

"Let's do it" agreed Hampton. "We paid your private detective guy less than we expected, so we still have some funds to offer her for the information we want. It won't take long; and we don't have to let London know yet. Nothing terrible is going to happen in the next few days."

That evening, as soon as it was morning in the US, Warburton called Harvey Green and got 'Irina's number. Green had not, in fact, contacted her again. Some casual sex was one thing, but he recognised that he could get quite fond of this Russian beauty, which would not go down well, given his new partner in life back in California. Showing a degree of abstemiousness that he had rarely demonstrated before, he let the connection die.

Warburton promptly rang the number, got an answering machine; and left a message saying he would love to meet up in the bar of the Four Seasons hotel at 10 pm that evening or, failing that, at 10 pm the following evening. In the overall context, either would have been okay, but Warburton was impatient to find out the truth of the matter. Fortunately, and somewhat to his surprise, she arrived shortly after 10 pm that evening. She did not attempt to scrutinise the people there – obviously confident that whoever had rung would know her.

Warburton went up to her. Another time he would have been impressed at how striking she looked, an unquestionably beautiful face, a shapely body, and provocative clothes. But Warburton had other priorities on his minds. "I'm the person who rang you. Can I buy you a drink?" she replied that a tonic water would be fine. He ordered himself a whisky and soda; and they headed for a sofa in the bar area. Warburton then pitched straight in. He put an envelope on the coffee table in front of him. "In the envelope is five hundred dollars. It is yours if you will just give me some information."

Given that the offer of money merely for information, rather than sex, must have been something of a surprise, Warburton was impressed at how unsurprised she looked. "What information is that?" she asked.

"It is my belief" said Warburton "that a high-ranking figure in the Russian government, or someone on his behalf, paid you to attend an international trade affair posing as his daughter; and then gave you a schedule of hotels and dates when you should ….seek to meet up with people wanting an escort for the evening." The horrible circumlocution was Warburton's way of avoiding any reference to 'clients' or 'customers', still less 'sex'. He somewhat nervously took a gulp of his drink as he awaited her answer, fully aware that a major element in Anglo-Russian international relations, not to mention the prospects of his Prime Minster being re-elected, depended on it.

"I will tell you for one thousand dollars" was her unanticipated reply.

"I don't have another five hundred dollars on me" replied Warburton.

"But I'm sure that you have a credit card; and there is a cash machine in the lobby, which will give you dollars" was her calm repost.

Warburton was too tense, beaten up by events, and too desperate to object if the truth were known. He nodded and headed off to the lobby, taking the envelope with him. He got the extra money, put it in the envelope and returned. "Fine, there is now one thousand dollars in the envelope." Having seen how she handled herself in Green's bedroom, he did not expect her to check it, but she discreetly inspected the contents of the envelope and dropped it in what even Warburton could see was a very stylish, and no doubt expensive, bag.

"You are right" she said. "I never said I was his daughter – he just introduced me that way. So, I have not infringed the law, beyond the usual" she smiled. So, there it was – everything he had worked out and feared. To his surprise, unlike sixty hours ago, he was now extremely angry that Gudanov should dupe him this way, that he could have fallen for it, but he managed to hide any sign of this.

"Thank you" he said. "That is all I wanted to know. I hope you have a good evening" which, he registered could, in the current context, have a very diffcrent meaning to its usual one.

The next morning, he reported back to Hampton; and they agreed that there was now nothing for it but to see Palmer. Warburton flew to London the next day, having fixed to see Palmer at 6.00pm that evening at number 10. Palmer had no reason to think that the visit should be kept away from prying eyes; and, from Warburton's point of view, provided the Foreign Office didn't know, the arrival there of a middle ranking embassy official would cause no interest on the part of anyone who mattered.

Palmer poured them drinks and said how brilliantly the ploy Holt and he had devised was going. He was clearly about to go on to describe some of the forecast of emerging benefits to the UK economy as a result, but Warburton couldn't allow that. "I'm sorry to interrupt" he said, "but I'm here to tell you that a problem has arisen or, to be more honest, a complete disaster." He found that his mouth had gone so dry that he couldn't for a moment continue.

"Tell me" said Palmer, with the sort of intimidating look for which he was well known. Warburton took a deep breath and, as succinctly as he good, described how he had found out that Gudanov did not have a daughter, that Gudanov had completely conned him, Warburton, and that while, therefore, the gas was flowing, exactly as planned, they had no hold over Gudanov. If the stakes were high enough, the Russians could therefore threaten to reveal that the UK was breaching the embargo, exactly the fear that had initially prevented Holt's plan from being adopted.

Warburton braced himself for a tirade, a dressing down of Rolls-Royce proportions, knowing that his only response would be to accept it and say that he was resigning his post. To his surprise, Palmer simply said "what a fucking mess" and sat there, arms tightly crossed, no doubt fuming, but not exploding. Only later did Warburton work it out. Palmer used intimidation, ranting, bullying, every nasty trick in the book if he needed to, but to achieve whatever ends he was pursuing. Rage or worse, for its own sake, clearly didn't figure in his way of working. There was nothing he wanted, nothing he could seek from Warburton to help the situation, so it wasn't worth it. Worse, it might cloud his thinking; and there was no doubt that he was now thinking very hard indeed.

For his part, Palmer instantly recognised that, in one important respect, he had been here many times before. So often in the past, faced with a tricky situation, he had taken his time before finally deciding what to do, but nearly always that was merely to confirm his immediate and instinctive response. He knew what he would have to do almost before Warburton had finished explaining. They must quietly set about cancelling all the contracts. If news got out, or if Gudanov played his card, Her Majesty's Government would deny previous knowledge of the contracts; and point out that as soon as they had found out about them, they had, of course, sought to cancel them. If the news broke after they were all cancelled, the same line would hold, with the added advantage that it would be of only historical interest and not even a nine-days wonder.

He also immediately saw the two big problems. First, it would no doubt be expensive to cancel the contracts. Well, Seymour would just have to solve that. Second, far worse, all the gains that they anticipated, both economic and then political, would reverse. That would need to be considered, but there was not even a second's questioning in his mind that this would be infinitely preferable to a forced admission that Seymour had deliberately breached the embargo. Simply no contest.

Into the silence that followed Palmer's expletive, Warburton said that he would offer his resignation from the Foreign Office. But Palmer's reaction was similar to Hampton's. "You can't" he said flatly. "You screwed up royally, but no-one else knows, except Hampton, and we must do nothing to draw any attention to the possibility that anything is wrong. You can go on health grounds in a year or two, maybe" he added, which promptly terminated the relief that Palmer's first response had engendered, "but nobody must do anything at the moment unless I tell them. Is that clear?"

"Very" said Warburton. "Do you want me to do anything?"

"See that chap Fielding, the one who set it all up" replied Palmer. "Explain that it's all off, everything to be cancelled, in complete secrecy. As soon as possible, ask him for a report on what will be involved and what it will cost. He's had his two million dollars, hasn't he?" Warburton nodded. "Well remind him that the other two million still depends on none of this coming out in public. Get his report back to me. Other than this, just forget that the whole thing ever happened. Same goes for Hampton. What a fucking mess" he added again; and stood up. Their meeting was clearly at an end.

CHAPTER 26

Conveniently for Warburton, Fielding was due to be in his London office the next day; and so, after dinner and a restless night at his club, he saw him the next morning. He explained, without saying why, that he had been given instructions to call the whole thing off, cancel the contracts, pay whatever penalties were involved and then forget the thing had ever happened. Fielding's response was to stare at Warburton with a curious look, that he eventually realised was incredulity.

"I'm not sure you know what you are asking" he said. "I guess that, in principle, the contracts could be unwound with the same degree of opaqueness with which they were set up. But the contracts are like so-called 'take-or-pay' ones. You pay for the agreed amounts, whether you can actually take the gas or not. The prices agreed in these contracts reflect estimates that there may be times when the buyer can't take delivery because he has run out of storage at times of reduced demand. Because of this built-in flexibility in the contracts, the penalties are huge if you decide to cancel them. And if you don't pay them, they will sue you. I can't think of anything more likely to expose the whole venture to the world."

Warburton was, quite literally, dumbstruck. He had begun to see, or thought he had begun to see, a possible way out; but what Fielding had said look like destroying the plan completely. What sort of sums are we talking?" he asked.

"I don't know off-hand. I will check and get back to you. But, given the number of traders involved and the scale of the contracts, we are talking billions rather than millions."

"Oh, Christ" was Warburton's passionate, but unhelpful reply. "Will you text me an estimate, as soon as you have one? Is there nothing we can do?" he lamely added.

"Not if you want to keep the whole thing secret" said Fielding. "If the British government is prepared to cough up, I do not doubt that the Russians, and everyone in the network, would be quite happy with that. They get the compensation and keep the gas. But I guess there would be real difficulty in the government keeping such payments secret."

Warburton thought for a while. "I suppose the government could claim that this was the cost of pulling out of an embargo busting plan of which it had no previous knowledge; but I can't see the Treasury buying that. It would radically screw up their budgeting. Text me an estimate of the likely cost, just the number, as soon as you can." He passed over his phone number, but could think of nothing else to say, or ask, and got ready to leave.

"Just one other point" said Fielding. "If the thing does come out, and the government seeks to deny any foreknowledge of it, you know that I am not going to carry the can for this? If they come for me, I'd have to say where the proposal came from. It might not save me, but it would certainly divert attention away from me."

"I see" said Warburton. "I don't think there would be any intention to drop you in it; but it would, of course, be your word against No. 10's if it came to it."

"I'm afraid not" was Fielding's worrying reply. "Like all my meetings, I have our earlier one all on tape. So, let's not go down that route. The simple fact is that it is massively in both our interest to keep the network of interlocking contracts, which is working very well, completely secret. Why you should want to backtrack now, I don't know; and I don't want to know. I just know that it isn't on except at very considerable cost."

So, there it was. He had been outgunned by Gudanov, and now it was clear that he had been outgunned by Fielding as well. But that wasn't the worst of it, The worst, the very, very worst, was that he had assumed any attempt by the Government to deny any knowledge of the breach of sanctions would put culpability on the gas traders involved, who might well evade any prosecution. But now it was clear that, if the government went that route, he, and Palmer would be in the firing line. Palmer was the type to live another day, whereas he, Warburton, merely an official at the British Embassy in Moscow, would be hung so far out to dry that he'd never recover.

As he headed back to his club, he felt such a wave of utter despondency flow over him, so complete a devastation of his soul, that he scarcely cared if he got run over or not in London's traffic. Its grindingly slow progress was all that saved him, and for what? Another awful meeting with Palmer, to relay what Fielding had said. Twenty-four hours after he had last seen him, Warburton was back, in the same room in No. 10, with Palmer. As he explained the situation, including Fielding's clear threat that, if he was made a scapegoat, he would not be a silent one, he felt so depressed, so mentally battered. that he no longer really cared what Palmer's reaction would be. He just wanted to get it over with.

"Did you, or Holt, ever check out these contract terms?" was his daunting first response.

"I don't know if Holt knew about them" said Warburton. "I didn't, but neither of us contemplated that you would want to cancel the contracts. That would be bound to be expensive; and like Fielding said, almost certain to blow the whole thing wide open. So, we just didn't see it or think of it as an option."

"We might need a conversation with Fielding" was his next, even more daunting comment. "Make certain things clear to him....." he trailed off, clearly deciding that he didn't want to pursue the particular train of thought any further in front of Warburton.

"Well", he concluded "I need to talk to Seymour. Go back to Moscow, carry on normally, and do not say or do anything, anything at all, on this unless you hear from me. You and I will be for the high jump if it comes out. I can't let anyone think that the PM knew about this. Are you married?" Warburton nodded. "Does she know?"

"She knows I have totally screwed something up, and will probably have to resign, but not what has actually happened."

"Keep it that way" replied Palmer "not a word to anyone. Tell Hampton as well. Christ, I could fucking well murder that bastard" was his parting shot; and Warburton hoped that it was Gudanov, not Hampton, to whom he was referring.

Late the next evening, as Warburton was sidling back into his house, wanting to see Valerie but anxious beyond words as to what he would say to her, Palmer caught up with Seymour in his flat above No.11. Palmer was too tough, too confrontational, to feel any great emotion, still less anxiety about what news he had to deliver; but he knew it would need very careful handling. For Palmer, that meant getting on top of the issue, focusing Seymour's thought, rather than allowing him to just go berserk at how they had been fooled.

Seymour fixed then a couple of drinks, but before they had even sat down, Palmer weighed in. "Graham, I'm sorry, but this is going to be your worst nightmare. That video we have of Gudanov's daughter? It was a set-up. He doesn't have a daughter. She was no more or less than she seemed, an expensive Moscow prostitute. Gudanov set the whole thing up - he had found out that we previously killed the Russian gas supply idea because of the leverage it might give the Russians over us. So, he fooled us into thinking we had a reciprocal threat over him. But we don't. As he doesn't have a daughter, the video is worthless. And he has right royally screwed us. I've already been looking at possible ways out of this, but it doesn't look good." He wanted to keep talking, stop Seymour re-acting before he had thought more about it, but he'd gone on long enough.

"Of, fucking Christ, no" was Seymour's less than considered first response. "Fucking hell. Are you sure?"

"The guy at the embassy got hold of her; and she confirmed it. Said she was in the clear because she never said to anyone that she was Godanov's daughter. He just introduced her that way at some trade fair or whatever." He was anxious to move on from the sheer shock, and useless cursing. "I thought we might start to cancel the contracts – just get out - and if the plan was exposed, say that we were unwinding illegal contracts that we had only just discovered." Noticing the slight look of optimism that this brought to Seymour's face, he rapidly ploughed on. "But there are three really big problems with that. According to the guy who arranged all the contracts, cancelling them will be hellishly expensive – he talked billions. We can't deny previous knowledge because he taped my meeting where we set the thing up with him." Seymour, still standing, looked as if he might keel over. "And third, if we could find a way to cancel them, then the UK economy will shudder back onto the downward trajectory we were on before, which will almost certainly lead to defeat at the polls." He paused for breath; and was relieved to see that Seymour was still too shocked to be able to offer any useful thoughts. "There is an alternative, of course. Do nothing, no embarrassment, help the economy massively. But you would have to go along with whatever the Russians wanted for the rest of your time in office."

Seymour finally clicked back into some semblance of thought. "That simply isn't on. It wouldn't just be supporting them on the Eastern Ukraine, about which I don't give a shit by the way, or even muscling in on the Baltics. What if they wanted us to pull our forces out of NATO; or just scale down our armaments in Europe? The US are not dependable on this; no one but the French have any appreciable ground forces; and they are useless when it comes down to tough talking. No, I can't – I won't be in that position. If, or I suppose it's when, they try to pressurise me, I will just have to walk. 'Overstepped the mark in my enthusiasm to help my country, terribly sorry' and resign in disgrace." Maybe he was hoping for Palmer to tell him this was all wrong, maybe not. Either way, Palmer's silence spoke volumes. "Can you see any alternative?" Seymour asked.

"It will take a miracle" was all Palmer could offer.

CHAPTER 27

Three days later, a period in which neither Seymour nor Palmer could, in their free moments, think of any way out of the now impossible position Seymour was in, a miracle, at least in outline, unexpectedly arrived. It did not initially show any signs that it was a miracle, indeed quite the contrary.

Two days after he met with Seymour, Palmer's secretary came in to see him. The PM's office had been in touch. Would Palmer join the PM for a meeting the next day. The Minister for Energy and Climate Change, Stephen Marlowe, had requested an urgent meeting with the PM. He had asked that no official be present; and would not be bringing his Permanent Secretary or any of his staff, but needed to bring along a senior industrialist, Anthony Preston, CEO of EnergiCorp. The PM had agreed that, even though unusual, neither the Cabinet Secretary nor his No. 10 Chief of Staff would be present. But he would wish to have Palmer there, as an adviser who was outside the formal hierarchy of Whitehall; and Marlowe knew that he could not object to this.

On hearing of the meeting, Palmer feared the worst. If the head of a major energy company had been speaking to the minister; and the minster thought the matter must, under conditions of extreme secrecy, be brought to the PM's attention as a matter of urgency, then it could, thought Palmer, mean only one thing – that the breaching of sanctions against the Russians had been discovered. Which almost certainly meant that Seymour was finished. So, it was with a heavy heart that Palmer headed for the Cabinet Room the next day.

Marlowe and Preston sat opposite Seymour and Palmer. Palmer was interested to see that Preston had quite a commanding presence, even in the exalted company of the Prime Minister. No doubt being the CEO of a major international company helped. A somewhat chiselled face, a good sun-tan and immaculate suit all exuded affluence and confidence. He carried no briefcase or notes, clearly very familiar with whatever he had come to say. Marlowe introduced him; and kicked off by saying that Preston had come to see him, unofficially, two days ago. He, Marlowe, felt that what Preston had to say should go straight to the PM. With that he asked Seymour if he might invite Preston to re-count what he had said two days earlier. Seymour nodded . "Please, go ahead" he said to Preston.

"By way of background, Prime Minister" said Preston "my company, EnergiCorp, is one of the world's major oil and gas exploration companies, with activities in the Gulf of Mexico, the Middle East and, of course, the North Sea, to mention only some. Of late we have been drilling for gas in the Irish Sea under licenses granted by the Department. Our geological surveys suggested that there would be strata there suitable for fracking. It took us longer than expected, but we have been successful. More than successful. The test drillings we have done in recent months indicate that the area is one of the biggest sources of fracking gas we have ever discovered – even the lowest estimates are considerably in excess of all the gas we have had from the North Sea. The strata is not difficult to access; we have all the technology needed to develop the field. Better still, because the gas lies under the seabed, all the objections to fracking that have, effectively, caused this source of gas to dry up on land sites, won't be a problem."

In just the slightest pause in this utterly unexpected statement, Seymour interjected "Mr. Preston, that is, if I may say so, fantastic news, most welcome. Do you have any estimates of the likely production?"

"Early days" cautioned Preston "but the UK should once again become self-sufficient within a year, two at the most, and then a significant gas exporter, provided your government doesn't try to tax us out of operation" he added with a smile.

"I'll endeavour to ensure that" said Seymour, with a laugh. But behind the bonhomie, three jumbled up thoughts were racing through his mind, and no doubt Palmer's as well. It was, first and foremost, extraordinarily good news – he could scarcely believe his luck- and clearly Preston's visit had nothing to do with the Russian embargo, a fear he had not communicated to Palmer before the meeting, but he certainly shared. Second, could this, in some way that he couldn't begin to fathom at the moment, offer some way forward on the Russian gas problem? But this was not something he could dwell on in the present meeting. And third, a faint cloud, perhaps slightly more than that. This was tremendous news, but why had Preston not only talked to Marlowe privately but insisted that they come to see him about it? He wasn't about to wait for an answer.

"That is, I must say again, most welcome news" he re-iterated. "You will be as aware as anyone of what this will mean for the British economy;

and I'm delighted that you could come to see me in person. Is there anything you were hoping to discuss before the find is announced?"

"I requested this meeting Prime Minister, because there is a problem, quite a serious one" said Preston. The strata of which the fracking gas is one were originally laid down horizontally for millions of years. Over still more millions of years, these layers have been subject to serious upheaval; now all slope down to the West. Our initial find was close to where the gas layer hits the seabed, about fifteen miles off the Northern Ireland coast. Our subsequent drillings have all been progressively deeper as we move westward, but none is at a difficult depth. In fact, the strata then goes right under the land mass of Northern Ireland, but the geology and our technology are such that we can access that horizontally; so no need for drilling on land. However, it means that most of the gas field lies under the Irish Sea within about ten miles or so of the Northern Irish coastline."

Palmer saw where this was going only a millisecond before Seymour. Preston continued.

"My team at EnergiCorp are well aware that, following the Scottish example, there is growing pressure in Northern Ireland for a referendum on whether to leave the UK and link up with the Republic of Ireland; and your government has always said that, while opposing it, this is a matter for the population of Northern Ireland to decide. If Northern Ireland were to vote to become part of the Irish Republic, then virtually all of the gas deposits we have discovered would accrue to the United Ireland which, with its population of less than seven million, would make it one of the richest economies in the world. I asked to see you because, the moment we announce the new gas field, and the scale of the deposits, this might, indeed almost certainly would, trigger precisely that demand for an independence vote which you would want, more than ever, to avoid."

For the second time in three days, Seymour felt like he had been punched hard in the stomach. Palmer realised that the 'miracle' that had appeared at their doorstep was wrapped around a time bomb. Neither could find anything to say at first, and Preston continued.

"I'm sorry to be the bearer of such bad news. All I can add is that I have, for a long time, been a supporter of your government and its policies; and I was quite sure in my mind that EnergiCorp would not make any public statement until you have had a chance to advise us on how you would like to proceed. Hence my rather dramatic request that no officials be present when we met."

"I quite understand" said Seymour "and I very much appreciate your coming to see me before taking any action. I will need to think hard about this. What are your time scales on this?"

"We still have a lot to do on mapping out the field, and how best to exploit it, so there is no immediate urgency. But we would hope to start developing the field in around six months. We will shortly start work on a pipeline back to the coast, north of Liverpool. So, knowledge of the find will leak out by then. But knowledge of the scale of the find could, I think, be kept secret for at least a year, if not somewhat longer. Does that help?"

"It certainly does" responded Seymour. "As you may imagine, I will address this as a matter of the greatest urgency, and then get back to you. Meanwhile, my thanks again for your timely warning and your restraint. I will not forget either." Palmer was probably not alone in noting that this probably indicated a knighthood, maybe even a seat in of Lords, in due course. Preston would deserve it a lot more than the usual load of washed-up, failed politicos that filled out so many of the benches there. Seymour then discussed with both Preston and Marlowe arrangements for staying in close touch on the matter. This concluded, the two men took their leave.

"I'm not sure" said Seymour quietly "if I can remember why I went into politics; but for sure it was not for this. I'm already likely, courtesy of the Russians, to have to resign in utter humiliation; and now I am going to preside over the break-up of the United Kingdom. I thought we might, if we were clever, hold on to Scotland but, once the Northern Irish learn what wealth they have on their doorstep, theirs, and theirs alone if they leave, there will be no stopping them. What a fucking disaster"

Palmer, perhaps the most experienced man in Whitehall for dealing with disaster, with handling crises of all kinds, could see little to challenge in what Seymour had said. He would go down with Seymour, but that didn't bother him that much. There was always employment for a person of his character, skills and experience. But it genuinely grieved him that Seymour, whom he regarded as an able leader, with his heart in quite the right place, should have had the double trouble now facing him. The old adage, that all political careers end in failure, was no doubt largely true; but the extent of failure in Seymour's case was, Palmer thought, not remotely deserved.

"Let me think about it" was all Palmer could offer. "I agree it all looks beyond repair. But we have only just heard about it. We've got to give ourselves some time; and that is something which, fortunately, we do have. So, I'm going to sleep on this, think about it, and I'll come back to you in a couple of days, if that is okay?"

"If you would, yes" replied Seymour. "I don't know how much time I will have to concentrate on it, but I will try to do the same. It seems like we need two miracles now."

CHAPTER 28

It was the following night before Palmer could get a sustained period on his own. He returned to his flat in Notting Hill where he lived alone. A marriage having ended in divorce and a live-in relationship having ended in acrimony, he now had a sometime girlfriend, which suited them both. He wouldn't see her again until the weekend; and so, after cooking himself a light supper, he settled down with a malt whisky to reflect on Seymour's – and his – problems. He prided himself on being able to think coolly, calmly, rationally about whatever almighty mess-ups his political masters managed to create; and he forced himself to do so this time, however daunting the prospects. And, by midnight, cool, calm and rational had done the trick or, at least, given him something to work with – a strategy, or rather a set of strategies - that might, just might generate a way forward. Not an entirely promising way forward, he had to admit, but better than the great fat zero with which he had started the evening. He just hoped that, in the morning, when the effect of several glasses of malt had fallen away, the tiny wormholes to a better future which he had identified would still seem feasible.

The morning did not disappoint him; but he decided to mull over what he had developed for another day or so, before going back to Seymour, not just reviewing his ideas but trying to address every objection he could conceive of. Because if he didn't, for sure Seymour would. He wanted to make notes and write it down so that he could survey it more comprehensively, but he recognised that what he was dreaming up could never appear in black and white. If his plans worked, then history would, for a very long time, be none the wiser, if ever.

He also needed to check some aspects of what he was planning to put to Seymour; and they needed to be checked very discreetly – checking a number of documents, confirmation of the identities of some people, the whereabouts and current activities of certain individuals, plus some highly sensitive technical advice. This last item required invoking Seymour's name, without the PM knowing, but Palmer did not let that trouble him. If he was successful, no-one would know; if he was unsuccessful, this deceit would be the least of his problems. None of these investigations took that long, however; and so it was that, only four days after his taking a somewhat despairing leave of Seymour, after Preston's visit, the two men again met, this time, very deliberately, quite alone. "Any thoughts?" was Seymour's brief introduction to their discussion.

"I have had some, yes" said Palmer. "By no means definitive, but maybe the start of something we can construct to get us out of this mess. It's a series of interconnected plans. We will be lucky to pull it all off, but I think it is worth the try. Anything's better than just waiting for the shit to hit the fan. I'll start with the gas deposits in the Irish Sea." He paused to see if Seymour wanted to intervene, but Seymour just waved him on.

"The first thing is to buy us some time. I'll explain in a moment why this is important, but I'm hoping this will not be too difficult. Preston has already signalled that he could give us a year; and I think we could ask him to spin this out to at least eighteen months, maybe more – not stop gas field development but just slow the pace. Why do I think Preston would do this? In the first place, he is, in principle, supportive of us. But more importantly, I think we can offer him some really attractive incentives to slow the field's development rate, just enough that it doesn't seem like some new Eldorado. We can offer him an easier tax regime than we deployed in the North Sea, easier, I'm sure, than his financial wizards are expecting – we will need to get the Chancellor on board, but he is going to be as keen as anyone to stop the potential tax revenues on the gas supplies disappearing to Ireland. Also, I've checked. The licences that EnergiCorp has at the moment are for exploration. New ones are needed for actual exploitation of oil and gas fields. In the North Sea, we ensured they were reasonably distributed amongst several energy companies; we'd have to have more than just EnergiCorp in the Irish Sea. But we could easily swing the distribution significantly more in its favour than otherwise. And the great thing is that the delay we will be asking for is just that, a delay, in the profits the company will make, whereas what we are offering will be a permanent increase in its profitability. I don't think it will take him long to decide; and if there is any hesitation, there is always a knighthood or a seat in the House of Lords."

"Andrew" said Seymour "you are, I am glad to say, at your most persuasive. I buy it so far. But how do we use the time?"

"That's the next element. It's simple logic really. If the true scale of the gas deposits goes public before any Northern Irish vote on leaving the UK, then it must be heavily odds-on that Northern Ireland will leave the UK. That we cannot have. Therefore, the vote must take place *before* the information becomes public. So, this part of the plan has four main steps. First, we must ensure that those in Northern Ireland who want a vote, so that they can leave the UK, are triggered to demand it, irresistibly, and quite soon. I won't go into this right now, but I'm pretty sure there are ways we can do this without our fingerprints being anywhere near the scene. The issue is hovering there, only just below the surface; and won't need much to bring it right out into the open.

"The second step is that, most regretfully, your government gives into this demand, saying you will campaign against but, as you have always said, it is for the people in the Province to decide. Third, however, you say that you absolutely refuse to get into the ludicrous situation that has developed in Scotland, where a referendum was supposed to settle the matter but, as soon as the SNP lost, it started, and now with ever increasing passion, to demand another referendum. And no doubt a third until it gets its way – which of course will be irreversible. So, the Northern Ireland referendum comes with the condition that it is absolutely final for, say, twenty-five years – no ifs no buts. And this will be enshrined in Westminster legislation. Of course, the Province will go berserk later, but no Westminster government is going to cancel legislation, the impact of which is to hand a vast amount of wealth to a tiny proportion of the population of the UK." He paused, possibly for breath but, more likely for effect. "And the fourth step is that we must win the vote."

"A rather important piece of the jigsaw" interjected Seymour. "I see all the logic, but can we be confident that we would win? People have been saying for years that, with the higher birth rate amongst the Catholics, it is only a matter of time before a majority of the voting population want to leave; and a lot of people, especially younger ones, will vote to join the Republic as an insurance, a way of staying in the EU if the Brexit movement ever gets its way."

"I have had several thoughts on that" replied Palmer. "At least it gives us a chance, whereas if we do nothing we are, I think, bound to lose. But the situation is better than you describe. The influence of the Catholic Church has massively declined in recent years; many 'Catholics' are not Irish nationalists. The EU point will hurt us, but the EU is in such a state of dysfunction at the moment, and with potentially very large bills heading towards the northern countries, of which Ireland is, of course, one, to bail out the southern bloc, I think this argument can be resisted. Plus – my third element of the overall plan - I have put together a strategy which, given these points, should give us every chance of winning.

As Palmer paused, Seymour poured them some more drinks, feeling faintly like the butler to Palmer's Master of the House. "Keep going" he said.

"Apologies that it is another list, but I think that way; and I hope it makes everything clearer. There are four strands to our winning the vote, some of which you won't like, but this is a serious game we're in. First, we have some straight-talking arguments to put forward. Northern Ireland gets a very substantial subsidy from the rest of the UK and, subject to checking, it is far more than the Republic is likely to cough up; or be able to afford. The Province now gets virtually nothing from the EU, because its regional support policies have to deal with the very much lower standards of living that have now appeared in the recently joined Eastern countries. In short, we can offer a much better standard of living. If needed, we can add some big infrastructure promises that Dublin could never match, even including a bridge or tunnel to Scotland. And we shouldn't forget that the Province does far more trade with the rest of the UK than it does with the Republic. So, there is quite a lot of straight self-interested economics going our way.

"Second, we can indulge in some fake news, untraceable leaks that Dublin really doesn't want a poor neighbour dumped on it, that it will retain all governing powers in Dublin, will resist attempts by the Province to get either significant devolution of powers or substantial regional aid from it. Actually, I'm by no means convinced that this *is* fake. There are still some totally backward-looking sentimentalists in the Republic who think that all that matters is a United Ireland; but I suspect that, these days there are not that many, compared with hard-headed bean counters. But whether true or not, it will ring true; and will be a cause for concern for many living in the north.

"The third strand, with apologies, is straight character assassination. We will identify the key figures pushing to leave the UK, put their past lives through the ringer, and leak every last bit of scandal or, better still, corruption we can find. If we can, we will twist whatever we find out to suggest that their stance on leaving, to the economic detriment of the majority in the Province, is all linked in some way to their own interests. Not pretty, I know, but it will all help to present a sense of malaise about the leave vote, which could be quite important to the outcome.

"And, finally, there is the terrorist card. The Protestant paramilitaries have, understandably, been very quiet, in fact they have rather withered away since the pressure from the IRA and Sinn Fein for unification ended. But there is a latent infrastructure there, with which we have retained a few informal links; and it would not be difficult to gear them up again, to make it quite clear that, if unification happens, then the Republic will have a civil war on its hands. Most in the north, whatever their views, will absolutely not want to see a return of the Troubles; and Dublin wants a warring Province inside its borders like a hole in the head. It might even demand some completely undeliverable commitments about no return to armed struggle, as a one- way bet. No Prots or no unification. Put that lot together, and I think we have a pretty good chance of winning."

To say that Seymour was impressed was the understatement of the year. He had no idea if any of it, let alone all of it, would work, but he clearly saw that it gave him and Palmer much to work on. "We need to discuss how things would play out if we did win" he responded "but before we do, there is, as I guess you will have recognised, one potentially very large hole in you plan - the IRA."

"You are right on both. I have recognised it; and they are a big hole in the plan. They have retained quite a lot of their basic structure, although with various spin-off groups of more or less violent intent; they still have access to weapons and they were always much better organised than the Protestant paramilitaries. A threat from them that, if Northern Ireland rejects this democratic opportunity to leave the UK peacefully, then the Troubles will start again in earnest, undermining all the benefits that the Province has seen in recent years, that will have real force. In fact it's worse than I originally thought because, if Northern Ireland does join up with the Republic, the Prots' cause is lost however murderous they get. Ulster will never decide to leave; whatever they do, they will know it, that will undermine their credibility and in time, any terror campaign they launch. But if the vote is to remain, the IRA will clearly still have everything to fight for; and everyone will know that. So, their threat to commit mayhem indefinitely will be all too credible, and could win the day. I'd go so far as to say that, but for the bloody IRA, I'm confident we can win this battle. But, can I park it for the moment, as the only real objection so far, to complete the overall plan first?"

"Certainly," agreed Seymour. "So, we win the referendum. What then?"

"Well, you will see now why the delay is so important. If we move fast, I estimate we will need around six months to get the referendum to be agreed and voted on. During that time, and for another twelve months, EnergiCorp will be completing its exploration, getting its first supply licences, developing its pipeline infrastructure, and then, at a modest level, start suppling gas to the UK. The main location from which they will initially be sucking the gas, where the gas strata hits the seabed, is significantly more than twelve miles from the Northern Ireland shore; this should help to allay any concerns. In fact, the technology is such that quite a lot of gas can be sucked out from under the twelve-mile limit, but that will only take them so far. The key thing is that the referendum should be done and dusted, by upwards of a year or so, before the true scale of the deposits, and their location, becomes known. By which time, it's too late."

Seymour was about to comment, but Palmer went straight on. "But that's not all. We still have the Russian issue to deal with. Now this could be really beautiful. We take Preston into our confidence – he seems loyal – and get him to take over the European gas line contracts. He then progressively cancels the contracts, building up his Irish sea supplies as the Russian gas declines. EnergiCorp pays the cancellation penalties and we, out of the very substantial tax revenues that are going to flow from the Irish Sea field, reduce the future tax burden on EnergiCorp, by substantially more than the penalties, which should be enough for Preston to persuade his board. If Gudanov seeks to reveal what he knows, we just deny that the British government knew anything about it. I suppose we might say that we asked EnegiCorp to close it all down as soon as we knew about it, but I don't think we need to. That leaves Fielding, but some sticks and carrots should convince him to keep what he knows secret. Say a further million pound carrot to keep quiet and a life in hiding from men with chain saws if he doesn't. I know it is all wild; and I know we need to review it all, piece by piece; but I think it will work. I really do."

"Have you counted how many?" asked Seymour, with deliberate opaqueness.

"How many what?" asked Palmer.

"How many laws your proposals will break. If any of this came out, they'd lock us up and throw the key away."

"I don't think so" was Palmer's unexpected reply. "Certainly, you wouldn't have broken any. Neither stirring up the loyalist paramilitaries nor threatening Fielding would come anywhere near you. If anything else came to light it would see you out of politics, I accept, but I don't think either of us would be in line for any prosecution. Fake news, character assassination – it's a grim world – but no one gets prosecuted for them. But, anyway, it is the only way I can think of to secure the benefits of what EnergiCorp has discovered and, remember, get us out of the Russian mess. I really think we should go for it."

"Okay, say we do" said Seymour, but without conviction, "We still have the IRA problem. If we can see that their threatening a return to violence - bombings, killings – and all the economic consequences of that, might make people think it's better to leave the UK - then undoubtedly so will they. I can't believe I am quite saying this, but that seems to be the only weak link in the scheme. But it's one hell of a weak link – it could just about scupper the whole thing."

"That's certainly true" replied Palmer "but, if the IRA can threaten the whole enterprise, then there is, logically, only one way forward."

"Which is?" asked Seymour.

"Eliminate it."

CHAPTER 29

In what, at any other time, would have been seen as a theatrical gesture, but on this occasion was totally real, Seymour literally choked on his drink. Though it was only for an instant, he recalled from somewhere way back an allusion about the thirteenth chime of a cuckoo clock – it wasn't only obviously wrong, but raised considerable doubts about the mechanism as a whole. Suppose Palmer was seriously contemplating 'eliminating' the IRA, which no British government, backed with vast military resources, had been able to achieve in nearly a hundred years. In that case, he must be suffering some sort of mental disturbance – he flinched from the word 'illness' – which must bring all his other proposals into question, however plausible he had made them sound to Seymour.

"What on earth are you saying" he blurted out, anxiously leaning forward in his chair. "You and whose army are going to eliminate the IRA?" What he did not know, what Palmer would never reveal to him, was that he, Palmer, had thought about the wording he would use when putting his final proposal to Seymour; and had been deliberately ambiguous. He positively wanted and intended that Seymour would think he was somehow proposing to get rid of the IRA – clearly a fatuous proposition – in order to make what he actually wanted, which could still be seen as quite reckless, rather less unpalatable.

"No, of course I'm not proposing eliminating the IRA, Graham" he assured Seymour "I'm only proposing that we eliminate the threat they pose to the referendum result. It's a much more modest proposal, time-limited and, I think, achievable if we go about it the right way." Exactly as Palmer had intended, this sounded distinctly less mad a proposition, which certainly stopped Seymour in his tracks. He sat back in his chair, now feeling slightly silly that he had thought Palmer was suggesting all-out war in Northern Ireland; and that he had revealed to Palmer that he had drawn such an absurd inference.

"Christ, thank God for that" he said. "I've had more extraordinary proposals put to me in the last half hour than in all my political life to date; and I'm beginning to suffer overload. So, what do you mean by 'eliminating the threat'?" And with that question, Palmer knew that, while he was not home and dry yet, his ploy had succeeded in getting over what might well have been immediate and total rejection of the last, critical part of his overall plans.

"I estimate" said Palmer, "that we need to make them ineffectual for about three to six months, while we hold the referendum. To do that we need two things; first incapacitate the leadership. I spoke yesterday to an old acquaintance of mine, now in the Ministry of Defence. He reckons that, since the current settlement in Northern Ireland, the leadership of the IRA has got not just very quiet but quite small – only half a dozen or so key people to keep the flame alive. So, not an impossible number to neutralise. Second, we would need to stop outraged lesser figures in the movement from retaliating, which means getting to their munition dumps. It looks like there are now very few of these. Their armaments controller is, apparently, quite well known, one of the top six or so, and living quite openly in the Republic; so, we shouldn't face too big a difficulty in getting their location. With, at least temporarily, no effective leadership, and no weapons, that should see us through the referendum period without too much alarm."

Alarm was precisely what Seymour was now beginning to feel again. "Are you seriously suggesting that someone , the British Army I suppose, 'neutralise' – no. let's be accurate, assassinate – the top echelons of the IRA and, I also suppose, torture information out of one of them at least as to the location of the arms dumps that they have held onto?"

"No, not at all" replied Palmer. "There would be no assassinations and no involvement of the British army. This would all be carried out by a quite independent and deniable group; and they would simply detain the IRA leadership for several months. There would no doubt be speculation that they had been murdered, but they would re-appear; and it would all be staged to look as if the protestant paramilitaries were responsible. They would, no doubt, be quite happy to claim responsibility for such a coup, or at least not deny it. You may think this is all too extreme, but it is certainly feasible; and the alternative, for both of us, for your political legacy, not to say obituary and, let us not forget, the future of the economy and the living standards of millions of Brits, is all in the balance. If you have a better idea, Graham, then let's discuss it; but for me, now, this looks like the only way to pluck a glorious victory out of an otherwise hideous defeat."

Part of Seymour wanted just to scream a very loud 'no'; but Palmer had reminded him, if reminder were needed, of what they were facing. And there was another factor, lodged at the back of his mind. The IRA had murdered his predecessor, Alan Gerrard, right outside Chequers. Seymour wouldn't be PM otherwise, but he had been not only a colleague but a good friend of Gerrard. He therefore had a visceral and quite understandable hatred of the IRA, which tempered his more dominant thought that this was all madness. So, instead, partly just to buy time for himself to think he asked "And how would you get the information you need on the ammunition dumps? However high the stakes, I won't sanction or condone torture."

"I give you my absolute assurance, there would be no torture, no harm meted out to any of those detained. Just the threat of losing one's limbs, one by one, and then one's life, or those of one's family, would be quite enough – a bluff, but no one is going to risk that."

Seymour allowed a slight doubt to cross his mind as to the validity of even an 'absolute assurance' from Palmer; but decided not to pursue it. "Who, then would carry this out?"

"Better that you do not know," said Palmer, but be assured that I do know a group with the necessary training and would, I suspect, be prepared to do this, indeed more than prepared and extremely willing. I have worked with them before, and on that previous occasion, the IRA got the better of them; they'd be delighted to have this opportunity. As I say, a few clues left behind will undoubtedly point to the extreme wing of the Protestant paramilitaries as the perpetrators. I have given it a lot of thought. You will just have to trust me on this."

Still wanting to find some chink in Palmer's thinking, anything that would save him from having actually to decide on everything Palmer was suggesting, Seymour asked another question. "But if one of these key people is seized, the others will immediately go to ground. And I doubt any group could co-ordinate a series of simultaneous kidnappings. That's strictly for the movies. I don't see how it could be done."

"We would need to get them together" was Palmer's unexpected reply. "That's all it needs. One operation."

Seymour found the cuckoo clock coming back to mind. "And how, on earth, would you achieve that? Oh, yes, of course. Some Brit gets in touch, says could you all get together please for a chat, nothing suspicious, have a few beers; and these guys, some of the most suspicious and, let us not forget, some of the most successful terrorists of modern times are going to say 'sure, begorrah, always up for a few beers. Just leave your armoured vehicle at the door, would you?"

Despite the heightened tension of the conversation, Palmer could not suppress a smile at this. "No" he said, "not quite like that. We find a Brit prepared to contact them, or" he added darkly "doesn't really have a choice about it; and whom, the IRA leadership would totally trust. I think I have worked out how such a person could get them together."

"But you'd never find such a person – ready to betray them but entirely trusted? You're still not making sense, Andrew."

"Just two corrections there." Said Palmer. The chosen person wouldn't know that the purpose was to remove the leadership from circulation; and it may come as a surprise, but I know just the person.

CHAPTER 30

Looking back later, Seymour identified this as the point of no return, not literally perhaps, because he was still struggling to absorb everything Palmer was telling him and trying to put off anything remotely resembling a decision on what was being proposed. But effectively, it was the point of no return because, as was now clear, Palmer had thought everything through. He had an answer for every question, every objection Seymour could raise, no matter how outlandish his proposals had seemed minutes earlier. The bottom lines were that Palmer was confident he could do it, and equally confident that none of it could ever be traced back to Seymour. He doubted that was really the case, but as long as nothing illegal could be placed at his door, the prospect was better than the alternative. He knew that this was his gut talking not his head; and that he would have to bring his brain to bear on every single stage in Palmer's plans. But his gut instincts had served him well in the past. He wasn't the PM by virtue of forever thinking through a situation's pros and cons. He was still by no means committed to what Palmer was proposing, but the psychology had, not so subtly, changed. He was looking for objections but from the perspective of someone who wanted to overcome any that presented themselves, not someone seeking reasons to run away.

"So, who is this remarkable man, who is trusted by the IRA but is going to stitch them up royally?" asked Seymour. Palmer's reply practically induced another coughing fit in Seymour.

"Not a man, a woman" said Palmer. Her name is Kate Kimball. I've thought through how we will do it; she will carry it out, no question; and for reasons that will become clear, the current IRA leadership will trust her completely."

Seymour was dumfounded. He thought he had been subjected to every shock that Palmer could possibly produce; but here was yet another absolutely inexplicable notion from Palmer, someone who, he now realised, had depths so hidden as to make him truly dangerous. The textbooks said that the British government system, unlike the US one, was not presidential – the PM ruled via cabinet government and support in Parliament. Well, what he was witnessing – what he was now part of – was so far from that textbook idea as to be unrecognisable. Thanks to Palmer, he and an unelected official were planning something not unlike a coup, not against the government of the day but in its support; and using any and every means available to achieve it.

Seymour was now almost too drained even to ask Palmer to go on. But he managed one more question "Who, for Christ sake, is Kate Kimball – some MI6 spook?" He waved his hand to indicate that Palmer needed – by God he needed – to explain.

"No, she's a science editor with Oxford University Press" said Palmer. This did nothing to quell Seymour's astonishment, indeed, quite the contrary. But by now he really was too overwhelmed to say anything; and let Palmer proceed. "You know, of course, that the IRA murdered Alan Gerrard in a car outside Chequers. I was in the car with him. I thought they were going to shoot me as well, but instead they forced me to call Alex Tyson at *The Times* to explain why the IRA had targeted Gerrard. It was - you know all this but it's important to go over it – because Gerrard, thirty years before, had ordered the killing, in the Republic, of a five-man IRA team that, unsuccessfully as it turned out, tried to blow up Sellafield nuclear power station. So that all came out in the Press. But there is a whole other background to these events that no-one knows about except me, the IRA and Miss Kate Kimball. And that history is what is going to get us where we want to be."

"Miss Kimball is as unlikely a participant in all this as you could hope to find – she is just a senior manager in a successful academic publishing house. But her partner, a guy called Paul Emmerson, is a professor at Oxford who, in the course of some research work, discovered, just a couple of years ago, that some sort of attack on Sellafield had actually occurred but, having failed, was then hushed up – that's why the IRA team who carried it out had to be eliminated. Their breaching of Sellafield's security really threatened Gerrard's position at the time, responsible for domestic security – so he had organised their cold-blooded murder and, if this had all now come out, he would have gone to prison for a long, long time; and the fact is that he panicked. The Americans were desperate for him to assist them with airbases in the UK for their attack on Iran's nuclear facilities for tactical and diplomatic reasons, so he asked them to 'deal' with Emmerson. They duly obliged. They snatched him one evening, while Kimball was in the US, but they then kept him on ice in Germany, as a sort of sword of Damocles over Gerrard's head.

Now, Miss Kate Kimball is a very ballsy lady. She wouldn't accept Emmerson's disappearance; and set out to trace him. During the course of this, she found out what had happened at Sellafield and, would you believe, went off to Ireland, hooked up with the IRA guy who had master-minded the attack on Sellafield – a certain Victor O'Connell – and who, up until Kimball told him, had never found out what had happened to his Sellafield team. There's a whole lot more, but the main thing is that Kimball worked with the IRA, blackmailing Gerrard to get Emmerson released. I don't think she had anything to do with Gerrard's murder, but she had certainly collaborated previously with the team who carried it out; and knew all about what Gerrard had done. So, she had to be silenced."

He paused, just possibly for dramatic effect, as Seymour managed to overcome his shock at what this might have meant. If Kimball was to assist, then she had to still be alive. He said nothing, and Palmer continued.

"To ensure her silence I forced her to make a set of recordings on a tape that apparently implicated her in the IRA's pursuit of Gerrard. If I say so myself, the tapes were quite clever. All phoney – Kimball was forced to make them under threat of a very unpleasant end – but they purported to confirm that the whole story of Gerard having the IRA team murdered was pure fabrication, dreamed up by the IRA so that they would have a basis for blackmailing Gerard, with Kimball involved as go-between. This was the price if she ever wanted to see her beloved Emmerson again. She played the part I have to say, rather well – amazing what the threat of violent death can do. So - and these are the two crucial points - if the tape recording were to be released, she'd go to prison for a very long time, for her role in the supposed blackmail attempt. We might even try to link her to Gerrard's assassination. So, I think she could be persuaded to do more or less whatever we want her to do to avoid that. And second, the IRA will totally trust her. She revealed to them what happened to the Sellafield team; and she worked hand in glove with them to try to corner Gerrard. They won't know about the recording, but Kimball can tell them about it, and therefore why she has been forced back into being an intermediary. She is, in short, just what we need."

Seymour poured more drinks, aghast at what he had been told, but trying as hard as he could to focus on what this meant for Palmer's plan

– was this Kimball woman really the answer? He felt he was losing his grip, not just on the conversation – that had happened a while before – but on the situation, where they were headed, and what could be achieved. Rather plaintively, he asked, "How do you *know* all this Andrew?"

"It was all Gerrard's plan" he replied. "He only brought me into it later when the IRA and the Kimball woman contacted him, to blackmail him. I was astounded. I was his *alter ego* and I hadn't known any of it. But I was his man; and so I helped out. It was me who arranged for us to pick up Kimball; and it was me who fixed the recording, to ensure her silence. In the end, the Americans were happy – they got their bases and their attacks in; Gerrard was in the clear, Kimball got her man, Emmerson, back, it was just the IRA who were pissed off to hell; and now they knew who to blame, which is why they assassinated Gerrard. So, yes, I know it all; and it was Kimball – her existence and her position – around which I dreamed up a way of tackling the current IRA leadership. Because, guess who are the two main guys running the IRA nowadays? Would you believe, Vincent and Declan O'Connell, who are Victor O'Connell's two sons. Victor is still around but is now in his seventies and more of an *eminence grise*. Kimball knows them all; and after what she did for them, they will not doubt her. She worked closely with them; and the British Government colluded in an enterprise to have her partner murdered. As clear a case of 'my enemy's enemy is my friend' as you will ever hope to find."

"Okay" Seymour heard himself saying, when everything was far from okay in his mind. "So, you have someone whom the O'Connells will trust. But how does that help us, especially if the plan is to remove them from the scene? Kimball presumably won't go along with anything that endangers them; and she is not, I presume, as an academic publishing editor, a highly trained, female James Bond?"

Palmer allowed himself another short smile. "No, nothing like that. My plan is actually quite simple. She will bear a secret and conciliatory proposal from the British government to the IRA. She will be told, and she will tell them, that she has been asked to do this precisely because she is someone whom the IRA will trust enough to let her near them. She could certainly say that she didn't want to be involved, but was told that if she didn't, then her liaison with the IRA would be brought to the attention of the security forces, after which charges might follow."

"And this conciliatory proposal is what exactly?" asked Seymour.

"I'll get to that" replied Palmer. "As long as it is important enough, it barely matters. The point is that Kimball will propose a further meeting, with the IRA leadership, which is when a team who will have been tracking Kimball will move into action. If any important players are not present, they will be tracked down the same evening, as will the weapons dumps. I suggest you ask for no details of how either of these will be carried out. But our mission will be accomplished."

"Aren't you forgetting something?" asked Seymour. "What about Kimball? It will become apparent that you have used her as a tethered goat to seize her friends. She doesn't sound the sort to take that lying down. She may not understand how she is being used at the time, but she could go very public with it afterwards"

"That's true" confessed Palmer, "but we still have the recording of her supposedly plotting with the IRA to attack Gerrard. I agree she will be mightily annoyed, but she isn't going to risk spending most, if not all, of the rest of her life in prison because of that. There will be no witnesses, no comeback, at least, not on us. Ammunition at the site, and one or two 'random' sightings that we will engineer will lead straight back to Ulster and its paramilitaries."

"Andrew, you do know, don't you, that you will burn in the hottest part of hell?" was Seymour's response. But before Palmer could come up with a pithy response he continued. "What will the message be that Kimball will take to them?"

"That's still work in progress" said Palmer "but the referendum will have been announced; and so I think it will need to be linked to that. I'm rather attracted to the thesis that, if you are going to lie, make it such a big lie that it just couldn't be anything but true. So, how about this. The referendum has been called. The British Government's position is that it is for the population of Northern Ireland to decide, but that it is opposed to the Province leaving the UK; and will campaign for it to remain. Then Kimball arrives with a top-secret communique. There is a growing group within the government – and it now, belatedly includes the Prime Minister - who would be quite content to see Ulster leave the UK. In part it is just that they think, in the end, Ulster is bound to leave, not least since the disintegration genie is out of the bottle following the Scottish vote; and so it might as well be now and peacefully. More strongly, the Province is a big drain on the UK's economy and public finances, at a time when it is under huge financial pressures. Why spend large sums to prop up a split and semi-detached community who will probably leave one day anyway. There is also a sub-group who are keen to hold onto Scotland; and think the best way to do this is see Northern Ireland suffer, as it surely will, if it leaves the UK for the Republic."

"But how does that message help?" asked Seymour.

"Because, on the back of that message, Kimball will say that the UK government has learnt, from the contacts it has retained amongst the Prots – the IRA will undoubtedly buy that one – that the protestant paramilitaries are planning a war against Northern Ireland leaving the UK; and the government is worried that that threat might lead people to vote for the peace of the status quo. It does not want a flare up of Protestant violence to influence the outcome. There is no way that it can itself intervene – chasing after bombers after they have brought death and destruction to communities in Ulster is no solution. So, Kimball's second message is that she will return, accompanied by a well-trained and highly experienced, but retired, military man, completely without links back to the UK government, who will offer to assist the IRA, mainly with information about the protestant paramilitaries but maybe with weapons as well, so that *they* can prevent the Prots from undermining the referendum. Depending on how things develop, they might want to raise their own threat of a bombing campaign if Ulster looks like rejecting a peaceful exit. That would be enough for them to agree on a second meeting."

Seymour looked at Palmer in astonishment. "You are planning to encourage them to carry out precisely the bombing campaign that you have spelt out, oh so clearly, is the main threat to our project? Am I missing something?"

"Yes, you are" replied Palmer. "Because the people Kimball meets up with aren't, after the second meeting, going to be around to bomb anything."

Palmer hadn't said anything that he hadn't clearly intimated before; but the starkness of his latest words nonetheless shook Seymour to the core. Part of him could barely believe what they were discussing. For the moment, too shocked to formulate any proper response he rather feebly fell back on another objection. "And you think that this Kimball woman, a nice little science editor for God's sake, is going to be able to deceive the O'Connell's, father and sons, who have no doubt had a lifetime of rooting out infiltrations of their organisation – you can't really believe that."

"I don't" replied Palmer. "As far as she knows, she won't be deceiving anyone. She'll hate being involved again; but she will be exactly what she professes to be – an innocent, rendered, by what happened before, the one person whom the IRA know we can use as a go-between they will trust. As far as she will be concerned, what she is being asked – told if you like – to do is no threat to her erstwhile pals in the IRA. She will know what we are proposing, why we want her to go back with an experienced mercenary. She won't have to dissimulate anything."

"Wouldn't it be easier" said Seymour, "if the straightforward message from me is that, if the IRA start a bombing campaign, to try to intimidate the population into voting to leave, I will simply cancel the referendum?"

"I did think about that possibility" replied Palmer, "but it is too risky. If they didn't buy the bluff, the one thing we can't do is cancel the referendum. We have to get it out of the way before the new gas field starts delivering. Hence my more devious, but I think quite plausible message."

Seymour recognised the sense in this, but was still seeking objections. "You will have to track her, won't you?" Seymour responded. "Put a tracker bug on her somehow. They are bound to be suspicious. They will take whatever precautions they need to ensure that she isn't followed, that no-one knows where they will meet."

"I'm working on that" was Palmer's less than reassuring reply. "It won't be a problem." Rather suddenly, Seymour knew that he had run out of objections. He felt exhausted, almost dizzy, but it was clear that Palmer had thought through his plan in minute detail. Seymour couldn't 'discuss' the matter anymore. It was decision time.

"It's not on" he said, to Palmer but almost to himself. "I'll go along with the deals with EnergiCorp; and with the referendum; and even with the dirty tricks you want to try to secure a vote to remain. But stirring up all the old animosities in Ireland; and cold-bloodedly planning the incarceration of the top echelon of the IRA. Yes, yes, I see the logic; but that is a step too far, in fact it's madness. It's not on."

There was a long silence for the first time since they had met up. Both men sat, impassive, avoiding each others' eyes. Eventually Palmer spoke.

"I can understand your reluctance. But let me just point out three things. First, the O'Connells and their pals are some of the worst thugs in Europe. For over thirty years they murdered, tortured, maimed and generally terrorised innocent men, women and children. They murdered Gerrard and why? Because he got rid of five guys who nearly succeeded in killing hundreds of thousands in the north of England with a nuclear fallout from Sellafield. I don't want to sound pompous – it's not my style – but they are just not the sort of people that a civilised society should tolerate in their midst. And these are the very men who could jeopardise everything we want to achieve. Why would you let such people do that?

"And that's the second point. If they swing the referendum, they would ruin you and me – well I guess we can bear that – but the Russian gas deal would blow the UK's international standing for years; and the Irish gas field going to Ireland would ruin the economic well-being of millions of Brits, and for what? So that a tiny proportion of what is currently the UK, plus the population of a small island off the north west tip of Europe can become ten times richer than the Swiss or the Saudis. Why should they be allowed to get away with that? Why should half a dozen or so ruthless, murdering bastards be allowed to bring that about?"

If it had been a boxing match, Seymour would have been on the ropes, but the knock-out blow was still to come. "So, what is your third point?" he asked.

"Well" said Palmer slowly, with unaccustomed caution, "I hesitate to point it out, but the operation I have in mind will, for obvious reasons, be set up so far away from you, or anyone near you except me, that it doesn't actually need your approval. This conversation never happened. You would just wake up one day to the news that there had been some sort of terrorist infighting in Ulster, the police investigating etc. Later found to be the incapacitation of some individuals who were planning to terrorise the population into voting to leave the UK. Very regrettable.

Hope we can all return to the peace of the current settlement etc. You'd have to put out a statement – usual perfunctory stuff – and on we go."

"You would just go ahead anyway?" asked Seymour, incredulously.

"The key to all this" said Palmer "is not that I answer that question, one way or the other; but that you don't ask me the question. Just retract it. In any event, I won't answer it. Then we can move on to more detailed planning of the whole sequence of events."

Seymour was not unintelligent, but it took him a few moments – fortunately a few moments in which he desisted from speaking – before he fully took on board the lifeline that Palmer was throwing him. Trying to block Palmer might fail; if he succeeded in stopping him, the plan would be dead; which would almost certainly ruin his own career and place in history – not the most inviting of options. But the alternative *wasn't* having to agree with Palmer. He was now clear that he could not do that. All he had to was……. not oppose him. As Palmer had said, the discussion never happened. Why would the PM have any particular knowledge about internecine warfare between terrorist groups in Ireland?

He noticed that he was not breathing normally – rather short breaths, almost like he was panting. So, he focused on calming his breath – and with it himself - while the second, long silence of the meeting developed. In that silence, both men knew that what Palmer had said could never stand up - Palmer would never get the funding he needed from a suitably obscure fund at the Treasury without Seymour's backing – and both men knew that the other knew it. But, staring disaster in the face, the fiction was just enough to edge Seymour through the critical moment. After a minute or two, he threw in the towel. "Let's see if we can sketch out a rough time- line for what we need to do" he said. It didn't remotely sound like a declaration of war on the IRA, but he was under no illusion that that is what it was.

PART THREE

CHAPTER 31

Only relatively few people with whom Palmer regularly worked noticed that, over the next month or so, he seemed less in evidence, less on top of anything and everything that came Seymour's way. Few mourned the loss of his usually abrasive style for this slightly more considerate way of working, and none thought to contemplate what might have brought it about. Still less did anyone suspect that he was now a man on a mission, totally focused on what he understandably saw as the make-or-break issue of Seymour's tenure of No. 10 Downing Street. He did not – he could not – give up on the usual matters that he had to troubleshoot, mainly but not exclusively with the media; but his time and his attention were much more focused on the scheme that he had developed in the isolation of his home. He could not see why it wouldn't work; and he was determined that it would.

Given this, it was slightly paradoxical that the first step was one from which he was excluded entirely. If EnergiCorp was to be induced to play the role Palmer envisaged, then the Chancellor, David Flemming, would have to be brought on board. Seymour was adamant that he, and he alone, raise the matter with Flemming. The Chancellor was by no means the only cabinet minister who, with varying degrees of bitterness, resented Palmer's hold on Seymour, and the immense power, far more than any minister's, that this gave an unelected official – and not even a regular Whitehall official at that. Palmer didn't argue the matter. He recognised that his presence might be counter-productive; and he was sure that Seymour would be pushing at an open door. Flemming was being offered the opportunity to be, with doubt, the most successful Chancellor since the war, presiding over a booming economy and tax revenues pouring into his coffers. He would also clearly see that this could – almost certainly would – buy the government re-election and, with it, the likelihood that the next PM would be another Conservative. Flemming had strong views on who that might be.

Seymour duly saw Flemming and, as he and Palmer had anticipated, had not the slightest difficulty recruiting him to their cause. The next step was the two of them meeting with Anthony Preston, CEO of EnergiCorp; this time Seymour insisted that Palmer join them. If what they were about to discuss became, to any degree, public knowledge, it was Palmer who would have to manage the media coverage.

Seymour took the lead, rather than the Chancellor, partly because he was better informed of the propositions to be put, but also to impress on Preston the importance of what he had in mind. As succinctly as possible he said that, if EnergiCorp could initially only exploit the Eastern end of the gas field, outside any territorial waters that an exit of Northern Ireland from the UK could create; and then slow the whole development over a period of up to two years, then the Chancellor could guarantee a tax regime sufficiently favourable to EnergiCorp to compensate it very generously for the delay; and would pull some strings to ensure that EnergiCorp was able to get the lion's share of the subsequent supply licences that would need to be applied for. If Preston was content with that, then some confidential calculations could be worked on, to ensure that EnergiCorp came out a long way ahead of where it otherwise might be.

It was no surprise to Palmer and Seymour, given what Preston had said at the previous meeting with him, that he was entirely amenable to this – he'd have to look at the figures but he was clear that this could help to put EnergiCorp into a different league globally. But it surprised Preston when Seymour said they had an additional suggestion, which should also benefit EnergiCorp.

"What I'm telling you now must remain completely secret for reasons that will become obvious." Preston nodded as if to say 'of course'. "You will know as well as anyone that energy supply to the UK is on something of a knife edge relative to likely demand. To help ease that situation, we have been increasing gas imports from a range of European suppliers, via a series of interconnected contracts; but the origin of these supplies is Gazprom." Preston gave Seymour a meaningful look, to register that he understood the seriousness of this admission; but said nothing.

"Desperate times required desperate measure" Seymour said, by way of explanation, "but with the forthcoming development of the Irish deposits, we wish to terminate these contracts as quickly as possible" Again Preston just nodded. "But just cancelling them, as you would know, is hugely expensive, prohibitively so for the government. We could not find the money on such a scale without its use becoming public. But it has occurred to us that EnergiCorp could take over the contracts at this end, at prices which will secure a profitable return to the traders involved; and then run the contracts down yourself. This would be just as expensive for you as it would be for us, but the government could provide exploration and development grants to EnergiCorp, exactly as happened in the early days of the development of North Sea oil, which it wouldn't particularly matter if and when they became public; but would be set so as, in total, to more than compensate the company for the cost of the cancelled Russian gas contracts."

"Leave that one with me" replied Preston, in a very relaxed tone. Palmer thought only afterwards that one didn't become the CEO of a global energy company without some experience of the ways in which governments and corporations scratched each others' backs; but it was nonetheless, he thought, a cool performance. But Preston wasn't finished. "I can't promise anything but, as a matter of fact, we may be in a position to help you here. We have some gas operations in Europe, not huge but significant. We might be able to take over the contracts as you suggest and then sell at least some of the gas on to other European countries, at a very competitive price relative to their renewing whatever contracts they have coming up for renewal. Obviously, we'd take a loss, which you could compensate, but the amount would be only a fraction of what would be involved if the contracts were just cancelled."

Neither Seymour nor Palmer was the type to display great emotion; and in fact, outwardly, all they did was catch each others' eye. But it was the best news they had had since the whole ghastly Russian mess had blown up. It was left to Flemming to say, with a broad smile, that that was extremely good news; and that they should liaise once Preston had looked into how best to move that all forward. How quickly, Palmer wanted to know, might EnergiCorp be in a position to take over the contracts. Preston said that they could get moving within a month, subject to checking it all out. This time, Seymour could not contain himself.

"A month would be absolutely brilliant" he said. "As you can imagine, the situation has been a considerable worry; having this off our backs so soon would be such a relief." At some underground level, so deep in Palmer's mind he barely registered it, still less voiced it, was one major worry, that all this good news, with the prospect of escaping from under Gudanov's influence, critically depended on the British Treasury being able to provide the compensation promised to Preston; and that could only be forthcoming if the Irish referendum went the right way. The government could call it, but - by Palmer's own choice he acknowledged - it was down to him, and increasingly it felt like him alone, to ensure the right result.

Palmer was by now anxious to get moving on the referendum strategy he had outlined to Seymour, but knew that that would have to wait. First, he had to be sure that his plans for the IRA would work; and for that he needed to ensure the co-operation of two individuals.

Retired Major-General Frederick Sykes, DSO, MC was in the study of his Hampshire home, an attractive Georgian pile set in its own grounds of around ten acres, when the call came through from Palmer. Now in his seventies, he retained a fitness, and almost athletic physique, with powerful shoulders, a soldier's bearing and a large head covered in short grey hair. His rugged, still quite handsome features had a weather-beaten hue. He was not a man easily crossed, nor did he look it.

It was two years since they had been in touch and two years since, at Palmer's request, Sykes had set up a dedicated team to seize an IRA courier at a disused mansion near Sykes's residence. The operation had been a disaster. The whole situation had been a carefully constructed IRA trap, designed to force Sykes, if he wanted his men to survive, to confirm that his operation had been sanctioned by Number 10. And that mattered, because it was no issue of national security that had prompted No. 10's action, but an altogether squalid attempt by the then PM, Alan Gerrard, to cover up his literally murderous past. The surrender of Sykes' team to a well organised and well-armed IRA terrorist group had been a humiliation, for them and for him, the only one he had suffered in what had otherwise been a rather illustrious career in her Majesty's armed forces. He did not hold it particularly against Palmer that he had been comprehensively outmanoeuvred – the fortunes of war – but it had caused him little grief that they had had no contact since. With Gerard dead, murdered by the IRA, with a new prime minister in office, and Sykes enjoying a comfortable retirement, his life had moved on. He retained a semi-executive directorship in a successful security firm, Trojan Security Ltd., which employed a number of his former service men when they left the army, which kept his interest, supplemented his pension and, from time to time, provided for some enjoyable travel around the world. His response, therefore, to Palmer's call was polite but cautious.

Palmer had given considerable thought as to how to approach Sykes; and, given their history, recognised that he would need to engage his interest, even his enthusiasm, quickly. "I apologise for calling you without warning" said Palmer "and I hope this finds you well." But he didn't pause for an answer, knowing that Sykes would not welcome the renewed contact and giving him no time to back away from the call. "I'm calling because I would greatly value a meeting – not a matter I can discuss on the phone – but let me say that what I have in mind would allow you to reverse the unfavourable outcome of our last joint effort."

Palmer could be absolutely brutal when he needed to be, but he also had very sound instincts for how to play people; and this approach to Sykes, direct, which Sykes would like, a form of peace offering, and a clear opportunity to assuage the anger, however latent, that he knew Sykes would feel about the one late blot on his record and his reputation, all combined to generate the result Palmer sought, in the form of a long pause before Sykes replied.

"I will lunch at my club tomorrow, the Cavalry and Guards, at 1pm. Can you make that?"

"Thank you General" replied Palmer "You won't regret it. Until tomorrow" he added; and ended the call. Palmer had not been confident that he could get Sykes to meet him. Now that he had that fixed, the next stage, he assured himself, would be a lot easier.

The two men duly met the next day, in the refined setting of one of London's long-standing 'Gentlemen's Clubs' though, like most of them now, it was also open to women members. Sykes offered Palmer a drink in the bar, ordered himself a whisky, and they went straight into the long, elegant dining room overlooking Piccadilly. Palmer took a moment to realise just how much he was looking forward to the encounter, not just because he was fairly sure that Sykes would help him in his project, but because he genuinely liked the man. And that, he also realised, was because Sykes was one of the very few people Palmer had come across professionally who was not remotely intimidated by him. Palmer hoped to persuade him of their joint interest in what he was going to propose; and he would try hard to succeed. But he knew, very clearly, that if Sykes didn't want to be involved, then there was nothing that Palmer could do about it. He had nothing on Sykes and, even if he did, Sykes was the type to tell him to go to hell. Indeed, given the General's 'connections' Palmer might find himself winding up in a hospital bed if he ever tried to strong-arm the General. But Sykes would agree, he was sure, if only he could make the case persuasively.

Food and wine having been ordered, Palmer came straight to the point. "It is not public knowledge yet, but the Prime Minister has recognised that there will soon have to be a referendum on Northern Ireland's continued membership of the UK. It is absolutely vital to the future of the UK economy that the vote is to remain. This is not some vague feeling, still less historical nostalgia. I presume that I can count on your absolute assurance that this conversation remains completely secret." Sykes merely nodded, in a manner that not only agreed to secrecy, but indicated that he was of a class of people for whom such assurances meant what they said.

"One of the largest gas fields ever found has been discovered in the Irish Sea, which will transform the UK economy and the living standards of its population; but the gas field is on the western side of the Sea; and if Northern Ireland leaves the UK, virtually all of that wealth will accrue to the very much smaller population of a United Ireland. That is why the vote must be to remain; and all our indications are that this will be the outcome. But we now have intelligence that the IRA are planning a renewed bombing campaign, with the threat that if the vote is to remain, it will mean a return of 'the Troubles' in spades, and indefinitely; and our concern is that this may scare enough floating voters to vote to leave. The PM has, therefore, asked me to consider how the IRA may be stopped. I have formulated a means of getting most, if not all, of the current leadership of the IRA together - a known spot at a known time - and I need a team, I estimate around twenty or so minimum, of people, trustworthy people, with army experience and expertise, to intercept them, obtain all necessary information as to the location of their armaments dumps, and then keep them completely incommunicado until after the referendum. I should add that the three most prominent members amongst the current leadership were all present the last time you engaged with the IRA. The whole operation would, of course, be completely deniable on the part of Her Majesty's Government."

Sykes, though he had just been asked if he would organise a major military action against one of the European continent's most successful terrorist organisations, was not the type to overreact or, indeed, at first, to react at all. When, eventually, he responded, he very much took Palmer by surprise.

"Is 'incommunicado' a euphemism?" he asked. It took Palmer a moment to understand.

"I'm asking that you keep them under lock and key in a safe house, preferably abroad for three to six months if they can be taken without bloodshed. If they resist overwhelming force, your men would have to take whatever action they deem necessary. Does that answer your question?"

"It does" replied Sykes. Another pause. "When would you want this operation carried out?"

"Immediately after we announce the referendum, so, best guess, in around two months."

"Why after the referendum is announced?" asked Sykes. "Surely you want them out of the way before you start the process?"

"I can't give you the answer to that" said Palmer, "but I presume that you will need that sort of lead-in period to set the operation up?"

"I will, yes" Sykes replied "but if there is any element of your plan that I don't know about, then the answer is 'no'" and he returned to the medium rare fillet steak which had now arrived. Palmer could see that this was non-negotiable, so he explained how he intended that Sykes's men could get to the IRA leadership, and that for that to work the referendum would have to be public knowledge.

"How will you contact the IRA?" asked Sykes.

"You will recall the woman who was present when you last encountered the IRA?" replied Palmer. Sykes nodded. "Her name is Kate Kimball. My plan is for her to make contact – the present leadership of the IRA will trust her – and then offer to return with someone who was previously with our security services with links to the Protestant side. You will need to recruit that person; and then track them when they go back to Northern Ireland. The rest will be up to your team." That 'the rest' would certainly involve extreme intimidation, maybe worse, kidnap, and possibly murder was left unacknowledged by either man.

In seeking to recruit Sykes to his plan, Palmer was very aware of competing emotions within him. On the one hand, Sykes would no doubt review every last detail of the plan; and the sooner Sykes engaged with that, the more likely, Palmer thought, he would become attracted to the operation. On the other, the whole thing had been dreamed up in his study, and been subject to no critical review other than Seymour's – who was far from able to offer a dispassionate assessment – and if Sykes saw any flaw, or just thought it too great a risk, then the plan, Palmer's plan, would be dead in the water.

To his great relief, Sykes made no critical comment. "What is the budget?" asked Sykes, not exactly abruptly but with his usual economy of words.

"Assuming twenty to thirty men, three million pounds for them, untraceable source, payable anywhere, plus all expenditure, on weaponry, transport, safe house facilities and surveillance. And may we say a £5 million fee for the project? I trust that would be sufficient?" Sykes made no reply to the question.

"What about the Kimball woman?" asked Sykes. "She was supposed to be a courier for the IRA; but turned out to be the decoy that led us into their open arms." He did not deign to identify any options available for dealing with her. "Can she be trusted?"

"Once she has led your team to the IRA leadership, just send her on her way" replied Palmer. "She is quite capable of finding her own way back."

"And if things don't go quite according to plan, if she ends up as collateral damage?" was Sykes overly deadpan reply.

"Then she must disappear, completely and irretrievably" was Palmer's equally deadpan instruction. "I can control her if she returns alive – she knows that any attempt to publicise what happened would result in her being prosecuted for involvement in Alan Gerrard's murder, followed by a very long prison sentence - but she could be a major embarrassment to all of us if she turned up dead in Northern Ireland. Get her out of there as soon as you don't need her anymore, but if there is any problem, then she is an unresolved missing persons case. I trust that is no problem, General?"

"We will try to ensure that she returns unharmed" said Sykes. "If she does become collateral damage, then it will be of no concern to her what happens thereafter. So, yes, no problem. Now, talk me through your plan again, in as much detail as possible, for me to take away and reflect upon." Palmer, hoping that it was not just wishful thinking, took this as a good sign; and it took him only a few minutes to rehearse his view of how the operation could be carried out, with minimum risk, provided that Sykes's team was familiar with, and experienced in this type of 'search, seize and contain' activity.

"I'll discuss it with a couple of my people – purely operational matters, not the context, and I will need to get board approval. I'll call you a week today. If it's on, I'll want three million up front, and access to maybe another two million for equipment and the like. Final payment just before we go live. I'll also need to consult on the surveillance issues involved.

Palmer, who had never for one moment anticipated that he would get a reply from Sykes immediately, was more than content with that outcome. Sykes seemed prepared to countenance the operation, and the budget was adequate. He needed to know whether it was a feasible operation, and that he would now check out with 'people' who knew this territory.

The two men ate for a while in silence. Eventually, Palmer asked about Sykes's house in Hampshire, which they discussed briefly; but neither man was given much to small talk, they finished their main course and prepared to leave.

"Seven days, I'll ring you" Sykes confirmed.

"You have my mobile number" said Palmer. "Just a 'yes' or 'no'. If it is on, we can meet again to sort out the details." Again, Sykes just nodded, and they left, with Palmer recognising that it would be a long seven days.

CHAPTER 32

Though he found it very frustrating, Palmer spent most of the next seven days on what he now saw as a very mundane day job, once again injecting the type of authoritarian, not to say, on occasion, menacing approach towards all who would criticise, weaken or undermine his lord and master. He would have been happy to know that Sykes wasted no time in pushing matters forward, later that day contacting the two men who would be critical to the project. The first was Captain James Russell. Ironically, in all the deception that was involved in the operation, the one accurate element was that Russell had, indeed, for over two years been the link between the Government's armed forces in Northern Ireland and an informant in the Protestant paramilitaries. He now worked for Sykes's security firm but, crucially, was familiar enough with the paramilitaries, how they operated, to a limited extent who they were, and what supply lines they used, that he could appear perfectly credible to the IRA for as long as Sykes's men needed before they shut down the planned meeting.

The second was Lieutenant-Colonel Alastair Ferguson, an ex SAS officer, also now on Sykes's payroll and, in Sykes's view, very much the man to lead the operation. Well respected in military circles, with over 25 years, experience, much of it leading men into difficult and dangerous situations, in both the Middle East and in Northern Ireland, he had been a key factor in Sykes's ability to recruit former soldiers to his company. While capable of leading extremely violent operations when needed, his natural style was calm, careful and, above all, very logical. Sykes was confident that he would ensure a well-thought-out approach to their latest task.

Sykes arranged to meet them both at his company's office in Mayfair. Russell arrived first. He was neither particularly tall nor particularly powerfully built, but had a rather commanding presence, stemming from a rather penetrating gaze and a quiet solidity of manner, both of which accurately conveyed that he was not a man to mess about with. This was equally true of Ferguson, who arrived a few minutes later, but the message was rather more immediate in his case. Comfortably over six feet tall, clearly of very muscular build, but with a lightness of step that spoke volumes of his fitness, there could be no doubting his physical potential. Coupled with what Sykes knew of his mental abilities and discipline, he was formidable, as his past senior role in the SAS testified.

He and Russell knew each other through Sykes's firm, but not well; and had not worked on any operation together. But both recognised in the other that indefinable military bearing that somehow never seemed to disappear entirely, however long it might be since leaving the army; and Sykes was pleased to see that they appeared to establish an instant rapport with each other.

Coffee having been brought in, Sykes got straight down to business.

"We have been offered a major commission, completely off the radar. The task is to find, seize and hold a number of the IRA's current leadership, for several months – to be put into operation quite soon, probably within two months. A woman who will have previously established contact with the IRA leadership will take you, James, to meet up with them on the pretext that you can fill them in on the Protestant paramilitaries' identity, location and plans. You can gen up enough to make this credible for the short period of time before Alastair and his team come in and make the seizure.

"Subject to any observations that either of you have, I've split the project into eleven semi-self-contained sections: personnel, armaments, tracking the woman – her name is Kimball - and James to the site of meeting, delivery of our team to the site, taking control of the IRA men involved, tracking and seizure of any key players not at the meeting, locating their arms stores, extracting all of us – our team, the IRA and any weapons or explosives seized, establishing a holding centre for them for what will be at least several months, guarding and managing it, and establishing alibis for most or all of us covering the duration of the operation. Have I left anything out?"

"Where do Kimball's loyalties lie and what do we do with her?" asked Russell.

"She is an unwilling participant" said Sykes, "has no idea that Alastair's team are coming in; and will be very pissed off when it happens. But she is no threat to us or those commissioning this operation, so she can just be let go, to find her own way home. However, this relates to a wider issue. While there may be some casualties – it depends how quickly the IRA perceive their lack of options – I do not envisage any fatalities. If they should occur, and this applies to Kimball as well, the bodies must be destroyed, and any remains removed to a location where they will never ever be discovered. If neither of you is content with that possibility, now is the time to say so." There was a grim silence, with neither Russell nor Ferguson moving a muscle.

"Good" said Sykes. "So, let us get down to the details of each operational component." The three men moved rapidly into a logistic planning routine with which they were all very familiar. There was no certainty as to how many IRA personnel they would have to deal with; but Palmer and Sykes had thought it might be up to half a dozen or so, essentially the IRA's so-called Army Council. They decided they would allow for up to ten; and Ferguson was tasked with recruiting around twenty-five 'operatives' – a term they preferred to 'mercenaries' - to carry out the operation. He and Sykes were confident that they could recruit at least half from the pool of people that Sykes's security firm, Trojan Security Ltd., regularly used; and they would no doubt be able to recommend a similar number from among their contacts in what was a rather small world of ex-military and ex-intelligence services personnel. Ferguson would also take responsibility for arming them from the undisclosed store which Trojan Security had built up over the years.

"The next element is tracking James and Kimball to the meeting" said Sykes. The Irish will no doubt make absolutely sure that no-one can track you or the Kimball woman – I assume that they will check for any bugs on either of you or your clothing. But, no problem. I'm arranging for two high altitude drones with cameras, together with their operators, to be available, much the same as we used last year in the Nigerian operation you were on, Alastair. They are supplied by a specialist firm, James, which we have used before; and they are very good at what they do, so you can rely on us being right behind you. These drones fly at several thousand feet – quite impossible to hear or see – but their cameras can pick out details of less than a centimetre – they'll know whether you shaved or not that morning. The beauty of them is that, with half a dozen or more of our vehicles in the area, we can direct them in from multiple directions so that if the Irish stake out the road to see if anyone is trying to follow them, they won't find anyone."

"Sounds very satisfactory" was Russell's slightly cautious reply "and you say you have used them before. Do they know what our operation entails?" He forbore to spell out that it involved kidnapping, false imprisonment, and maybe worse.

"They do know, yes" Sykes assured him. They have worked for security and intelligence services here and in the US; including the US Drug Enforcement Agency, but I'm fairly sure they have done work for the other side, so to speak as well. In any event, they will be pulling out just as soon as Alastair and his team go in to support you. By the time you are done, they will be long gone, without a trace."

Russell gave an affirmatory nod. "Next" Sykes continued, "getting to the site. I think that some of the team should go singly to Northern Ireland by ferry to Belfast, some to Cork. The rest I'll come to in a minute. Once there, six or seven of us will hire cars, using phoney driver's licences, plus two teams of two will go over in two medium sized trucks. We will need one for our equipment and both for the return journey. The trucks can be kept well away from wherever the meeting is, until needed, but the cars will each meet up with other team members and then, with four men in each of them, will station themselves at various points around Belfast Airport – I'm assuming that will be Kimball's initial route in, but we can adjust if not - and wait for information from the drone operators. We can't risk the drones being intercepted on their way to Northern Ireland, nor any of our weaponry, so my plan is for all of it to be taken across the Irish Sea a few nights before in a powerful but undetectable inflatable. Those not going across by ferry will go in with the equipment and then get picked up by one of the trucks. Everyone will converge on James and Kimball, as indicated by the drone operators. The team can then track you to the meeting site, deal with any guarding forces that the IRA may have installed, and then break into James's fireside chat. All okay?"

Both men nodded. "Assuming our superior numbers and fire-power, and with the element of surprise" mused Ferguson, "I don't think it should be too difficult."

Another nod from Sykes. "The next three elements I will leave in your hands, Alastair" said Sykes. "Immobilising the Irish, getting them to confirm to your satisfaction that there are no other key people missing, or their location if they are; and the location of their arms dumps, such as they are. Seizing any explosives they may be hoarding will be particularly important. We don't know how many secret sites they may still have, but I'd suggest that they need to reveal at least three if they want to come out of this alive and intact. If they can persuade you it is less, then that's fine – I've no doubt that you can be quite persuasive enough. I don't know how long it will take to round up any other personnel or weapons, but the team won't be under any great time pressure, so reckon it could take some hours. Once that is concluded, we then come to the issue of finding a safe house. Our client wanted us to shift them abroad, but he left it up to us; I think that raises all sorts of problems we don't need. So, James, could you find somewhere on the mainland? it could be anywhere, but must be remote and with a large cellar or something similar. It will need proper plumbing; but we can get that installed if we need to. A remote old farmhouse would be ideal, but it depends on what is readily available."

"I'll get on to it straight away" replied Russell.

Sykes moved on. "Alastair, you will need to identify maybe ten of your team who can readily go off on an 'overseas' project for the firm but, in reality, run the safe house for a few months. I'll dream up a suitable cover project."

Alastair confirmed that he would get onto that. "Which" said Sykes "leaves us with the trickiest part, getting everyone to the safe house. My plan is to use one of the trucks to take them to the coast, where they can be transferred to the boat – it can't remain at its landing site so will have to make a second journey across the Irish Sea. As for any weapons or explosives seized, our weapons and the drones, they will all have to go back by sea that night or, if needed, over several nights. Any questions?"

The three men spent the next half hour going over each strand of the project, making no notes but mentally absorbing the logistics and all the various actions that would need to be put in place. They concluded with a discussion of a timetable, and how long therefore, before they could commence the operation. Sykes indicated that speed was of the essence, but that they had several weeks, and would not go ahead until every last risk had been identified and a response determined. After lengthy discussion they concluded that, subject to Russell finding a suitable property, and Ferguson finding suitable launch and landing sites for their boat, they could be ready to go in a month. Russell and Ferguson would allow themselves five days to examine and resolve all the various logistical issues involved and, assuming no insuperable obstacles, Sykes could then, subject to Board approval, let the client know that they would in principle, be ready within a month. In due course, Russell would need to fix a rendezvous with Kimball before their trip to Ulster. The men, weapons, drones and transport would all be in place by then; and Sykes would ensure that false IDs and solid alibis for all of the men involved were all ready to be deployed by then.

Ferguson was well aware of Sykes's ability to conjure up false IDs – it was a standard part of numerous operations in the past - but was curious about the process of providing the alibis they would need if any hint of Trojan's involvement should emerge.

"We have a small, ad hoc team" replied Sykes, who use various methods. We have people who will use your credit cards, mobile phones, or cash machines from sites in England while you are in Northern Ireland. We have contacts who will swear you were with them in a pub, a restaurant, wherever. We can rig up photos showing you were at a party, we can have tickets for a match, a show, and make sure you know the score or the cast or the plot. For one or two we will put new photos on your passports and driving licences, have you hire cars abroad, and so on. Some will have their security access cards to the office used; and a few will just say they were at home watching TV, but we will brief them on what they watched. We don't want absolutely everyone to be rock solid – that would look suspicious – but, overall, if anything should appear to link the operation to the firm, it will appear impossible that the company could have carried it out. And we will rotate the guards at the safe house, so no-one is away very long. Plus, let me assure you, the whole thing will be stress tested, with one of the team playing a very determined detective inspector. It will be fine."

"I don't doubt it" said Ferguson. "Sounds quite a fun element." And on that cheerful thought, Russell and Ferguson left, both very energised by Sykes's plans and the quiet intensity with which he had presented them. It was a good feeling to have as much confidence in Sykes as he clearly had in each of them.

CHAPTER 33

Five days later, Sykes, Russell and Ferguson again met at Trojan Security's London office.

"Let's start" said Sykes "with the item with the longest lead time. James, any luck with a property we can use as a safe house?"

"I think I have somewhere," was Russell's very welcome reply. "Googling estate agents threw up a surprisingly large number of vacant properties that seemed to fit what we are after. I've narrowed it down to three or four, but the best option is a house in Cumbria, not the Lake District but a rather bleak stretch of territory to the east of the M6. It has been empty for three years – the owner hasn't found a buyer in all that time – and has a large workshop-cum-storage area attached. The owner is a now retired local builder who has moved into a new house he built about five miles away, so that's no problem. It's very isolated, down a long track to nowhere; the workshop could be just what we need to house our guests. I've told the owner that it might be what I'm after, but I'm not sure, so I suggested I rent it for three months or maybe six months, and then decide whether to buy it. He's not had any success to date in selling it, so he is happy to agree that if we want to go ahead. Do you want to see it?"

"How would you set up the workshop?" asked Sykes.

"That's the best part" replied Russell. The workshop is on the same cesspit drainage as the house; we could easily arrange secure fencing all round the inner walls; and I'd suggest that we acquire several camper vans to house the men. They can be kept securely in the vans most of the time; but can't get out if we let them get some exercise inside the building. And our guard team have the run of the house for their accommodation. It all looks to be just fine."

"I don 't need to see it then" said Sykes. Go ahead. Talk to finance about paying via one of our less traceable companies. And contact Engineering about the internal fencing." Not uniquely, but quite unusually, Trojan Security had its own engineering department. This had come into being when a major international famine relief charity offered them a large contract. Over half their aid was getting lost en route, due to theft and bribery. Sykes had seen an opportunity. His firm took over security for delivery, resulting in over 95% of the aid getting through, earning the company a nice fee in the process. However, some of the delivery problems in various African states had simply been the state of the roads, rivers that had broken their banks and flooded access, and numerous similar problems. So Trojan Security had simply set up a dedicated civil engineering unit to tackle every one of those problems as they arose. It had been a great money spinner for the company, but the fee to the charity was dwarfed by the hundreds of millions of pounds of extra aid that actually got through to its intended recipients.

Russell nodded agreement that he would contact the department. He and Ferguson then each gave Sykes an account of the detailed plans they had put together since they had first met, covering personnel, equipment, transport and alibis. Ferguson first confirmed that he had identified and secured the recruitment of twenty-four operatives, four of them women. Sykes was not surprised at this, as Trojan Security had found, on numerous occasions, women could much more stealthily achieve close observation or a final approach to a target; and they might well come in very handy for an operation such as this. Second, he described two sites that he had identified, one in Scotland from which they would launch their inflatable, the other in Northern Ireland where they would land their weapons and equipment. Both were remote, with virtually no risk of being intercepted at night. They then reviewed the arrangements for the vehicles they would need; and plotted out everyone's required movements throughout the operation. At each point, Sykes played 'Devil' - Trojan shorthand for considering anything, anything whatsoever, that could go wrong at each stage - and how the team would respond. They then arranged for the team to meet for detailed rehearsals at Trojan's so-called 'training ground' - a once derelict industrial site surrounded by open countryside some miles outside Swindon. As a result of Trojan Security's developments over the years, this now comprised over twenty 'sets' or backdrops to possible areas of action – offices, warehouses, commercial premises, residential premises, all of various sizes and types, farm buildings and some rural locations – of which Hollywood would have been proud. Not knowing where they would encounter the IRA, the plan was to rehearse on as many of these as time allowed. But Sykes did not have to wait for this to be completed He now had enough to know that they were in business.

The following day, Sykes met up with Sir Simon Fawcett, Non-Executive Chairman of Trojan Security Ltd. Fawcett, after a distinguished military career, had become something of a legend as, eventually, Deputy Secretary at the Ministry of Defence, where one of his major responsibilities was liaison and co-ordination with the UK's intelligence services. This was widely known to be an almost impossibly difficult remit, only partly due to inter-service rivalry; but Fawcett had been seen on all sides as a safe pair of hands. On retirement and, after a suitable gap of 18 months, he had been an obvious person to chair an organisation like Trojan Security; and had been in post for several years. Though of unremarkable features, his impressive height, elegant silver hair, and an indefinable, but unavoidable, sense of being in control of any situation in which he found himself made him a man of immense presence. He was the only man that Sykes, General though he was, regarded as a true peer; and the two had established a rapport at Trojan that was worth more than anything that could be written down about the firm.

Despite having a natural flair for summarising the main issues of anything he wishes to say, clearly, concisely and around the main points, Sykes had nonetheless prepared for the meeting. In a few minutes, he described the proposed contract, how his team thought they would go about meeting it, the risks and the finances. The two men sat silently when he finished as Sykes waited for Fawcett's response.

"Three things" he said. "Operationally, it sounds fine, but I know that you will not proceed unless you yourself are convinced that it is watertight. So, I have no concerns on that score. Second, there must be no possibility of the operation being traced back to us; and so I would like you personally to review and test, to destruction if necessary, the arrangements for distancing our operatives from the action. I'd like your personal confirmation of that." Sykes simply nodded. "Third, I am not clear how Trojan accounts for the profit on this operation while having no traceable association with it. Has that been looked at?"

"A key point" agreed Sykes. All the expenses will be financed from accounts unrelated to either Trojan or, indeed, the client. As for the £5 million fee, I have asked one of our men, Roderick Holland, to set up a shell project – a phoney operation - somewhere overseas, which will invoice overseas banks where the funds are held for the costs of that operation; but the costs will in fact be more-or-less zero. He will establish all the necessary paperwork; Trojan's receipt of the funds will have no connection to the Irish project."

"Sounds okay" was Fawcett's low-key response. "So, I'm content to give you the go-ahead. The total size of the project is above the level I can authorise without going to the full board; but if none of the expenses come anywhere near us, the £5 million via the shell operation is just within my delegated authority, so let's do it." Sykes regarded it as a very satisfactory meeting.

A week after they had previously talked; and bang on time, almost to the minute, Sykes rang Palmer.

"It's on." He said, in a flat tone that totally belied the significance of those two words, for him, for Palmer, for Seymour and, indeed, for the future of the UK. "Come down to my house this week-end and I'll introduce you to a couple of my men who will direct matters. We can check out with you what we are planning. Let me have the funds for our costs by the end of the month at the latest. I'll give you details of where to direct it when I see you."

Whether relief and adrenaline can simultaneously diffuse through one's body or not Palmer did not know, but it nonetheless very much felt like that to him. Less given to hyperbole than almost anyone on the planet, Palmer still couldn't escape the feeling that this was a truly pivotal moment, one that could never be revealed while he was alive, but which he hoped, in some way could be recorded for posterity, so that the UK – and it would be the UK, not Great Britain – would know what he had done for it and for its prosperity. The original motivation - getting Seymour re-elected - was sufficiently far from his mind to pass him by at that moment. But the brief moment of self-delusion would not last long. Palmer merely said he was pleased and would call on Sykes on Saturday. "Come for lunch" said Sykes, and their conversation ended. A truly delighted Palmer immediately turned his mind to the next step, and to the second person whose co-operation he would need.

This other person, so key to his plans, was blissfully unaware of the disruption to her life which was about to descend upon her. In all normal circumstances, Kate Kimball could not be further from the world which Palmer inhabited, still less the vortex of forces into which he wished to cast her. In her mid-thirties, she had risen just as fast as her publishing abilities warranted, to head up the Science Division of Oxford University Press. This traditionally published both learned academic treaties, which were part of the onward march of scientific research but made little if any profit, and more popular books on all aspects of science, destined for a wider readership. But of late the Press, as it was generally known, and her division in particular, had branched out into a wave of internet publishing and e-learning, completely demolishing the view that the internet signalled the demise of traditional publishers. On the back of this, Kate was into all manner of TV and film projects on scientific issues; and was widely recognised in the industry as being a very successful innovator in this field.

Though she would only acknowledge it quietly to herself, she knew that her career success had to some extent been assisted by her appearance. Her height and fulsome figure made her immediately noticeable; and her undoubtedly good looks – high cheekbones, wide mouth and rather large blue/grey eyes, – all made her a striking presence in any company. But her resulting attractiveness to men, which she had well understood since her teenage years, had necessitated her developing a rather tough streak to her character, fending off a succession of alpha males whom she found at best patronising and at worst predatory. Perhaps this, more than any physical appearance, had underpinned her success as a businesswoman, though normally well hidden behind outwardly engaging social skills and an amiable seeming personality.

What she regarded as a fortunate upbringing, a good education, some luck in getting into publishing in the first place and both an interesting and exciting career since was all marred only by the terrible, and terrifying, circumstances that had surrounded her two years previously. Her partner, Paul Emmerson, a modest, unassuming and increasingly distinguished Professor of Engineering at the University, and the love of her life, had disappeared, without leaving a trace. Eventually, she accepted that he was dead, but then odd clues emerged that suggested that he was alive, but something very strange - certainly not just a mindless mugging as the police increasingly concluded – had been going on. She eventually found out that he was still alive, effectively a hostage in an appalling military-political nightmare involving the US, the UK and the bombing of Iran. Against all the odds she had managed to rescue him but the cost to her had been high – twice threatened with death, twice threatened with something a lot worse than death, co-operating with Irish terrorists to get Paul back, and being forced by an appalling servant of the then Prime Minister, Alan Gerrard, to make a secret tape incriminating her in their plans to assassinate Gerrard. She had a resilient character; and had more or less put all of these traumas behind her. But she still occasionally had nightmares, not least of the time when two men attacked her in her own home and came close to faking her suicide. She would wake up in a cold sweat, trying to pull the rope they had used from her neck, until she came fully awake and tried, once again, to focus on the simple fact that she had survived all of it; and that her life now was once again very much what she wanted it to be.

One major contribution to this was the annual Frankfurt Book Fair, a major event in the publishing world's calendar; and a time when Kate marketed books, sold rights, discussed propositions and met old friends whom she had accumulated over her years in the business. It was one of the highlights of her year, but brought with it a degree of tiredness and anti-climax the Monday morning after she returned, as she headed for her office to pick up on everything that had been carrying on in her absence. This particular such morning was not helped by the fact that she had developed quite a cold on the flight back.

Her P.A., Janice who, despite her name was a Pole from Warsaw was delighted to see her back after four days away, provided coffee and muffins, and was keen to hear how matters had gone at the Fair. Kate gave her a quick overview, they pencilled in a time thoroughly to go through everything Kate needed to follow up from Frankfurt and then turned to Kate's schedule for the day. This included two internal meetings, a meeting with some independent illustrators, and two meetings with authors, current or potential. The former had nearly finished a book on the history of the internet; but given that new developments were happening almost daily, was having some difficulty knowing how to bring the book to a conclusion.

The latter was an American professor whom she had not met, but had been in touch about the non-US rights of a book he was planning on dark matter and dark energy, which together apparently made up 95% of the universe, but about which very little was known; and the process of discovery of these strange phenomena. Kate had doubts about how a book could be written if so little was known about the subject matter; but the Professor was briefly in the UK and had suggested lunch, so there was little to lose. He had suggested the Trout Inn, not surprisingly thought Kate, as it was the standard tourist-book recommended stopover for all Americans visiting Oxford; but Kate knew it got crowded and noisy – not ideal for a business meeting – and had got Janice to switch the lunch to the Perch, another timbered, though rebuilt, inn on the river but much more off the beaten track. It also had the advantage that, in fifteen minutes, on a pleasantly sunny day such as today, she could walk to it, which would make a welcome break in the middle of what would be a busy day, if not evening as well.

On arrival, she said that she was meeting a Professor Kowalski. The waitress said that he had already arrived, that he was at a table in the garden, and led Kate through the low timber beamed dining area to the garden. As her host rose to greet her, Kate felt her whole body go rigid. For this was no American Professor Kowalski , not Kowalski, not a professor, not even an American, but her nemesis, the stuff of nightmares, Andrew Palmer, the one person who terrified her, whom she never wanted to meet again, not now, not ever.

Kate felt her head and her heart start to throb uncontrollably. She managed to steady herself by holding on to the corner of the table, and turned to ask the waitress for help, but the waitress had already gone. Kate's one thought was to leave immediately, without a word but, even as she prepared to do so, she was paralysed by the knowledge that if Palmer had gone to this much trouble – a false identity, a phoney c.v. an elaborate book proposal – then she was unlikely just to be able to walk away.

"Sit down" said Palmer in a quiet but firm voice. "You know that you have to speak to me if I want to speak to you. You know that, so just sit down, have a stiff drink to recover and let's take things from there." Kate wanted to scream that she did *not* have to speak to him; or doing anything he said; but there was no point, worse till no validity. For two years, she had generally managed to suppress the knowledge that this devious bastard still had a hold over her, a recording that could send her to prison for a very long time. Still, the thought was always in the background, and now her worst fear was coming true.

A stiff drink seemed very appealing at that moment, but Kate was determined not to accede to Palmer's proposal. She stood there for a long moment, staring at him, trying to regain her composure, and not even prepared to sit down if he had suggested it. For his part, he sat there, motionless and expressionless. "What do you want?" was eventually all she could manage.

"I want you to sit down" said Palmer. We need to talk; and I'm not doing it with you hovering over me like this. So just sit down. If you don't, I'm on my way; I can assure you that you do not want that to happen." His voice was quiet and controlled – no-one at any other table, had they looked across, would have heard or, indeed, noticed, anything unusual about the two of them; but the menace in his words, the explicit threat they contained, was as if someone had slapped Kate very hard in the face.

She stood a moment longer, but if it was meant to indicate that she might or might not accede to his request, it was an idle gesture; and they both knew it. She sat down and, in barely a whisper said "I'd like a glass of water - nothing else." Palmer forbore to show any sign of victory in the little battle of wills; caught a waitress's eye and ordered a glass of wine and a glass of water.

For a moment, neither spoke, Palmer reviewing in his mind how he proposed to handle the meeting; and Kate, trying to recover from the shock of seeing Palmer again, consciously seeking to access the rage, as opposed to fear, she felt towards this man, anything to bolster her resilience and her determination not to be subservient to him. But she also wanted to get away from him as fast as possible. "What do you want?" she repeated.

"I want you to carry out a small task for me" said Palmer. "It is not difficult, it is not dangerous and it is not illegal. But, as you will see, you are the only person I know who could do it for me."

Although Kate felt that she was as distrustful of this man as someone could be, she also felt herself calming down slightly at this declaration despite that extreme distrust. But she had little idea of what she could contribute to his purposes that only she could provide. "What is it?" she said, deliberately as terse as possible, her face a grim mask of hatred for the man sitting comfortably across the table.

"On behalf of the Prime Minister I need to get a completely confidential message to what remains of the IRA in Northern Ireland. It is a message that they will welcome. But, you will understand that the government cannot be seen to be having any sort of dialogue with the IRA – it is still a terrorist organisation. So, the contact must be in complete secrecy – purely verbal so that there is no paper trail or electronic evidence - and, if it ever came to light, totally deniable by the PM. It will be completely unexpected; and so they will be highly suspicious. This is why the message has to be delivered not only in person but by someone that they will trust. As you may imagine, there is no one in government or anywhere in Whitehall whom the IRA would remotely trust; in any event, that would be too near to the PM to be deniable. But you fit the bill perfectly. You worked with them, you assisted them in their efforts against Alan Gerrard. Even if you tell them why you are acting as courier - in fact you certainly can tell them that you have effectively been blackmailed into it - they will still trust you to be straight with them. All it will take from you is two brief trips to Northern Ireland, one to deliver the message and one subsequent follow-up. And, before you ask, if you do this, then I will hand over to you the recording – in fact there are two copies and you can have both – of your complicity in the IRA move against Gerrard. Two short trips and you will be free of me and, I can assure you, that is a much better place to be." He stopped, leaving Kate with just an unflinching stare.

Kate had sufficiently recovered from the shock of seeing Palmer, of being cornered by him, to be able to take in his little speech; and it did seem to have a logic to it. But the emotions and the questions it generated were still deeply unsettling; from somewhere inside her came the need to get back onto something like even terms with him. Her words preceded any careful thought.

"I've known for some time that you are an odious little shit, but only now do I find that you are a total moron as well" she began. She had not expected any reaction, so she was not disappointed when Palmer did not try to interrupt her. "I had some brief contact with a rather tangential group in the IRA two years ago. I knew nothing of their leadership then, I know nothing of who leads it now and, even if I did, I have no way on earth of contacting them. You can threaten me all you like but even you can't be so stupid as to think I can do something impossible, however much you may want it. If that's all, I'm going."

To her immense irritation, Palmer just smiled. "Two years ago, you were in bed with Victor O'Connell and his two sons, Vincent and Declan. You may be surprised to know, or maybe not, that Victor is now very much the elder statesman of the IRA, a sort of *eminence grise* since his attack on Gerrard; and the IRA, such as it is at the moment, is run by Vincent and Declan. So, you see, you do know the current leadership. As for contacting them, you managed it before so I do not doubt that you can manage it again. Hurl as much abuse my way as you feel you need to, but you can, and you will do this. The sooner you accept that the quicker we can get on to the messages themselves – not difficult but they need memorising."

Kate was almost as shaken by this information as she had been by seeing Palmer in the first place; and felt her position, which she had tried to bolster, once again slipping away. But she was conscious that this was not only because Palmer seemed, in the end, to hold all the cards. It was also because Palmer's project now had a human face; and the prospect that a couple of conversations with people she knew and had collaborated with would get her freed from Palmer was altogether much more manageable. However, she was not yet in any state of mind to capitulate.

"What possible guarantee could I have that you would not keep a third recording of those stage-managed phone calls?" she asked, barely able to look at Palmer as she spoke."

"None, other than my word that I won't" he replied "in which, no doubt, you will place little confidence but, frankly, as I keep saying, you don't have any choice. If it helps, it will become clear from the message itself, and the answer to it, that the whole purpose of this enterprise is to resolve both the tensions and, more than that, even the need for any further contact between the government and the IRA. In which case, your, how shall I say, special value, will no longer exist. In short, I would have no need to keep a copy. You can accept that or not but, either way, we need to move on."

Kate felt a strong urge to stand up and slap Palmer hard across his smug face; and a half-formed idea surfaced that she could accompany it with a scream that he had sexually assaulted her, groped her breasts, propositioned her in some way. She'd never make it stick, but she could cause such a well-known figure a lot of grief if she had a mind to. But the moment passed – no slap, no scream – and she was left with the reluctant task of accepting, as Palmer said, that she had no choice in the matter.

"What is it?" she said. "What is the message?" Palmer eschewed any acknowledgement, any sign at all, that he had just won a battle.

"There are two. They are quite simple, but you will need to understand the background. The world does not know it yet, but there is to be a referendum on whether Northern Ireland should remain in the UK or leave and unite with the Republic of Ireland. Her Majesty's government does not believe that it can any longer ignore the growing demand, from some quarters at least, for such a re-alignment of the Province's constitutional position; and has always held the view that, ultimately this is a matter for the people of Northern Ireland – hence the referendum . But the government has always said that it wants the Province to remain in the UK; and it will campaign for that outcome. However – and if you were to repeat what I am about to say to anyone, anyone at all, even your professor partner, I would not only deny it, and no-one would believe you, but I would take the greatest pleasure in seeing you locked way for ever and a day – however, the Prime Minister has come to the conclusion that he would rather see Northern Ireland leave the UK.

The reasons are, first, that he sees it as inevitable in the end; second, that being so, he would rather get shot of the economic burden of the Province, at a time when the economy of the UK is struggling and, with apologies for the cynicism, seriously denting his chances of being re-elected. But he is also convinced that the move will be detrimental to the economy of Northern Ireland – as a poor region in the UK it gets a lot of support, but it's not at all poor by EU standards, on which it would then have to rely – and when this becomes clear it will kill off any further moves for Scottish independence, about which he is altogether much less sanguine. So, the first entirely confidential message is that for the first and no doubt only time in history, the PM's preference coincides with that of the IRA. He will not admit this in public for one moment, but that is his view."

"I can tell the O'Connells that" said Kate, "but so what? And why would they believe me anyway?"

"The answer to both questions lies in the second message" Palmer replied. "The PM 's view is that the momentum lies with those wanting Northern Ireland to leave the UK and, for reasons I have explained, the government's campaign against may prove a little lack-lustre, but there is one potential obstacle. As the IRA has always suspected, there are corners of Whitehall that have, over the years, retained discreet links to the protestants in the North, including both the politicians and, even more discreetly, some of the loyalist paramilitary groups. It has become clear, from these sources, that if there is a referendum, they will re-start a bombing campaign. It will be accompanied by the clear threat that this will lead on to, or rather back to, civil war if the Province joins the Republic. Their strategy is quite crude, but potentially effective, to frighten the population of Northern Ireland that a vote to leave the UK will lead back to the 'Troubles' from which they feel they have finally escaped; and induce the Government in Dublin to go very lukewarm about re-unification. It will not want to become a war-torn country with an indefinite terrorist presence in its midst; if it does not want that, it can easily leak messages that will deter voters - low funding, second class status for the Province, etc.

If that were to be successful, then the UK would end up with the millstone of Northern Ireland round its economic neck for ever. So, these terrorist groups must be stopped before they start. The UK government is in neither a political nor military position to do this; and so the second message is that, if they agree, sufficient information can be supplied to the IRA to ensure that they can neutralise, completely neutralise, this threat before it has time to get off the ground. If they give you a positive response, you will return with someone else who is also completely untraceable back to the government, but who, nonetheless, will have all the information they need to prevent the loyalists stealing the referendum vote."

It is plausible that someone can receive so many shocks, one after the other, that they become immune to any more but, if so, Kate had definitely not reached that point. As the full import of what Palmer had said struck, she was seized by an incandescent rage, so much so that, most unusually for her, she was, if not speechless, certainly incoherent for a moment. "You mean…. I can't believe…. you can't…. Do you mean that you will use the IRA to precipitate a new sectarian war in Northern Ireland, just to ensure that you get the referendum result you want? What sort of animal are you?" She realised she was almost shouting, but was about to explode even more when Palmer cut in.

"On the contrary, Kate. You're not listening. It's the loyalist paramilitaries – as nasty a bunch of violent thugs as you could ever meet – who are planning a new war. I plan to stop it - do you understand - before they blow some helpless innocents to pieces and immediately start a process of retaliation. We must stop them, but the government can't do it without the IRA. We need a committed, clandestine organisation's assistance if we are to halt the equally clandestine operations of a very ruthless group of people. There's not a lot of them, and they do not have any great support in the community these days, but they can do immense damage, to lives, property and the democratic process. So, just calm down and think it through. Anyway, I'm not asking you to take sides, or be any way involved in the thrust of what the PM is trying to do. We just want you to take the message, because we don't have any credible alternative."

Kate was still not so shocked that she couldn't see what complete bullshit this final peroration from Palmer was, and said as much. "So," she continued, you want me to tell the O'Connells that you secretly support Northern Ireland leaving the UK; and that you will help them with secret intelligence so they can locate and, as you so primly put it, 'neutralise' the loyalists, before they can create fear and panic over a 'leave' vote?"

"Exactly" said Palmer. "And we can help them with foreign-sourced, untraceable weapons if their stocks are, as I am fairly sure is the case, now too depleted to be effective."

Now, it finally happened. This latest add-on from Palmer, almost a throw-away line, left Kate so stunned that she was temporarily devoid of words or proper comprehension. She noticed her hands were shaking; and her mouth was dry. Eventually, her lips also shaking, she half mumbled her next words. "You're going to *arm* the IRA? Are you completely insane? I can't sit here and listen to any more of this. Just fuck off for Christ's sake" and she stood up to leave.

With more agility than Kate might have anticipated, Palmer grabbed her arm and, right in front of her, almost eyeball to eyeball and, with more intimidation than she thought possible at a table in a pub, snarled at her. "Shut up and listen, or I will be preparing a brief for the Director of Public Prosecutions before the end of the day, I promise you." he forced her back into her seat. "The arms, if needed, are there purely to ensure that the loyalist paramilitaries can be prevented from destroying both the peace and the future of Northern Ireland. You are quite intelligent enough to understand the paradox that peace can often be secured only through maintaining overriding force. Only the dumb think peace movements, or disarmament, bring peace. For God's sake, even in Northern Ireland itself, the Good Friday peace agreement only came about when the IRA finally recognised that, although they couldn't be defeated, they could never actually win – that is, achieve a United Ireland – by military means. So, get off whatever high horse you think you are on, focus on *real politique* and know, beyond doubt, that you are going to Northern Ireland with these messages, or you are heading for a very long period of imprisonment. Know also, that you must decide now, right now. You agree, right now, or you leave, and that is it."

Kate sat very still, almost trance-like, now staring at Palmer, dumfounded by the events of the previous ten minutes. Part of her still screamed in her head, just to get up, go, leave this despicable situation, this despicable man. But a wiser part forced her to focus on what Palmer had said, what he had threatened. She did not doubt that he would go through with his threat if she left; and his insistence on a decision now absolutely terrified her. She was about to say something, perhaps ready to concede, though she was very far from clear what would emerge, when Palmer spoke again. "How old are you?" he asked.

"What has that got to do with anything?" she spat back at him, relieved that he had provided her with something to say. Palmer more or less ignored her.

"You will get a minimum of 14 years. So, if you are, what, early, mid-thirties, that will effectively rule out ever having children. I know you are very career-oriented, but do you really want to decide that now? Rather sad I'd say, and quite unnecessary."

This stab at any composure she had left, at a future she had not to date thought much about, was so vicious, so uncompromisingly brutal, that through some unknown chemistry it galvanised her thinking. In a moment of sheer inspiration, a second of absolute clarity, she saw her way forward or, rather, two ways forward. "When do you want this done?" she asked.

Unsurprisingly, Palmer thought that his final threat must have done the trick and, to some extent, had. It convinced Kate, beyond any doubt that she had still harboured, that she would have to go along with Palmer's plan. He would have been less pleased had he known the other strand of her thinking. "Shortly after we have announced the referendum, probably about a month or so from now, with the return trip a few weeks beyond that."

"Two messages, and I arrange to take your intelligence man back with me? That's it?" Kate now just wanted to get away.

That's it" said Palmer. Shall I go over what you need to say?"

"No" said Kate, less emphatically than she felt. "I've got it. You support Northern Ireland leaving the UK; and you will offer information and weapons to assist them in ensuring that the loyalist elements in the Province don't scare the population into remaining."

"You've got it" said Palmer "The man you will take to meet them, who will supply the information they need, can do so wherever the O'Connells choose, but he does need to meet their leadership group, - I think they still call themselves their Army Council. We do not want to risk getting involved in a highly risky operation, only to find that some dissident faction doesn't agree and goes off on its own trail of destruction. But I'll give you an update on what to say, just before you go. The distinguished 'Professor Kowalski' will get in touch to fix another meeting, maybe in London. Don't miss it."

Kate stood up and walked out without a word or even a glance at Palmer. She was silently grateful that she had walked to the pub, because she did not feel in any sort of mood to drive safely. The walk back also gave her what she needed most, which was time to think through what she had to do, how she would do it, and how she would scupper everything that Palmer wanted.

CHAPTER 34

Back at her office, Kate managed to carry on with the day's commitments, but only with some difficulty and, as soon as she could, headed home, at least an hour earlier than normal. If Janice noted any change in Kate's demeanour, she did not comment on it, though she was a little surprised that Kate did not comment on her lunch meeting with Professor Kowalski. Once back at the home which she shared with her long-standing partner, Paul Emmerson - a large flat on the ground floor of a listed Victorian building off the Woodstock Road – she poured herself a welcome glass of white wine and rang Paul on his mobile. Rather predictably, she was transferred to an answer phone – Paul was either in a meeting or working in a part of the engineering laboratory where he held a University professorship that banned mobiles as potentially disruptive to electrical or electronic experiments being carried out. She left a message asking him to phone her back as soon as he could and then, in a somewhat calmer and more organised frame of mind, set out to plan the rest of her week.

Paul rang back about an hour later. Palmer had warned Kate not to tell anyone, even Paul, about their conversation, and if she had just told him that she had to go off on another work-related trip, it would have been no surprise whatever to him. But Kate had immediately decided, even as she was walking back from the meeting with Palmer, that she would have to tell Paul what had happened – she would be quite unable to disguise here anxiety - and discuss with him what she was planning.

"That bastard Palmer has been in touch" she said. "Can you get back now? I really need to see you as soon as possible." Paul instantly recognised that asking more on the phone was a waste of time, just not what Kate needed.

"I'll be back in five minutes" he said. "Stay calm if you can" and set off down to where his bicycle was parked. A three-minute journey brought him to their flat and, in the five he had promised, he had Kate in a supportive embrace. A tall man, with an unquestionably handsome face, and quite a commanding presence for someone whose modus vivendi was calmly academic, he immediately comforted Kate. He poured them both glasses of wine; and settled next to her on their large sitting room couch. He didn't need to ask her to explain.

Kate, in normal times, had a talent for organising her thoughts, and being able to present them clearly, and was determined not to let the appallingly exceptional circumstances she was now in to disrupt that. In brief, stark summary she told Paul how Palmer had fooled her into meeting him, and what he had asked – in reality, told – her to do. She concluded by saying that she did know how she could almost certainly be in touch with the O'Connells – Palmer had been right on that point – and could tell them what Palmer wanted her to tell them; but then she might add a twist of her own.

Paul, very familiar with the part Palmer had played in Kate's life previously – an intervention due solely to Kate's determination to save his life when no-one else would act – waited, but with growing concern, for her to explain.

"The thing is" said Kate "I am the only connection between Palmer and the O'Connells – that's why he needs me to contact them. Palmer expects that they will welcome his proposal with open arms; and expect me to return shortly afterwards with someone who can supply the intelligence and maybe the arms, they need. But what if the reply is that they regard Palmer as a duplicitous bastard, a representative of their sworn enemy, whom they want nothing to do with. What then?"

"Do you think they might take that view?" asked Paul

"They might if I suggest that Palmer is not to be trusted" said Kate. "but the beauty of the situation is that I could give that answer to Palmer whatever the O'Connells say. He has no way of contacting them or, therefore, ever finding out what they might think of his offer. In fact, it has only just struck me, maybe I don't need to contact them at all – just go off to Northern Ireland, get lost, tell Palmer that I spoke to them but they won't play ball with him. What could he do?"

Paul made no immediate reply. Kate had had half a day to absorb Palmer's re-entry into their lives, and what he wanted from her. Paul had had maybe fifteen minutes. He was horrified that Palmer was back, even more so at what he wanted but, with a growing pain in the pit of his stomach, most anxious of all about Kate's plans to sabotage Palmer's intentions.

"Not making contact would be a very dangerous game" he said. "I know there is no obvious way Palmer could find out, but he might, somehow, and then I have no doubt that he would exact a very nasty vengeance on you. But your other plan – tell them Palmer is absolutely not to be trusted, so they don't buy into his scheme – that could work. It is utterly plausible that they wouldn't do business with the British Government, however much at one remove from anyone official. You would only need to make the first trip, and you'd be completely safe from Palmer – he'd need you for the return trip – not your problem if the IRA won't play ball."

Kate sat silently, thinking this over. Before she replied, Paul floated another thought to her. "I realise that they wouldn't allow me to accompany you, but I could follow you, discreetly, so would be on hand to help if anything started to go wrong?"

Kate smiled a rueful smile. "I'd feel so much better if you did, but I know these people. They won't even talk to me until they are sure I haven't been followed. They'll be thinking in terms of the military rather than you but, either way, they would take extreme precautions. But, as you say, I will be safe enough. The O'Connells will trust me after what happened before, especially when I explain just why and how I have been forced into this; and Palmer needs me. so, I'll be okay. Anyway, nothing is going to happen for some weeks, so I now just want to get on with my life. Let's have another glass of wine, then go out for dinner, and just forget all this for as long as possible."

In sharp contrast, Palmer was now galvanised into further action. Having set up links to the two people who were critical to his plans, and with considerable confidence that they could and would carry out what he wanted, he turned his attention to the next step – securing the funding he needed. Palmer, as a result of his many years at the heart of the UK government machine, was well aware of a number of semi-secret and totally secret accounts dotted around Whitehall, that could be used for more or less clandestine activities; and he was fairly sure that, with Seymour's backing, he could get access to one or other of them. But he also recognised that this was nevertheless dangerous, unavoidably running some risk that the funds and their use would be uncovered and, with it, the risk that Seymour would be implicated. Fortunately for him, Palmer had worked out that, in any event, he didn't need to take these risks. The day after seeing Kate he rang Anthony Preston at his EnergiCorp headquarters from his mobile. As soon as the receptionist understood that the call was from Palmer, she put him through. Preston had someone with him, but explained that he needed to take the call, Palmer said that he would like to meet up with Preston, with no risk of them being observed together.

"Is anything wrong?" asked Preston, calm but concerned.

"Not at all" Palmer assured him. "In fact, everything is moving ahead well, but I wanted to get an update on how things were going at your end; plus, I need you help on something – not difficult, I think. Could you make lunch, either Thursday or Friday?"

Preston fully understood that Palmer, sensibly, did not want to talk on the phone. "Just a moment." He consulted his diary, "I can do Friday, yes. Where and when?"

"Could we meet at the Reform Club at one pm. Tell the major-domo in the main reception area that you are Mr. Sullivan, coming for lunch with me in a private room. I'll arrive slightly earlier than you, having fixed a cold lunch, wine opened and will meet you in the room he will direct you to. So, no record of you being there, and no-one will see us together, not even a waiter if the food and wine are already laid out. All a bit cloak-and-dagger I know, but best to be careful."

"Got it" said Preston cheerfully "I'll see you on Friday".

Palmer spent some of the intervening days starting to sketch out in his mind his plans for the referendum campaign, what he could discuss with others, maybe even delegate, and what would be kept very close to his own chest. By Friday, as he made the way to his club in Pall Mall he felt that everything, bit by bit, was coming together.

Preston duly followed Palmer's instructions, so they met in a small upstairs dining room without anyone knowing Preston was there, with no chance of them being seen together. As they sat down to eat, Preston, with a wry grin, indicated that he was very curious to know what the meeting was for. Palmer kicked off by asking for an update on Preston's plans for the slow development of the Irish Sea gas field. He was aware from Press reports that EnergiCorp's discovery of gas had been seen as, to date at least, rather exploratory and small scale, rather than anything more substantial; and all well away from the Northern Irish coast, but wanted to check that this could readily be maintained. Preston assured him that all was in hand; and that he saw no difficulty in spinning this out for the year or two that Palmer had requested. He reminded Palmer that he was relying totally on trust that the government would later deliver on Palmer's promise of an unusually large share of the field when fully developed. He did not mention that EnergiCorp, equally of course, now had plenty of clear evidence of the first stages of its project to take over the 'Russian' contracts at a loss; and could clearly provide very convincing support for any allegation of duplicity by Palmer should he later try to back away from his side of the bargain; and Palmer did not need Preston to spell that out before assuring Preston that he had absolutely no cause for concern regarding Seymour's commitment on the future licencing regime. They then turned to Palmer's more immediate pre-occupation.

"The other thing is this" said Palmer. We have quite well-developed plans for ensuring that we win the referendum, but there are one or two points at which it would be good insurance to oil the wheels a little. That will cost money, money which needs to be untraceable. So, I can't raid any convenient government budget. I wondered, therefore, if EnergiCorp might be able to provide the funds – it's a global company and must, I assume use offshore tax havens and the like. The funds would, therefore never go anywhere need the Government and, while we could specifically reimburse you later, via the gas field licences, the sum involved would be absolute peanuts in comparison to what EnergiCorp will gain from the development of the new gas field– literally lost in small change. Do you think you could arrange that?"

Preston remained impassive, no doubt not at all phased, or even necessarily surprised, by a suggestion of this sort. "How much would you need?" he asked.

"Around ten million pounds" said Palmer.

"When?" asked Preston.

"By the end of this month if possible, though timing can be adjusted to fit with what is feasible at your end."

Preston's tone remained quite inexpressive. "That should be okay, yes. There are a small number of shell companies that we indirectly own with registration in the Cayman Islands. We occasionally use them for transactions which are quite legitimate but where, for one reason or another, we do not want various others to know about them – an investment in exploration for example, which of course, this would be. I can arrange for that sum to be deposited in the Cayman account of one of those companies and if you let me know where you want to transfer the funds, I can arrange that too. If you can guarantee anonymity, it would be very difficult for anyone to follow the trail back to EnergiCorp."

"I can certainly guarantee that" replied Palmer, "The funds will go to a numbered account, probably in Switzerland, to which only I, via a password and pin code, will have access. Nor will the funds be traceable from there on." He could have just said that he would be turning the funds into straight cash, and then closing the account, but he felt it detracted from the pleasant fiction they were playing, that all of this was above board and perfectly defensible. So being 'untraceable' would have to do.

"Then I think we can do that" concluded Preston. "Give me a few days, then let me know your account details. If I can trouble you for another discreet lunch, it would be best to do this in person – nothing on paper, nothing electronic."

"I'd be most happy to oblige" Palmer said with a rare smile. "but the same arrangement here might possibly create a question mark in the Club. Let's just both be in the queue for a taxi at Charing Cross Station, say at one pm on Friday week, and we can both get in the same taxi. We can close the glass behind the driver; and that will give us plenty of time to swap bank details away from any possible interception. We can just go to the park for a walk if we have any concerns. When this is all over, I will buy you the best lunch you have ever had" he added.

"That all sounds good to me" replied Preston. "I'll head off now; and will see you in two weeks."

After he had gone, Palmer reflected that, while he had had little doubt that Preston could come up with the funds he needed, he had been surprised at just how easy it had been. He concluded that, worldly and cynical as he knew himself to be, he was perhaps a little naïve regarding global corporations and their financial arrangements. In any event, everything was now in play about the IRA threat; and he now needed to be ready for the announcement of the referendum.

CHAPTER 35

Palmer had outlined four separate strategies to Seymour to ensure the right result in the referendum; and he now set about setting these in motion. The first requirement was a very robust, indeed aggressive, but entirely above board PR strategy highlighting the economic foolhardiness of Northern Ireland leaving the UK; while the second comprised an altogether below the board, not to say below the belt, attempt to portray Dublin as an unsympathetic and unwilling recipient of the province. But, different as these two elements were, Palmer knew exactly who he wanted to carry out both. In a more normal situation, he would advertise what he was seeking, invite a number of PR firms to make a bid, and select the most cost-effective one. but, in the present circumstances, he had no time for all of that and, in any event, for the second operation, he needed a tried and trusted ally, someone he could be sure would act in an entirely discreet, not to mention, invisible way. Peyton Brown was a well-established lobbying and PR firm, active in many places worldwide, and a frequent supplier of PR-type services to Seymour's government, and Gerrard's before that. One of its founders and current CEO, Stephen Peyton, was not only a very accomplished spin doctor and powerful lobbyist on behalf of whomsoever had the money to hire his firm – some with decidedly unappealing reputations to be massaged away - but, as a result of past contracts, a friend and political supporter of Seymour's and a substantial donor to his party. Palmer needed no job spec or beauty parade to tell him that Peyton was the man for the job, or rather jobs, he had in mind.

Palmer duly invited Peyton to Number 10, a simple way to ensure that he got to Peyton very quickly, got his focused attention even before they met, and no doubt a ready disposition to take on whatever Palmer might offer him. Although they weren't very well acquainted, they had met on several occasions before, in connection with work that Peyton Brown had done for either the government or the Conservative Party; and so some small talk was appropriate; but fairly soon, Palmer turned the conversation to the purpose of the meeting.

"What I have to say is, for obvious reasons, completely confidential – you know the rules – some of it temporarily, some of it for ever and a day." Peyton nodded that he fully understood. "The fact is, Graham has come to the conclusion that he cannot put off a referendum on Northern

Ireland's membership of the United Kingdom indefinitely; and thinks his chances of winning it are better now than they might be later on. The Republic of Ireland, with which it would presumably unite, is not in the best of shape economically speaking at the moment, and unlikely to be of much economic support to the Province, but that may change. But its economic prospects within the UK are not great either, and that may feed growing resentment. So, to be brief, the next time there is any significant call for a referendum, which is likely to be quite soon, he will accede to it. He wants you to consider taking on master-minding the campaign to remain. We are talking all aspects here - the whole media campaign, including advertising, interviews, research on what will have resonance with the population, surveys designed to help the remain cause, and so on, you know this game inside out so anything that you can come up with to win the vote, but particularly focusing on the economic consequences, or more accurately, the economic costs, to everyone living there, of cutting itself off from its major trading partner. I know that message may not keep the UK in the EU for ever, but that doesn't mean it is destined to fail. Plus, how much more support the Province can and will get from the UK than from Eire or, as fallback, the EU. This will be backed by some fairly hefty pledges from the PM for various infrastructure and regional investment projects. All in all, there is a lot to go for."

Peyton later reflected that he didn't pause for even a nano-second before replying that he would be delighted to put together a detailed and properly costed proposal. Such a project was as much his working life's flesh and blood as he could imagine; and he knew, without any undue arrogance, that his firm was one of the best, most experienced firms anywhere in the world, certainly in the UK, to carry it out. and if experience was anything to go by, he would not get bogged down in any long wrangling over the charges his firm would make, given the customer and the importance of the issue.

"When will the referendum be called?" he asked.

"I hope, in about two months' time" replied Palmer. "It depends on when we get a good opportunity."

"Then I will have to talk to my team now" said Peyton. "It will take time to research the issue, work out the main lines of attack, so I will need to let them know what is coming".

"Okay" said Palmer, rather cautiously, "I see that, but as few as possible and only experienced people you know you can absolutely trust. At the moment only you, me and Graham know about this, so that should help to keep them honest."

"I think I can guarantee the confidentiality you want" replied Peyton. He was about to elaborate on this, but Palmer cut him off.

"Good, but just to make it watertight, I propose that part of the remuneration is a very fat bonus if the remain vote wins, distributable to everyone involved, which should reinforce their trustworthiness with a strong incentive to keep it confidential until the announcement. After that, the world would be surprised if we *didn't* recruit a firm such as yours to handle the campaign."

"All fine", confirmed Peyton, "I'll get on it right away. But you said that there was an aspect that had to remain confidential for ever. Do you have an additional project in mind?"

"There is, yes" said Palmer, rather hesitantly and looking rather thoughtful as he said it. "It's not clear that everyone in Dublin is as enthusiastic about Northern Ireland joining the Republic as most people think. It will be an economic burden, with little help from the EU now it has such much poorer areas to assist in Eastern and Southern Europe; and there is the distinct probability that the Province will bring with it a resurgence of 'The Troubles' from disaffected protestant paramilitaries, even civil war. I don't know just how strong or how widespread such sentiments are in Dublin, but it would certainly help the remain cause if it became clear that a significant element in the Irish government just did not want the unification; it would not be well disposed towards Northern Ireland if it happened. Some well-timed leaks to that effect could be ….quite powerful."

Palmer did not need to spell out, and Peyton did not need to inquire whether or to what extent such 'leaks' could or would be genuine. Both were quite experienced in the darker arts of what had lately come to be termed 'fake news'; it was better for both of them that any movement of the proposal in that direction would be left unexpressed.

"I'm sure they could be" agreed Peyton. "I think any such activity would have to be at one remove from the firm, but it probably won't come as a surprise that we have had contact in the past with individuals or small organisations that could assist on this front. Leave it with me. I'll get back to you with some possibilities if I can."

Palmer had anticipated that Peyton would be able to help on this, the second of his four strategies, but was nonetheless surprised at how easily Peyton had bought into the idea. Perhaps another example of how he was somewhat more naïve about the world's ways than he had thought. But it immediately emboldened him to explore whether Peyton might be able to help on the third of his stratagems.

"That would be very helpful" he said." I wonder if that means that you might, indirectly at least, be able to help me with another strand of the campaign - not entirely pleasant but standard fare in this sort of game – which is to look closely into the background of our opponents, to see if there is anything that might suggest they are not to be trusted or supported. I'm not really thinking of sex scandals and the like, but financial ones, anything to do with public money or abuse of public office – the public would have a right to know about such things."

The utter cynicism of this pompous observation was so brazen that even Peyton, an old hand at this sort of thing if ever there was one, could not restrain a tolerant smile. "I quite take the point," he opined. "There are certainly firms that will research people's background – I know one in particular that is very good, very discreet, whom we have occasionally used. I'll, talk to them, if that's okay, and see if they could help." Palmer was quite aware that 'research' would entail the most extensive intrusion into certain people's private lives that could be achieved without them knowing; but if he wasn't up for that he would never have mentioned the idea.

"That would be good, he assured Peyton. "I can't tell you how helpful this discussion has been."

"Well, much to be looked into, no promises at this stage" cautioned Peyton "but this is all fairly familiar territory to me; and I can't see at the moment why we could not provide what you need, ultimately I'd hope, on all three fronts. Best, of course, if the billing is all done on the basis of the first project."

"As you say, 'of course'" confirmed Palmer. "but there will, I'm sure, be other elements of compensation to be factored in, pole position for future contracts, some recognition of dutiful service. Let me know when you have a proposal, some feedback from your contacts, and we can meet again to start agreeing on the details." Palmer's parting comment was not, for a moment, lost on Peyton. As he took his leave, it was not clear which of them felt more delighted at what had transpired.

CHAPTER 36

Palmer's plans had gone so well this far that he decided to hold off on his fourth strand - playing the protestant rebellion card. For that he would need to access what the security services did or did not know about the current disposition and strength of the paramilitaries; and he knew it would be difficult to achieve that unless there were very good reason for the PM to know. That situation did not currently exist, but it almost certainly would once the referendum was announced, so that would be the moment to pursue that final line of the strategy he had outlined to Seymour. With not a little adrenaline pumping around his body, he faced the fact that they were ready to announce the referendum as soon as they could.

Palmer had always had some misgivings about this part of his plan, simply because it was the one part which relied on external events, on something he could not control. And to his dismay, the next six weeks offered not the slightest glimmer of an opportunity for Seymour to announce a referendum, no public statement or other type of pressure on him to address the issue of Northern Ireland, simmering though it was, just below the surface. There were, however, some silver linings. It gave Palmer ample time to arrange the financing from EnergiCorp through to an account he had established in Switzerland, and then on to a number of much smaller accounts in Jersey, the Isle of Man and elsewhere. He also finalised a contract with Stephen Peyton, so that he could start very detailed preparations for the day a referendum was announced. It also gave him some time to think about Sykes's operation.

At the lunch Sykes had arranged for them at his house, Palmer was very impressed with Sykes's thoroughness and attention to detail as the General took him through the various strands of the operation, the plans, the risks, the fall back actions that might be needed. He was equally impressed with the two men whom Sykes had with him, introduced to Palmer but without names as the team commanders on the day. Palmer noted that Sykes did not mention where the IRA men would be held; and knew better than to ask. He doubted anyone, least of all the IRA would ever discover where it was. Sykes concluded by saying that they were ready to move at short notice any time from one month on.

Palmer had anticipated that the men in Sykes's security firm would not have been given quite such a task before; but would nonetheless be very familiar with each and every one of the individual components that the plan required. However, for the third time in a short period he felt slightly like an innocent abroad as it became clear that a track, seize and hold operation was not at all new to them, only the location – on UK soil rather than in the Middle East. From their perspective, this would just make the operation much simpler, much easier to disguise, and the consequences of failure much, probably very much, less extreme.

Six weeks after Palmer's second meeting with General Sykes, everything just fell into place – into Palmer's, or rather Seymour's lap. An outbreak of food poisoning in three care homes in the Province led to the deaths of five elderly residents. The outbreak was traced back to an American food supply company; and it was then very publicly claimed, with what accuracy no-one, least of all Palmer, could seem to identify, that this was because of either lower standards or less rigorous inspection procedures applied in the UK in comparison with the Republic. Whether valid or not, this was simply too good an opportunity for Sinn Fein to miss. Not only was re-unification of the island an historical mission it said – not a great crowd winner Palmer thought - not only would the Provence's economic prospects improve within a United Ireland – well, false news was everyone's prerogative thought Palmer – but the UK's weaker controls, in terms of trade, regulation and health and safety, with Northern Ireland trapped in it, were directly killing vulnerable people, Protestant and Catholic alike. This, claimed Sinn Fein, was intolerable; making the choice facing the Province absolutely clear. The government had always said it was up to the people of Northern Ireland to decide its future, so now was the time to make good on that claim.

Palmer saw Seymour the next morning. Neither needed to identify the agenda item. "It's one hell of a risk" was Seymour's rather defeatist opener.

"It is" agreed Palmer, "but we won't get a better opportunity; and if we don't take it, you, me this government, the economy, all are lost, not to mention your reputation when the Russian contracts story unravels. But for me the clincher is this. If we don't do it now, the Irish Sea gas field will be developed anyway; there is no doubt that Northern Ireland will secede from the UK – why would they not with all that gas in their coastal waters? So this is our only opportunity to keep the UK together. The decision may need cast iron nerves, but it really is a no-brainer".

Whether or not Seymour conceded the point, he made no sign either way. "How are your plans shaping up?" he asked.

"The only thing that you need to know" said Palmer, "is that I have Peyton Brown on standby to provide the campaign, all aspects, but checking in with me on a daily basis. You know them well, what they are like; no one is better placed to help us on this. It just needs your say-so."

There was a long pause, but Palmer, in his gut, was quite relaxed, because what he had said was unerringly right. There really was no sensible alternative but to go with the plan; and seek to block Northern Ireland leaving the UK before the gas field became public knowledge. It might not work, but not to try was to invite the worst of all possible outcomes.

"You are, of course, right" was Seymour's rather magnanimous response. "I'll call the others in, let them know that I am going to call the referendum. Meanwhile, could you start preparing the announcement that tries to get us on the front foot as soon as possible. The care home deaths are not an auspicious place from which to start. Plus, fire the starting gun with Stephen. The sooner his team swing into action the better."

Palmer noted that Seymour had said all the right things but, more importantly, had not said any of the wrong things – no questions, no reference to any of Palmer's other plans. He had not forgotten them because he was clear that he had not really heard them, still less sanctioned them. If they ever came out, Seymour would, of course, be appalled. Palmer would carry the can, but then Palmer fully understood that, had in fact invited and accepted that responsibility.

Seymour and Palmer agreed that they now had to act fast. Sinn Fein's statement had come out on a Thursday; and Seymour and Palmer decided on the following Tuesday to announce the referendum. Rather to their surprise, they had found that, legally, they could call it for as little as three months; but decided to go for somewhat longer, otherwise there was a real risk that the IRA would seek to act fast – either threats or actual bombings – as a matter of urgency, disrupting Palmer's carefully laid plans. On the other hand, the longer the campaign, the more that might go wrong; and so they agreed on four months.

Dealing with the food poisoning and care home deaths proved paradoxical to a degree that even Palmer, experienced as he was in the world of mass media communications, found curious. Highly relevant was the fact, that rapidly came to light, that the problem had been caused by one operative working for the food supply company failing to follow proper storage procedures. The outbreak had nothing to do with the ownership of the company, or UK health and safety rules, either in themselves or in relation to those in the Republic. But none of that counted for very much at all, if anything, in the media coverage, where this aspect was either side-lined, as not a very exciting story or, at worst, a suspected cover-up of either corporate greed, or regulatory failure. On the other hand, completely irrelevant, it emerged that the food in question was lamb imported from the Republic of Ireland. The same problem would have arisen if the meat was from Timbuctoo, but this fact was leapt upon as an indication of the lackadaisical approach adopted by the Republic, in contrast to the severe rules of the UK. So Palmer found that, for absolutely bizarre reasons, he could prime his media contacts to paper over the original health scare story that led to the referendum call, emphasising the potential health dangers of forming a United Ireland instead. At least, he felt, they started from a reasonably level playing field. That was not a situation he intended should last long.

CHAPTER 37

With Peyton Brown now in crash-drive mode to develop a PR campaign and, very much more quietly, exploring contacts to carry out Palmer's two other commissions; and with the finances he needed secured, Palmer could turn his attention to the final piece of his jigsaw. In the guise of Professor Kowalski he rang Kate at her office in Oxford. Her PA, Janice took the call, and said that Kate was in a meeting. Palmer, in his most soothing Americanised tones apologised profusely, but said it was urgent, he only need one minute of Kate's time and he was sure that she would take his call. Rather to Janice's surprise, he was not wrong about this.

"What is it?" said Kate when she got to the phone, less brutally than she would have done had Janice not been nearby.

"One pm. next Monday, same place as before; and be ready to go on Tuesday, or Wednesday at the very latest. I would say 'don't let me down', but the only one going down if you don't do as I say is you." he immediately rang off with that. Kate found herself mouthing a mumbled 'okay' to a dead phone line, so as not to alert Janice to the nature of the call, but whether this was successful she couldn't tell, and certainly couldn't ask.

At one level, Kate was shocked by the call and its abruptness and brutal tone. She needed quite some presence of mind not to betray any of that to Janice. But at another level, she was better prepared for what she knew would happen than she had imagined. The people she was to meet held no terrors for her, unbelievably dangerous though they were. Her help for them in the past would see to that. She had a quite reasonable plan to undermine Palmer, one that would not have her finger-prints anywhere near it; and she had, since their first meeting, come to recognise that, if anything went wrong and Palmer sought to prosecute her, she would have a considerable amount of information – information that the O'Connells would no doubt be happy to back up - that Palmer had ruthlessly sought to undermine the government's stated position on Northern Ireland. It might not be an absolute guarantee, but she now had much, much more of a bargaining position against Palmer than she ever had before, which gave her considerable strength for what was to come.

Later that day she invented a reason to have to go to Belfast the following Tuesday, asked Janice to re-arrange her appointments, and book her a flight from Heathrow. She had no immediate idea how to respond when Janice asked if she would need a hotel for the night in Belfast, but said that she should – any other answer would have seemed strange to Janice; and Kate just couldn't allow that possibility. At one pm the following Monday she once again walked to the Perch Inn to meet Palmer, feeling considerably more resilient than when she had last left it. Palmer was already there, a glass of wine in front of him. In reply to his invitation to join him in a drink, she ordered tonic water, but otherwise made no acknowledgement of his presence, no 'hello' no question. She sat and waited for him to say what he had to say, a look of distaste, if not complete contempt, on her face.

"Are you ready to make a trip to Northern Ireland?" was his opening line. Kate's rebellious response was to simply stare at him.

"I've no time for fun and games" replied Palmer. "I'll take that as a 'yes'. When are you going?" There was no point in further rebellion, however minor.

"Tomorrow" was her one-word answer.

"Good" replied Palmer with a more down-to-earth efficiency tone. "I presume that you have worked out how to contact the O'Connells?"

"I know how to, yes" was Kate's deadpan reply.

"Good" repeated Palmer. "I just want to go over the messages you need to impress upon him." Kate was about to interrupt, but Palmer held up his hand to stall her. "Yes, I know you know, but this is too important to leave anything to chance or just plain old ambiguity. So, bear with me. First, you can be absolutely truthful about how or why you are there, why you have no choice, why I chose you, as someone they would trust enough to at least get through to them. Anything else they ask, just the truth. Second, the referendum will be announced tomorrow morning, so they will have had time to digest that by the time you get to them. Any incredulity on their part as to why you are there can be met by the single phrase 'the referendum'. That will get their interest. Then the first of the key messages, that while the government will campaign against the Province leaving the UK, Seymour, and quite a number of his cabinet, would rather see it dispatched to the Republic. Make sure you know the reasons – it's an economic drain at a very difficult time for the UK economy, it will need a lot more investment, in infrastructure and much else, and why should the UK cough up if, as they believe, the Province will eventually leave, for demographic change reasons if no other. Better for it to go now, peacefully. Plus the hidden motive – they think it will be economically disastrous for Northern Ireland, and this will serve to ensure that a second Scottish referendum goes the same way as the first. They don't mind seeing Northern Ireland go, good riddance, but they definitely do not want to lose Scotland. Have you got all that? In your mind – you cannot, at any point, write anything down, on paper or electronically. Is that clear?"

Kate was not about to parrot the message back to Palmer, like some kid in a primary school class, but she did enumerate them in her mind, with a heading for each – honesty, the referendum, economic drain, leaving anyway, and Scotland. She sat in silence while repeating this to herself several times.

"Yes, it's clear" was all she eventually said.

"Right" Palmer went on. "Now for the second message. A narrative that you must again just commit to memory. We have at least one agent amongst the senior Protestant paramilitaries and we therefore know that they have been planning, for some time, that if and when a referendum is called, they will start a bombing campaign, accompanied by the threat of ongoing civil war if the vote is to leave the UK. That has to be stopped, lest it might succeed. The British Government can't get involved in that, so the IRA must stop it, and stop it now, dead in its tracks, before it can get going. But, in entirely deniable ways, the mainland can provide help. You have therefore been instructed to return, exactly fourteen days later, with a retired army colonel who has recently acted as an invisible but key link to our man in the Prots. – his so-called 'handler'.

He will therefore be able to give them a lot of detail about who they are, where to find them, what weaponry they have and where to find that too. From there on it shouldn't be too difficult for them to incapacitate the paramilitaries. If, for good measure, they think this needs more weaponry than their very reduced remaining stock piles can provide, then the same man can give them supply contacts who will, within reason, given them what they want without charge – to them at least. But he wants confirmation of the deal from the whole Army Council, not just the O'Connells. We will not risk helping the IRA, only to find that some key people, or even just some hotheads they control, go on a bombing rampage of their own. That's key. So, to summarise, in five sentences, the Prots plan to bomb themselves to victory. Only the IRA can stop them. But our man can give them what they need to neutralise that threat. And, if needs be, the weapons to achieve it. But only if the IRA leadership are all agreed - dissension in the ranks and it's all off. If they say they want to know more, tell them, truthfully, that you don't know any more, but the colonel can tell them a lot more, indeed everything they need to know. Can you remember all that?"

Kate went over the four points in her mind, then the points from the first message again. She then went over them all again but, in truth, it wasn't difficult. She'd go over them again a few times, but she certainly wouldn't have difficulty in remembering them for a day or two, and that was all that was needed.

"Yes" was another flat reply from her. "Is there anything else?"

Palmer produced a card and gave it to Kate. "Call me on this number when you get back to Oxford. Do not mention your trip – we will just make another appointment to meet."

Kate took the card, without any further conversation, got up, and left Palmer with the remains of his glass of wine. Just as with their first meeting, Palmer felt very pleased with how things had gone. He would have been less happy if he had known what other messages Kate was planning to give the O'Connells.

CHAPTER 38

Palmer spent the rest of the day sequestered with Seymour as they planned the referendum announcement for the next morning. By the evening, both felt relatively pleased with what they had constructed. It recognised, without condoning or condemning, the historical pursuit of a unified Ireland , but quickly emphasised the benefits of the peace that had come upon the Province since the Good Friday Peace Agreement, and the desperate need not to now disturb that . It went on to emphasise the significant economic benefit that the Province gained from its membership of the UK, benefits that to very little extent could or would be matched by any from the Republic or from the EU. It painted a rosy picture of a future within the UK – new infrastructure projects and the like – and concluded that by far the best arrangement for the Province was the devolved governmental powers that currently existed, ones that it darkly hinted might not continue in a unified Ireland. All in all they were very satisfied, their only concern being that it might be thought so persuasive as to undermine the message they were sending to the IRA via Kate. But she would explain why the UK government had to take this line publicly, and if it did seem likely to have traction with the voters, then all the more reason from the IRA's point of view to stop any reinforcement from the protestant paras by threatening a bombing campaign.

In contrast, Kate finished her day at the Press, rehearsed her lines a few times, and headed home to tell Paul of the latest developments. They were both comfortable that Kate should go the next day, she would have nothing to fear from Palmer – doing his bidding – nor from the O'Connells, who would be, if suspicious, nonetheless old friends, and with a potentially very welcome message being put to them. Where things went from there was another matter, but that would just have to play itself out.

The next morning, Paul drove Kate down to the central bus station in Oxford, where Kate got a coach to Heathrow; and by lunchtime was in a taxi from Belfast Airport to that city's bus station. Just as she had done two years ago, she caught a bus to Bambridge, then a taxi to Loughgannon, and asked to be dropped off at the garage, more or less in the middle of the small border town. She felt much more relaxed than she had expected; but was delighted when entering the garage shop, she recognised Bridget, the daughter of the owner, Dermot McGuiness, who had been so very hospitable to her when she had come searching for any news of the brother and sister who had died – not by accident – in a car crash thirty years previously, a quest that had led, in a very direct line to her presence there again.

They had only met the once, and it had been two years before, but Bridget immediately recognised Kate. At the time, Kate had given her name as Kay, but this was clearly rectified later, as Bridget stood up to greet her.

"Kate, my dear" she said with the most welcoming smile, "How grand to see you! Are you well? What brings you back here?"

"A long story, Bridget" said Kate, with what could only be described as a smiley grimace. "It's very nice to see you as well. The short version of why I'm here is that I need to talk to someone I met when I was here before, and the only way I know to contact them is through your father. So that's why I'm here."

"He's over in the repair shop" said Bridget "I'll get him in a moment, but first, tell me what you have been up to since you were last here. Is all going well for you?" So Kate talked a little about her publishing work, and 'no' she wasn't married but had a long-term partner; and 'no' she didn't have kids, but there was plenty of time for that. Bridget, she found out, in contrast, had got married that year, no kids, but soon, so that by the time that Bridget said she would go and get her Dad, Kate was psychologically a long way away from the terrifyingly serious venture into which she had been forced.

When Bridget's father arrived, he weas even more effusive in his welcome than Bridget had been, and Kate instinctively realised that he must have heard from the O'Connells of the help that she had given them the last time she was here. It being just after 2 p.m. it was too late for lunch and too early for tea, but he and Bridget led Kate through to a small back office and made her comfortable.

"Bridy says you want to get in touch with someone" said McGuiness. " Now, would that be Victor O'Connell by any chance?" So, that confirmed Kate's instinct that her past activities had been conveyed to McGuiness, and his question made her task a whole lot easier.

"That's right" she said. "I do need to talk to him, and the only way I know to find him is the same route as last time. So, here I am" she added with a smile.

"Well now" replied McGuiness, "I've only met him the once, some time after you were last here; and I don't have any contact details for him. But if you hang on, I think I can probably get a phone number for you. I won't be a moment." He got out his mobile, then headed into the shop to make the call. Then Bridget had to leave the office to serve someone, and Kate was left alone to review progress. All she could think was that it was all going quite well.

McGuiness was on the phone for quite some time, whether one call or several Kate couldn't determine, with Bridget popping in and out, but he eventually re-appeared in the office. He picked up the garage's landline phone, dialled a number that he had written down on a piece of paper, and handed the receiver to Kate.

"It's Victor" he said. Kate, now, belatedly perhaps, felt adrenaline beginning to pump into her system.

"Hello Victor" she said, in a sturdier voice than she had feared.

"Kate, Kate, Kate" came a slightly growly voice down the line, "What a surprise. How wonderful to hear from you. Now what on earth could be bringing you back to us?"

Kate had had her reply to this question prepared for some time. "I'd love to see you Victor, if we could meet up. I really would. There is much for us to catch up on. But the sad answer to your question is, the referendum."

The pause from the other end of the line was as eloquent a silence as Kate had ever experienced. Eventually, O'Connell replied.

"I see" he said, in a manner that clearly indicated that he saw nothing. "Well, yes, we must meet, and doing so will be the greatest pleasure. There are more than a few who hold a torch for you in these parts, but none more than me. Tell me, how did you get to Loughgannon? Did you drive?"

"No" replied Kate. "A taxi from Bambridge".

"Good" was Victor's slightly baffling reply. "Could you put Dermot back on the line, and I will make some arrangements." Kate wasn't entirely sure why any such arrangements had to be made via McGuiness, but dutifully handed the phone to him. For a second time, McGuiness was on the phone for quite some time, while Kate and Bridget chatted amicably. When he had finished talking to O'Connell, McGuiness made another call; when that finished, he turned to Kate.

"All fixed" he said, with a cheerful smile. "I've got someone coming round now who will drive you to meet Victor, who is, I must say, very keen to see you. He'll just be a few minutes." None of this was particularly odd, but for some reason, Kate began to feel a little uncomfortable for the first time since she set out from Oxford. But she could not identify any particular cause, so she continued chatting to Bridget.

It wasn't a shock, but it was certainly a surprise when the person who had agreed to drive her to meet Victor O'Connell walked into the garage office and Kate recognised him – Connor O'Brady – the man who had, very gently but very firmly, escorted her to meet O'Connell two years ago. That first time he had clearly had a brief to keep hold of her until the O'Connells found out what she was doing in Northern Ireland. She hoped they would see that that was hardly necessary this time, so maybe he was just acting as chauffeur this time. She certainly hoped so because, friendly, even a little charming as he was, he certainly had the air of someone whom you would not wish to cross.

"Dermot, here, says you'd like to go and see Victor again. Is that right?" said O'Brady; and when Kate nodded, added "Well I'd be very happy to take you. It's good to see you again. Can I tell people that I've seen you?" he added with a totally conspiratorial smile. Kast couldn't stop herself joining in with his laughter.

"I didn't know I was that famous" she replied. "But I think a low profile is the best, don't you?" and she tapped her nose.

"Got you" said O'Brady. "My lips is sealed." And so it was in quite a good mood again that Kate said farewell to the McGuinesses and got into O'Brady's car with him. As they set off, Kate realised that, although she assumed that they were headed back to Belfast, as that was where O'Connell lived – or at least he had done two years ago – she didn't actually know where they were going. She asked O'Brady if they were heading for Belfast, but his only reply on the point was to say 'nearby'.

They chatted inconsequentially on the journey but, after a while, O'Brady said "its funny you turning up today of all days. Have you heard the news? They just announced this morning, there's going to be a referendum vote on whether we stay in the UK or join the Republic. I really didn't ever think that I'd live to see this day, but it is great news. But you're a Brit. What do you think?"

Oddly, Kate had not, in all the time since Palmer first approached her, been asked that question, nor had she given the issue any thought either. For someone now so inextricably linked into the issue and its fortunes, that was, to say the least, ironic. But she had no difficulty in forming an answer.

"The government has always said that it is up to the people of Northern Ireland, and that sounds about right to me. So a referendum seems sensible, in fact inevitable I'd say. I just hope it all goes through peacefully."

"That's well said" commented O'Brady. "Exciting times" he added, rather to himself, but did not continue with the topic. As they drove, Kate stated to focus on her forthcoming meeting; and then on what she thought about Victor O'Connell. He had absolutely terrified her when they first met, genuinely afraid that he might have her killed. Still, their shared interest in finding out what had happened, to his comrades and her partner, the former murdered by Gerrard the latter incarcerated by him, had brought them together. She knew that she was genuinely looking forward to seeing him again. At the same time, she had to remember that he had planned to devastate the north of England with a nuclear cloud from Sellafield; and had gunned down the former Prime Minister. There was no real way to reconcile these conflicting views, conflicting emotions, and she didn't try. She would just have to live with the paradox and get on with what she had to do. The prospect that she would fairly soon be free of Palmer's influence was a welcome alternative thought on which to focus.

After a little under an hour's driving, they entered what could have been a small town, but Kate didn't actually see a sign, so it might have been a far-flung suburb of Belfast. In the distance, Kate could see some traffic lights. There were no cars immediately in front of O'Brady, but he approached them rather slowly and, Kate noticed, kept looking in his rear-view mirror. What, if anything, he could see was not observable from where Kate sat in the front passenger seat. O'Brady continued to approach the traffic lights, now at green, slowly, and then, as they went amber, shot through them and turned sharp left. He halted the car for less than two seconds, during which time someone opened the rear passenger door behind Kate and jumped into the back seat. Before the door was properly shut, O'Brady was driving off again. Kate turned, but the head rest of her seat meant that she couldn't really see who had got in, but she did not have to wait long to find out.

"Hello again" said Victor O'Connell.

CHAPTER 39

Kate was, she thought, mentally geared up to meet O'Connell again, but his sudden appearance in the back of the car, a manoeuvre he had clearly worked out with O'Brady in advance, surprised her, and slightly threw her off balance.

"Hello, Victor" she managed, before regaining some equanimity. She re-called that it was important not to be intimidated by the O'Connells if she could help it, or at least not appear to be. "All rather cloak and dagger isn't it?" she added.

"I can't deny it" replied O'Connell with a laugh. "But just think about it. You turn up on the day a referendum is called, tell me your trip is connected to it and I think to myself – there's officialdom in here somewhere. And if so, what's to say that you are not being followed, or even have a tracker device – I know you didn't come in a car, but it could be in your clothing. So, if there is any such thing going on, they will think you are still on your way to me, whereas we can have a good conversation in the car; and then I'll disappear just as easily as I arrived. Neat don't you think?" he added with another short laugh.

"Makes sense," Kate agreed. "But I can assure you I do not have any tracker unit about me, and I very much doubt that I'm bring followed. Anyway, you seem to have taken care of any such worries. Victor, it's good to see you again. How are you these days?"

"Just fine, just fine" O'Connell replied. I'm rather retired these days, leave most things to those two lads of mine. How about you?"

Kate filled him in a little on her life back in Oxford, while O'Brady, silent beside her, drove she knew not where. But there was no surprise that O'Connell wanted to get onto the reason for her trip. What, he wanted to know, was her connection to the referendum. It was time for Kate to perform.

"You will remember that ghastly man, Andrew Palmer, Gerrard's supposed Press Secretary but in fact his evil genius?"

"Indeed I do" interrupted O'Connell. "He was in the car with Gerrard at Chequers. I threatened to shoot him if he didn't relay what was happening to the Editor of the Times so the world would know what Gerrard had done. He saw the wisdom of meeting my request."

"Well, I'm sorry you didn't finish the bastard off" said Kate, with more vehemence than she had intended. "It would have made my life a lot easier." She then, in a few succinct minutes, explained to O'Connell about the phoney tape recording that Palmer had forced her to make, falsely implicating her in the IRA's murderous activities, the hold this gave him over her, and his re-appearance in her world a few weeks previously.

"I'm doing this because it is the one way that I can retrieve the tapes Palmer made, assuming I can trust him to keep his side of the bargain. I can't, of course, but I didn't have much choice; and I can't see that he will have much use for my connection to you once this trip is over."

"And what, exactly, is 'this'" asked O'Connell.

"Palmer, on behalf of Seymour, wanted to contact you, in secret - deniable - but it clearly had to be through someone you would trust enough to meet; and I fitted the description. He could hardly send one of his senior mandarins."

"Very clever" commented O'Connell. "And successful. So, what does the British Government want to say to me?"

As Kate got ready to explain, it struck her how surreal the circumstances were. The whole situation was bizarre. She had expected that she'd be sat down somewhere with O'Connell, face-to-face, focused on supplying Palmer's information and invitation. But instead, here she was, in a car, unable to see O'Connell in the seat behind her and talking to him through her seat's head rest. That the future of Northern Ireland as an entity might depend on this conversation just didn't seem to make much sense, yet that was what the matter had come to.

"The Government will, as promised, campaign for Northern Ireland to remain part of the UK" said Kate. "But Seymour, and a significant number of ministers in the cabinet would, reluctantly no doubt, rather it voted to leave. I'm supposed to tell you that, explain why, so that you will see that you and Seymour for once have a common interest; and then put a proposal to you for how to achieve your shared aim. If that sounds completely unexpected, please don't blame me – I'm only the messenger here."

Kate had no idea whether the silence from the back seat of the car which followed this was shock, delight, caution, curiosity, suspicion or any combination, but she decided to wait for O'Connell's initial response before going any further.

"Only the messenger," repeated O'Connell. "Hmm. Some message to be sure. You are going to have to spell this out for me."

It took Kate only a few minutes to explain what Palmer had told her, the continuing cost of the Province to the UK at a time when its economy was threatening to remain too weak to provide any re-election chance for Seymour; the wish to avoid further infrastructure investment in a region that Seymour was quite certain would eventually leave the UK, so why not get it over with now; and the signal Seymour wanted to send Scotland, that leaving the UK was going to be an unpleasant economic experience for any population that chose it. "So," she concluded, they'd be quite happy to see the Leave vote win."

There was another long silence while O'Connell digested this information. Eventually, he replied.

"Well, if that is right, I'm a happy man, but why does Seymour want me to know all this? If the official line is to be for Remain, he and I will hardly be standing shoulder to shoulder at a sequence of rallies, promoting a United Ireland, are we?"

"I think their official campaign will be as low key as it can be without raising any suspicions" said Kate, "but they have one big worry. Palmer says that they have an informer high up somewhere in the Protestant paramilitaries, who says that they have been planning for some time against the day when a referendum is called, to start a major bombing campaign in the Province, basically threatening that if the vote is to leave, then they will see to it that a new civil war gets going, in the hope – which Palmer thinks is a real threat – that this will swing enough votes the other way. The main reason he sent me is to say that the British Government can't do anything to stop that, but you can; and if you do, he can help."

The silence that followed this was not unexpected on Kate's part, and it was just silence; but it had a tension, almost a menace, that really unsettled her for the first time. She was not one given to panic, even in these extraordinary circumstances, but in that silence, the full force of what she was doing and saying hit her hard. The thought she had resisted for weeks - that she just couldn't do this, that she just had to stop - couldn't any longer be consigned to some remote part of her brain. It was here, it was now, and she was inextricably involved – even if only the bloody messenger – in what would no doubt be unspeakable violence. She wanted to say something, anything to break the silence, but there was nothing she could say, except to go on, to explain what Palmer had in mind. And with that thought she now realised that there was no way back.

She was about to go on when O'Connell, finally, broke the silence.

"Jesus, Kate, you're not short on surprises, are you?" was his response, one so pedestrian, almost comical, that Kate felt herself breathing more normally again. "Just what does your Mr. Palmer want us to do; and how is he offering to help?"

"It's horribly simple" said Kate. "If you agree, Palmer insists that I come back again, in the next few days, with some man he has in mind – I don't know who but he is clearly ex-army and works as a link between the British security services and their informant. He will meet up with you and provide two things - all you need to know to be able to find and disable the protestant paramilitaries; and the names of some suppliers if you need to re-build your weapons store, with no payment required. He leaves it to you to decide how best to ensure that the Protestants are in no state to intimidate the population during the referendum campaign. That's it, that's everything he wanted me to tell you." She paused, but could not stop herself adding "I think it is terrible, repulsive - I wouldn't have dreamed of being here if I hadn't been forced to; and I hope your reply is to tell Palmer to get lost."

"Well, I can see that you might think that" said O'Connell cautiously, "but you'll understand that this is somewhat of a surprise to me, one I'll certainly need to consider. If his information is even half right about the Prots, then it could jeopardise finally achieving what my people and I have wanted, and wanted for over a hundred years." he paused, maybe to let that sink in but also because he was now, Kate could sense, even though she still couldn't see him sitting behind her, furiously thinking through what he had heard. His next words were to O'Brady, still patiently driving them along.

"Connor, sorry but you are going to need to keep going somewhat longer than I expected." O'Brady merely nodded, not indicating what he thought of what he had just heard.

"Where are you staying tonight?" he asked Kate. She told him the name of the hotel that Janice had booked, though she had hoped she would not need it.

"Okay" said O'Connell. "In a moment I'll leave you; and Connor here will take you to your hotel. I need to talk to my lads this evening. Someone will pick you up from reception at nine a.m. tomorrow, okay?" Kate wasn't at all sure if 'my lads' referred to his two sons, who, Palmer had said were now effectively running the IRA, or if he meant his IRA associates more generally, but she confirmed that was okay. However, she wasn't finished with the day's conversation.

"Victor, listen to me. Don't trust Palmer. People, powerful people, aren't frightened of him for no reason. He has royally ruined a lot of people - politicians, journalists - he has certainly messed me up, and he has no time for anything except his own ends. I think he is just trying to use you, put you in the firing line, and there will be no sign of him if anything goes wrong, I don't want to have any further role in this; and I don't think you should either."

"Don't worry, I hear you" said O'Connell soothingly. "I just need to think it through; and if we do hook up with Palmer's plans, I'll make sure that he leaves you alone. You said yourself that he only needed you as a credible messenger. Once that's done, you're home free, or Palmer will know that he is a hunted man. We aren't the force we once were, but I can assure you that he will not want that sentence of death hanging over him."

What shocked Kate was that she was not more shocked by this statement of extreme violence. Maybe it was because it was directed at the man she hated more than anyone or anything she had ever hated in her life, but maybe also that she was losing the ability to be shocked by the world she had once again been sucked into.

"That's some re-assurance" she said "but I'm not just thinking about me. If Palmer can get what he wants and leave you carrying the can, he will, I've no doubt. So do think very hard before going along with this."

As she finished talking, the car went round a left hand corner, slowed for a second and O'Connell, without another word, leapt out, slamming the door as it pulled away. "Sorry about that" said O'Brady. "Just standard precautions. I'm certain we aren't being followed, and Victor doesn't really believe you've got a tracker bug stitched in your clothing, but he hasn't survived this long without being a belt and braces sort of man." Kate nodded her understanding, but O'Connell's abrupt departure had left her feeling very deflated.

"Can you tell me where we are?" she asked. "Anywhere near Belfast?"

"We will be at your hotel in about twenty minutes, " replied O'Brady. "Just rest yourself and we will be there in no time." Kate appreciated the polite offer not to feel she had to make conversation; and so she put her head back against the headrest of her seat, closed her eyes and reflected on what had happened. The surprise was the dawning realisation that she had not actually seen O'Connell except for a few half seconds when she tried to turn to talk to him, and then only a flash of the side of his head. She had no sense of whether he had changed much since she had last seen him or had aged much in the intervening two years. but, on a more positive note, she had done what Palmer wanted, she had warned Victor, and she had for the first time seen that she might not have to rely just on Palmer's good will to let go of her after this was all over. So, all in all, not too bad an outcome so far.

O'Brady dropped her at her hotel, the Maldron, a twelve-story glass and steel tower. Kate thanked O'Brady for his time, checked in, and was thankful to Janice for choosing such a central location and comfortable facilities. Though only late afternoon, she already felt very drained by the day, but rang Janice to catch up on matters back at the office in Oxford. She knew Janice was dying to ask her what she was doing in Belfast, but was too sensitive a P.A. to ask, if Kate wasn't offering to tell her. Later, she rang Paul and recounted how the day had gone, saying she would be back the next day. Chatting to him about his day at his lab brought a semblance of normality to what, by any measure, were the utterly abnormal events of her day. Dinner in the hotel was a further source of relaxation; before ten p.m. she was ready for sleep.

CHAPTER 40

The next morning, after a rather leisurely breakfast, Kate headed for the hotel's reception area. No-one was holding up any sign with her name on it but, rather to her surprise, a short and rather bulkily built woman in her mid-forties Kate would have guessed, clearly recognised her from some description she had been given, came up to Kate and introduced herself as Aisling.

"Before we leave" she said, in an inoffensive but rather commanding tone, "Could you ask reception for a late check out. Two p.m. will be fine." Kate had hoped to be away before then, but didn't object, and duly arranged for her to leave by two p.m. She had, wisely it now turned out, not yet booked a flight back to Heathrow, but they were frequent – it wasn't a problem. Aisling then led her outside, but instead of heading, as Kate had anticipated, for the car park, they headed off down the street and arrived outside Central Belfast's Marks and Spencer store in a few minutes. Aisling then announced, in a rather more formidable tone, clearly brooking any opposition before it arose,

"Could you please buy yourself a complete new outfit, including underwear and shoes. I'll pay for it all on my credit card." Kate stared at her, rather incredulously, about to ask for some explanation for this bizarre request, or rather bizarre order, when the reason clicked. O'Connell was still not convinced that Kate's clothing wasn't in some way bugged, so that she could be tracked to wherever he was. She was going to have to change into a totally different set of clothes, just to assuage any lingering suspicions that he might have. So, it wasn't worth questioning, still less protesting. They entered the store, Kate quickly chose a blouse, skirt, underwear and a woollen top. The shoe selection was limited, but she found some that were, at least, comfortable.

"Do I put these on now?" she asked Aisling.

"No, we will go back to the hotel. You can change there and leave your own clothes in your room. You will be able to change back later." Even as Aisling was speaking, Kate realised what a silly question she had asked. Given O'Connell's concerns then, they couldn't take her clothes with them, so they would have to go back to the hotel. Plus, she realised she would have to change in front of this woman - O'Connell would want her to report back that there was no scope for any type of device to be switched from one set of clothes to the other. No surprise then, she mused, that O'Connell had lasted so long when there must have been many people who would happily have seen him dead.

They returned to Kate's room in the hotel and, as Kate had surmised, Aisling sat in the room, discreetly but observant, while Kate changed.

"Could you leave your mobile phone here as well" said Aisling. It wasn't a question; and, again, the reason was obvious. Kate duly left her phone on the room's chest of drawers. Only then did they head for the car park; and soon headed out of Belfast. Kate thought she recognised their route as heading back towards Bainbridge, to where she had travelled on the bus the day before, but wasn't certain. Either way she was, once again, heading to nowhere Kate knew. Apart from asking a few questions about Kate's stay at the hotel, and whether she yet had a flight booked back to London, Aisling made little in the way of small talk; and the journey was largely in silence.

Around half an hour later they entered the small market town of Dromore and pulled up outside a small tea and coffee shop just off the market square. Aisling led the way in; and there, sat nursing mugs of tea or coffee, was Victor O'Connell, and this time he had his two sons, Declan and Vincent, with him. They seemed genuinely pleased to see her, and she felt rather the same, in a nonetheless slightly schizophrenic way, given that one of them, Vincent, had openly suggested killing her when they first met two years ago. Now, in rather more hospitable mode, he asked her what she would like to drink, and went to the counter to order her a coffee. Aisling left them; and Kate sat, waiting for Victor, no doubt for all his protestations of being retired, the driving force of this terrorist family, to kick off the meeting.

"My apologies for requiring the new clothes" he said. "You'll know why. When this is all over, do keep them, a small enough thank you for all that you did before, and now as well."

"Well, thank you, as well" replied Kate. "I guess I'll have to stop myself from telling people back home just who bought them for me. Not that they'd believe me anyway" she added with a smile.

"Probably just as well" O'Connell echoed, adding his own laughter to the proceedings. "Still, you'll be wanting to get back, so I'd better get on to giving your Mr. Palmer his reply."

"Don't ever call him that" Kate interjected quickly, but left the matter go.

"Point taken" said O'Connell. "Okay, so, I have talked this through with Declan and Vincent – it's really for them to decide. But we all agree, two things. The first, on the upside, is that what Palmer is offering, if it is genuine, is a mighty fine opportunity; and we shouldn't just walk away. But the second, on the downside, echoes what you yourself said. He is a scheming British bastard, who we can't, for one moment, trust. But we have reviewed everything you told me yesterday; and we think there is a neat way forward. So, tell Palmer that we aren't saying 'yes' and we aren't saying 'no'. We will meet his security services man, just you and him, hear what he has to say, and then decide. Palmer doesn't appear to want anything from us until then, so that shouldn't be a problem. If he wants more of a commitment before he sends his man over, then there's no deal. Got that?"

"Straightforward enough" said Kate, managing to keep to herself her disappointment that they hadn't just killed the whole idea. "Makes sense" she agreed "How do you want to meet up once I have his man in tow?"

"We've discussed that" replied O'Connell. "Just head for the garage in Loughgannon, just like before, by bus to Bainbridge and then a taxi. You will be escorted from there on, but don't be surprised at our arrangements. We will be even more security conscious with Palmer's military man present than we have been today."

"I understand" said Kate. "To be quite honest, I just want to put you in touch – that's all Palmer wants from me – and then get back to my attractively normal life in Oxford. From then on it is nothing to do with me what you arrange; and I absolutely do not want to know. I hope you will equally understand that."

"I do, I do" replied Victor with a smile. "If ever there was a Brit I'd like to have on my side it would be you, Kate. You're loyal, gutsy, determined, and wasted in publishing, but there it is. I don't know how things will develop when we meet Palmer's man, but I'll see that you can get back home immediately. I owe you a lot, and I don't forget debts like that. Now, tell me about your lucky man and that policeman who helped you. How are they doing?"

It was very easy and welcome for Kate to talk about her and Paul. The reference to Detective Sergeant Neil Hargreaves, who had supported her when she was hunting down what had happened to Paul two years ago, was altogether more problematic. Did Victor know that Hargreaves had fallen very much in love with her; that in a single, weak but sympathetic and not entirely dishonourable moment, they had had sex together on what they agreed was the last time they would meet? Victor might have intuited the first of these, but he couldn't know the second; and so it was easy to fall back on the simple truth that she had not seen Hargreaves since the events of two years before. Conversation about Paul led to much reminiscing of their earlier time together, which in turn led on to what the O'Connells had been doing since. From this it became clear, just as Palmer had told her, that Victor's two sons now formed the leadership of a relatively quiescent IRA, often more concerned about retaining unity in its ranks than pursuing its goal of a United Ireland, but with that goal always lurking there, waiting for its time to come again.

Eventually though, one of the sons, Declan, brought the discussion back to business, not, Kate noticed, without just the slightest questioning glance first to Victor and his even slighter nod.

"When does Palmer plan to send you over again" he asked, "with this spook?"

"I don't know" replied Kate. "Quite soon I think. I'm to call him when I get back. How should I get in touch with you to arrange another meeting?"

"Call Dermot's garage. I'll give you the number" said Victor, and got out a pen. "Just say that you are calling to say 'hello' to Darren, and add when you can get back to the garage. We can make arrangements from there on."

"Get there the same way as before" added Declan. "The bus to Bainbridge, a taxi to the garage. And don't be surprised if you think someone is observing you, will you?" he added with a slight grin. "We are going to be very, very careful."

"I've no doubt Palmer would expect nothing less" said Kate, "but as he seems, for once, to be on the same side as you for a small moment in history, I guess that isn't a problem for him."

The meeting seemed to have come to a natural end, but Kate had one more thing to say. "One other thing, Palmer wants the meeting to be with your 'Army Council' or your leadership group. He doesn't want to risk his man agreeing a deal with you, supplying information and arms, only to find some splinter group who aren't happy with the agreement going off on their own. Palmer's clear that unless his man comes away from the meeting confident that the IRA as a movement is on board, then the deal is off – just too much risk for him, for Seymour."

"I can see that" said Victor "but it shouldn't be a problem. We have a pretty reliable control structure. It will be a small group, but if they sign up, then Palmer can rest assured that we can meet our side of the bargain, no 'loose ends' if you get my meaning."

"I'll tell him that" said Kate. "So, I'll see you again soon; and then I am well and truly out. To use a phrase from my other life, my skill set is not designed to tackle …. all this." She waved her hand at no-one in particular.

"You are too hard on yourself" said Victor. "I think you're magnificent, and I don't say that of many Brits. We will miss you, you know."

Kate did not have any reply. A compliment but, she had to remember, from people who had bombed, maimed, killed, not recently bu t not that long in the past; and the intrusion of a personal note left her once again wondering what on earth she was doing here, how had her life come to this point? Well, it would soon be over.

They stood and, somewhat awkwardly, all three men gave Kate a small kiss on each cheek. Then Aisling, who clearly could not have been far away, and certainly must have been in line of sight, re-appeared, ready to drive her back to her hotel. After a change back to her own clothes, Aisling drove her to Belfast airport.

CHAPTER 41

Kate was too tired, and too unprepared to talk to Palmer when she got back to Oxford; and part of her was more than happy to make him wait for her report on her trip to Northern Ireland. So she rang him the following morning. He brusquely said that he didn't have time to get back to Oxford to meet her; and told her to meet him the next day at 11 am at the outdoor restaurant opposite Horse Guards Parade. Kate was furious at the disruption this would cause to her schedule, and presented still more problems in terms of explaining her movements to Janice, but recognised that she was in no position to refuse. At least she could, in the meantime, catch up a little on the job that paid her salary.

She duly met Palmer the next day as arranged, did not join Palmer in a cup of coffee and, as tersely as possible, said that the O'Connells had agreed to meet Palmer's emissary, nothing more. Only then would they decide whether to go along with Palmer's proposal. Palmer, equally terse, asked what, if any, arrangements the O'Connells had suggested or demanded for the next trip. Kate said that she and whoever would be accompanying her should repeat what she had done before – go from Belfast, via bus and taxi, to the Loughgannon garage; and the O'Connells would take things from there. Palmer inwardly digested this.

"Did you make it clear that this has to include all the key people in their organisation – full buy-in or no deal?"

"Yes I did" said Kate tersely. "They don't see that as a problem. The O'Connells reckon they run a tight ship. If you get an agreement, it will stick." This was rather tangential to Palmer's real concern, but he sensed that his message had got through to the O'Connells, and they themselves would not want to embark on a deal with the hated government of the UK unless the top echelon of the IRA were involved and all fully on board.

With nothing else to follow up on, Palmer said he would get back to her in due course, and left. While Kate still hoped that the O'Connells would turn Palmer down, she had no inkling that Palmer could not care less about that. For him, the second trip would be the endgame, the elimination of any prospect of an IRA response to the referendum. He promptly rang General Sykes and arranged to meet him at Palmer's club. There he told him that the project was confirmed, outlined the arrangements for meeting up that the O'Connells had stated, and said he would let Sykes know as soon as they had an actual date.

Sykes confirmed that his team would be ready to go from the following week-end. They would now factor in how the O'Connells wanted to meet up. The kicking off point of the operation being the Loughgannon garage, rather than as soon as Kate landed in Belfast was, Sykes noted, a real plus. Palmer was not entirely clear why, but was happy not to know any more than he needed. No doubt the O'Connells felt they had very tight security from there on, but Sykes seemed confident that he had the measure of whatever they might arrange.

"I'll await a final date from you" said Sykes. "I will need five days' notice, to get everything we have planned in place." He and Palmer confirmed the arrangements for Russell to meet up with Kimball at Paddington Station, once the date and timing, to fit with flights from Heathrow to Belfast, were known. Palmer agreed that the final £5 million would be transferred to Sykes before the week-end.

"I trust that is everything?" asked Palmer. Sykes nodded. "Apart from my letting you know the date, I don't think we will need any further contact" added Palmer "but if you do need to contact me, please use this" and he handed Sykes a mobile phone. "It is untraceable to you or me, and has only one number programmed in, namely this one" and he produced a second phone from his pocket. "Please destroy it once the operation is over, and I will do the same."

"A wise precaution" noted Sykes, "but I very much hope it will not be necessary."

"As do I" were Palmer's parting words.

Straight after the meeting with Palmer, Sykes contacted Russell and Ferguson.

"Some good news" he said. "We now know how the contact with the IRA is to be made; and it simplifies our job." He described O'Connell's requirement that Kimball, with James in tow, go to the garage in Loughgannon.

"That saves a lot of hassle" Sykes said. "We can set the drones up near there right from the start; and we will have no problem tracking them in such a rural setting. So, I've said we will be ready by the weekend."

A brief discussion indicated that they would definitely be ready by then. The safe house had been rented, the internal security installed, and the site provisioned. The men, weapons, boat and vehicles had been secured and all thoroughly checked, and the alibi team were ready to move into action. The last few days would be spent re-running their 'scenarios', seeking to identify things that might go wrong and, if so, how to respond, and co-ordinating with the drone operators.

Palmer then rang Kate, saying that she should now contact O'Connell again and, when she got through she should fix a date for her and the man she would bring with her to meet the O'Connells, for late the following week, and then let Palmer know the details. She should then fix a morning flight to Belfast, travel to Heathrow from Paddington on the Heathrow Express, and should meet up with the person she was conducting to the meeting at the Heathrow Express platform at Paddington, He would await confirmation from her.

"When you have put my man in touch with the O'Connells" he added "just head home – home free I might say. He will need to stay on for a while, but your job will be done." He knew that Kate had no choice; but thought this word of encouragement might not go amiss.

"I'll get back to you" was all Kate said in response; and put the phone down.

Later that day, Kate called the number of the garage in Loughgannon that Victor O'Connell had given her.

When a female voice answered, Kate asked if it was Bridget.

"It is" the voice replied. "Is that you Kate?" Kate confirmed that it was ; and Bridget said how pleased she was to hear from her. A few inconsequential words passed between them before Kate said that she needed to 'speak to Darren'.

"Ah, yes" said Bridget, fully aware of what that request signified. "Give me your number and I'll get him to call you. Will you be coming to see us again?" she added.

"I think so, yes" replied Kate. "Maybe in a week or so. Darren will let you know I'm sure." Bridget said she would get on to Darren straight away; and rang off. Though Kate was, by now, feeling quite comfortable with the trip she had to make – she'd done it recently, no-one was hostile towards her except Palmer of course, who needed her and from whom she would soon be free – but it was still an anxiety-filled ten minutes before her phone rang. The deep, unmistakably throaty voice of Victor O'Connell came down the line.

"Thanks for calling" he said, not mentioning his or, indeed, Kate's name. "Always a pleasure." Kate decided it would be both impolitic and insecure to remind him of the time when he had more-or-less decided to have her killed.

"And mine" was her automatic and, perhaps, half true reply. "I've sorted things out this end, all as agreed, and could call in to see you Friday of next week, if that is convenient."

"Give me a moment" replied O'Connell. Kate presumed that he was discussing this with his two sons; but could hear nothing. After a minute or so, O'Connell came back on the call.

"That will be fine" he said. "when will we expect you?"

"I'll fly over in the morning, so should be with you by early afternoon – maybe two o'clock or so?" O'Connell confirmed that that would be fine, neither of them referring to the meeting place they had already agreed. With conventional but, in the circumstances, rather meaningless phrases they wrapped up the conversation; and Kate was left to wonder once again at the disjuncture between, on the one hand a short trip to introduce some people who wished to do business with each other – at worst a bit of a distraction from her day job – and the safety, not to mention lives of a number of people, the politics of Ireland and the future of the United Kingdom on the other into which she had unwittingly stumbled. Her only comfort was that she would be free of the whole mess by the end of the following week. With that consoling thought, she called Palmer, relayed the arrangement, and said she would meet his representative as required, at Paddington Station on Friday week. Within minutes, Palmer had reported this onto Sykes. With a feeling that he hated, Palmer recognised that the matter was now well and truly out of his hands.

CHAPTER 42

The following Monday, D-Day minus 4 in Sykes's way of reckoning, three trucks left Trojan Security's site near Swindon. Three separate companies had rented them, each registered in the Cayman Islands, with a local director. Ownership was not revealed, but in any event comprised two South Africans and one Australian unconnected with Trojan Security but discreetly paid a worthwhile sum simply to have their names as the owners. The rentals were, therefore, entirely legal, but no amount of interest in them that might arise would lead back to Sykes or his company.

The smallest one was a three-ton box truck, not much more than a large van. Once rented Sykes's team had carried out one modification, welding metal bars along both sides of the truck. The truck was empty as two of Ferguson's men drove it up to Liverpool to catch the Birkenhead to Belfast ferry. At the end of a completely uneventful journey, including an eight-hour sea crossing, the truck made its way to a lorry park a few miles from Loughgannon and the two drivers got some sleep in a couple of hammocks set up in the back of the truck. A second, only slightly larger truck, with no modifications, went by the same route the next day, again with two of Ferguson's men, and also empty. It made its way to a lorry park on the outskirts of Balleywater, roughly due east of Belfast on the Northern Irish coast. The two men booked into a nondescript but comfortable hotel under their Trojan-supplied false IDs and settled in to await a call.

The third truck was a 7.5 tonner, with a length in the back of a little over twenty feet. Unlike the smaller truck, this one was crammed full of equipment. The main item was a twenty foot long boat made of reinforced plastic with two 190 horse-power in-board engines. It was stripped down to be little more than a hull, but with a small cabin near the front to provide some protection for a captain and one other. Under it was a wheeled trailer, with a wire to a winch installed near the front of the truck. Stored on and around the boat were two sizeable drones and a number of boxes. These contained drone control equipment, six crates of hand-held semi-automatic machine guns, a range of other weapons, including pistols, grenades, smoke bombs, ammunition and medical supplies, together with another box of what in the theatrical world would be called 'props' that Ferguson reckoned might come in handy. With two men up front with the driver and six more men wedged in the back, the truck set off north around 9 am. at a leisurely pace and, with a few stops on the way, arrived in Stranraer on the south-west coast of Scotland at 9 pm that evening.

After another short break they headed south down the Stranraer peninsula, eventually turning right towards the west coast. This was much the nearest point to Northern Ireland; but locating a launch point had initially proved problematic for Ferguson's team. There were a number of small roads and tracks down towards the sea that the truck could get down, but they all seemed to peter out too far from the sea for them to be able to get the boat launched. During his research, Ferguson had been near the point of giving up on the area, but fortunately found a route down to a small sandy cove called Ardwell Bay. The track was just wide enough for the truck and led to a sizeable grassy parking area. This was still too far from the sea, separated from it by around sixty metres of very rough sandy tundra but, to Ferguson's immense good fortune, the track carried on a little further, to another grassy area large enough to turn a 7-ton truck around and, to his surprise, a concrete ramp down to the beach itself. There was only one dwelling that could observe the site, but it was nearly a mile to the north and, with Ferguson's team using night goggles and no lights, would not see or hear anything.

The only risk arose from the fact that near Ardwell Bay the road passed right by one residential property, called a cottage but actually with the dimensions of a solidly built house. It might be a holiday home, but if anyone was in residence, they might be curious about a large noisy truck going past late at night. There was no landline in evidence, but a mobile phone call to the local police in Stranraer could prove fatal to the operation. Sykes, however, had come up with a solution. The truck would stop short of the house and one of his men would plant a mobile signal-blocking device, first developed by the Israeli intelligence services by the house. It could be recovered as they returned from the beach.

At shortly after 10 pm, Ferguson's team, with no lights showing, arrived at the bay, having planted the blocking device, and ran the trailer and boat down to the sea. They loaded the drones and all of the various boxes onto it and then, leaving two people in the truck, paddled the boat several hundred metres out to sea, before switching on the engines. With the sea relatively calm – had it not been they had allowed for up to three days delay if it were needed – they were soon doing a steady 15 knots. The night vision goggles meant that they needed no lights on the boat either; and so were quite invisible; and the plastic hull made them invisible to any radar that might be sweeping the area. Whether their route was one favoured by drug smugglers into Northern Ireland, which might have led to such security arrangement, they were not sure, but were confident that only a very unlucky break would lead to them being spotted.

Right on schedule, after a fairly smooth two-hour crossing, Ferguson, his team and equipment arrived off the coast of Northern Ireland. A call to the men with the truck parked at Balleywater brought them to the rendezvous point simultaneously. Whereas Ferguson had thought a launch point near Stranraer would be easy to find, which turned out not to be the case, he thought finding a landing point on the much more heavily populated east coast of Northern Ireland would be difficult, but it turned out to be quite easy. Near Balleywater, and quite close to a beachside holiday park – not normally ideal for an undercover operation – was a small cove, hidden from the holiday park and from the road by a sizeable and densely wooded copse of trees running along the waterline. Ferguson thought that they could probably have disembarked their equipment in broad daylight without anyone noticing, but at past midnight, the operation felt totally secure.

The two teams duly met up and transferred all the equipment to the truck, which then headed back to the Balleywater lorry park, with Ferguson and three others of his team on board. Having parked the truck, they all returned to the two hotel rooms the forward contingent had booked. Meanwhile the two remaining operatives started the two-hour boat journey back to the Stranraer peninsula. They were back in Scotland by 4.00 am, just before the dawn light started. They winched the boat on its trailer back into the 7-tonner, and unnoticed by anyone, were in a lorry park outside Stranraer in time for a breakfast in the transport café nearby.. As D-Day minus 3 dawned, all units reported back to Sykes that everything was on schedule, with no problems encountered.

During D - 3, and over the next two days, the remaining fourteen men and four women in Ferguson's team, plus the two drone operators, all made their way, singly and by various routes, some via the Irish Republic and at different times of the day, all with false IDs, to Northern Ireland, checking into twenty different hotels in and around Belfast. During D – 2, five of Ferguson's men rented cars; one rented some commercial storage space in a suburb of West Belfast, and one met up with the drone operators, who got in the car to check out two possible sites that Ferguson had previously identified around Loughgannon for a convenient, discreet and easily evacuated base for the drone control units. One, a small, currently derelict old timber yard, with protective fencing that was now so fragile it could almost be torn down by hand, proved to be ideal, less than half a mile from the centre of Loughgannon. On D – 1 another message was sent to Sykes indicating that everything was in place, and they were all ready to go. Sykes passed this message on to Russell, giving the final okay for his meeting with Kimball at Paddington to start the ball rolling; and then phoned Palmer on the one-use mobile with the same information. The final step was for Palmer to phone Kate, to confirm that the arrangement they had agreed for the next day was solid.

Palmer reflected that this must be what it is like for a theatre director. You plan and organise everything, you co-ordinate all the different elements, using all the diverse skills of everyone at your disposal, and then, when it is all in place, you can only sit back, powerless, redundant, and let events take their course; whether the outcome would be a triumphant success. or a desperate failure was now out of his hands. The only real difference was that the consequences of success, and even more of failure, were in this project so far beyond anything a mere theatre director could even begin to contemplate. Palmer was increasingly convinced that, with all his other plans maturing nicely, only the IRA stood between, on the one hand, an outstanding economic future for the UK, not to mention a brilliant political one for Seymour and, with him, in the shadows, for Palmer himself; and, on the other, utter reputational ruin at the least for Seymour and himself, and almost certainly, prosecution and, probably jail, for him. But it was a risk that he had finely calculated and was prepared to take. He had confidence in what he had planned, had confidence in Sykes and his team, and took much comfort from the fact that Sykes and his team were themselves confident it would work. If that was all misplaced, then so be it.

CHAPTER 43

Friday turned out to be an unseasonably sunny, warm day, which suited Kate's mood as she rose early, based on her calculation that in less than twelve hours she would be shot of her whole disagreeable and stressful situation. By 9 am she was at the entrance to platform five at Paddington, solely used for the Heathrow Express. As she arrived, a man walked up to her, of medium height, with nothing very distinguishing about him except a very confident manner and a rather penetrating gaze.

"Miss Kimball?" he asked, in a deferential, questioning manner, but without the slightest doubt that that was indeed who he was addressing. Whether this was more Kate's very noticeable appearance, taller than him, attractive, stylishly dressed, or more because there was just no-one else approaching the spot at that precise time was a moot point. Kate nodded.

"I'm John" he said, without bothering to ensure that there was no hint of this being false. "Have you bought a ticket yet?" Kate said that she hadn't, and 'John' went and bought two first class tickets from the Heathrow Express booth nearby. Only when they had taken their seats in the train, which was waiting in the platform, did they speak again.

Russell was fully aware that, given the situation, neither of them was the slightest bit interested in any small talk. Yet total silence seemed a bad way to start; and would make their enforced journey together much more tedious than otherwise.

"I've been made fully aware" he said, as the train set off, "that you are not here voluntarily. I do not know what has forced you to help me speak to certain people in Northern Ireland; but I assure you that I have had no hand in it at all. I simply have been given a job; and told that you could help affect the introductions I need. I hope you can see me in that light for the few hours we are working together?" The slight lilt upwards at the end of this last phrase turned what might have sounded quite pompous, even rather arrogant, into a much friendlier appeal, inviting some degree of co-operation in return.

Kate knew only that 'John' was Palmer's man; and had therefore been much disposed to dislike him on the spot. She had not envisaged any significant conversation with him on their shared journey, by train, plane, bus, and taxi. But she saw no reason to doubt either what he had said, or the accessible way in which he had said it.

"Why I am here I certainly do not want to discuss" she replied, "but I accept what you say. I'll be happy to get you to where you want to be; and then get back to my own life" this with a small smile, in part a response to his overture, in part just the thought of getting back to her own life again. With the ice thus broken, they did, initially in a rather desultory way but later in a more relaxed way, exchange snippets of information about their respective careers, for the fifteen minutes of the train journey. Then it was into the maelstrom that is the lot of anyone going through Heathrow at a busy time; and their conversation did not really take off again until they were settled in their seats on the plane to Belfast.

Meanwhile, in Ulster, twenty-two experienced mercenaries and two drone operators were getting themselves readied in their various starting positions, the drones checked over in their timber yard, the two trucks driven down to just outside Loughgannon, and four cars with five people in each one parked in different locations around the town, their weapons in the boot of each car. They were all quite warm as, under nondescript jackets – all that could be seen from outside the cars – the men wore full military camouflage dress over ordinary civilian clothing, not because they would need any camouflage, still less, in a sleepy provincial town, the patchwork clothing pattern developed for operations in the Middle East; but because, once they went in, they needed to establish very fast that they were a highly trained, militarily experienced unit well used to dealing with any and every type of opposition that might be thrown at them. The outfits would convey this impression very quickly indeed.

Kate and Russell's journey to Belfast and then by bus to Bambridge, was uneventful, and not unpleasant for either of them. Only Russell was aware that, as they made their way to the taxi rank at Bambridge bus station, somewhere way overhead a pair of drones was transmitting their every move back to the timber yard near Loughgannon. It followed their taxi; and saw them with total clarity as they got out at the Loughgannon garage where they had been told to report. As ever, Bridget was in the office and delighted to see Kate again. Kate introduced John; and then Bridget phoned 'Darren'. After a brief call, she announced that transport was on its way to pick them both up. It was no surprise to Kate when

Connor O'Brady arrived, with a pleasant grin that could not quite hide what a dangerous man he could no doubt turn out to be if provoked.

Slightly to Kate's surprise, instead of heading out to his car, he asked them both to accompany him over to an extension building on the side of the main garage repair shop. Once inside, he asked them to wait a moment while he went into an inner sanctum, and re-appeared with a detector of some sort. With his best attempt at an apology, he asked Kate, and then Russell, to stand with their arms up and legs slightly apart, while he ran the detector over them, seeking any tracking bugs.

"We would have done this last time you were here" he said to Kate, "but you caught us unawares, which was why Aisling had to go to the expense of a new set of clothes for you. I hope you got to keep them" he added.

The check proved entirely negative on both of them, but O'Brady was not quite ready to go.

"I'll need your phones" he said, again slightly apologetically. "They can be tracked" he explained, rather needlessly. Kate and Russell produced their mobiles and handed them over to O'Brady. "They will be safe here, for you to collect afterwards" O'Brady added. Only then did he lead the way out to the car. As they set off, Kate had not thought about where they would be taken but was, nonetheless, slightly surprised that they headed off back towards Bambridge from whence they had just come. Information on this from the drones was immediately relayed to the truck and four cars, which all then set off in that general direction, but only two of them directly on the same main road, and well over half a mile behind.

As they approached the outskirts of Bambridge, they pulled off left down a country road which seemed to skirt the back of the outer reaches of the town, with houses only on the town side of the road. Several of these were in groups of semi-detached dwellings, but some were detached and more isolated. To one of these larger residences, O'Brady drew up the car, right on the corner of a still more minor road heading rightwards into town. Russell immediately recognised the advantage of this location to the IRA – a house surrounded on two sides by road and two sides by open fields, making a hidden approach to the building very difficult. Whether it belonged to one of the people he was due to meet, to a helpful sympathiser, or was until now a safe house for the IRA he had no way of knowing; but it raised few qualms as to whether Ferguson's team would be able to carry out their plan. The sight of two men idly standing at the front door – obviously a welcoming committee of guards for the meeting – was neither a surprise nor any more of a concern for him. He could not see, but the drone operators reported that there was also one man at the back of the house.

Kate and Russell followed O'Brady into the house. A front and back room, both quite substantial in their own right, had been knocked into one long room. It would have seated twenty comfortably, but there were in fact seven men sat there, mainly at the near end. Kate immediately recognised Victor O'Connell and his son, Vincent, but not the other son, Declan. Some of the other five had a faint ring of familiarity, no doubt from two years ago when she worked with the O'Connells to bring down Alan Gerard, but the recollection was too faint to make much impression. Victor got up and gave Kate a perfunctory kiss on the cheek, no doubt to re-enforce some message that he must have been giving his men that these arrivals, though hated Brits, might actually, being planning something that could help the Cause. He greeted her with warmer words though, indicating that Vincent was again with them, but did not offer any other introductions. Kate then introduced John, the man they wanted to meet.

Some refreshment might have been offered at another time, but it was 2.30 pm and it didn't seem appropriate; and so Victor launched straight in.

"Before we get to the heart of the matter, tell us something about yourself John" he said "and the background that means you could be of service to us". Russell had been planning to do just that anyway, to give Ferguson and his team as much time as possible to join them; this was a very welcome start.

"I was twenty years and more in the British army, all over, but four years in Northern Ireland" said Russell. "During that time, I spent two years as the secret link – I guess you'd say the controller - to an informer in the Protestant Paramilitaries. He contacted us to offer help after some of his guys, quite wrongly he thought, kneecapped his brother for alleged disloyalty. Though not that high up in the organisation, he was a great asset, keeping us informed of their thinking, planning, personnel, weapons, strengths and weaknesses. We were able to curb some of their excesses, so in that respect I suppose we were working to the same end as yourselves, not, I confess, that we saw it that way."

"Well that's commendable honesty, anyway" said O'Connell. "How does that help you, or more importantly, us, now?"

"I'm based back in London now" said Russell, "in military intelligence, with more general oversight of what the Prots are up to in the Province; and we have been getting a series of signals, separate but rather confirming each other, that they are planning a terror campaign, a series of bombings and more individual assassinations, with the message that that is what Northern Ireland will look like if the referendum votes to leave the United Kingdom. I think Kate here as already explained that the Prime Minister, whatever his public stance, does not want them to succeed; and has asked me to give you as much as I can to allow you to take preventative action. That is my role here. I have no political views, am still less committed to any of this. I'm just here to do my master's bidding. My understanding is that you all here are the effective leadership of the IRA; and so it is to you I should provide what information I can; and then up to you to decide what you may wish to do with that information. I hope that is your understanding as well?"

While Russell had been delivering this carefully orchestrated speech, events outside were developing. All Ferguson's transports were converging on the area around the house. One of Ferguson's cars halted a few hundred metres from the house, to discharge two of his women operatives, with a child's collapsible buggy from the boot, one of Ferguson's little 'props'. With its hood up, no-one could see that there was no child in it. In rather plain attire, and with headscarves, they appeared like any two young women from a more rural Irish background walking down the road. As they reached the house, one called out to the men on the door.

"Could you help me a moment" she said as she pulled out a notebook which was apparently not giving her the information she sought. She walked up the path, calling over her shoulder to the other woman that she wouldn't be a moment. As she reached the men, she leaned inside the buggy, pulled out a taser gun and, in less than two seconds had shot and stunned both men, who both fell to the ground, all without a sound. In only two more seconds the drone operators had alerted all cars, and the truck, all of which were already only a few hundred metres at most from the house. As meticulously planned, one car arrived before the others, two men went round the house to the left, the other two to the right and then converged, silently and totally unexpectedly, on the one man guarding the back of the house. The first he knew was when he also was rendered completely incapacitated by a taser shot. One of the men radioed back "house secure". Within a minute, just as Russell was beginning to expound on the types of information he could supply, the house was surrounded by twenty of Ferguson's team, with no-one inside any the wiser. Each man had a semi-automatic machine pistol in his hand, with a silenced pistol in his belt. They as yet had no idea how many of the opposition were inside but, judging by the size of the building, there was little chance that it would exceed Ferguson's estimated number and, with the element of total preparedness and total surprise, there was an air of supressed confidence about the operation.

Inside, Kate gently interrupted Russell. "I think I've done my part, John" she said. "Is it okay of I leave now. I have nothing to add; frankly, the less I know, the better. Is that okay?" she repeated. Before John could reply, the two doors to the room, entrances to the originally separate ones, flew open and Ferguson's men, all now stripped back to their military clothing, surged in, screaming to everyone to get down, get down, get down on the floor, their machine pistols at the ready. The surprise for the IRA leadership was so total that, on the plus side, no-one made the slightest move to oppose Ferguson's men. On the minus side, they were so stunned and completely shocked that none of them made any move to comply with the order being screamed at them. Only when one of the intruders went up to one of the Irishmen, punched him very hard in the face and literally dragged him by his shirt collar to the floor did the others start to comply. As they slipped to the floor, Vincent O'Connell caught Kate's eye.

"Your dead, you fucking bitch, do you hear". He might have added more but one of the men hit him hard on the side of his head with his pistol; and he sank, half unconscious to the floor.

"Hands behind your backs" shouted Ferguson, now reasonably confident that all would go well – seeing only eight totally unprepared men, including O'Brady. However, he might have to smoke out a few more. But his instruction was somewhat lost as Kate, turning to Victor O'Connell, spoke simultaneously.

"Victor, I don't know who these men are, I have no idea...." Her voice trailed away. "Oh Christ, I said not to trust Palmer. I swear to you, I didn't know, I don't know how...."

Russell cut her off. "Kate, you're right. Your work is done here. Just get out, go back into Bambridge and go home, now." With that he gently pushed her towards the door. As it happened, this brought her right past where Victor O'Connell, older and stiffer than the others, was lowering himself to the floor. Ignoring both Russell and Ferguson, he stood again.

"You have to believe me Victor" said Kate again. "I don't know who they are or what they want, but it isn't anything Palmer told me about. Why would I betray you, after all we went through?" Victor stood motionless and silent before her.

"Out, now" said Russell to Kate, but she didn't move. O'Connell gave her a look of such penetrating intensity that she almost lost her balance.

"Best be gone" was all he said, but delivered in a tone of utter finality. Before Kate could respond, O'Connell turned away and began to sit down again. Shocked beyond measure by the sudden turn of events, Kate stumbled out the door. 'Best be gone'? Did that mean best be gone from the criminal scene occurring in front of her, or did O'Connell's words have a more sinister meaning, best be gone somewhere, anywhere so that he or his men could not catch up with her; and hand out what they would consider appropriate retribution? Kate knew instantly that, if she managed to get out of her present predicament those words could haunt her, terrify her, for ever.

CHAPTER 44

Kate somehow managed to propel herself out of the room, out of the house and, almost on autopilot, turned right down the small side road that she instinctively felt would take her towards the centre of Bambridge, to the bus station, away, please God, from the appalling scene she had just witnessed. But she had not gone more than a hundred metres or so when a car pulled up by her. The driver leaned across and wound down the passenger window.

"What's going on Kate?" said Declan O'Connell.

Kate stopped. "I don't know, I don't know" she said, more a gasp than words. "I brought Palmer's man to the meeting – that's all – but then an army of men suddenly poured in and forced Victor, Vincent, all of them to the floor. Then they sent me away."

Declan O'Connell got out of the car and came round to where Kate was standing.

"Get in the car" he said.

"No, I can't" said Kate "I've just got to go. This is not my business. I've got to go."

"I said, get in the car" repeated O'Connell and forcefully took hold of Kate's arm to make it quite clear that this was not a request. This startled her, but what really shook her was that he marched her round to the driver's side of the car, opened it and pushed her in.

"Drive" he ordered. "To the corner, left, past the house and keep going". He climbed in the back of the car behind her. "Mess me about and I will fucking throttle you". Kate started the car. She started to say again that she didn't know what was happening but O'Connell told her to shut up and just drive. There was no sign of any action at the house, and when they were a few hundred metres past it, O'Connell told her to stop, reverse and park by the roadside.

"I was supposed to be there" he muttered, almost to himself. "Got delayed by a phone call. If you've led the Brits to us you will pay a heavy price, be sure." Almost overwhelmed by a rising panic, Kate fought to stay calm.

"I said to you, to Victor, I said, 'don't trust Palmer'. But you didn't listen."

"I said, fucking well shut up. Let me think." His focus was concentrated on the house.

Inside, Ferguson was organising the next stage of the operation. The seven men plus O'Brady were handcuffed as they lay face down on the floor.

"Now" said Ferguson, "this is all very straightforward. First, anyone tries to look up, I will shoot one of you. Do not make the mistake of thinking that I am bluffing. Second, I need two pieces of information, and then you will all live, no doubt to fight another day. But if I don't get them, my men here, some of whom have not the best of memories of dealing with your lot in years gone by, will start shooting you, one by one, first in the ankles and then good old-fashioned knee-capping. If they get really angry, they will kill a few of you, for old times' sake, but the real unlucky ones will be those left to spend the rest of your lives in wheelchairs. Please do not make the unfortunate error that thinking any of this is a bluff or that anyone can ride to your rescue. We have enough manpower and weaponry here to take on any back-up you might have thought of. So, I hope that is all very clear." No-one made any response.

"The two pieces of information are quite simple. First, the names of any of your central committee, army council, or whoever who is not here. I have a list, not necessarily complete I'm afraid, but if, after you have spoken, there is any name on it not mentioned, then you know what will happen. Second, I need the location of your remaining weapons dumps. I don't know which of you knows those locations, but I say to whoever does know, your pals here are totally in your hands." No-one spoke. None knew that Ferguson had no such list.

"Now, I know that speaking up is going to be difficult for you – no one likes a grass – but I'm going to make it very easy for you. We will take you, one by one, into another room. I *will* get what I need, but none of you will ever know who spilled the beans, so to speak. you will all be able to go on your way unharmed. All you will ever know is that if every one of you is stubborn enough to keep quiet, your reunions will not, I suspect, be happy ones, those of you who get to go to one." He then pointed to one of the men.

"Let's start with him". Two of Ferguson's men went over to him and, without ceremony, lifted him to his feet.

"Before we start, let me appeal to you" said Ferguson. I don't want to send you off as a load of cripples, though I will if I have to. But the IRA has a long career, whether you regard it as glorious or inglorious. You have had spectacular triumphs and equally spectacular failures; but you have always bounced back. I suggest you think of this as just one of the latter, on a long, long road, from which you can bounce back again, but not if you fail to give me what I want. Okay, let's get going" and he nodded to the two men holding the first object of interrogation.

"Stop" said a voice at once slightly frail but nonetheless commanding. It was Victor O'Connell. "I will not let you destroy the lives or livelihoods of the men I have worked with, for one simple cause, over many years; and I will not allow them to be placed in the dilemma your obscene requests have created for them. If anyone is to go down for this enforced betrayal, then it will be me. I have few, if any, years left to me; and I would rather spend them in the continued hope of a United Ireland, some day, than in the destruction of all I hold dear by you. I will speak to you in another room."

One of the men on the floor said "Victor" and was, it seemed likely to say something to him, but Victor cut him off. "No, don't say anything now. I'll do this, for all our sakes, and you must decide later what the consequence for me must be." He just nodded, making it clear that he was ready to be escorted elsewhere.

Elsewhere was, in fact a kitchen at the back of the house. Ferguson and three of his men followed. One pushed O'Connell into a chair. Ferguson sat opposite O'Connell, while his men, all with machine pistols to hand, stood behind O'Connell. "Well?" asked Ferguson.

"There are three people of note in my organisation not here. One is my son, Declan. He was due to be here; and I don't know why he isn't. Another is Shaun Kelly, but he is quite ill – possibly terminally so. I suggest you ignore him. The only other one is Michael Murphy."

"Where can I find Murphy, and your son?" asked Ferguson. O'Connell gave Ferguson addresses in Belfast. "And the weapons dumps?"

"There are two" replied O'Connell.

"You will need to take me to them" said Ferguson. O'Connell merely nodded.

"Excellent" said Ferguson. "You will not appreciate any words from me, but for what it is worth, you showed true leadership in there. If your men behave, you will all escape this safely." This provoked only a stony-faced silence from O'Connell.

There followed a lot of action but a sense of anti-climax for Ferguson's team. Ferguson allowed the IRA men to sit more comfortably on the floor, decided that he would skip Shaun Kelly, and dispatched two five-man teams to locate and pick up Michael Murphy and Declan O'Connell. He then radioed in the first of the two trucks – the unmodified one - by now waiting near by and then, with eight others, escorted Victor O'Connell to it. Declan O'Connell, unobtrusively parked down the road, watched as his father climbed into the passenger seat, with the driver one side of him and another man the other side of him. The rest climbed in the back and the truck set off.

"Where are they going?" asked Declan asked Kate.

"I don't know," replied Kate. "I keep telling you, I don't know anything, why do you keep asking me what's happening?" Declan made no reply to this question.

"Follow them" he said abruptly. Kate did not respond immediately. "I said, follow them, or by Christ you'll not leave this car alive. Go on, now". He almost screamed the last word at her; and Kate started the car. She had to reverse again to be able to follow the truck; but was soon following it quite easily.

"Where are they going?" asked Declan again, but this time just musing to himself. They headed in a generally western direction, on main roads, which was presumably why no-one in the truck noticed that they were being followed. But then after about 25 minutes, the truck signalled it was turning off left onto a more minor road.

"Oh, Christ, oh Mother of God, oh no" said Declan. "I know where they are going. Don't follow, go straight on. Stop where you can." Kate complied with this; and they ended up a half mile on in a parking area at the side of the road.

"He's taking them to the arms dump" he said, as if Kate cared. "He's fucking well giving them our weapons. Shit, shit, shit." Kate remained silent. "Okay, get going again. I'll give you directions." They set off and Declan soon had them heading in quite a different direction. About thirty minutes later he told her to stop in a layby.

"Get out of the car" he said. "Head for those trees. I have a small but very effective pistol here; and if you do anything other than what I say, if you make a sound, I will shoot you right here and now. Do I make myself clear?" Kate nodded, feeling so disorientated that she could imagine her head falling off. They walked for about a hundred metres, until they were opposite a farm gate. "Sit down by this tree and do not do anything" he instructed. "We may be here some while."

Once he had calmed down from the shock of it all, Declan O'Connell had readily worked out what must have happened. His men had, somehow, been taken by surprise; and now Victor, no doubt under threat of retribution on Vincent or the others, was being forced to reveal their somewhat depleted weapons store. They were now opposite the entrance to the second of these, with his expectation that, after a while, the truck would turn up, load up, and he could at least try to find out where it was headed.

Meanwhile, Victor O'Connell had taken Ferguson to the first dump, in a cellar under a lock-up garage near Craigavon. The dump consisted mainly of Armalite rifles and ammunition, all in a set of crates, not a vast amount but enough to fill over half the truck. Ferguson's men removed their military outfits before removing the crates, so that they would appear to be engaged in a quite innocuous loading operation, should anyone come close by. They then set off for the second dump, in another cellar, this time under a farm outbuilding near Lisburn. Declan O'Connell watched them as they arrived. He saw them enter; and knew perfectly well where on the site they were headed, but from where he was could not see Ferguson's men as they set about loading up the contents of the second armaments dump. He saw a car arrive and follow the truck into the farm but, like the truck, then lost sight of it.

It was clear to Ferguson's team that not everything in the second dump would fit into what space remained in the truck; but a significant percentage of the contents in this cache was explosives. Ferguson's men loaded up the weaponry, which did just about fit in; and then went in search of a hose. Using this they flooded the rest of the cellar and all its explosive contents, before driving the truck off to the storage space they had rented three days previously in West Belfast. Declan and Kate went back to their car and once again followed. They failed to notice that Victor O'Connell was no longer in the truck, but in the car they had seen arrive. On arrival, Ferguson's men unloaded all the weaponry they had taken, transferred it to the rented storage unit and locked it up. With the truck now once again empty, they then headed to the timber yard to pick up the drones and associated equipment which had been so vital to the operation, and which, given the very recent development of this type of technology, the O'Connells had fatally failed to anticipate. Meanwhile, with four men to guard him, Victor O'Connell was headed elsewhere.

As Declan O'Connell watched this, he realised that he had made a bad mistake. He had followed Victor, which had seemed sensible. He knew where their stolen armaments had been secreted – which could be crucial in keeping them in the game – but it looked very much as if the operation was now winding up. In consequence of following Victor, he had completely lost track of what had happened to all the others at the meeting. He told Kate to forget the truck and drive back to the house at Bambridge.

In the period since Victor O'Connell had left, Ferguson had summoned up the other truck. Once informed that it was outside, his men had checked no-one was around to see, and with the IRA men still handcuffed, had taken them, one by one, out to the truck and handcuffed them to the two steel rods fixed along either side of the interior of the truck. Before leaving the house, Ferguson fired a series of rounds from a make of pistol which he knew from Russell was favoured by Protestant militia gangs, which should, he hoped, create some confusion. Then, with two of his men in the front and the whole of his remaining team in the back, Ferguson set off from the house. Four men were dropped off to pick up and return the rental cars. The rest set off for a layby near Balleywater. By the time Declan and Kate got back to the house they were long gone.

Once they were in the layby, Ferguson's men waited, for almost an hour before a car arrived with a subdued Michael Murphy in it, and then the car in which Victor O'Connell was being held. The men in a third car arrived with the news that they had been unable to locate Declan O'Connell.

The other truck, with the drone equipment in it, joined them in the layby, where they all sat until 1 am. Meanwhile, the men with the 7-tonner had driven it back from Stranraer to their original launch point, unloaded the boat and again set off across this narrowest strip of the Irish Sea. They met up at 1.30 am with the two other trucks on the Irish coast, after which all the equipment and the now nine senior IRA men, still all handcuffed, were loaded aboard. By 5 am. guarded by ten of Ferguson's men they were back in Scotland and by 7 am, locked in the back of the 7-tonner, were at the site that had been prepared for them in East Cumbria. Ferguson introduced his Irish prisoners to the motor caravans that would be their new home, giving them a guided tour of the electric fencing that had been installed all around the inside of the large farm building housing the caravans. He explained that food would be delivered to them, CCTV would monitor them but, otherwise, they would not know that he or any of his men were there. But he cautioned against any approach to the electrified fence, as contact with it would certainly be lethal. With that he ordered them to be uncuffed, and left. Meanwhile, the rest of his men had made their individual ways back to Britain, with two of them bringing the two smaller trucks back across on the ferry to Heysham, to be returned to the hire firms from which they had been rented but minus the steel rods that had temporarily been installed; and the 7-tonner set off to return the boat, weapons and drone equipment to Trojan Security's backlot, before being returned to the truck rental firm from whence it had come.

As he departed, Ferguson felt that the whole operation had gone almost perfectly, very much as planned, with no need for violence and only one loose end – Declan O'Connell had not been amongst those he had taken. He would have to report that to Sykes, but with no support and no weapons, he couldn't see that one O'Connell junior was likely to be much of a problem. The only thing he did not know was that Declan O'Connell, with Kate very much his hostage had seen and followed the truck with the weapons; and so knew where Ferguson had stored the stolen weaponry

CHAPTER 45

Declan O'Connell was now in what amounted to an advanced state of shock. In a few hours - quite how he did not know – their whole operation had been discovered and wound up, his top men, including his father and brother, and all his armaments gone. The only saving grace was that, because of the lucky break of his delayed arrival, he was free at the house in Bambridge, and he knew the storage unit in West Belfast where the weaponry had been stored. But he had no idea what had happened to the other members of the Army Council; and he couldn't imagine how he could function without getting the men back.

He needed to consult, discuss options, but anyone obvious was now in the hands of the Brits. Then he remembered that Shaun Kelly would not be there, suffering from a nasty lung infection or worse that left him breathless much of the time and exhausted all of the time. But his mental faculties were unaffected – he could still offer some wise counsel.

Declan directed Kate to drive to Kelly's house, arriving early in the evening. With Kate in front of him, literally at gunpoint, he approached the house and rang the front doorbell. Kelly opened the door, a tall and heavily overweight man, with a too florid complexion, with an off-putting wheezy breath as a result of his illness. He was surprised to see a tall, quite elegant but clearly highly distressed woman at his door, until he saw Declan behind her and let them in. Kelly got out two beers as Declan, as succinctly as possible, told Kelly what had happened. He said they needed to discuss urgently what they could do.

"Well, not in front of her" said Kelly, indicating Kate. "Put her in my garage out the back. There's a padlock on it." Kate tried one more time.

"Please, I'm not you enemy. I've been stitched up as much as you have…." But neither man was listening. Declan grabbed her arm and marched her outside, to the small garage behind Kelly's house, thrust her inside and padlocked the bolt on the door. He then went back to re-join Kelly.

"It's a total fucking mess" was Declan's unhelpful summary. "I've no idea what to do." Kelly wheezed but otherwise was silent.

"There's not a lot you can do" he said. "We can get some boys together to try to get back the arms, but that'll take a day or two at least;

and where they are may be a very temporary resting place. They may try to move the weapons, but I doubt there is any way you can seize whatever truck they use. If they try to move them, we could get a team to follow it and see where they are taking them. Either way, we can't do anything fast enough. But the first thing is, what will you do about the girl?"

Declan looked up somewhat startled. He had thought about the first two suggestions himself, and he knew he couldn't drag Kate Kimball round with him; but he had not, up to this point, followed the logic of that last point. Kelly continued.

"You can't let her go. My guess is that she is in this up to her neck, but even if she wasn't. like she says, she knows what has happened; and we cannot risk that getting out. You have to get rid of her."

Declan looked pensive. "She came through for us before, you know. Told us what had happened to Victor's team at Sellafield, all those years ago; and was key in us trying to get Gerrard, even if she wasn't in at the kill."

"All no doubt true" relied Kelly. "But we are facing catastrophe. It could take years to recover from this, if we ever do. I think she must have connived at this, in some way or other, but as I say, even if not, we have got to keep this to ourselves until we can re-group, Christ knows how, and that's not going to happen if she goes home. It's not as if our men won't press, as hard as it takes, to find out what part she played in all this. If anyone knows that history matters, we do, but whatever she did before, you can't take the risk, Declan, you just can't."

There was a long and, though she was not there to hear it, from Kate's point of view, a very ominous silence. "Okay, okay" said Declan. Leave her in the shed and I'll come back for her tonight. I'll take her to a spot where it's unlikely anyone will find her unless it's a nocturnal animal. She will just disappear."

"It's for the best" said Kelly.

Kate, alone, locked into a rather squalid garage, at the mercy of two very angry members of the IRA, was now absolutely terrified. No attempt by her to convince Declan O'Connell that she was an innocent in all that happened had had any effect whatsoever; and she recognised that if he continued to think she had been part of the entrapment, then he wasn't going to let her head of home, not now, not ever. She had the presence of mind to try the door and a rather flaky looking window, but it was too heavily welded in, and probably too small for her to get through anyway. A garage, she thought, ought to have something with which she could, perhaps, defend herself; and quite quickly found a potentially useful tyre lever. She could inflict real damage with that, but it was large and unwieldy, with no way to conceal it about her. Better, and the only other thing she found, was a small screwdriver. She tucked it inside the waist of her skirt, with the handle up behind her blouse. It was hidden, but she doubted whether she would ever get an opportunity to pull it out and use it.

It was three hours later and, by now, dark, when Declan O'Connell went back to the shed and let Kate out.

"My friend and I have discussed the situation," he said. "We are prepared to accept, for the moment at least, that you didn't know what was going to happen but, if so, if we are to get anywhere near rectifying the situation, we are going to need your help, basically eye witness information. It's that or… well no, that's your only option."

"I'm happy with that" said Kate. "I just want out, and if that is the only way then, yes."

"Good" replied Declan. "Back in the car then, you drive; I'll tell you where. We need a very discreet meeting with one of the few people I can still get to."

They said farewell to Kelly and set off across the southern territory of Northern Ireland once again, Declan giving Kate directions. Eventually, driving alongside a forested area, he told her to pull into a layby.

"Let's go" he said as he got out of the car; and Kate got out too. With the car lights out, total darkness descended on them.

Where are we going?" asked Kate.

"I'm meeting almost the only man I can think of who might be able to help; but he has been a fugitive for past actions for a lot of years; and he will only meet in a very remote location. There's an old disused hut about fifty metres into the forest, down that path through the trees. We'll meet him there."

Kate had gone only a few paces when she realised the whole thing was a sham. Declan was going to kill her, miles from anywhere in amongst the trees in the dark. She stopped, turned to Declan. "You're going to kill me aren't you" she whispered.

"Just kneel down" said Declan. "I'm sorry, I genuinely am, but we can't let you go back home, not after what you know, and maybe what you've done. Just kneel down" he repeated.

No-one knows if it is true, as is often alleged, that those about to die see their previous life rise up before them, but Kate, in that moment, saw Paul, who had made so much of her life a joy. Whether because of this thought, or because she was just paralysed with fear, she did not attempt to kneel, as Declan had ordered.

"Please, don't do this" she sobbed, but Declan just raised his arm and pointed the pistol at her. As he did so, Kate clutched at one last, illusory straw.

" Declan" she said, with as much force as she could muster, "when I was marched out of that house, Victor said two words to me." she paused, desperate to try to engage O'Connell's curiosity.

"Which where?" asked O'Connell.

"He said, 'find Declan.' Now she knew that she had to keep going. "He said that because he was there and knew I was innocent of this disaster, but not just that. He'd worked it out, and he knew I would work it out, and he saw that I was the one person that could help you to retrieve the situation. That's why he told me to find you."

"You're going to have to explain that to me" said O'Connell, with little enthusiasm. Kate clutched still more tightly to the straw.

"You know what message Palmer told me to give you, that he wanted you to deal with the Unionists gangs who might try to frighten people into voting to stay in the UK. But you've seen what happened. He was playing you from the start. It's *you* he's trying to close down – you – because he clearly wants Ulster to stay, not leave. The whole thing was a colossal sham; and Victor realised. And he knew I'd realise as well. And that's not all. Palmer's men could have shot the lot of you – no-one would ever have known who did it, and no-one would have suspected Palmer. But they didn't. They've taken them off somewhere, which means that they must plan to hold them until they can't do any damage to Palmer's plans – until the referendum is over. So, you have an opportunity to do something about the situation – Victor saw that as well; and he saw that that must mean getting to Palmer somehow. That's why he told me to find you – because I'm your way to Palmer and, believe me, after all this, I want to see that bastard pay as much as you do. I know you don't trust me, but trust your father's instincts. They haven't let him down before today."

Throughout this plea, Kate had become increasingly emotional, so much so that she completely lost sight of the fact that it was based on utter fantasy. Victor's words to her had, in fact, been horribly threatening; and had made no reference whatsoever to her finding Declan. But Victor was gone; it would be a long time, if ever, before Declan knew the truth.

Declan was silent, the only hopeful sign for Kate being that he slightly lowered the gun while he reflected on what she had said. Kate saw that she had to press home whatever minor advantage she had temporarily gained.

"I'm a publisher from Oxford, completely out of my depth but, like I explained before, Palmer has a tape recording – a completely fraudulent one, but I'd never prove that – that can send me to prison for the rest of my life. I couldn't ever kill anyone, but I'll happily do whatever I can to help you get your men back and then settle with Palmer. We *can* do that; and Victor will be relying on you – there isn't anyone else now is there?"

"Were you supposed to contact Palmer when you got back?" asked Declan. The truth was that Palmer had not suggested this; and Kate had had no intention of ever being in touch with him again. But that was clearly not the right answer at this still horribly precarious moment. In a moment of inspiration, she saw that she needed to distract Declan's thinking, away from shooting her to how he might begin to retrieve the situation.

"I'm supposed to phone him. He'll be getting a report from 'John' whoever he really is, but he also wanted to hear my assessment. But I think we could work out a way to get to him, especially when he hears that you weren't in the round up – that will certainly worry him. I can't think straight at the moment but I'm sure we can use that in some way so that he wants to see me again." The key word, by some long way in that pronouncement was 'we'. She just had to get Declan thinking of how he could use her, not dispose of her.

Declan was ominously silent again. Kate filled the void.

"If you sacrifice me, you sacrifice everything" she said, now far too emotionally strained to recognise the grandiloquence of this utterance. "Can't you see that?"

"I can't just let you go back" said Declan finally. "I've no way of keeping track of you, no way of keeping you quiet about all this."

"Then I won't go back" said Kate, finally seeing a way forward. "I can phone Palmer from here. He won't know where I am. And I know what I can say. Look, can't you get together some men, urgently, if not tonight then tomorrow. Then we break into that storage unit, recover whatever weapons or explosives they took. Then I call Palmer, say that you are holding me and that I am to deliver to him the message that unless he releases Victor and the others, you will start a succession of bombings and assassinations – maybe prominent Unionists, maybe ordinary people, people who can't possibly protect themselves, day in day out; and that you will publicly promise to continue this for ever and a day, until either the referendum votes to leave, or there is a second one, or a third, however long it takes. That will mean the loss of everything he has been trying to achieve unless he releases the others. He won't care that I'm in danger at all, but he will care about the vote. He may not believe me at first, but when he finds out from John and the others that the arsenal they took has gone, he'll have to believe us."

Kate had no idea where all that had come from. She would later believe that while the prospect of imminent death may paralyse, it could do wonders for one's creativity 0f mind. Whatever the explanation, it finally persuaded Declan O'Connell that he might, just might, be better off working with Kate than without her.

"You've certainly got balls" was the much too prosaic way in which he indicated that he agreed; and confirmed that Kate would not die a lonely death on the edge of a wood in the bandit country that was the south of the province of Ulster. "Let's find somewhere to stay" he continued. "We can't go anywhere the Brits might be looking for me."

They headed back to the car and, half an hour later, were booked into a room in a small hotel in East Belfast. O'Connell then made a list of people he thought might be able to help at short notice; and got ready to go visiting. He would have much preferred to go alone, but he still wasn't prepared to let Kate out of his sight; and so she accompanied him. In the course of three hours that evening they visited around a dozen men, all to some degree signed up or at least sympathetic to the IRA's aims; and all deeply suspicious of Kate. But eight said they would help; and agreed to meet Declan at the storage unit at 12 noon the following morning. This would give them time to hire several vans to remove the arsenal they hoped to retrieve.

They picked up takeaway pizzas and bought some beer on the way back to the hotel. Once back in the room, and having had their makeshift supper, O'Connell said Kate could sleep on the bed. He moved the one small armchair in the room right up against the door and settled into it, tucking his pistol into his belt.

"Don't dream of trying to leave" he said. "you'll be dead before I've woken up properly."

"Don't worry" replied Kate. "I'm not going anywhere. I want Palmer finished as much as you."

Declan recognised that the weapons could have been moved in the night, but he doubted it. Palmer's men had no reason to believe anyone knew where they were; and probably planned to leave them there indefinitely. After an uneventful night, the problem turned out to be access. The unit was essentially a large garage, with a large single rolldown metal door. They had brought some tools, mainly tyre levers and the like to force their way in, but the rolldown door was secured with two very large bolts going into a rigid metal frame around the doorway; and no amount of trying to lever up the door proved any use at all.

"We will need metal cutting equipment" said one of the men to Declan, but he shook his head.

"We'd wake half of Belfast if we did that" he said. "No, the only way will be with oxyacetylene. If we park a van in front, and do it in daylight, then it shouldn't be noticeable, and it is a lot quieter." This was generally agreed to be the way forward, except that no-one had access to either an oxyacetylene torch or the gas canisters needed to fuel it. Feeling frustrated beyond measure, Declan saw that they would have to wait util Monday – a whole week-end missed – before they could arrange to hire what they needed. It was arranged that they would all meet again at noon on Monday; and Declan, keeping a close eye on Kate, headed back to their hotel room again.

CHAPTER 46

Ferguson rang Sykes that Saturday afternoon to report on the operation. As Trojan Security never regarded any telephone link as secure, he said he would report in person on Monday, but that all had gone well, with no 'mess' and only one minor hiccup. Sykes had been reasonably confident of success, but was pleased to hear it first hand; they arranged to meet at the firm's office on the Monday. Sykes decided he would not contact Palmer until he had a full de-brief.

Rather less happy were Victor O'Connell, his son Vincent and their seven colleagues, not least because they had no idea where they were, not even whether in Scotland or England. Their quarters were comfortable enough, but that just confirmed their suspicion that they would be held for some long time, presumably until after the referendum had taken place. It was re-assuring that the Brits would let them live – they'd never have gone to all this trouble if a few bullets would have been sufficient back in Bambridge; and if the referendum was lost, they would, as ever, live to fight another day. But the enforced idleness was desperately depressing; made worse by the knowledge that they had been so comprehensively out-manoeuvred. Quite how, they still didn't know. But it hardly mattered now.

Despite knowing that they were under surveillance, they thoroughly reviewed the security arrangements within which they were restricted. But it didn't take long. There was simply no way past the electric fence; and food would only be delivered through a tiny space in it when the men inside were all out of sight in their caravans. With no human contact with their captors, they could not even contemplate somehow trying to bargain their way out, not that any of them had any idea what sort of bargain arrangement they were in a position to enter into if they ever did make contact. In the absence of anything else, they fell to discussing Victor O'Connell's acquiescence in the Brits' plan to take their weaponry, but quite quickly agreed that, as a group, they had no choice if they were to survive. Victor had taken the load of guilt that anyone would nonetheless feel on his own shoulders, for which they were grateful. Victor, for his part, consoled both himself and the others with the thought that someday, somehow, the perfidious bastards who had so massively stitched them all up would pay, and pay dearly.

Also very unhappy were Kate and Declan. With Declan not prepared to go anywhere he might be known or intercepted but equally certain that he could not let Kate out of his sight, they were forced to spend what turned out to be just about the dreariest week-end either had ever spent, locked in each other's company in Declan's hotel room. One of his recruits for the Monday morning assault on the lock-up brought them food and drink and, at Kate's insistence, toothbrushes and some other odd toiletries. But their arrival made little impact on the hours and hours of sitting, while Declan brooded, and Kate tried to watch some television, with minimal enthusiasm. They rehearsed Kate's proposal again, that once they had the weapons, they should contact Palmer and make it clear beyond doubt that unless the men he was holding were released, and released quickly, then Norther Ireland would once again become a very dangerous and violent battleground, with absolutely no-one able to feel safe, unless and until the province voted to leave the United Kingdom. They did not, they recognised, have any idea as to whether their threat was sustainable, but they were sure it was credible; and ought to give Palmer reason to back off – neither he nor Seymour could think that holding onto Ulster was worth such murderous chaos, especially given that, in the absence of such an outbreak of violence, they might well win the referendum anyway.

Kate did not have to keep reminding herself that she was not a principal player in this tortuous game. She had no view whatsoever on the referendum result, nor Northern Irish politics more generally, she just wanted the present stand-off settled so that she could, as she hoped would be the case, then get back to her own life, her career and her partner Paul. Without her phone she could not contact him, not that Declan would have allowed it even if she hadn't been forced to leave her phone in Loughgannon. If he was ringing her, he'd be getting increasingly worried at the lack of reply. But, if she spoke to Palmer on Monday, then with luck she would be back with him by Tuesday or Wednesday.

As Palmer waited for news, as Victor and his men resigned themselves to their incarceration, and as Declan and Kate, struggling with the boredom of the week-end, anticipated a more successful week ahead, none of them, not one of the people sucked into Palmer's devious web of lies actually knew the true, the overall situation. No-one other than Palmer and Sykes knew about the gas field in the Irish Sea that was the overwhelming prize being sought. Only Ferguson, Declan and Kate knew that Declan was still at large; and no-one other than Declan and Kate knew that Ferguson had not hidden the IRA's armaments sufficiently well as to be out of reach. Absolutely no-one, therefore, knew that the economy of the United Kingdom, the future well-being of its population, the constitutional status of Northern Ireland, Seymour's government and Seymour's place in history, all currently rested on the resilience or otherwise of two metal bolts in a lockup garage in West Belfast.

At 9 am. on Monday morning, Ferguson and Russell met up with General Sykes at Trojan Security's office in Mayfair. They gave a thorough and detailed account of the whole operation, noting that Declan O'Connell had not been seen, but otherwise, ignoring one ill member of the Army Council, they had all the men they needed under secure lock and key; had destroyed the explosives they had discovered; and had hidden away all the IRA's now quite limited store of weapons. They concluded that it was 'job done' and that Sykes could report as much to his client.

"What about the girl?" asked Sykes.

"I sent her on her way as soon as we had taken them" said Ferguson. "We have had no contact since. She was within walking distance of Bambridge bus station; and so I presume she made her way back to Belfast airport and is now snugly back home.

"Do you want me to contact her?" asked Russell.

"No" replied Sykes. "That's really a matter for the client. I'll leave it to him. If that's everything, can you check out the admin., make sure everyone is paid properly. Meanwhile I'll report back to the client. Well done both of you. A great success; and a very profitable one for Trojan. Well done" he repeated. "Just remind everyone – no meeting up to celebrate. Nothing to draw attention to themselves. The usual." Ferguson and Russell nodded; and headed out. Sykes picked up the phone to call Palmer. On getting through to him, he said only that he had good news; and that they should meet up as soon as was convenient for Palmer. They agreed to have lunch at the Reform Club, the arrangement being the same as Palmer had organised with Preston, so that at no point would anyone see them together. It was, almost certainly, a quite unnecessary precaution but, the operation having happened, and with Palmer as yet having no feel for how the loss of the IRA men would become public knowledge, it seemed nonetheless wise.

While Ferguson and Russell were reporting to Sykes, Declan O'Connell, Kate and two others, having hired a transit van, made their way to a small engineering works on the outskirts of Belfast where a cousin – somewhat distant but close enough to generate some camaraderie – worked. They had no problem hiring out an oxyacetylene jet and fuel tanks for the day; and set off for the lock-up. They arrived at 10 am. where six others were already standing around, waiting to help, with two more transit vans parked nearby. As they had discussed on the Saturday, they lined up two of the vans right in front of the lock-up and then, having set up look-outs at both ends of the access road in front of the lock-up, one of Declan's men proceeded to cut his way into the metal frame of the door, all round where the security bolts entered it. Progress was much slower than Declan had anticipated; but eventually both bolts lay on the ground. Moving swiftly, the men then loaded all of the contents of the lock-up into the three vans and set off for a farm near Dromore owned by one of Declan's men. They each took a different route, so it was almost midday before they arrived. The vans went into a barn, the doors were locked shut and, by early afternoon, all those involved were back to their regular routines. Declan and Kate returned to his hotel room, buying a small mobile phone on the way. It was now over to Kate.

While this was happening, Sykes was lunching with Palmer in Pall Mall. Sykes repeated in considerable detail what Ferguson and Russell had told him, not disguising either his feeling of success overall nor his disappointment that they had not scooped up Declan O'Connell. Palmer was inwardly furious, less that Sykes' men had missed someone – that was always on the cards – but that it should be one of the O'Connell brothers, one of the two lynch pins of the IRA's current organisation, was very unwelcome news. But he had the sense to realise that it wasn't Sykes's fault in the planning nor his men's fault in the execution. If Declan O'Connell had failed to turn up, and wasn't at his home address when they went looking for him then there wasn't much that could be done about it. There wouldn't, he surmised, be much that Declan could do by himself. He might get more men together, but they would not include any of the skilled and experienced leadership; and, unless they had totally fooled Ferguson, they had no explosives and no arms left with which to cause much trouble. So, unless he was very unlucky, Palmer's plan had worked. He could, he thought, put the IRA threat out of his mind; and get back to steering his other stratagems designed to ensure the right outcome of the referendum.

He had just arrived back at his office in Downing Street, contemplating what, if anything, he would say to Seymour, when his phone rang, no caller ID.

"Hello" he said into the phone, abrupt as ever.

"This is Kate Kimball" came the response.

"Well, hello Kate" said Palmer in a more welcoming tone, "I was wondering if I would hear…" Kate, with a degree of enjoyment that reflected all the mountain of strife she had suffered at Palmer's hands, cut him off.

"Just shut and listen, you little shit of a man" she exploded. "I don't know if you know, but your bloody little plan misfired. You didn't catch Declan O'Connell; and he is sitting here with me right now."

"I did know" said Palmer, in a tone designed to imply that Kate was just a tiresome nuisance.

"I said, shut up" repeated Kate. "Declan has a gun in my ribs; and I have had great difficulty in assuring him that I knew nothing of your bloody double-cross. He may still decide that I can't be trusted on this, which will not go well for me, not that you would care, but he wants me to give you a message. Your men didn't only screw up in not catching him. He has tracked down where they stored the weapons they took; and he, together with a large number of mightily angry supporters of his, have reclaimed them. If you don't believe this, check it out – a large lock-up storage facility in an industrial slip road off Cliburn Street in West Belfast. If he does not hear from Victor and the others within twenty-four hours, and has them in his sights, alive and well, within forty-eight, then they are going to commence the worst round of random assassinations of Unionists since the height of the Troubles. The political fallout will no doubt be somewhat unpredictable, but if they link it directly to the prospect of something like a new civil war if the vote is to remain in the UK, then he thinks you might well lose just what you have been trying to achieve. So, twenty-four hours, or your plan is well and truly off the rails."

There was a long pause from Palmer. He could barely believe that the weapons had been lost, but Kate had been so very precise, on something he could check in a matter of minutes, that he was inclined to accept what she said. For a few seconds longer he failed to reply, trying to think how best to respond. And then, it suddenly hit him – they had made a big, a very big mistake.

"Put O'Connell on the phone" he said. Kate passed the phone to Declan but, before Palmer could say anything, Declan spoke.

"You've got the message. There will be no negotiations, in fact no further contact. You have twenty-four hours" and switched off the phone. "Let's hope that concentrates the bastard's mind" he said, as much to himself as to Kate. "You did that well" he added. "I'm beginning to agree with Victor – you're the one Brit we can trust." Kate felt it unwise to point out that Declan had been on the point of shooting her in the back of the neck less than three days ago. She wasn't out of the woods yet.

Palmer was incandescent at being cut off, made all the worse by the fact that he had, in no time at all, thought of a way to manage the situation. He really didn't want to give them the satisfaction of his ringing straight back, but realised that, unfortunately, that was precisely what he was going to have to do. He brought up the number and called back. At the other end, Declan smiled and let it go to answer phone. This only increased still further Palmer's outrage. So he left a message.

"Listen you bag of shit. You really didn't think this through. For me it's just politics. So, your crummy little province goes and bleeds money from Dublin not London to keep it afloat. What the fuck do I care. But for you, its personal, it matters. So here's what's going to happen. The first murder you lot commit, one of the fucking bastards I'm holding will disappear, for ever, and maybe not in a very good way. Next assassination, down will go another, and so on. and just to really focus your fucking stupid minds, the first one to go will be your father, Victor O'Connell himself, followed by your brother Vincent. As you said, there will be no negotiations, no contact. All up to you. Sweet dreams." He switched the phone off. Let us see what you make of that he thought, as he prepared to report to Seymour on what he now, once again, regarded as a reasonably satisfactory state of affairs.

In Belfast, Kate and Declan listened to the message. "Oh shit" was all Declan could manage.

"He's right though, isn't he?" said Kate, and it wasn't really a question. Declan was very still for a moment, but then nodded.

"Yes, he is. I've no idea where Victor and the others are. Palmer could order their disappearance – their murder – and we'd never be able to stop it, or even prove he'd done it. I can't take that risk, but I can't do nothing." The two of them looked at each other, as unlikely a pair of conspirators as either could imagine.

"I think there is only one thing we *can* do" said Kate. It wasn't what Declan was expecting. "We must go after Palmer."

PART FOUR

CHAPTER 47

"What do you have in mind?" asked O'Connell cautiously.

"I think we may be in a position to do each other rather large favours" was Kate's somewhat intriguing reply. She certainly had O'Connell's attention. "The only way to free your men is to get hold of Palmer, threaten him unless he releases them. I could never do anything like that, but I've no doubt you could – you've got a very strong motive and experience of violent confrontation that I could never cope with. However, and it's a big however, you need to get to him. That's my favour. I can get you to him. But, as I say, you can help me too. Palmer has this concocted recording of me – a complete fabrication but that won't save me from prosecution. Palmer said that he'd return what he said were the only two copies if I helped him out, contacting you and Victor; but given just how trustworthy he has proved to be, I don't think there is any chance at all that he would actually give up his hold on me – I know too much. I'd always be a risk for him without the recordings. So, when we get to him, you can force him to give up the recordings – I'm sure you could be very credible. He'd just laugh at me. So, we have a mutual interest in this and, as I'm saying this, I think it won't be that difficult."

"Because?" interjected O'Connell.

"Because, think about it. When he was Prime Minister, Gerrard must have been the most closely guarded person in the country, but you got to him. I suppose Palmer might have a personal detective, just because he works in Downing Street, but I doubt much more. We need to think out a plan, but I really don't think it will be that difficult for us to intercept him somehow, and take matters on from there. What's more, he is such an arrogant bastard, if there are no violent incidents in Northern Ireland, he'll assume his threat is working. He won't see us coming."

"You know, Kate, you really are wasted in publishing" said O'Connell, with a rare, broad smile. "Can't you find some Irish blood in your ancestry and join us?" Kate returned his smile, not just because what he had said was, in the circumstances, genuinely amusing, but because, for the first time in over two years, she could actually begin to see a way back to her everyday life, free of the Sword of Damocles that Palmer held over her.

"Let's go back to Kelly's place," said O'Connell. "I think we can risk it. I know he is not well, and looks worse, but he has one of the sharpest minds on the Council. We can work out a plan of action and let him test it. If there are holes in it, he'll spot them."

Kate nodded agreement, but said she had two requests first. Could she ring her partner Paul, to say that she was fine, but would be delayed returning home for a day or two – he could call her office and say she was at home and not very well – and could she buy a change of clothes, as she had thought she would be home by the previous Friday night. O'Connell agreed to both, but emphasised that her call should be short, with no indication of exactly where she was – just enough to give her partner some re-assurance.

Paul Emmerson, unsurprisingly, was in a state of utter frustration and crippling worry about Kate. He hadn't necessarily expected her back before the week-end, but it was now Monday afternoon with no word from her; and so his relief was palpable across the ether when Kate got to him at his laboratory office in Oxford. She assured him she was okay, making no mention that she had been close to a lonely death in some woodland where her body would probably not have been found for a long time, if ever. She also assured him that she would be back in Oxford very soon, but she had lost her phone, so he shouldn't try ringing it. To try to minimise both his worries and his inclination to ask questions, she asked how things were with him.

"Fine, fine" he replied, not for one moment distracted. "Are you sure you are okay?" he asked.

"Definitely" she said, with a touch of laughter in her reply. "I'd better go, but will see you soon my love." She left just enough time for him to say goodbye before switching off the call.

"Thanks" she said to O'Connell, reflecting that although they might be planning an operation as equals, he was still very much in control of her. That was fine with her if that is what it took to get her out of her predicament. They went out to O'Connell's car and headed for some shops. O'Connell insisted that the clothes she bought were put on his credit card, not because he was now wanting to buy her things – they both even had a slight laugh at that idea - but because he wanted no electronic trace of Kate's whereabouts, not at a shop nor even a cash machine.

"You can pay me back when this is all over" he said

"Do you know what the phrase 'fat chance' means?" asked Kate. "Think of it as my fee for my services to your organisation."

"If this works, I'll throw in a crate of beer," said O'Connell. Kate welcomed the camaraderie, but had no illusions that it was anything other than paper thin, to be ditched at the slightest sign that she was a hinderance not a help to O'Connell.

As they drove, Kate started to contemplate a plan; and quickly came up with one that was so easy to formulate in her mind that she worried that it must be crazy. Well, Declan O'Connell and Shaun Kelly could give their views on that.

The drive back to Shaun Kelly's house gave Kate time to flesh out her plan, and even do a bit of testing of her own. She worked through a few variants of the basic plan, depending on how Palmer responded when she contacted him. By the time she arrived, she was ready to present her proposition to O'Connell and Kelly – no power point but, for once, an activity not totally out of keeping with her former and – please God, future – life back in Oxford.

Kelly poured them drinks and O'Connell, having taken a sizeable swig, looked at Kate, expectantly.

"We need to go to London" she started. "I will phone Palmer and tell him I must see him; that I have a message from you that he will want to hear; and he has two tape recordings to hand over to me. I will say that I don't trust him and will need to meet him outside somewhere. Fortunately, his thinking was very similar before, and we met at the outside restaurant in St. James's Park, opposite Horse Guards Parade – it's very convenient for Downing Street - so I will suggest the same place. Her may suggest somewhere else, but as long as it is outside, we can go along with it.

"So, we meet up. I just don't know if personal protection goes with his job, but let's assume it does – a personal police officer of some kind, probably armed. If he arrives with Palmer, my guess is that he will take a seat at another table but aim to be just a few feet away from Palmer at the most. I don't think either will be that worried – it's a public space in the centre of London; and he is meeting a woman he will feel he has absolutely nothing to fear from, either physically or in any other way. He will be curious to know the message; and no doubt looking forward to telling me that he has no intention of handing over the tape recordings.

"We will need five men altogether" said Kate. "You, Declan, two others armed with silenced pistols, and two in cars. They will need to know how to steal cars at short notice. She then explained the details of what she had worked out during the drive to Kelly's house. O'Connell and Kelly listened intently, but Kate's plan was sufficiently simple and, they thought, relatively riskless that they had few questions. Both, in fact, were rather impressed, but the only compliment was O'Connell's repeated comment that Kate was wasted in publishing. Kate herself had one moment of introspection, when she slightly panicked at what she was, to all intents and purposes, now organising; but for the rest of the time she was now well and truly hooked into a new persona. She was inwardly furious, explosively so, with the way Palmer had treated her, had threatened her and manipulated her, and she had, quite simply, had enough. She had seen a way to thwart him, and with luck get herself out from under his influence once and for all; and she was entirely focused now on achieving that. She realised that she could never have done this on her own, but the same fate that had conspired to put her in this position had also provided her with the means – with Declan O'Connell and his men – to overcome Palmer's plans; and she was determined to use them.

CHAPTER 48

Once O'Connell and Kelly had approved Kate's plan, she and Declan bought a new pay-as-you-go mobile for Kate, who tried to ring Palmer. She only got an answering service saying he wasn't currently available, and Kate declined to leave a number for him to call, saying she would ring at 6 pm, and he would want to hear what she had to say. They then spent the intervening time contacting and recruiting four of the team of IRA members or sympathisers who had helped then reclaim the weapons Sykes's men had taken. Two brothers, Patrick and Liam O'Sullivan, rather a rather dour pair of thirty- year- old construction workers, could not hide their delight at the prospect of helping Declan out, against the Brit who had so royally screwed over bigger IRA fish than them. Both assured Declan that they were comfortable with pistols from previous 'activities'; and picked up two Glock 16s with silencers from the relocated weapons store. The next recruit, Ryan Mendes, for some reason rather proud of his long-lost Spanish roots, no doubt going back to the time when part of the Spanish Armada was washed ashore on the rocky coast of Ireland on their way home, was equally happy to volunteer to be one of Declan's drivers, a skill he had acquired which went far beyond his day time activity as a Belfast taxi driver. The final member of the team, Michael Flynn, was a much older man, in his fifties, but had been a minor motor racing enthusiast in earlier times, and was also very keen to be involved. Neither were unpractised at breaking into cars, and hotwiring them, usually Mendes said with evident pride, in about eight seconds. Kate explained that it was doubtful that any advanced driving skills would be needed, but it was good to know that the potential was there if needed.

At 6 pm Kate phoned Palmer again and, as expected, got through this time.

"Hello Kate" said Palmer with a deceptively pleasant but slightly condescending tone. "What can I do for you?"

"You can shut up and listen" said Kate, consciously allowing her anger with the man to infect her. "I have a message from people here, potentially to your mutual advantage which they want me to deliver. So, I need to meet you – I suggest the same place as before in London, noon on Wednesday – and I want those tape recordings. That's it." There was a long pause, and Kate could, in her mind's eye, see Palmer pondering, calculating but, as she had surmised, he didn't see any reason to worry about what Kate was proposing. He held all the cards, the men tucked away somewhere in Sykes's good care, and the recordings of Kate indicating her willing involvement in terrorist activity.

"Make it 11 am – I'm busy at noon" he replied. Whether he was, or just didn't want fully to comply with anything Kate suggested, she did not know, but it didn't matter.

"11 am at the restaurant" she confirmed, and rang off. "Right" she said to Declan, "let's get ourselves organised, get to London tomorrow, and be ready to deal with Palmer. I may end up terrified on Wednesday, but I think I'm going to enjoy it."

After fixing up accommodation in London for the following night, and a convivial supper at a local restaurant, Kate and Declan spent the night at Kelly's house; and then, the next day, Flynn drove them to London via the Belfast to Heysham ferry, while Mendes drove the O'Sullivan brothers. The six of them booked into six different hotels in the Paddington area, all rather unprepossessing but perfectly comfortable for a night, paying cash in advance and providing no identification. Curiously, or perhaps not, the only one to object to this was the one Kate had booked, as if female discretion was more suspect than male discretion. Kate explained that she was trying to avoid her husband – soon to be ex-husband – and felt safer leaving no credit card trail. This rather implausible story seemed to do the trick, however, and she was welcomed in. The six of them then met up for supper in an Italian restaurant nearby; and they spent the time going over every inch of Kate's plan. Back at her hotel, Kate rang Paul, to re-assure him that she was fine, and would be back home the following evening, finally able to put the nightmare of the last days behind her once and for all.

At 10 am the following day, Mendes and Flynn both broke into two anonymous looking saloon cars parked in residential parking spaces near Paddington station. They hot-wired them and then, while Flynn picked up Kate and Declan, Mendes picked up the O'Sullivan brothers. Mendes and Flynn then both drove to Birdcage Walk, round the corner from Horse Guards Parade. There they waited until shortly before 11 am. Their four passengers then made their way the few hundred metres to the restaurant in St. James's Park on foot. A few minutes before 11 am, Kate, with a coffee from the café, sat at an outside table in the restaurant, while

Declan and the O'Sullivan brothers stood by a side wall of the café, apparently having a discussion, perhaps, to any observer, temporarily getting some fresh air from their nearby office jobs.

At 11 am Kate saw Palmer approaching from across Horse Guards Parade, accompanied by one very tall and rather burly figure, who couldn't, she thought, really be anything other than a personal protection officer. Well, that was what they had anticipated. Palmer saw Kate and headed over to her. As he arrived, his protection officer took a seat at the next table along, only some three metres away.

"Hello Kate" he said, with a smile, and sat down at her table. "Before you say anything else" he said, "let me apologise for the deception I involved you in, but it was in a good cause, with a good outcome." His tone, however, conveyed no sense of apology whatsoever. In a moment to savour, Kate said nothing in reply. She merely smiled, as the O'Sullivan brothers approached the protection officer, one behind him the other sitting down at his table, while Declan, just a second or two behind, came up behind Palmer.

Liam O'Sullivan, under the cover of a light raincoat over his arm, pressed his silenced pistol into the protection officer's neck, while Patrick O'Sullivan pressed another, also hidden by a raincoat, into the man's ribs.

"This is a silenced pistol in your ribs" said Patrick. "Any sound, any movement from you and you will be dead. My colleague here will hold you upright, no-one will notice anything, and we will be long gone before someone finds a dead body here. Do I make myself unmistakably clear?" Palmer's man was armed, but he saw immediately that he had no room to manoeuvre. He might just be able to grab and re-direct one gun aimed at him, but two was impossible. He could explode out of his chair, cause a degree of mayhem, but he had no doubt that he would not live long enough see it. So, this round to the opposition, whoever they might be. He sat quite still, silent, and looked across at Palmer.

Declan, coming up behind Palmer, had employed a similar technique. He pressed the silencer of his pistol into Palmer's neck.

"Do not move an inch or I will kill you" said Declan. "No one will hear, no-one will notice, not until it is far too late; and do not look for help from your guard dog over there because, as you will see, he is well taken care of." Palmer was shocked beyond measure, but his only outward response was to look, very quizzically, at Kate.

"You stupid fucking bitch" he said, almost airily." Do you have no idea what you have just done ? I simply cannot calculate how much you are going to regret this".

"Just shut up" said Kate. "For once in your life you are going to do exactly what you are told. You will hate it, and I will love every minute of watching it." Palmer just shook his head, partly in exasperation, partly in feigned, or maybe real, disbelief. "So, what happens now?" he asked.

"Nothing, for the moment" was Kate's unexpected reply. They appeared to be just a man and a woman at a café table, with third man standing but maybe involved in their conversation. No-one paid them any attention. At the next table, Liam O'Sullivan spoke to his hostage.

"We will all now stand up and casually walk over to Horse Guards Parade. Anything else, anything at all, and I or my companion here will slot you. Even if anyone notices, we will be in a car and far from here before anyone can do anything about it, so I suggest, for your own sake, that you do exactly as I say, is that clear?" There was no response but, as Patrick and then Liam O'Sullivan stood up, the protection officer stood; together they set off across the slight stretch of park that separated them from Horse Guards Parade. With immaculate timing, that had been carefully planned the night before, Mendes drove round from Birdcage Walk and, as the O'Sullivans got to the street, he pulled up in front of them. Liam got in the back with their quarry, while Patrick joined Mendes in the front and they sped away. They would drop Palmer's guard dog two hours later in a remote part of the New Forest, none the worse for his experience, but with quite a long walk before he got back to civilisation. Once dropped, the three IRA men headed for Bournemouth railway station, dropped the stolen car in a side street, and got a train, to Reading and then another back to Paddington. They picked up Mendes's car and returned to Belfast via the Heysham ferry.

Once the O'Sullivans had disappeared with Palmer's protection officer, Declan told Palmer to get up and walk the same route. Palmer, determined not to lose all control of the situation, however dire it appeared did not move.

"So, Kate, no message from these bastards? Or is this goon going to deliver it himself?"

"You'll have your message soon enough" said Declan. "Now, get up, and I mean now, or say goodbye, to Kate and the world." To emphasise his intent, he dug the barrel of the silencer still deeper into Palmer's neck. Palmer slowly got to his feet, and the three of them slowly followed where his officer had gone only a minute or two previously. At the road, Michael Flynn in the second stolen car was waiting for them. Kate joined him in the front, while O'Connell forced Palmer into the back and stuck the pistol firmly in his side.

"So, where are we going?" asked Palmer, is as insouciant a manner as he could manage.

"We are going to your place" was O'Connell's somewhat surprising reply. "Tell our driver here how to get there. It's really tedious if I have to accompany every instruction to you with a reminder of what will happen if you don't follow them, so just get on with it will you? Anyway, it's there or a suitably isolated spot where it will give me great pleasure to extract the address from you." Palmer could see that there was no point in resisting; and still felt remarkably untroubled by the turn of events. He accepted that he needed to play along.

CHAPTER 49

Palmer lived in a large, rather stylish ground floor flat in Notting Hill. Had he not bought it some twenty years previously he would never have been able to afford it. Now separated from his wife, it was too large for him, but he loved the property, and the area, and the cache that went with it. He told Flynn to do a U-turn, then directed them to Victoria, Park Lane, Paddington, and Notting Hill. He directed them to a resident's parking space almost in front of his flat.

As Flynn parked the car, O'Connell told Palmer to get out of the car, very slowly and very carefully. His pistol would never be more than a few inches from Palmer's back. Kate also got out, leaving Flynn in the car, to drive round the block if any traffic warden intervened. O'Connell gently pushed Palmer towards his front door, the pistol firmly in Palmer's back, with Kate following. Palmer let them all in; and they headed for a large, very comfortably furnished living room, with large double glass doors onto a garden at the back of the flat. O'Connell told Palmer to sit in a larger armchair while he sat down on an elegant sofa, the hand holding the pistol resting on the armrest. Kate felt too agitated to sit down, so leant against a sideboard to one side of Palmer,

"So, what now?" asked Palmer, in as casual a voice as he could manage. O'Connell nodded to Kate.

"First" said Kate, "I want those tape recordings you promised me. My bet was that you would keep them here, not at your office. I hope for your sake that I was right?"

"In my safe" said Palmer, still outwardly very calm and, almost it seemed, unconcerned.

"Which is where?" asked Kate.

"Behind that picture" said Palmer, pointing to a Paul Nash print – or maybe it was an original – on the wall behind Declan. Kate went over to the picture and was about to lift it off the wall when Palmer said that if she undid a latch at the side, the picture would swing forward to reveal the safe. When Kate did this, she saw a small safe behind, not unlike those regularly found in hotel rooms, with a keypad of numbers on the front.

"7273" said Palmer before Kate could actually ask for the combination, slightly disconcerted by how co-operative Palmer appeared to be. She punched in the code, the door came open and, inside, apart from two small boxes, which looked as if they might hold some jewellery items, a few papers and an exercise book, there was, Kate was pleased to see, a cassette tape, which she took out.

"I'll need to listen to this before we depart, but where is the other one? You said there were two."

"There are indeed two" said Palmer with just the slightest smile. "The other one is in a safe deposit box. Sorry about that. I hardly need to point out that the bank will not give access without me and confirmatory ID. Anything happens to me, the bank has instructions to notify my office. I think they will be able to take things from there."

Kate was so shocked, as much at her stupidity in not anticipating this as the information itself, that she could not think of any response. Her brain, drenched with adrenalin, rushed through a series of absurd scenarios – taking Palmer at gunpoint to the bank, maybe threatening a loved one if he didn't go and get it – but she knew that this was all totally unrealistic.

"Which bank?" she asked.

"It's not in a bank" replied Palmer. "It's in a dedicated secure storage depo in Hounslow, quite near Heathrow – I imagine that is not a coincidence."

"What's the address and your box number?" snapped Kate

"It's just called STL Ltd – I don't think I even know what that stands for" said Palmer. "It's in Arlington Street, you can't miss it, and the box number is 158; but you can't get access, so you might as well stop this whole charade now. Apart from you not being me, they photograph anyone wanting to enter the vaults; and then digitally compare the photo with one they already have on their files. Their whole raison d'etre is that no-one, but no-one, other than the owner of a box can get access to it. You can walk away now, and I might just think about not using the other tape. If not, you are in more trouble than you can imagine. A bad decision now, Kate, and you are going to be out of circulation for a very long time."

Kate had rarely felt such rage as at that moment, not least at herself, at how easily she had been so completely fooled. She wanted to slap Palmer very hard, but just about had the good sense not to; and wanted to respond, say something, anything to wipe the smug smile off his face; but nothing, absolutely nothing, came to mind. In a quite involuntary movement, she looked, rather helplessly, at Declan.

"Let's just park that for moment" he said to her. Then, turning back to Palmer, and leaning forward towards him to indicate the earnestness of what he was about to say, or possibly do, he moved onto his own agenda. "Now, Palmer" he said, deliberately slow and determinedly, "you have my father, my brother and some of our colleagues under wraps somewhere. So, you are now going to call whoever has them and order their immediate release. And let's not bugger about. If you do not, I will kill you right here and now. After the stunt you pulled, it would give me the greatest pleasure. No-one will hear anything" – he nodded to the long silencer barrel on the pistol – "no-one knows we are here. So, make the call please."

"You really are a bunch of fucking amateurs, aren't you" was Palmer's surprisingly brave response. "Do you not think that I might have suspected some left over thugs like you would come calling? Christ no wonder you lost out in Northern Ireland. Piss-ups and breweries come to mind. So, words of one syllable, so to speak, I call a guy every third day and give him a single code word. If I don't, he waits another twenty-four hours for my call. If there is still no call, he arranges the disappearance, with extreme prejudice, of your dear family members and their nutter pals. So, fire away. You couldn't be more directly responsible for the deaths of your mates. The alternative is that you both just fuck off out of here, go back to wherever you've come from, and in a few weeks, once the referendum is over, they will all be released, unharmed, all ready to fight another day - they might even win next time – but at least they will *have* another day."

It was O'Connell's turn to look helpless. "Nice try Palmer, but I don't believe a word of it." Even Kate noted that this was said with less than total conviction.

"Oh, for fuck's sake, do you really think I'd allow myself to be in the position of having to call off my, if you'll excuse me saying, rather carefully arranged plans without a simple expedient to counter it. You lot really are fucking morons, you know. So, do you want them to live or not? Make up your bloody mind. Kate, if this goes the wrong way, tell everyone I was worth eight fucking IRA will you?"

Though this was addressed to Kate, Palmer kept his eyes firmly fixed on O'Connell, who just stared back at him, at a loss what to do. In the silence, Kate slowly stood up straight from where she had been leaning against a desk; and moved the foot or two that separated her from O'Connell. Then, without any warning, she leant down and, with both hands, grabbed the pistol, which O'Connell had been loosely resting on the arm of the sofa, out of his hand. O'Connell was so taken by surprise that Kate had the pistol firmly in her two hands, pointing at O'Connell's back before he had fully registered what had happened.

"What the.." he started to say, but her face boiling with rage, Kate screamed at him.

"Just shut up Declan, shut up." O'Connell started to turn round to look at her, but she yelled again . "Don't turn round, don't bloody well move, nor you Palmer" and for a second she levelled the pistol at him rather than O'Connell. But, despite Kate's order, O'Connell couldn't help himself.

"What the hell are you doing, Kate? He said, in a low voice, quite menacing given that he had a gun pointing at his back.

"I have just had enough, is what I am doing" said Kate, rather less grammatically correct than her usual conversation. "Apart from a day's clay pigeon shooting, which I didn't enjoy, I have never held a gun, still less shot anyone, but you'd better believe that that could be about to change – and even I can't miss at three feet – if I get any resistance from either of you. The fact is, I'm in a win-win situation here." It was Palmer's turn to join O'Connell in blank incomprehension. "So, there are two ways forward, and I'm happy with either. If, Palmer, you make the call, then O'Connell's lot are safe, we two can go home, and you will get me my tape." Palmer raised an eyebrow. "Because, if you don't, then as a 'thank you' to me for saving them all, they will find you and without doubt kill you – they got Gerrard alright so you will be very easy to get to. The knowledge will haunt your last few weeks, that every day will quite possibly be your last. I quite like that. Is it a deal, Declan?"

"We'd be very happy to oblige" said Declan.

"Good" said Kate. "Now the tricky part. If you don't make the call, I will put a bullet in you, Palmer. You have mucked up my life quite long enough…" O'Connell interrupted her

"Kate, you can't, you heard what he said."

"I did" said Kate, and to descend to the language of the moment, I don't give a fuck if your lot disappear. They're just a bunch of mentally arrested thugs – most will have cold-blooded murders at their door, and the world will be as well rid of them as it will be of Palmer."

"Kate" said O'Connell, in a very low sombre tone "If you do that, I will personally kill you myself, and not quickly."

"No, you won't" said Kate, "because straight after Palmer's bullet, you will get the next one. I don't know what the police will make of a dead senior government official and a dead IRA man, but they certainly won't be looking for an academic publishing agent from Oxford. I'll wipe the desk clean; and dispose of the gun in the Thames. I'll be out of it. And don't think I won't. You're the bastard who was about to execute me three days ago. You should have finished me off when you had the chance" she added viciously.

"What about the tape?" said O'Connell. "That will lead them straight to you."

"Not so" said Kate. "I only saw the way forward when I realised that nothing on the tape could lead to me except a voice match. But for that they'd have to know I was involved; and how would they know that if Palmer is no longer with us? They can hardly check every adult woman in Britain can they? So, Palmer, you little shit, I simply don't care which way you go. You decide. I hope any wish you might have to see O'Connell here get what he deserves doesn't unduly influence you towards not making the call?" She stared hard at Palmer.

"Kate…." said O'Connell, but she interrupted.

"Not a word, Declan. Let the man make up his mind." She stared at Palmer, her face still flushed with every sign of extreme stress and anger. Palmer neither spoke nor moved. Kate raised the barrel of the gun a fraction, so it pointed straight at Palmer's chest.

"To echo what you said to me a moment ago, Palmer, 'bad choice' "and visibly tightened her grip on the trigger. Palmer remained immobile.

"So be it" she added. "End of the line, for both of you." Now holding the pistol in both hands she began to squeeze the trigger.

"Okay, okay" said Palmer, raising his hands in a rather futile defensive gesture. "I'll make the call. Though why O'Connell here would seek to help you get the tape after what you have just said, just threatened, I do not know. You are a long way from out of it yet."

"I'll take my chances" said Kate. "I think Victor will call the shots, and he will be very grateful that I have just saved his life. Anyway. Make the call."

"I need the phone in the draw behind you" said Palmer.

"Get the phone" said Kate to O'Connell, without taking her eyes of Palmer When O'Connell had got it he asked Palmer what the number to ring was.

"It only has the one number stored in it." O'Connell saw that this was correct and pressed on the retained number.

To his mild surprise, General Sykes was in his Mayfair office when he saw Palmer calling him. He asked his P.A. to give him a moment with whom he was talking. When she had left, he replied, no names being necessary or prudent.

"Yes" he said in a flat tone, neither welcoming nor unwelcoming. O'Connell passed the phone to Palmer.

"The consignment that you are holding for me," said Palmer, "I'd like you to release it. Earlier than planned, I know, but it would now suit me better." Sykes's surprise was considerably more than mild this time; but was far too well disciplined to reveal this.

"Are you sure?" was all he replied.

Even Palmer didn't know whether the slight pause before he answered was deliberate or unconscious, but he did pause, unnoticed by Kate or O'Connell who could only hear Palmer's end of the conversation. "Yes" Palmer said eventually, very flat. A 'yes' as far as Kate and O'Connell were concerned, but not a totally convincing one to Sykes's acute ears. There was a pause. As far as Kate and O'Connell were concerned, Palmer's telephone call recipient might have been talking, but Sykes was, in fact, just thinking. A man with a long history of action, but also of shrewd thinking, and decisiveness as well.

"Are you under pressure, under restraint at all?" was his eventual question.

"Yes" said Palmer in a definite but almost jovial fashion, as if he was just signing off on what had been agreed. Another silence followed as Sykes reviewed his options.

"So, would you like me to ignore this request?" he said.

"That would be good, thanks" said Palmer, this time very evidently, or so it seemed in his room, to be confirming some detail or other. "Bye" he added, as nonchalantly as possible, and switched off the phone. "He says they will be on their way home in twenty-four hours at the most" he informed Kate and O'Connell.

"Thank God for that" said Kate "Here, Declan, do take this gun back. I can't hold it anymore." O'Connell was once again caught totally off guard.

"You can't *hold* it anymore" he said, incredulously, "yet, apparently, you were all ready to shoot both of us?" Looking extremely suspicious, he took the pistol from her.

"Oh, don't be a clot, Declan. I could no more shoot someone than fly to the moon. It was clear that Palmer here didn't think you'd risk Victor and the rest, and he was right, but I thought he might think twice if it was me holding the gun. Apologies for those rather nasty things I said about you all, but I needed to persuade him, really persuade him, that I was serious, little miss maniac."

O'Connell was staring at her again, this time the incredulity mixed with some degree of awe. "You mean that little performance was all….. just a performance?"

"Spot on, Declan. Do keep up" Kate added with a smile. "It was my hidden acting talents that got me into this mess, so it's good that they've also helped me out. I know it's not quite what is normally meant by a feminine touch, but it did the job, didn't it?"

"I don't believe it" said O'Connell. "I fucking well don't believe it. Wait 'till I tell the others about this. They'll be pissing themselves.

Amazing. You had me totally…" He never finished the sentence. Palmer had said nothing. He now launched himself out of his chair towards Kate. "You fucking bitch" he shrieked, "you…" But he too was destined not to finish his sentence. There was a quiet 'plop' sound; and it was as if Palmer's body, coming out of the chair, had hit a brick wall. It seemed to defy gravity for a moment, suspended, half in the chair, half out of it, and then it sank back as another 'plop' accompanied a second bullet from O'Connell's pistol into Palmer's chest.

Kate would have screamed, but so shocked was she that she could produce no sound at all. She felt as if she had stopped breathing while simultaneously starting to pant rapidly, her mouth stuck open and soundless. O'Connell filled the void.

"Sorry, Kate, but we would never let him survive. He could easily have rescinded the message to let Victor and the others go. He could even have finished them off and, in any event, he knows far too much about us. So, he had to go. I'm sorry we didn't tell you, but you'd never have gone through with this if you'd known, would you?" As he spoke, he bent down to examine Palmer more closely. He didn't want to touch him, but it was clear that Palmer was dead.

Kate was still too traumatised by what she had just seen to be able to speak. All she could think about was that she was undoubtedly some sort of accomplice to murder; or that, no, she wasn't - she'd had no idea that O'Connell planned all along to kill Palmer - but would have no chance of avoiding such a charge if they were caught. When she finally got herself together enough to speak, it was at the most prosaic level.

"Get a cloth" she said. O'Connell, duly picked one up from the kitchen and, when he returned, he had a pedal bin liner with him. He gave the cloth to Kate who, rather trance-like, wiped down the desk and the sofa, then gave the fabric to O'Connell and told him to dispose of it with the gun. Meanwhile, O'Connell took everything that was still in the safe and put it in the bin liner. "It doesn't look worth stealing, but the police won't know what might have been there, so this will make it look very like a burglary gone wrong, or interrupted at least."

"Let's just get out of here" she said. As they left, she picked up Palmer's phone from where it had fallen to the ground when O'Connell's first bullet hit him. She gave it to O'Connell. "That needs to go as well" she said.

"The whole lot, gun, phone, cloth, stuff from the safe, they're all going in the bin bag with a big brick and dropped into the Irish Sea on the ferry home" said O'Connell. "I can't see there's anything to link us to Palmer."

They had one more look round, then left Palmer's flat, got back into the stolen car with Michael Flynn at the wheel. "All okay?" he asked.

"Fine" said O'Connell, without elaborating. "Just get us back to near your car, drop this one off somewhere out of the way, then meet me at the car and we will head home. We can drop you at Paddington, Kate, if you are heading back to Oxford?"

"Drop me by your car and I'll walk from there" said Kate. She felt she just had to have some time outside, fresh air, to collect her wits after what had happened. As they drove, she looked through the things that O'Connell had taken from the safe. It mainly seemed fairly inconsequential, a watch that looked valuable, Palmer's passport, some cufflinks, but with two exceptions. One was a key. Kate had never actually seen a safety deposit box key, but some instinct told her that this was exactly that, the key to the box where the other recording was lodged. She realised that she couldn't hope to use it even if she was right, but decided to keep it anyway. The other was the exercise book, which on inspection looked very interesting. It wasn't a diary; it seemed mainly filled with brief references to times, dates and places for meetings with various people, plus occasional short notes. But the writing was such casual-looking scribble that she had great difficulty making much out of it.

A few dates were recognisable, but virtually none of the names; and Kate even wondered whether maybe this was deliberate, so no-one but Palmer could read what was written there. But, under one indecipherable name, she did make out two words, which she was fairly sure were 'little boys'. As she told O'Connell, this was enough to indicate what the exercise book was – clearly Palmer's 'little black book' recording what hold he had on various people with whom he had to deal. Even armed with that information, she could only decode one other note, the word 'pros' which presumably meant prostitutes. Whether Palmer had evidence of the transgressions he had noted was unclear; but no doubt even the possibility that he did would have given him considerable leverage, with politicians, civil servants, journalists, significant businessmen, if they ended up in Palmer's book.

"Maybe we should hold onto that?" suggested O'Connell. "We might be able to cause mayhem with information like that."

"I don't think so" said Kate. "I can't decipher any of it to the point where it might be useful; and holding onto it and anything that could link us to Palmer is just madness. No, it has to go with the rest."

"I guess you're right" conceded O'Connell. "Pity. We might have royally fucked the whole British government with something like that. But we will be back in action soon. I can't wait to tell Victor and Vincent, all the boys, what you did back there. They'll make you a fucking saint."

"Too high profile for me just at the moment" replied Kate. "I've just got round to thinking a bit more clearly about the situation. Specifically, can anyone link us to Palmer? I've got two major worries on that score. First there's the men who carried out the kidnapping. They never saw you, but they certainly saw me. If any of them get caught, I doubt I'm going to escape attention. Ant then they've got someone to check against that ruddy tape."

"I've been thinking about that" said O'Connell "and I don't think you need to worry." Kate pulled a doubtful face. O'Connell pushed on. "What those men did was not just very dangerous, it was highly illegal and politically potentially catastrophic. I don't think, for one moment, that Palmer could or would have used regular army, or any part of the security services to carry out the operation. They may have been ex-army or whatever, in fact they are almost bound to have been I would say but, Kate, they were mercenaries. Believe me. And I'll bet that the only connection from Palmer to them was via the phone we have in our binbag. There's no way for the police to contact them, when they read about Palmer, the last thing they will do is announce themselves, or any connection to him. And even if somehow the police did get to them, would they know who you are? I bet no-one used your surname; and there are rather a lot of Kates in the world. Probably think you're Irish. So, I tell you, you're not at risk from them. Who else?"

"Palmer can't have done this all alone," Kate said. "Why would he? There's got to be some group, maybe small but some people, who hatched what you have to agree is a highly political scheme - a military style operation, sure, but with a purely political end in mind. If there are people in government who know what Palmer was trying to do, explicitly aimed at the IRA, and now he is dead, they will quite easily work out who did it. Once they're onto the IRA, do you think your security is good enough to keep something like this completely secret. You may say it is, but I can tell you that won't let me sleep at night."

"You're missing the point," said O'Connell. "Just because the operation was so risky, I very much doubt that Palmer discussed his plans with many others. Palmer of all people knows – sorry, knew - not to leave himself open to leverage, frankly blackmail, by others. He will have needed some sort of secret authorisation, but I'm willing to bet that he kept that to the minimum necessary. And the minimum necessary is one man, Seymour. I very much doubt Palmer will have mentioned you, even as a player, let alone by your name to Seymour; and even if he did, the very last thing Seymour - or anyone else if there is anyone else - is going to do is offer up the name of the one person who could reveal the whole operation to a stunned world. There is no-one, absolutely no-one who has any incentive to identify you, even supposing they could, quite the reverse in fact."

As he concluded this, Flynn announced that they had arrived. Kate and O'Connell got out; and Flynn headed off to dump the car they had been in. Kate confirmed that she would walk the few hundred metres to Paddington station. Both found parting to be quite awkward. They had collaborated on a matter of extreme danger; they were somewhat dependent on each other, they had each threatened to kill the other, albeit only one threat was genuine, and now they were going entirely separate ways to quite different lives, extremely unlikely to ever see each other again and, both indeed knowing that it would be highly unwise to contact each other. So 'goodbye' didn't really feel quite adequate to the situation. O'Connell rose to the occasion.

"Kate, we should not be in touch again, but thanks for what you have done; and if things do go pear-shaped, and you need the sort of help I and the others can give, then do ask."

"Thanks" said Kate. "I will. Do give my best to Victor. Maybe, in a few years, we can have a little re-union if it is safe. Go carefully." She turned and headed off to the station, already mulling over what O'Connell had said, why he thought she was safe.

CHAPTER 50

As O'Connell and Flynn made their way back to the Heysham ferry and on to Belfast, Kate, now starting to tremble with shock as the adrenalin generated by what had happened at Palmer's flat began to wear off, stumbled towards Paddington station, her mind unable to focus on anything very clearly. Buying a ticket from a machine and looking up the next train to Oxford seemed like major tasks. Fortunately, travelling first class in the middle of the day, she had no-one near her in her carriage; and she almost collapsed into a seat. As the train pulled out, and she fought to pull herself together, the effect, paradoxically, was to make the whole morning somehow recede into a surreal memory, almost of something she had observed but not been part of. She held out her ticket when the train's ticket inspector came past, but she had no reserves left to say anything or even acknowledge his presence. She felt completely disorientated, in such a daze, she worried she might pass out. One thought came to dominate, that she must just hold out, forget, ignore any thoughts on anything until she could get back to her home, contact Paul and then, only then, with him by her side, start to face up to her predicament. She got out the phone she had obtained in Northern Ireland and called Paul. Predictably it went to voice mail – no mobiles were allowed in the engineering lab where he spent much of his working day – so she left a message, that she'd be home mid- afternoon, was not in a good state, and could he get back as soon as possible.

In fact, the human mind, she reflected later, is extraordinarily adaptive. Half an hour later, before they had reached Reading, she was starting to go over in her mind what O'Connell had said, why he thought she was safe, why no-one would ever come looking for her. And she could start to see his logic. It might well be that no-one, now Palmer was dead, knew of her involvement, and anyone who did could only know because they were part of, or party to, Palmer's scheme, in which case they had, just as O'Connell had said, every reason to keep very quiet about her. So maybe, just maybe, she would be okay. She could go back to the life she had had before, to the partner and the career she loved; and forget, bit by bit, the nightmare she had been through. By the time she got to Oxford, though hardly the confident and self-assured person she had been until recently, she was, nonetheless, starting to get back in control of her thinking and even her emotions. What she now needed was to talk, to Paul, to hear what he would say, perhaps even advise, though it was already occurring to her that there was absolutely nothing to be done but sit tight and hope for the best. Nothing she might do could remotely help the situation.

Kate walked to their flat from the station. She still felt she needed to be outside, though she couldn't have explained why; and Paul wasn't likely to be home any time soon. Though only the middle of the afternoon she poured herself a glass of wine, to help steady her nerves and then, feeling a little revived, called her p.a. Janice, to say that she'd be back to work the next day, and to set up a de-briefing meeting on what had been happening while she had been away. She could tell that Janice was at once concerned and curious -Kate's behaviour had been decidedly odd - but restricted herself to just asking how Kate was. Kate, only remembering in time that she was supposed to have been unwell since her trip, said she was fine, and looking forward to returning to work. That seemed to satisfy Janice, at least for the moment.

Kate was now desperate to get some semblance of normality back into her life and thinking, but it proved quite beyond her. All she could do was go round and round in her head what O'Connell had said. Was there a weak link, an omission perhaps? Then she froze as she realised that, for the second time in her life, she was, though no fault of her own, tied into a sitting Prime Minister. It was Seymour's predecessor, Alan Gerrard, who had orchestrated Paul's disappearance – the action that had precipitated everything since – and now, if anyone knew her name, her involvement, it would have to be Seymour. But, as O'Connell had said, even if he knew her name, he would be the last person to offer it to anyone investigating Palmer's death. And then she almost fainted as she realised what she and O'Connell had missed – that Seymour would have every reason to see her silenced. That would give him total protection, could no doubt easily be arranged, and the death of a publisher's agent in Oxford, no doubt made to look like an accident, would have no obvious connection to Palmer's murder. Kate felt panic once again rising, engulfing her. Another glass of wine was this time accompanied by two tranquilliser tablets, normally taken only to help her sleep on long flights. Now scared that panic attacks could be dangerous she sat, immobile, traumatised, waiting for Paul to return.

Paul arrived around 5 pm, a mere five minutes after getting Kate's message. He was shocked beyond measure when he saw her huddled up in a corner of their sofa, her arms loosely wrapped around herself. He had never seen her in such a state – normally a quite striking presence in any company. His alarm grew as she looked up at him, stress written all over her face, but didn't rise off the sofa to greet him. He sat beside her and put his arm around her. She leant into him, but for the moment had no words; and Paul knew now was not the moment for him to say anything either. They sat silently, neither knowing how to begin.

Eventually Kate sat up straight. I may be in some trouble" she said.

"Only if you feel up to explaining" Paul replied. "maybe just some TLC first?"

"No" said Kate. "I've got to tell you – I'll go mad if I don't." And then, as calmly and completely as she could, she told Paul everything that had happened to her since she headed off to Northern Ireland only a few days – but it seemed like weeks – before: the hook up with the O'Connells, as planned, Palmer's betrayal of the whole operation, Kate being picked up by Declan O'Connell as she left, and their plan to get Victor O'Connell and his men back. She omitted to say that Declan had come close to killing her; and stressed that her thinking had been that if she could facilitate putting Declan in contact with Palmer, he could get his team back and get her tapes. She then explained, in painful detail, what had happened at Palmer's flat that morning, Palmer's indifference to being threatened, because Kate could not get access to the remaining tape without him; and O'Connell would lose all his men if he tried to force Palmer to release them. Kate had, however, managed that, and then O'Connell shot Palmer dead – had planned to all along. She ended with the fear now permeating her body, that while no-one still alive might know of her involvement, or if they did, they would have every reason to keep quiet about her, the Prime Minister, Seymour, who must, she thought, have known what Palmer was up to would, if he knew her identity, have a strong reason to arrange a fatal accident. And there was nothing she could do about it. She could hardly go to the police with such a story. If she persisted they'd lock her up as quite insane. And if someone did reveal her role, they'd lock her up as at least an accessory to murder. "I can't deal with this" she concluded. "I don't know what to do. All I can think of is to disappear somehow, go abroad, change my name, just start again…." Her voice trailed off, perhaps because she knew, even as she said this, that it was entirely fanciful, a way of not facing the reality of the situation.

Paul heard her out in silence. His mind was already moving into problem-solving mode, but he had the good sense to realise that this was not – at least not yet – what Kate wanted or needed. He kept his arm around her, gently moving some hair away from where it had fallen before her eyes.

"Let me think about all this" he said. "There will be a way through it. For the moment, let's just concentrate on your comfort and your safety. Let's take it a day at a time, and today you are quite safe with me. I'll be with you all the time; and we can talk more tomorrow about what to do." He might have tried more soothing words, thought Paul, but knew they would sound hollow. Maybe any words would be ineffectual, but Kate gave him a very slight, rueful look, that nonetheless indicated acquiescence.

"I've told Janice that I'll go into work tomorrow" she said. Given the situation, Paul wasn't sure whether this was wise, but this was not the time for debate.

"Fine" he said. "I'll come in with you, and then let's meet for lunch; we can start unravelling the whole thing."

"Okay" agreed Kate. "I'll have a shower, let's eat early, and I'll try to sleep. It may take some time."

CHAPTER 51

Kate and Paul stayed up long enough to watch the ten o'clock news, but there was no mention of Palmer. Either he hadn't been missed, or missed enough to cause concern; or the matter was being kept secret for the moment. Nor, after a restless night, was there anything on the early news the next morning. This only underscored Kate's sense of disconnect from the previous day's events, but she knew this would not last. Paul walked to work with her, less than ten minutes, and arranged to pick her up there for lunch at the long-established but still somehow fashionable Brasserie Blanc, a couple of minutes from Kate's office. Kate spent the morning busying herself with her regular publishing work, as best she could, but she was very aware that she was not fully functioning, and Janice, though saying nothing, was quite concerned at Kate's degree of distraction.

Paul and Kate arrived at the restaurant shortly after one pm, and Paul immediately consulted the BBC News on his phone. And there it was. The Prime Minister's Senior Press Adviser, Andrew Palmer had been found dead at his flat in Notting Hill. The police had not yet put out an official statement, but it was rumoured that his flat had been burgled; and speculated that Palmer might have unexpectedly interrupted the burglary during the day. A statement from the Prime Minister would be forthcoming. There were no other details, not even how Palmer had died.

Paul could see how distressed Kate was but, perhaps worse, how resigned she looked. Having ordered some lunch Paul decided it was time to take the initiative, something one very rarely ever had to do where Kate was concerned.

"I've done a lot of thinking" he said. "Is now a good time for a briefing?" Kate even managed a small smile at Paul's terminology but nodded. "Okay, the bottom line is that I really do not think that anyone is coming after you on this; and there's a good chance you will hear nothing more. I'll explain. Palmer's operation was so illegal that, if he were found to have orchestrated it, he'd have gone to prison for a very long time. We know he is not a fool, so I don't think he would have involved anyone in Whitehall in this, except he would have had to have Seymour's say-so. So, I think Seymour - apart from the IRA and they won't be talking - will be the only person who will know that this is not a robbery gone wrong. It's him we have to focus on. Now, there is no reason why Palmer would have mentioned you at all, as the means to contacting the IRA. It's an operational detail that Seymour wouldn't need to know. If he did mention the way he planned to get to the IRA, there's no reason why he would have mentioned your name; and even if he did, who were you in all this? a means of contact. You had no role once his men had met up with the O'Connells. In fact, you left. But for the bad luck of getting caught by Declan O'Connell, you would have been back here days ago, simply not involved any further with Palmer. So why would Seymour even think you might have been at Palmer's flat? And, like O'Connell said to you, even if he suspected that, he wouldn't want any investigation to discover what you know. So, there's non-one with any motive to mention you to the police, quite the reverse."

"I can see that" said Kate "but that last point terrifies me. If Seymour doesn't want me talking to anyone, isn't he going to want me to disappear?"

"I don't think so" said Paul. "In fact I'm sure not, because Seymour will know that at the moment, no-one is going to connect you to any of this. But if you were to be harmed, he'd have to worry that you had told someone, someone like me, maybe even a lawyer, and everything would come out. From his point of view, the less attention on you the better. To put it another way, the very best outcome, from Seymour's point of view, is that this is put down to a burglary gone wrong. Very sad, but nothing to do with him or any political objectives that he and Palmer might have had. Don't you think that's right? I'm not just trying to cheer you up" he concluded, with a small smile.

Kate sat silently for a while, thinking over what Paul had said; and she had to admit that it did make a lot of sense. Coupled with the fact that there would be absolutely nothing of a forensic nature to link her to Palmer's flat even if the police had known who to check such evidence against, she might just be okay. Eventually she nodded. "It does make sense" she said. "I just hope to God you're right. Anyway, there is nothing we can do. We will just have to sit tight and hope that the police go for the obvious, if completely false, explanation."

When they arrived, Kate had not felt like eating anything, but Paul's line of thinking must have had some traction with her, because she began to feel a little hungry. They had a pleasant lunch, even talked a little about other things – his work, her work – and then Paul walked her back to her office.

"Call me when you are ready to leave," said Paul. I'll make sure I'm in my office not the lab, and I'll cycle over to pick you up."

"You don't need to do that" said Kate, but Paul indicated this was non-negotiable. "Thanks" she added. Somehow this very minor act of consideration moved her close to tears but, with her emotions having been through the shredder in the last twenty-four hours, it wasn't perhaps surprising.

That evening there was a lot more news. A police spokesperson said that Palmer had been shot; and that belongings had been stolen from his safe. To the rather too confirmatory question from a journalist, as to whether the police thought Palmer had encountered a burglary in progress, she got a short "yes". A little later there was a statement from Seymour, saying that Palmer had been a giant of support to the government, a dedicated official, a close colleague and a good friend as well. Seymour was devastated by his death, which would leave the government so much the poorer for the loss of his expertise. All in all a very glowing testimony, though both Paul and Kate wondered just how many others, any others at all, would endorse much of this. It was quite openly known how ruthless Palmer could be, and perhaps rather few would be remotely troubled by his passing. Seymour ended by expressing the ardent hope that whoever was responsible for this crime would be brought to justice.

There was nothing noteworthy about this final comment. It was no more than anyone might have said in such circumstances, a platitude, even if mildly comforting. But both Paul's and Kate's spirits, quite independently, rose as this tripped off Seymour's tongue. Both saw that the other had responded in similar fashion. Quite why was hard to fathom – it weas just a predictable platitude. But would Seymour have said it unless it was, not a steer but, at some subconscious level, a note of support for what the police had assessed was likely to be a burglary? The logic was unclear, but Paul and Kate had a much better night's sleep than the previous day.

Over the next two days, Kate's life began to return to normal, both in terms of her work schedules and her mental capacities and emotional resilience. She still worried from time to time about the potential aftermath of Palmer's death, but at some deeper level, her psyche, her soul perhaps, started to relax, little by little; and there were even glimpses of a sunny upland to which she might return. It was then that Declan called her.

"It's me" he said, which could have been a pointless tautology but, because of the accent, iy immediately informed Kate who was calling. Kate was about to say an hello, her nerves already beginning to tauten, but Declan O'Connell pushed straight on. "It's been nearly four days now, and there is no sign of ……the people I was expecting. Something has gone badly wrong." There was a long pause.

"I don't know what to say" was Kate's highly accurate response. "I don't understand."

"Neither do I" replied O'Connell "but not one of them has appeared."

"Could Palmer's call have been some sort of hoax?" asked Kate.

"I wondered that" said O'Connell, "but I don't think so. There was only one number on that phone; and I heard the guy answer at the other end. You heard what Palmer said, about early delivery. If the man at the other end of the phone wasn't whoever orchestrated the kidnap, then none of that would have made any sense. So, I'm sure the call was legit."

"So why hasn't he done what Palmer asked?" was Kate's obvious but not very helpful question.

"I don't know. Maybe Seymour knew more than we thought and, with Palmer dead, has somehow made contact, somehow overruled what Palmer said?"

"But that just doesn't make sense" said Kate. "The Prime Minister will never get involved in conversation with a bunch of mercenaries carrying out a highly illegal operation. He just wouldn't be that stupid."

"I agree" said O'Connell, But in that case, I just can't explain it."

"What will you do?" asked Kate

"There isn't much – nothing – I can do, except wait, and hope to God that they are still alive. Palmer threatened to kill them if we started a new campaign, and he's dead, so I've no way of knowing whether that threat remains or not - our hands are still tied." Kate registered that a 'new campaign' might mean death and mutilation for a lot of innocent people; and it was a sign of how far down a terrible road she had travelled – been forced to travel - that she didn't even think to comment, still less register any horror at O'Connell's words. Meanwhile, O'Connell continued. "But, if you think of anything, Kate, anything that might lead us to the bastards who did this, let me know straight away."

"I will" replied Kate. "I'm not hopeful, but I'll think it through. Meanwhile, as you say, let's just hope they are released as soon as the referendum is over.

Kate did give the matter some thought that evening, and talked it over with Paul, but she could think of no way to even start to find out who Palmer had employed to deal with the IRA leadership. Plus, it also struck her, was keeping Northern Ireland in the United Kingdom *so* important for Seymour and Palmer to have played such a dangerous game? In any event, while it was obviously critical for O'Connell, she couldn't see that it may any difference to Paul's and her hope that she was in the clear. She would later have cause to look back on that as being more naïve than she could possibly have imagined.

CHAPTER 52

The next morning, around 8 am., while Kate and Paul were having a quick breakfast together, before heading off to their respective offices, the front door bell rang . Kate answered it. On the door step were a woman and a man, maybe mid-thirties and mid-forties, both smartly and soberly dressed, and with rather expressionless faces.

"Miss Kimball?" asked the woman.

"Yes" replied Kate, feeling her whole body tensing up.

"I'm Detective Sergeant Miller, from the Thames Valley Police. This is my identification." She held out a wallet with a card that included a photograph, but Kate was already too stressed to look it at all closely. "And this is Detective Inspector Leyton from the Metropolitan Police." The man held out a similar looking identification.

"What is this about?" Kate managed to say, in a slightly hoarse voice, realising as she said it that it did not remotely sound like someone who was genuinely surprised to be confronted at 8 am by two police officers.

"We would like to ask you some questions" said DS Miller in a polite, quite respectful tone.

"What about?" was Kate's still more tense repetition of her first question.

"We'd prefer to put our questions to you at a police station, if you would accompany us" replied Miller, still very calm and polite in manner.

"Why can't you ask them here?" asked Kate, trying, without a great deal of success to get back onto something like equal terms in the conversation.

"I can see that that would be much more convenient" said Miller, "but we would like to have a proper recording of the interview, so we'd be grateful if you accompanied us." Her tone continued to match the reasonableness, as she saw it, of her request.

"Do I have to?" asked Kate. DI Leyton spoke for the first time.

"We would much prefer that you accompany us voluntarily" he said, rather mimicking Miller's respectful tone, "but if not, then I have a warrant for your arrest, in which case, yes, you would have to."

At these words, Kate felt herself starting to feel giddy. Fortunately, she was saved from having to make an immediate reply as Paul appeared from the kitchen. "What's going on?" he asked, in a fairly peremptory manner.

"These people are from the police" said Kate, a sense of panic by now pulsating through her body. "They want to question me, not here but at a police station, and say they will arrest me if I don't go voluntarily."

"What is it about?" Paul said to the two police officers, going to stand right in front of them.

"I'm sorry but we can't discuss that until we start a proper interview at the station" replied Leyton.

"I don't think that is good enough" said Paul, somewhat belligerently. "You must be able to give us some idea of why you are here."

"I'm afraid not, sir" said Leyton, not for a second dropping the polite tone that both officers had adopted since they arrived. "Now, Miss Kimball, if you would be so good as to collect whatever you wish to bring, we have a car waiting." Kate looked, in utter despair, at Paul.

"What can I do?" she asked him, aware of the uselessness of the question.

"Where are you taking her?" Paul asked Leyton.

"It's a Metropolitan Police matter" said Leyton. "DS Miller is here from the Thames Valley police because Miss Kimball lives here. I will escort her to Charing Cross police station in London, as the issues we wish to discuss arise in the Met's jurisdiction, but DS Miller will accompany us."

"Does she not have a right to legal representation, if you are going to interview her?" Paul asked, now fully into damage limitation mode.

"She does indeed" replied Leyton. "We can arrange for a solicitor to join her while we drive to London." Paul instantly knew that he could not allow Kate to be represented by some unknown duty roster solicitor in London, of equally unknown experience or concern for a client parachuted onto him or her. But, at the same time, the only solicitors he and Kate knew at all were ones who had dealt with property conveyance in Oxford, when they were selling and buying their properties – hardly any use for what must, of course, be a criminal case in London. But then, a lightbulb flashed in his brain.

"No, that won't do" he said, in as definitive a voice as he could muster. "Kate, I think you should go with them – you don't appear to have any choice – but, listen to me, do not say a word, not a word about anything, absolutely nothing, to anybody, until your legal representation, which I will get onto straight away, arrives." Kate had a slightly blank stare, which Paul couldn't interpret but it didn't look good. "Kate, have you got that?"

Kate, fortunately, was beginning to get herself together. Recognition that she would have to go to London curiously helped her to regain some equanimity, perhaps illustrating the near-universal truth that it is often uncertainty, more than any particular outcome that causes the worst anxiety.

"Who will you get?" she asked.

"Just leave it with me" said Paul. "If you get a coat and your bag, I'll get onto it immediately." Kate paused a moment, seemed to nod to herself and disappeared into a back room of the flat.

"Please do not attempt to interview Miss Kimball until her legal representation arrives." He said. "I'm sure she will wish to co-operate, so don't force her into being uncooperative initially." Neither detective responded to this request.

"Please get her solicitor there as soon as possible" said Leyton. "We can only hold off for so long. Then we will provide a solicitor ourselves."

"Give me a number and I will keep you fully updated" said Paul, whereupon Leyton pulled out a card and handed it to Paul.

"That would be helpful" he said. "Keep me informed, and then I will have your number if I need to contact you." At this point, Kate re-appeared. Paul kissed her.

"Try not to worry, my love" he said. "Help is on its way; and I'll come down to London so I'll be there when they have finished their questions." She returned his smile with a rather wan one of her own; and then she was gone, across their forecourt and into an ordinary saloon car plus driver, waiting by the kerb, Kate in the back with Miller, Leyton in the front passenger seat.

As soon as Kate had gone, Paul rang the Lodge of Wadham College, where he held the college post that accompanied his University post. He told the Porter on duty who it was that was calling, and asked for the home number of his close friend and colleague at the college, the Fellow in Law, Peter Watson. He then rang Watson.

"Peter, I'm really sorry to bother you so early" he said, when Watson answered "but I've got a crisis, and a great favour to ask." Watson immediately said he'd help in any way he could. "Kate had been arrested", said Paul "or rather she hasn't been, but under the threat of arrest has had to go to a police station in London. I desperately need a lawyer to meet up with her and represent her."

"What on earth can it be about?" asked Peter, knowing Kate quite well, and finding it rather incomprehensible that she would ever be involved in anything more serious than speeding.

"They haven't said" replied Paul but, absolutely just between you and me, I know it's to do with the murder of Andrew Palmer."

"But that's.... I don't know what to say. Surely it can't be right?"

"She is totally innocent" said Paul "but the immediate thing is to get her a lawyer. All they have offered is some duty hack. She needs more determined support than that, and I don't know any solicitors with the needed expertise. Can you help? I know it's a lot to ask, and no notice at all, but we really are at our wits' end."

There was a prolonged pause before Watson replied. "Look, Paul, I'd do anything I could to help, and I once practiced Law, but I'm purely an academic lawyer now, mainly working on Constitutional Law. I'd be hopelessly out of date on her rights, proper procedure, etc. I'm really not a good person to ask."

Paul's spirits, if it were possible, fell even lower than they had been. "Is there anyone at all you know who might be able to help, and today?" He asked, knowing how completely hopeless the question sounded.

"Well, I don't think......." Watson trailed off. "Actually, I've just had a thought. It's totally off the wall, but it's worth a try. Do you know Charles Irwin or, rather, know of him, Sir Charles as he now is? He chaired the Commission which produced the Irwin Report, on the Met's handling of the environmental protester riots two years ago. I was the

Commission's token academic, and Charles thinks he owes me a big favour. He doesn't, but he thinks he does - I'll explain later – and he is one of the top criminal lawyers around. He would never normally be involved in a case this early but if he wants to pay off his supposed debt to me, big time, this could be his chance."

"That would be brilliant" said Paul, if he would, and if he can get free in time."

"Only one way to find out" replied Watson, "I'll try to contact him now. It may take a while, but I'll get back to you with any news. Okay?" Paul could barely express his gratitude, but got off the call to let Watson get going. Watson, for his part, immediately called Irwin's chambers in London. Having established that he was a former colleague and very good friend of Irwin's, he learnt from the Chambers Clerk that Sir Charles was due in at 9 am, but had several pre-trial meetings scheduled, starting as soon as he arrived.

"Could you just tell him that I called" said Watson, "that it is very urgent, and could I just have two minutes of his time on the phone before he starts his meetings?" This may or may not have been a familiar occurrence as far as the Clerk was concerned, but he showed not the slightest discomposure.

"I will pass that onto Sir Charles as soon as he arrives" he said, in a tone that indicated Watson could be assured this would happen. Watson thanked him profusely, and got ready to wait the half hour or so until 9 am.

At only just past the hour, his phone rang.

"Peter, what on earth have you got yourself into?" was Irwin's opening conversation piece. Watson quickly disabused Irwin that the crisis was anything to do with himself. He explained that the partner of one of his fellow dons at Wadham – a high-up with Oxford University Press and the last person on earth who would have anything to do with crime or criminals, had been taken from Oxford to London to be interviewed by the Met. She desperately needed powerful legal representation from someone who knew what they were doing. He said that he knew it was an unreasonable request, but could Charles help her?

"You, or rather she, needs someone now?" asked Irwin.

"She is on route to Charing Cross police station as we speak" responded Watson. "Her partner has told her to say nothing until she has spoken to a lawyer, but there is only so long before they allocate her someone, so they can start questioning her."

"Peter, I'd like to help, but that is going to be difficult" said Irwin. I've got wall-to-wall meetings scheduled, and they tend to be time-sensitive, if not urgent." Watson could sense that he was losing Irwin. "What is she being questioned about" he added.

"Andrew Palmer, the PM's Press supremo, who was murdered a few days go." Watson had the good sense to realise that this reply had a real 'wow' factor; and he let his response to Irwin's question hang in the ether.

"Good God!" exclaimed Irwin. "I can see why you rang me. Let me think" There was a pause, no doubt of only a few seconds, but it seemed much longer to Watson.

"I'll tell you what" Irwin said eventually. "Can you go and hold her hand this morning, and I will re-schedule my afternoon. I could be there by around 1.30 pm"

"Charles, you are an Ace. I can postpone a couple of tutorials and head off straight away. I presume she should continue to keep quiet until you arrive?"

"Yes and no" said Irwin. "Now, this is very important. Very. Ask to speak to her alone – demand it if they cause any fuss. Then say this to her. First, with one exception that I'll come to, she is to say 'no comment' to any and all questions, other than her name and address. They will try to get round this –standard technique – by saying 'we know that you did this or that, we know you were in such and such a vicinity', and so on, trying to indicate that there is no point in her not answering their questions. When they do this, she must say, firmly, 'no, you don't know that'. That's all. Just 'no, you don't know that'. Have you got that?"

"I have" said Watson, "the point being?"

"Their approach will tell us what they know or claim to know, but what we need to know is *how* they know, whether it is real evidence or just them fishing. If she – what's her name by the way?"

"Kate Kimball" said Watson.

If Miss Kimball *asks* how they know, the police will merely say they are conducting the interview. But if she just contradicts them, not the facts – that runs the risk of them catching her out as lying – but contradicts that they know what they claim to know, they will get very frustrated. I've seen it a number of times before. And that is when they will start trying to show her that they do know this or that; and that will start to tell us how strong or weak any evidence against her is."

"Got it" said Watson. "I'll see you around 1.30 pm. I can't say how much I appreciate this, Charles."

"And you didn't once mention that I owe you" Irwin chuckled. "I appreciate that! One other thing. Tell them you are temporarily holding the fort, that her lawyer will be there around 1.30 pm but do not, absolutely do not tell them who it is. Let's not give them any forewarning of what will, I'm sure, be something of a shock to them." He chuckled again.

Watson confirmed that he had got all that and they ended the call. Before heading off for London, Watson called the college to postpone his tutorials – his excuse, if he ever got to be able to tell his students, would do wonders for his street cred – and then called Paul. He explained what had been arranged. Paul was once again effusive in his thanks.

"Can you tell me how Kate has got involved in this" asked Watson, "or at least, why the police might think she is involved?"

"It's just too long a story to tell right now," said Paul, apologetically. "It goes right back to two years ago, when I went missing, if you remember. Call me when you are on the train, and I'll talk you through the whole thing. Okay?"

"Will do" replied Watson. He was about to ring off when Paul asked a question.

"What is the favour that Sir Charles thinks, incorrectly apparently, that he owes you? I only ask because it must be quite a favour to get him to drop everything for Kate."

"Make no mistake," replied Watson, "Andrew Palmer's name got him. Favour or no favour, I don't think he would have gone for it but for Palmer's murder – you can't get much more high profile at the moment than that. But, for what it's worth the supposed favour goes back to the

Irwin Report. Charles assessed that several members of his Commission of Inquiry were either just out to get the Met, or worried that anything less than a damming report would be dismissed by the media as a whitewash; and so, in his view, they did not remotely treat the evidence properly. He saw me as one of the few who was prepared to look at the evidence objectively which, properly assessed, showed that there had been some cock-ups by the Met, none major, and a lot of bad luck in terms of what the protesters were doing versus what the Met, quite legitimately was trying to do. Anyway, he sees me as someone who, at some risk to my reputation, stuck to their guns on this; and that the report, as a result, was fair and accurate, or at least a lot fairer and more accurate than it would have been. We all got some stick of course, but over time, the report has stood up well, Charles' reputation has been enhanced, note the knighthood, and he thinks he owes much of it to me. I just think I was doing what I was asked to do, but if the result is that he will help now, that's great. But I still thought he would decline, until he heard what the case was; and then – no problem. Anyway, I must get going." They rang off.

All this time, Kate was sitting in silence and in such a state of anxiety and stress that she felt as if she would either feint or explode. The dilemma which kept going round and round in her head, one she could kick herself for not trying to resolve earlier, in case she was questioned, was what, when it came to it, to tell the police who would interview her. Simply denying any knowledge of, or acquaintance with Palmer would be pointless, indeed foolhardy, because they had obviously somehow linked her to him. So that suggested that she would have to tell them about her trip to Northern Ireland at his directing. But then, that would generate the inevitable questions, why her, and why agree to go? She could answer neither without the tape recording – the wretched tape recording in a safety deposit box in Hounslow -becoming known; and that would probably be it as far as she was concerned. Even if she could dream up some other explanation – Palmer wasn't round to gainsay her – there was still the question of whether to admit to having been at his flat the day he was murdered. If she denied it, but they had some evidence that she was there, then she would have been found to be lying to the police, which would massively worsen her situation; but if she admitted it, then she would have to tell them that it was Declan who was responsible for the murder; and she didn't give much for her life expectancy if she did that. These questions just kept going round and round in her head, without resolution. The only relief, and it would no doubt be very temporary, was that a lawyer was coming to help; until then, she was saying nothing.

CHAPTER 53

Charing Cross police station is a very large, remarkably imposing four-storey building, just of the Strand in London, built entirely of white stone, almost completely covered in large period windows, and with an extremely grand porticoed entrance. At another time, Kate might have wanted to stop to take in the architecture, but she barely noticed it on this occasion as she was led into the building by DI Leyton, with DC Miller by his side. Some sort of processing of her admission occurred, but she barely registered it, as she tried to prepare herself for the ordeal to come. The formalities completed, she was led to an interview room on the second floor, rather bare but with a large table, recording equipment and five reasonably comfortable chairs, four round the table, two each side and one against the wall. DC Miller took this, and it was clear that she was only present to represent the Thames Valley force and, more importantly, ensure a woman was in the room besides Kate. Leyton was joined on his side of the table by another man, introduced as Detective Sergeant Cooper of the Metropolitan police. Kate was invited to sit on the other side of the table and, when they were all settled, DS Cooper turned on the recording equipment, announced the date and time, who was in the room, and looked to DI Leyton to begin.

"As you will no doubt know" said Leyton, "Andrew Palmer, the Prime Minister's senior Press Secretary, was found dead at his flat in Notting Hill last Monday. Could you tell me what you know about this please?"

Part of Kate wanted to say that she didn't know what he was talking about, what it could be to do with her, there was clearly some problem of mistaken identity, but another part of her recognised that that road would lead to disaster. But she absolutely couldn't tell them what she knew. "I really don't want to be difficult" she managed to say, in a restrained voice, "but I have been advised not to say anything until I have had a chance to consult a lawyer, and then have him or her present. I believe someone is on their way here now."

"I understand that" replied Leyton, "but you do at least know what we are talking about, do you not?"

"I'm sorry, but all I can say now is that I have no comment to make; that must remain the case until I see my lawyer. I'm sorry" she added rather lamely.

"Well, we have good reason to believe that you were with Mr. Palmer the day he died. It would be useful if you could at least confirm that. We can go into more detail later."

This time, Kate didn't respond, at least not verbally, at all. She just looked at Leyton briefly, shook her head and looked down at her hands, gripped together with tension in her lap. "It is not clear to me" said Layton "why you should not be able to offer even a minimum amount of co-operation." It was said politely, but the threat that this was indicative of something to hide was clear and rather ominous.

"I just wish to speak to my lawyer first" said Kate. "I believe that is my right, proper procedure, and it was no doubt established for good reasons. So, could we just stop now? I'm sure it won't be long before we can proceed."

Leyton was only too aware that, recorded or not, anything Kimball said before her lawyer arrived would be challenged as inadmissible. He just hoped, while she was no doubt still feeling very anxious and probably flustered, that she would reveal some useful information they could return to with the lawyer present. But it seemed clear that this wasn't, on this occasion, going to work.

"Very well" he said. "We will leave you here with DS Miller and return in an hour. You have your phone, so could you find out when we may expect your legal representative?" Kate nodded her assent. "Good. In the meantime, I'll arrange some coffee for you both." With that somewhat unexpected gesture of goodwill, he and DS Cooper left.

As soon as they left, Kate phoned Paul, who explained that Peter Watson, whom Kate knew quite well, would assist by late morning. But he was only temporary, to give immediate advice. By 1.30 pm she would have one of the top criminal barristers in Britain, Sir Charles Irwin, to act for her, but that she must not reveal this until he arrived. Kate felt a slight upturn in her spirits for the first time since the doorbell had rung at eight am that morning.

"How on earth did you manage that?" she said, genuinely amazed. Paul explained that Watson had called in a favour, omitting to mention that Watson thought it was more the likely prominence of the case that had hooked Irwin in. That was the last thing Kate needed to hear just at the moment.

"I'm just heading off for London" he said "and will wait for you at the police station, no matter how long they take. Just do whatever Peter and Sir Charles say, and I'm sure things will start to improve." He tried to sound confident, but neither of them found his words that convincing. But at least Team Kate was up and running.

On his way to London, Watson rang Paul to get some background. It took nearly half an hour for Paul to explain how Kate had ever got involved with the IRA, had been forced by Palmer, under the threat of her being 'disappeared' or worse, to make a recording incriminating her in the IRA's activities and, now, using that had used her as an intermediary with the IRA. One of them had shot Palmer in front of Kate, but she had had no idea that that was going to happen. With a copy of the tape recording still in a safe deposit box, it might be very difficult to persuade a jury that Kate was blameless. Watson wasn't by any means sure that he had grasped the whole story, but that would be for Irwin to sort out. What was clear was that Kate definitely should not say anything until Irwin had briefed her.

On arrival at the police station, he explained why he was there, and was shown up to the interview room where Kate and DS Miller had sat in silence since DI Leyton and DS Cooper had left. Kate was clearly pleased to see him, but still in a state of extreme anxiety, still failing to see how she could ever extricate herself from the catastrophic situation she was in. Watson asked Miller to give him and Kate some privacy, so that he could advise his client, to which Miller agreed, but said she would be just outside the door. Watson then told Kate that he would explain to whoever was in charge that he was in a temporary capacity, that her legal adviser would be there by 1.30 pm, and that they should try to delay their interview until then. If the police didn't agree, he would be with her until then, but in that case, Irwin had instructions for her until he arrived. He then explained how she should handle the questions that would be put to her, and why. He said it might not be easy, but she must stick to Irwin's instructions. In fact, Kate felt more relief from what Watson said to her than perhaps was wise, but it was the relief of having some sort of strategy, however negative or provocative. Anything was better than the paroxysm of uncertainty she had been feeling up until then. Watson then suggested that they not attempt to call Miller back until she came back in – every minute that passed being another minute without Leyton putting awkward questions to her.

Twenty-five minutes after leaving them alone. Miller returned to say that DI Leyton and DS Cooper were returning to continue the interview. They duly arrived, announced details of the interview for the tape recording, including who was present and then Leyton looked meaningfully at Kate. Before he could start, however, Watson spoke.

"I should explain, Detective Inspector Leyton, that I am here in a purely temporary capacity. Miss Kimball's lawyer will be here at 1.30 pm to represent her. You will appreciate that he didn't know or expect to be needed until this morning. Could I therefore suggest, or rather request, that this interview be postponed until then, or shortly after, to give time for him to talk to his client. The delay will not be much more than a lunchtime break."

Leyton sat passively, silent, thinking. "I cannot see why, as Miss Kimball has representation, we cannot start now, with some preliminary questions, until one o'clock. We can then have a one hour break, recommencing at two p.m. by which time she will have had ample time to consult her lawyer" Watson was about to argue the point, but Leyton held up his hand to stop him. "I'm afraid that is settled. So, Miss Kimball, I ask you again, what do you know of Andrew Palmer's death?"

"I have no comment" she said, still sounding more apologetic than she wished. Leyton looked at Watson with what was definitely a scowl, but kept addressing Kate.

"Well" he said "could you at least tell me if you knew him? If you don't you could say so, and save us all a lot of time and trouble."

"No comment" Kate repeated, this time in a slightly more forceful manner; and Leyton saw that these attempts to get her to say something, anything at all just to get her started, would fail. Which is when he went for exactly the strategy that Irwin had foreseen.

"Well, let me tell you then" he said. "You did know him. We know that. Moreover, we know you met him shortly before he died." Kate rose to the moment, as instructed.

"No" she said deliberately, "You don't know that." Watson fought to remain completely impassive as Leyton looked momentarily knocked out of his stride.

"Why do you say that?" he countered. To which Kate, now more in control of herself repeated "no comment." Leyton stared at her, part angry, part bemused but not without an element of menace. There was silence for a while; and then Leyton just nodded to DS Cooper. The detective sergeant clearly understood what this meant. He picked up a folder that had lain on the desk before him and took a set of photographs. Leyton picked up the first.

"For the benefit of the tape, I am showing Miss Kimball photo AP-C1" He put the photo in front of Kate.

"Would you care to tell me who you can see in this photo?" he asked her. Some part of Kate wanted, very obviously, to avoid even looking at the photo, but she couldn't resist the stronger urge to see what Leyton had. Having looked at it, she once again said "no comment."

"Given you reticence" said Leyton, "let me tell what *I* see. I see Andrew Palmer, you, and another man walking away from St. James's Park to Horse Guards Parade. For your information, it was taken from one of the many CCTV cameras in the area. There's rather a lot of them because it is so close to Downing Street." He then laid two more photos in front of Kate. "These were taken shortly after that first one; and show the three of you getting into a car, driven by a fourth person, and heading off northwards. There are several more photos which track the car as it drives north – I won't bother you with those – but this one – he put another one in front of Kate – shows the car turning into the street where Palmer lives; and where, shortly afterwards, he was shot dead. So, please don't tell me that I don't know you knew Palmer, and were with him shortly before he died. If you plan to talk to me at any point, now would be a good moment."

Kate said nothing, feeling quite numb again. It wasn't a surprise that the police had used CCTV evidence, but she had not expected to be picked up by it quite so easily. But of course, she realised, they would have interviewed Palmer's protection officer. He would not have seen Kate – he'd deliberately been removed from the scene beforehand - but he would have told them where to look in terms of CCTV surveillance. As she sat there, not even managing a 'no comment', Watson picked up the photos and looked at them closely.

"What makes you think this woman is Miss Kimball?" he said. "These photos are quite fuzzy. There may be some superficial similarity, but this could be one of any number of women with a roughly similar build." He wanted to add that he didn't think any jury would rely on these photos, but that seemed to be conceding too much about where this investigation might end up; and he left the point hanging.

"A very good point" was Leyton's surprising and alarming reply at once. "Indeed, you might ask why, having seen these photos, it occurred to us that the woman might be a publishing agent from Oxford, hitherto unknown to the police." Watson would have liked to parrot a 'why indeed' but the trap was far too obvious. "Let me explain" continued Leyton, with just an ounce too much self-satisfaction for either Kate or Watson to doubt that this was not going to be good.

"As you would expect, we trawled through Palmer's phone records. Having interviewed his secretary, we could understand almost all of them. But there was one to the offices of Oxford University Press; and another one to the Perch Inn just outside Oxford. We don't know the content of these calls, but it seemed reasonable to assume that Palmer, who I have to say very rarely left London, had arranged to meet someone from OUP at the Perch. We called in with a picture of Palmer and asked if anyone remembered him having lunch or dinner there, with someone else. A long shot, given they have hundreds of people eating and drinking there every week, and I thought we were out of luck; and then a waiter said that he did vaguely remember Palmer – though he was sure it wasn't that name – because he remembered that when his guest – a woman - arrived, they seemed to be having quite an argument – she didn't even want to join him. But the real reason he remembered wasn't just the argument – he remembered the woman's name, partly because it was unusual, but mainly because it was the same as the main character in his favourite film, *The Fugitive,* in which Harrison Ford plays someone called Richard Kimble. He was sure that was the name that Palmer, by whatever name he called himself, had given as the guest he was expecting. So, that was a real stroke of luck. We then checked back at OUP and, what would you know, there was a Kate Kimball on the staff. We got our picture from the OUP website and, imagine our surprise when we saw it and compared it to the CCTV footage from Horse Guards Parade. So, Miss Kimball, you may 'no comment' as much as you like – that is your right – but given the evidence, I think you would be much better advised to tell us what you know."

It was small consolation to Kate that Irwin's strategy had worked so well – they now very much knew what Leyton knew and how he knew it – but it was, she thought, utterly damming. Not any longer having much confidence in sticking to what she had been advised, she looked at Watson. He leaned across and whispered "don't go off piste. Just 'no comment'." Kate nodded, grateful for the guidance, even if it was not very re-assuring.

"No comment" she repeated.

"You should perhaps look at the last photo I have here" said Leyton. "For the benefit of the tape, I am showing Miss Kimball photo AP-C7. This shows you getting out of the same car as before, near Paddington station, leaving the driver and the other man you were with previously. There is no sign of Andrew Palmer. From the timing, we think he probably was by then…" he deliberately left a short dramatic pause "…dead."

Kate's latest 'no comment', barely loud enough for the tape to pick up, sounded more like a confession she thought. Her spirits were now absolutely at rock bottom.

"This might be a good point to stop" said Leyton. "You can explain all this to your legal adviser when he arrives, and he might see that there is a better way forward for you, Miss Kimball. Interview terminated at twelve forty-two p.m. Mr Watson, Miss Kimball must remain here, but if you wish to get some lunch sandwiches for her, please do. We will continue at two p.m." With that, he gathered up the photos and, followed by DS Cooper, left the interview room. DS Miller, sphinx-like, remained in her chair by the wall. Watson discreetly nodded in her direction and then, turning his back to her, held up a finger to his lips. Further discussion would have to await Irwin's arrival.

CHAPTER 54

Sir Charles arrived at the police station a few minutes earlier than he had forecast and presented himself to the reception desk. The officer on duty did not recognise Irwin, but he certainly recognised his name; and said he would get someone to take Sir Charles to the first floor interview room. There, in the ever-presence of DS Miller, he greeted Watson like the long-lost friend that, in a manner of speaking he was. Watson then introduced him to Kate. When she thanked 'Sir Charles' for coming to her rescue, he quickly told her that 'Charles' was fine; and that they had no time to lose. At Irwin's invitation, with DS Miller once more outside the room, and with Irwin using a small tape recorder, Kate took him, as quickly as she could, through the convoluted circumstances that had led her to this interview room and the imminent re-engagement with DI Leyton.

She explained why and how her partner Paul Emmerson had disappeared after his scientific discoveries at Sellafield nuclear power station had threatened to topple the previous Prime Minister, Alan Gerrard; how her efforts to find Paul had led her to members of the Irish Republican Army. Paul had eventually been rescued, but in the process she, Kate, had been forced, by Palmer, to make a bogus tape recording supposedly incriminating her in murderous IRA activity. After the IRA had murdered Gerrard, Kate had hoped never to hear from anyone involved ever again. Then, a few weeks ago, Palmer, using the threat of releasing the tape, had forced her to act as a means of Palmer getting in contact with the current IRA leadership. Kate had hoped, again, that that would be the end of the matter – Palmer had promised her the tape in return for her help - but then he had double-crossed everyone.

He'd returned one copy of the tape, but another was in a safe deposit box that only Palmer could access; and while originally offering to help the IRA achieve a 'yes' vote in the forthcoming referendum on Northern Ireland leaving the UK, he had used a bunch of mercenaries to abduct the leading figures on the IRA Army Council – who had since disappeared completely – in order to block them from bombing their way to a 'yes' vote. She then took Irwin through the events the morning Palmer died – her plan, with Declan O'Connell, to force Palmer to give up the tape and release O'Connell's men, their failure on both fronts, and then the shock of O'Connell shooting Palmer dead, pre-meditated but a complete surprise to Kate. Finally, she summarised how Leyton and his team had tracked her down, what CCTV coverage they had seen, and what they knew. She concluded that, apart from assisting in getting Palmer to his home, where she hoped to recover the incriminating tape, she had at no time, as far as she could see, committed any sort of offence; but with her involvement with the IRA, her presence in Palmer's flat, and the tape, she'd be very lucky to convince a jury of that.

While she went through all this Irwin, despite taping it all, was furiously making notes on a small pad, page after page. Apart from a couple of points of clarification, he asked no questions, made no comments. When Kate had finished, he said he needed a few minutes to think, but two minutes later, DS Miller came in to say that DI Leyton was on his way.

"Ask him for five more minutes, please" said Irwin, and Miller went off again. She met Leyton and Cooper coming up the stairs. Leyton was still somewhat aghast and out of his stride at the news, from the reception desk officer, that Kate Kimball's Brief was none other than Sir Charles Irwin, he of the Irwin Commission and Irwin Report which had restored some counterweight to the Met's recently rather poor reputation. He couldn't begin to fathom how Kimball had managed to recruit such a heavyweight to her side, in such a short time, and without a solicitor having been engaged first – very odd - and he realised, just when he thought he was likely to make a breakthrough - having shown Kimball how hopeless her position was - how much more difficult it was going to be, even to arrest her, let alone secure a conviction. But he did still have one trick up his sleeve.

Feeling that it would be best to start on as good terms with Sir Charles as possible, Leyton, with Cooper in tow, went back downstairs and out for short walk, reflecting on how best to proceed. Clearly his attempts to get Kimball talking were unlikely to prosper with Irwin, one of the country's most respected QCs representing her. Even so, the evidence against her was already quite damming, and his team was by no means finished with their investigation. In particular, they needed to identify the man who had been with Kimball when they met Palmer in St. James's Park, but he felt reasonably confident that they would, maybe from Kimball. With Irwin looking over his shoulder, he would have to be very careful to play everything by the book, but he had no intention of letting that prevent a successful prosecution.

As a gesture of goodwill, he let Irwin have ten minutes or more before returning to the interview room. During this time, Irwin had said little, in fact nothing, but had been scribbling notes to himself, pausing to think, more scribbles. By the time Leyton came in, he had what Watson thought was a slightly self-satisfied smile. He wanted to see what developed, but understood that his involvement was now at an end. He said he would be off, said goodbye to Kate, Irwin and Leyton and left.

Leyton was about to turn on the room's recording machine when Irwin held up a hand to stop him.

"Before we start" he said "could I say something?" His tone was ultra-polite, but nonetheless, for Leyton, brooked no rejection. Leyton merely nodded. "I would like to suggest that this interview be postponed until tomorrow." Seeing the predictable look on Leyton's face, he ploughed straight on. "My client will then be prepared to make a statement as to her knowledge of events surrounding Andrew Palmer's death."

"I'm glad to hear that Miss Kimball is prepared to make a statement" said Leyton, but why not now? If it is to be a statement of the facts as she knows them, and not some contrived….." he was going to say 'fabrication' but, with Sir Charles Irwin QC opposite him he paused "….statement, then I fail to see why she cannot speak now."

"The reason," Irwin said in an almost apologetic tone "is that I have only just become acquainted with the facts about this case, and perhaps only some of them so far. I don't think my client should make a statement until I have been able to advise her, on her rights, on the importance of telling the truth and the consequences of not doing do, and that she should not feel any need to reveal matters that are not relevant to your inquiries." Leyton was not entirely sure what the significance of this last, opaque, reference was, but let it go.

"I trust any statement that your client makes, today or tomorrow, will be entirely truthful" he said, not concerned that this sounded rather pompous.

"I will make it clear" said Irwin "that while it is my responsibility to defend Miss Kimball's interests, I will not be supportive of, or in any way be party to anything that I know or suspect is false." Irwin was more than a match for DI Leyton when it came to being pompous.

"I'm sorry" said Leyton, in a tone that had no hint of apology, "but I think we should proceed. What you've said should be enough for Miss Kimball to know how to conduct herself."

"Well" said Irwin "I'm sorry too because, in that case, I will advise my client to say nothing at all. I do not, of course, know how your investigation is going, but I suspect that it will go a whole lot faster if you listen to what my client has to say; and I imagine, in such a high-profile case as this, that there will be a lot of pressure on you to make an arrest as soon as possible. But I cannot advise her to recount what she knows until I have had time to discuss the position with her. So, that is the situation; and I must leave it to you to decide how best to proceed."

So, thought Leyton, there it is – the carrot and stick. It was now abundantly clear that Kimball knew a lot, perhaps everything, about this case; and Irwin was certainly right that, if he could access that knowledge, he would probably wrap the case up a lot quicker than otherwise. But if she remained silent, evidence on whether she or the mystery man with her killed Palmer – and he was quite sure it must be one or the other - might prove difficult to find, at least to the standard that a judge would require. Plus, he was prepared to believe that Irwin meant what he said, about seeking to keep his suspect to the truth, not least because he would know just how difficult it was to keep a storyline consistent once one started lying about it.

While he pondered Irwin's offer, Kate sat silent but shocked and even a little incredulous. Irwin had said nothing to her about making a statement, still less getting her to agree that she would do so if the interview was delayed. The extreme anxiety she felt as to what she could or would say was, fortunately, just about matched by Irwin's reputation, and that he must have a very good reason for pursuing this course of action. He had clearly been thinking hard about what she had told him, but he hadn't had long – could he really have a plan to assist her or, better still, get her out of her predicament? The only certain thing was not to interrupt.

"Very well" said Leyton. "I'm not happy about it, but if you can assure me that we will get a proper statement from your client tomorrow, then I will postpone this interview until ten a.m. tomorrow morning?"

"Thank you" said Irwin. "I do think you will find that that turns out to be the best decision." The meeting concluded, Kate left the room with Irwin. As they headed downstairs Irwin suggested that they proceed straight away to his Chambers in Lincoln's Inn, to plan the next day's engagement before Kate returned to Oxford. Kate rang Paul, who said he would catch up with them at Irwin's chambers

"I am very grateful to you" said Kate, once they were in a taxi. "The stress has been… well… very stressful…" she trailed off.

"I'm more than happy to help" replied Irwin, "and I have a strategy – it's only half formed, and I need to finalise it – which you will need to follow tomorrow. It won't be that easy, and so we need to rehearse, this afternoon, and maybe again this evening, so that you will be word perfect by tomorrow morning. But I think we can materially reduce the risks to your freedom, maybe completely if we are lucky. Are you okay for this?" These were the most promising words anyone had said to her since the police had arrived on her doorstep, and Kate's response was bordering on enthusiastic

"If you direct, I can perform" she said with a smile.

CHAPTER 55

Irwin's Chambers, in Lincoln's Inn, close to Holborn station, were surprisingly small, but very elegantly furnished, with a Georgian partner's desk, well upholstered chairs and wall-to-wall bookshelves lined with heavyweight-looking law books. They met Paul in the reception area. Irwin ushered both of them into two large leatherbound arm chairs, and took a seat himself behind his desk. He poured them all a glass of mineral water.

"We have three tasks today" he said to Kate, eschewing any small talk. "First, I want you to go over the whole account again, and this time we are not under any time pressure. I want every single detail you can think of, whether it seems relevant to you or not. And I will be interrupting a lot, with questions as we go. By the end, I want to know everything you know, and I'm very happy to hear any assumptions, guesses and the like that you have, to fill in any gaps, but just make it clear what you know as opposed to what you suspect. Is that all okay?" Kate nodded.

"Second" Irwin continued, "I am going to write out your statement for tomorrow – you will just have to be patient while I do it. You can read it out tomorrow if you have to, but it would be much better if you could learn it overnight – it won't be that long – and just say it. That would have much greater impact. The key thing is that I want you to check that every sentence is true, literally speaking - it won't remotely help DI Leyton's investigation, but that is his problem, not ours. And then, third, we are going to rehearse every single question I can think of that he may put to you, and your answer to it. That may sound too demanding, but I don't think there are that many points that he can usefully put to you. Still all okay?" Again Kate nodded. "Fine, let's get started."

It took nearly two hours for Kate to describe, yet again, but this time in as much detail as she could, the sequence of events that lay behind her present situation, with Irwin puncturing her tale repeatedly, while once again scribbling notes to himself. In some ways Kate was emotionally exhausted by the process, but still stronger was the sense that she, or at least Irwin on her behalf, was making some progress. Why she should have such confidence in someone she had never even met before that afternoon, and only been faintly even aware he existed, she did not know;

but perhaps it was just that, without his plan, whatever it was, she was dead in the water, with no other support of any kind. In any event, she ploughed on, concluding with her being dropped at Paddington station the morning of Palmer's murder, Declan O'Connell then calling to say that none of the other members of the IRA whom Palmer's mercenaries had kidnapped had re-appeared; and then nothing more until DI Leyton and DS Miller had come calling. She added that she had stuck to the 'no comment' formular in her interviews prior to Irwin's arrival. With that, Irwin promised her a rest while he drafted her statement.

This took him about half an hour on is computer. He printed off two copies, and they then went through it together, line by line. Kate quickly saw what a subtly constructed piece it was – nothing that Leyton could fault her on, but substantially exonerating her from any wrong doing. With a few minimal corrections, Kate started committing it to memory, until Irwin said that she should leave that until she was headed back to Oxford. They now had to consider what questions Leyton would undoubtedly ask – three in particular.

It was almost six o'clock before they were finished. They agreed to meet at Irwin's chambers at nine a.m. the next morning, to give themselves time to review their preparations before the interview with Leyton. Kate thanked him again for his help, which Irwin quietly brushed aside, and she, together with Paul, headed off home. The journey back to Oxford, and that evening at home, very much reminded her of when she was in student dramatics, learning lines and practising how to deliver them so that they didn't sound like lines that had been learnt. Because of her height she quite often was cast as any one of Shakespeare's women pretending to be men, or aristocratic Chekhovian ladies, but tomorrow she would be playing herself. A bad performance would result in more than just some poor reviews.

After an early start, she met Irwin as planned, Paul had offered to again accompany her, but she was clear that she could cope well enough now, and he headed for his lab instead. Kate assured Irwin that she was very geared up to play her part, and they set off for Charing Cross. By ten a.m. they were all set, with the tape recorder running. After announcing the time and date, and who was there Leyton kicked off.

"So, for the third time, Miss Kimball, could you please tell me what you know about the death of Andrew Palmer?" Kate launched herself.

"Two years ago, my partner, Professor Paul Emmerson, as part of a research project, found that there had been an unsuccessful terrorist attack on Sellafield nuclear power station. He then disappeared. My attempts to find him led me into contact with the IRA, while the government's concern led to Andrew Palmer being involved. That is how I met him. All that is now history, and has no bearing on his death. I mention simply to establish how Palmer and I met. We then had no further contact, nor any reason to, until a few weeks ago. He then contacted me, as you now know, at the Perch Inn just outside Oxford, to ask for my help. He wished secretly to contact the IRA, and hoped that my previous contact with them would mean I could act as a go-between to set up a meeting. I wasn't keen – hence the disagreement that the waiter observed – but Palmer said it was of national importance, and clearly could not be done openly. I reluctantly agreed.

"The CCTV evidence that you have shows me introducing a representative of the IRA – let us just call him Mr. X – to Palmer. As you now know, we all then went to Palmer's flat. Mr. X and Palmer went inside. Later, Mr. X came out and, my job done, as you saw, they dropped me off near Paddington, to return to Oxford. I hoped that was the end of the matter as far as I was concerned. You may imagine my shock when I saw that Palmer had been shot dead. I can assure you that I had absolutely no idea that his murder was planned, but was, I hope you will understand, frankly, panic stricken that it might be thought that I was in some way a party to his murder. Which is why I have not wanted to say anything until I had had proper legal advice."

Leyton, with DS Cooper once again at his side, looked hard at Kate.

"I see" was his prosaic, initial reply. "That's it, is it? Nothing else to add?"

"No" said Kate, very slightly shaking her head.

"Fine" said Leyton. "Then I have a few questions. First, if you were reluctant to act for Palmer – getting him hooked up with the IRA – why did you agree to do it?" Kate was primed for this.

"Because Palmer said that my contact with the IRA could prove very damaging for me if it were ever to become public knowledge."

"You're saying that he blackmailed you?" asked Leyton.

Well "said Kate carefully, "it was more that he guaranteed that no such contact would become public if I could help him, with what he described as a simple, safe and perfectly legal activity."

"Hmm" mumbled Leyton, clearly less than fully impressed with this reply, but not disposed to follow it up, at least not yet. "So," he went on "it would be very helpful if you could now tell me the identity of 'Mr. X'"

"That I can't do" said Kate, quite firmly.

"Why not?" asked Leyton.

"Because if you arrest him, or worse still prosecute him, I do not doubt that for disclosing his identity I will be killed." Kate let that sink in.

"You appreciate" said Leyton "that you can be prosecuted for withholding evidence?"

"Sir Charles has advised me so" said Kate. "But a sentence, even a custodial one, is very much preferable to spending my last few remaining weeks, at most, in fear for my life and how it will end. So, no, I cannot identify Mr X for you."

"We have his picture" replied Leyton. "We will find him."

"That's fine" said Kate. "I hope you do. Just not with my help." She had expected some sort of tirade from Leyton, but he remained commendably, and perhaps slightly worryingly, calm.

"I have two more questions for you" he said. "First, did you enter Palmer's flat with Mr. X?"

"I was in the car outside" said Kate.

"So you don't know what transpired when Palmer and this Mr. X went inside?"

"As I say" repeated Kate, "I was in the car outside."

"But you would agree that Mr. X must have been Palmer's killer?" Irwin was about to intervene but Kate got there first.

"That is for you to determine" replied Kate flatly.

"True" said Leyton. "So, I only have one more question." He looked across at DS Cooper, who responded by taking a flat transparent plastic bag out of a file in front of him and passed it to Leyton. Inside was a small tape cassette. "Can you explain this tape recording? We found it in a safety deposit box belonging to Palmer; it appears to be of a collection of phone calls you made to or received from the IRA. I don't think 'go-between', as you put it, quite covers it."

CHAPTER 56

Kate's whole body went rigid. She and Irwin had discussed the matter of the tape but, with Kate having taken what she thought was the key to the deposit box from Palmer, they thought there was a very good chance that its existence would not be discovered for some time, during which they could contemplate how they might access it. That Leyton had found it, and found it so quickly, was truly shocking; and even Irwin looked quite surprised. He was about to lean across to whisper something in Kate's ear but, unable to stop, she asked "How did you get hold of that?"

Leyton felt there was no problem in letting Kate know, letting her know also that she could not evade or divert his inquiries. "We found a safety deposit key in his office. We didn't know where the box was, but a trawl through his bank statements revealed a direct debit to a depository in West London. A search warrant did the rest." Kate felt a pall of dismay fall across her, that she had not contemplated that there might be a second key to the deposit box. Then she nearly fainted when she remembered that the key she had taken from Palmer was where she had first put it, in her shoulder bag, and that that same shoulder bag was now sitting at her feet, not a metre away from Leyton and Cooper. They probably wouldn't search it, but she was completely and utterly finished if they did. As she fought to retain some composure, Irwin again leaned across to whisper.

"Tell them what you told me" he said. "The truth is going to be better than the interpretation they will put on this if you remain silent." Kate took this in, and prepared herself to answer Leyton's question. Before she could do so though, Leyton decided to press home his advantage.

"This tape is obviously a compilation of phone calls that, unknown to you, were being tapped. There are only two organisations in the UK that could do that. One is the police, but I have checked very thoroughly. We have no file on you, of any sort - no permission to tap your phone calls or record of any such activity ever being carried out. That just leaves the security services, and if they carried out a tap on your phone calls then this is altogether a lot different, and a lot bigger, than you have made out. So, you really need to start telling the truth."

Kate took a deep breath. "Everything I have told you is the truth" she said. "No-one, not the police nor the security services tapped my phone. You have a completely false set of calls that I was forced to make."

Before she could continue Leyton made a scoffing sound and interrupted her.

"Oh please, Miss Kimball, don't be ridiculous. Why would anyone want you to do that?"

"I was temporarily held hostage, so that Paul would know not to make public what he had found out about Sellafield; but that couldn't continue indefinitely. So, I was forced to make these calls, so there would be a highly incriminating record that could be made public if either Paul or I were tempted to go public. Once they were made, I was released."

" I am having great difficulty in believing this story" said Leyton. "How were you, as you say 'forced' to make these calls?"

"I was threatened," said Kate.

"Really?" said Leyton, in a clearly disbelieving tone. "What sort of threats?" At this point, finally, Kate just lost her self-control. She couldn't even remain sitting. Almost leaping to her feet, kicking her chair backwards as she did so, she almost screamed in Leyton's face.

"For Christ's sake, you don't know anything do you? I would be handed over to a bunch of squaddies who had been seriously beaten up by some members of the IRA, violent military men who thought I was to blame for what happened to them, to be tortured for fun, gang raped, and then disposed of. Do you have any idea what that was like? Of course you don't. I was terrified out of my mind. And you know what? I'm past caring whether you believe me or not. So, can we just wrap this up? I don't care how."

Leyton took this all in, but remained passive. "Please sit down again" he said. "Who on earth would make such threats?" Kate gave him as foul a look as she had ever given anyone.

"Who do you think?" she said dismissively. "The government." Leyton looked incredulous.

"The government?" he echoed. "You have got to be joking. Who in the government could possibly……" he paused. "Oh, my, God" he said, very slowly. "It was Palmer, wasn't it? I thought you were just making this all up, but you aren't, are you? It was Palmer. That's why you had to comply with whatever he asked you to do in that Pub outside Oxford. It was Palmer, wasn't it?"

Kate picked up her chair, set it straight, and sat down again. "I'm not saying anything more" she said, with a finality not lost on Leyton.

"That is, of course, your right" he said, "but is unfortunate, because, you see, I now have a motive for you wanting Palmer dead. You clearly had the opportunity – you were there, with him, just before he died; and I do not doubt that even if you didn't have the means to shoot him on you, the mysterious Mr. X, of whom you are so frightened you won't tell me his name, would certainly have. So, I'm not sure I can charge you with murder, but I will charge you with conspiracy to murder. Do you wish to say anything more first? Please feel free to consult your legal adviser."

Kate now felt the symptoms of panic welling up in her. "What can I do?" she asked Irwin. In response he addressed Leyton.

"Are you sure that such a charge is wise?" he asked. "The evidence that you have put to my client is very circumstantial. I don't think it will hold up."

"It is, ultimately, circumstantial" agreed Leyton, "but, as you will know, if there is enough circumstantial evidence – and there is a bucketful here – then a prosecution can certainly proceed on that basis. Miss Kimball," he turned back to her, "is there anything else you want to say? You will appreciate that my view of what happened might be materially altered if I could get a statement from Mr. X." The blackmail involved in this attempt to get Kate to cough up the identity of Mr. X could not have been more blatant.

Kate paused a moment, then shook her head. "In that case, I am charging you that between the 17th and 19th of September of this year, you, together with one or more persons unknown, did conspire to bring about the murder of Andrew Palmer in his flat. You do not have to say anything. But it may harm your defence if you do not mention when questioned something which you later rely on in court. Anything you do say may be given in evidence." He turned to Cooper. "Could you please get DC Sharma in here as quickly as possible."

Kate sat, immobile, the same thought going round and round in her head. This can't be happening, it can't be. The Caution's words were so familiar, from television, but she never imagined that they would be spoken to her. She looked, with desperation written across her face, to Irwin. "Can you help me?" she said, knowing it was pointless.

"Stay very calm, if you can" said Irwin. This charge isn't going to stand up; I will get to work on ensuring that right away. You must return to remaining silent, no matter what you are asked. That way, I can keep a grip on the flow of information, and that's crucial."

"So what happens now?" she asked him. It was Leyton who replied.

"You will be taken into custody overnight, to appear before a magistrate tomorrow morning. That will be a mere formality. It is much too soon to say when you might be brought to trial, so the magistrate will just set a date, probably a month's time, when you must re-appear in front of him or her."

"Will I be allowed home?" asked Kate.

"Your counsel can apply for your release on bail, but I think that is unlikely given the seriousness of the charge. Irwin was already working on that in his mind, but forbore to say anything. Kate still had enough presence of mind for one critical thing.

"Sir Charles" she said, could you look after my shoulder bag, get it back to Paul when you can. I doubt I will be allowed to keep it." Irwin merely nodded assent and took hold of the bag, as unaware as Leyton or Cooper that it contained all the evidence Leyton needed to tie up his case against Kate.

"I'll be there in the morning" he said "I presume Bow Street Magistrate's Court?" he asked Leyton, who nodded.

"Can I just phone my partner, to tell him what has happened" Kate asked Leyton.

"Certainly" said Leyton. So Kate reached over, got her phone our of her bag, and rang Paul. Despite the enormity of what was happening, it took only moments to explain. Paul said he'd be there as well in the morning. During the call a female detective constable, no doubt DC Sharma came in. Having finished her call, and having returned her phone to her bag, Leyton and Sharma escorted Kate out of the room, down two flights of stairs to a cell in the basement of the police station. DC Sharma took Kate's shoes and checked that she was not wearing a belt. The door of the cell then closed behind her, and she was left to her own devices.

The cell was quite light, airy and, in some curious way, quite modern. It's only furnishings were a mattress on a concrete bed, a lavatory and a basin, both metal, but at least they were clean and all in good condition. For some unfathomable reason, as her predicament had worsened her spirits had slightly risen, from 'this can't be happening' to a more positive feeling. She was completely innocent of Palmer's death, had not in any way been involved in its planning or execution and, that being the case, it was going to be difficult for anyone to 'prove', and prove beyond reasonable doubt that she had been; and with Irwin on her side she felt at least a small shaft of hope.

The rest of the day and that night passed horribly slowly, with only a couple of meals to break up the monotony. There was no heating in the cell, but she wasn't cold, which helped. She spent a lot of time going over and over in her mind what had happened, what had been said, what she would say in a trial, but none of it was helpful. Her sleep was, at best, fitful; and it was a relief when she was summoned the next morning, taken through a back door to a police van and thence to Bow Street, all the time handcuffed to DC Sharma. There was another long wait, but she was eventually released from the handcuffs and propelled up some stairs into the Magistrate's Court. There was hardly anyone there, though she immediately saw Irwin at a desk and Paul in a gallery seat. Dominating all, however, straight across from her, was a rather formidable-looking fifty-something woman, clearly the presiding magistrate for today.

Kate was asked for her name and address, and then the charge was read out. The magistrate nodded and asked Kate whether she wished to enter a plea.

"Not guilty" said Kate, as forcefully as she could muster, feeling rather like she was in a play where she had been asked to appear. The magistrate nodded again, made a note, and then looked up slightly expectantly. Irwin rose to his feet.

"I would like to make an application for bail." he said. Before he could continue, his opposite number interrupted, clearly acting for the prosecution.

"Bail would be unusual and inappropriate given the severity of the charge laid at the accused." He said.

"It would be unusual, I agree" said Irwin, "but not, in this case inappropriate. Miss Kimball has never had any involvement in any civil or criminal matter, not even a speeding ticket. She has built a successful professional career in publishing, with an established position and reputation amongst colleagues and friends that would make a failure on her part to return to this court when ordered unthinkable. And the evidence against her at the present time is highly circumstantial. She has every intention of clearing her name. If granted bail, she will surrender her passport, report to her local police station in Oxford each day, and, if necessary, wear an electronic tag that will allow her position to be monitored twenty-four hours a day. Given these conditions, I would submit that no benefit is to be gained from incarcerating her for what may be some months."

Neither Kate, nor Irwin, would ever know what influenced the magistrate. Perhaps, just the force of Irwin's argument, but perhaps, subconsciously, some perception by the magistrate that the accused in front of her was not unlike herself, a successful, professional middle-class woman, certainly very different from the great majority of people who came before her. Or maybe it was a combination of the two, with Irwin, in his little speech, playing to what he thought, or maybe knew, were some hidden proclivities of the presiding magistrate. In any event, Kate was granted bail, though with all three conditions that Irwin had proposed being imposed. Only a notional £100 was specified.

It was, perhaps, the best moment Kate had had for some time. The relief was enormous, and with it came still more determination that she would fight the absurdity of the charge, with whatever weapons Irwin could deploy. They left together, Kate thanked him as they went, met with Paul, and went to a nearby coffee shop. Having got their coffees, Irwin took the lead.

"Kate" he said in a rather forthright manner, "you must now go home with Paul, try to forget about the case for a while, sort out what you're going to do in terms of your job; and, most important, be in touch with either the Press's or the University's PR people as to how they are going to handle the media, once this story breaks, and how they are going to protect you. Those are your top priorities. Rest assured that I will be working on the case; I already have the outline in mind of how I will deal with it. You really don't need to be involved with that for now. Just get back to Oxford and handle things there. Is that okay?" This was, if anything, still more relief for Kate, as she had no idea how she could or would handle the case. That Irwin was so completely taking this over gave a fresh boost to her growing resilience; and the jobs Irwin had given her, though in themselves new, were much nearer to her own world than the previous twenty-four hours. Coffees downed, they parted company, and Kate and Paul headed back to Oxford. Irwin headed back to his chambers in Lincoln's Inn. He was now clear in his mind how he would proceed. He was going to embark on potentially the most risky, maybe even dangerous, pursuit of justice in his entire career; but a gambit well worth playing and, he thought, I'm going to enjoy it too.

CHAPTER 57

Back in his office in chambers, Irwin rang the office of Sir Peter Carshalton, Permanent Secretary to the Home Office. Irwin had had considerable contact with Carshalton while conducting his inquiry into the Metropolitan Police Force, as it was the Home Office that, under the close eye of the Prime Minister, had formally initiated the Inquiry. The two had got on well, mutually respecting the others roles and expertise; and Carshalton had both publicly and privately commended the Irwin Report that had resulted from the Inquiry. Irwin didn't expect to get through to Carshalton immediately and didn't, but left a message asking Carshalton to call him at his earliest convenient moment. This, fortunately, proved to be later that morning.

"Charles" said Carshalton "a pleasure to hear from you. How can I help?"

"I'm working on a case that may have national security implications" said Irwin. I need, rather unofficially, to talk to Number 10. I thought you might be able to suggest a trustworthy and efficient contact there?"

"Oh, yes, that's easy" said Carshalton. "The person you need is Amanda Belling. She is the Home Office's official contact with Number 10; and she is really good. Does not suffer fools gladly, but is immensely intelligent, totally discreet, and a very good reader of both the political wind and, I think, the mind of the PM. She will, I'm sure, deal with whatever you've got very effectively. I'll call her to say that you will be in touch. Give it half an hour? Okay?"

Irwin had had no doubt that Carshalton could and would help him, but this was very good news. He thanked Carshalton, took down Belling's number, engaged in a little irreverent chit-chat, and rang off. After an hour spent on another case, he rang Belling.

"Sir Charles" she said. "Hello. Sir Peter said you would be calling, and said I was to help you if I could. Powerful endorsement indeed!" she teased. "How can I help you?"

Irwin repeated what he had said to Carshalton, that he was involved in a case that might well involve national security matters. He felt very uncomfortable just pushing ahead without a proper understanding of the potential ramifications. He therefore needed to speak, however briefly, with the Prime Minister.

"Can you not tell me more about the case?" asked Belling. "I'm very used to standing in for him. In fact, that is my main role here concerning Home Office matters." Irwin had predicted this response, and was ready for it.

"I would do" he said, but have been advised that this is a matter on which the PM would wish to be informed before he decides how best to address it, or who would be best placed to address it for him. I'm sorry about that, but I don't think that I can ignore that." Belling's response was another question that Irwin had anticipated.

"I see" she said, in a voice that didn't suggest she saw at all. "Can I ask where that advice originated?"

"From a colleague in my chambers who has done some confidential work with the security services. I do not doubt that he knows what he is taking about."

"I see" repeated Belling, in a tone rather more attuned to the words this time. "Well, Sir Peter said to help, so I will arrange a meeting. I'm afraid that if and when I fix one, you must take it, whatever else you might have had on; it might be at quite short notice, and it might be any time between seven in the morning and ten at night. Is that okay?" Irwin assured that it was; and Belling said she would get back to him on his mobile. So far so good, thought Irwin.

Over the next two days, as Irwin awaited a call, Kate faced up to her new life in Oxford, The news of her arrest duly appeared, initially without her name but, a day later with her name. The Press agreed that she should continue to work, but avoid face-to-face contact with anyone outside the organisation. Meanwhile, the University put out a statement, confirming the charge, but stating that the University would be passing no judgement until Kate's trial was concluded. Kate then moved in with her friend Sarah Jennings, who lived in a cottage in Old Marston, inside the ring road but a very rural setting. This allowed her to get into and out of work without any journalists, some of whom were camped outside her flat, from intercepting her. It all felt odd and surreal, but it worked after a fashion.

Meanwhile, Irwin got the summons two days later, to call into number 10 at 6.30 pm the next day, where Belling would meet him. He arrived promptly, leaving time for the inevitable security check at the entrance to the street, and was shown to Belling's office, a surprisingly cramped affair somewhere towards the back of the rambling set of rooms that houses the centre of government affairs in the UK. Twenty minutes later, he was ushered into a rather larger and more grandly furnished office, and introduced to Graham Seymour, Prime Minister of Great Britain and Northern Ireland.

Beyond Irwin's thanks to Seymour for finding the time to see him, barely a word was said before Seymour slightly nodded in the direction of Belling with an interrogative arched eyebrow. Irwin very slightly shook his head.

"Thanks Amanda" said Seymour. "I think I'll be okay to take it from here." If Belling was disappointed, she was far too professional to show the slightest sign of it.

"Let me know if you need anything" she said as she left the room, shutting the door firmly behind her.

"Right" said Seymour. "What is this about?" He had very little doubt that it was about the woman Kimball, who Palmer had identified to him and who was now charged with conspiracy to murder Palmer, but he was not about to reveal any of this to her lawyer. Irwin had thought long and hard how to proceed with Seymour. Getting him to accept what Irwin planned to put to him would never be easy.

"I represent Katherine Kimball, a Oxford publisher who, as you will have seen, has been charged with conspiracy to murder your former Senior Press Officer, Andrew Palmer. She is innocent of this charge, and I must do everything I can to see that she is acquitted. "He paused, but Seymour made no move to interrupt him. "I do not know how much of what I am about to say you already know, but I need to spell it out. Palmer used some faked recordings which he had forced my client to make to induce her to put him in touch with the IRA which, for reasons I can explain but will leave for the moment, she was able to do. Ostensibly, Palmer was contacting them to seek help to ensure a 'yes' vote in the forthcoming referendum on Northern Ireland leaving the UK – he actually had an explanation for this in terms of it being inevitable, so why continue to provide large amounts of taxpayers money to prop it up – but he was in fact setting a trap, arranging for a group of armed men, mercenaries I presume, to seize the IRA leadership and, as far as anyone knows, are still holding them. It was as part of an effort by one remaining member of the IRA Army Council to get Palmer to reveal their whereabouts that he was, intentionally or otherwise, shot dead. Miss Kimball's only role was, once again, to put them in touch. She had no knowledge of or participation in Palmer's murder. The police, however, see her as complicit in the murder, which is why they have charged her with conspiracy." He paused again, but Seymour still made no move to intervene.

"If I am to defend my client in court, all of this will come out; and I very much doubt, whatever the truth of the matter, that anyone will believe that Palmer engaged in this highly illegal activity without some backing, however tacit from higher up in government." Irwin left it unsaid that, in practice, that could only mean Seymour himself. "If that is to be avoided, the charge against my client needs to be dropped."

Seymour finally responded, choosing his words very carefully.

"I can see that Palmer's actions might lead to uninformed criticism of the government more generally. That would be unfortunate at any time, but particularly so with the referendum in progress. Such speculation could easily have a very detrimental effect on the perception of the population of Northern Ireland as to their best interests. But, there are two obstacles to what you suggest. The first is that I have no idea of what evidence the police have against your client – how robust it is – and second, much more important, there is no way that I can intervene in any case before the courts, particularly such a high profile one. It will be a matter for the Crown Prosecution Service whether the case goes ahead; and they would never allow a politician, even the Prime Minister, to have any say – indeed any influence at all - in a case presented to them by the police. It just couldn't happen."

"I fully understand that" replied Irwin, "and I didn't expect any different response. But the unfortunate truth is that either some way is found to persuade the Director of Public Prosecutions to authorise the case being dropped – I should say that even the police admit that the evidence is only circumstantial – or Palmer's activities will become public. If so, the government, and the referendum result must both bear whatever consequences follow. Clearly, Palmer thought that a 'yes' vote would be so damaging to the United Kingdom that he was prepared to countenance such criminal behaviour, with all the associated risks – a position I find it hard to understand – but, I think you may well agree, his actions, once public, will very likely result in the very opposite of what he intended."

The reminder to Seymour from Irwin, totally inadvertent though it was, of the absolute necessity of getting a 'no' vote in the referendum, if the UK's economic future and his government's political future were to be secured, was enough to stop Seymour from just repeating his previous response. Instead, he played for time.

"I see that" he conceded. "But what would you have me do. I can't just summon the DPP and tell him to drop a case. He wouldn't do it and, if my request leaked, I'd be out of this job before you could say 'corruption'." Irwin decided that they had now reached the point, a point he always knew would arrive in this conversation, when Seymour would have to ditch all the conventions, of civil behaviour, of political rectitude, in the face of an overwhelming threat to his political survival and, indeed, to his reputation in history.

"Nonetheless, Prime Minister, that is what you have to do. Difficult, yes. Unprecedented, probably. But there really is no alternative, if you wish to avoid what will otherwise undoubtedly be the biggest political scandal since the Profumo affair, which effectively brought down a government. I cannot suggest how you manage it, but I do not doubt that there is a way if you are determined enough. It brings me no pleasure to point this out, but I think that, when you reflect on the situation further, you will see that I am right."

"I think the only thing we agree on" said Seymour carefully, "is that I need to reflect on this. That is as much as I can say."

"Quite understood, Prime Minister" said Irwin. "But, before I leave, there is, I'm sorry to say, one further point, no less unwelcome, but it is integral to the situation. Once the case against my client is dropped, I assume that the file, with accompanying evidence, will be archived. I must ask you to ensure that the tape recording of my client – a maliciously fabricated tape I remind you – is retrieved and returned to my client. Without that, she remains completely vulnerable to future prosecution or, indeed, blackmail. So that is a non-negotiable part of extracting us all from the various predicaments we find ourselves in."

Seymour stared at Irwin as if he were almost mad. "You know that there is no way I can manage that" he said, shaking his head to emphasise the point.

"Normally, no" replied Irwin, as if they were discussing some minor administrative error, "but this is an abnormal situation, requiring abnormal solutions. With the case closed, no-one is going to give a second thought, much less inspect the material relating to the case. It will just gather dust on a shelf somewhere in the Crown Prosecution Service's' bailiwick, and so there will be no difficulty in this tape recording being extracted and passed onto you. None at all."

Seymour felt a strong urge to tell Irwin to just get out and not come back, but had sufficient sense of self-interest and, indeed, self-preservation, to restrain himself. The most infuriating thing was that he could perfectly understand the logic of what Irwin was saying, however unpalatable it was. In the end he concluded the meeting with a whimper.

"I do not know if I can do what you ask" he said. "That's all I can say."

"I quite understand, Prime Minister" said Irwin. "So, I will leave now. If you need any further information from me, please let me know." Seymour just nodded, and Irwin left.

The reflections of the two men on the meeting were rather different. Irwin felt that it had gone quite well. Seymour had, of course, totally rejected the notion of influencing the quite independent Director of Public Prosecutions; but he hadn't thrown Irwin out, in fact appeared to have quite understood the force of the argument, the needs of the situation and, most significant, had in the end, opted to 'reflect' rather than reject outright the course of action Irwin had put to him. So, all in all a good meeting. His client was a long way from home free, but he felt that her chances were a lot better than they might otherwise have been.

Seymour was in an altogether much more complex frame of mind. On the one hand he was absolutely furious, literally seething with rage, that his worst fears on hearing of Palmer's death had been realised quite so quickly, before he had had a chance to formulate some sort of plan to deal with the political fallout that was bound to follow in some guise or other. On the other, Irwin had given him a way of neutralising the impact of Kimball's arrest, if only he could find a way to act on it. And, the one silver lining, Seymour was quite long enough in the political game, quite cynical enough about human nature, and sufficiently motivated to avoid any threat to the referendum that, with an animal instinct, he almost instantly knew how he would proceed. He would of course, review this overnight, look at his options very carefully, but with an instinct borne of years in the political jungle, he was fairly sure of his way forward. He just needed to hold his nerve, and that was something he had been very good at over the years. He could yet be the UK's most successful PM since, well since a long time ago.

CHAPTER 58

Seymour knew that the most difficult part of his strategy was simply getting to meet Daniel Reynolds, the UK's Director of Public Prosecutions. The constitutional separation of the Executive of which Seymour was part, from the Judiciary of which Reynolds was a part, went very deep in the UK, so that, in the normal course of events, they would just never meet. This meant that any contact would be exceptional, and so would instigate speculation of a sort that Seymour at all costs had to avoid. There was only one person who he thought could help and whom he could trust, and that was the formidable, but also formidably loyal, Amanda Belling. But even with her he did not want his next move to appear related to Irwin's visit; and so he did precisely nothing for several days. The one thing he had was time, because it would be some time before the papers in the Kimball case would be sent across by the Met to the CPS. Only the high-profile nature of the case prevented it taking months rather than weeks.

When he did make a move, it was carefully orchestrated. He called Belling into his office. After some minor chit-chat he told her why he wanted to see her.

"I've been getting some backstairs complaints from some of my backbenchers that we just aren't doing enough to stop the escalating knife crime in London" he said. "The figures are quite horrific, and deaths have risen substantially this year. It seems to be very much drug related, gangs competing over disputed territory, but the Press is on to it and, of course, it's the government that is getting the flak. What I don't know is how much it is down to inadequate policing or, as one MP suggested to me, lack of prioritisation by the CPS in what they prosecute. I'm going to have to say something on the subject soon, but I don't want to be undermined by a lack of the facts. So, can you fix me two very discreet meetings, one with the head of the Met and one with the DPP. Let's see what they each have to say on the matter before I go public."

Like most good lies, thus was very largely true. Only the introduction, mentioning backbench MP pressure, was fabricated. Belling took the matter in hand without a backward glance and, by the next day, had scheduled both meeting on consecutive evenings. Both would access Number 10 via King Charles Street, into the Foreign Office building, then out the other side of it, directly into Downing Street which they could slip cross, into number 10, without ever going near the main access to the street or, therefore, running any risk of being spotted heading for the Prime minister's residence.

Seymour had half an hour alone with the head of the Met, Sir Colin Duggan, a tough, no-nonsense career police officer whom Seymour admired, but recognised had one of those poisoned chalice jobs in the public sector that can crucify a career; and so made sure that his interrogation of Sir Colin about rising knife crime in London did not in any way seem to be, or imply, any criticism of the Met's handling of the issue. The PM just wanted to hear about the problem from the horse's mouth, he said; and Sir Colin was rather pleased that the PM should think to consult him on such a sensitive matter before speaking out.

Seymour found the session quite illuminating, but was nonetheless fully aware of what a charade it all was – nothing more than a smokescreen to disguise his real reason for wanting to see the DPP. That meeting took place twenty-four hours later. Once Daniel Reynolds was settled in front of him, Seymour kicked off acknowledging that the discussion was supposed to be about knife crime in London. However, it wasn't.

"I need to speak to you," he said "entirely off the record, about a case that will be coming your way shortly. He meant to push straight on, but Reynolds immediately held up a hand to stop him.

"Prime Minister, you must know" he said "that I cannot possibly discuss a case with you. I cannot even hear what you might want to say. So, please, do not go any further."

"Ordinarily, I would totally respect that" said Seymour "but, unfortunately, a matter of national security is involved. There is, therefore, a public interest matter that must, on this rare occasion, trump such considerations."

"If that is the case" replied Reynolds "then I need to be informed through the proper channels, from the security services through the Home Office, to the Justice Department, with a no doubt secret but proper paper trail. No disrespect is intended, Prime Minister, but I could not possibly respond to a private, undocumented conversation with you."

Seymour had known all along that he would hit this brick wall. He had toyed with lines of argument that might persuade the DPP to drop the Kimball case, but none had felt sufficiently persuasive even to Seymour himself, to make it worth the while. The appeal to national security matters had already been kicked into touch. So, he would have to go for the jugular. It was high risk, but he recognised in himself the element of ruthlessness that had been an integral part of his rise to the top in politics; and he doubted that Reynolds, successful lawyer, bureaucrat and public servant though he had been, had ever really come face to face with naked political brutality. Well, that was about to end.

"Daniel" he said, in a deliberately low voice, aware that it added a sinister touch to his words "you will shortly leave this meeting, and fairly soon head off into one or other of two futures. The first, if you follow up on what I need to happen, will be a story of success. There will be items in the media as to the good fist you are making of a very difficult and under-resourced job. You will be re-appointed to a second term next year. You will around the same time receive a knighthood for your efforts and, when you finish your stint in the office, you will be given a peerage. This will allow you easy access to almost any further career in public service that you would like; and, or, access to a number of private sector appointments which will make you extremely well off. In short, you and Lady Reynolds will have quite a glittering time of it.

"If you do not provide me with what is required, your future will be very different. The media will hear rumours that you are seen as a great disappointment; and inquiries as to whether you have support will be met with revealingly ambiguous answers. Alone amongst former DPPs you will not be re-appointed for a second term, which will be the clearest sign of failure. You will be the first DPP in modern times not to receive a knighthood, still less a peerage. You and Mrs. Reynolds, as she will continue to be, will have to make the best of it, with you back, I guess, in private law practice, but there will be the stench of failure about you Be under no illusion that that is the choice before you at this moment, nothing less than the rest of your life. To access the former of these two futures I do not ask of you anything even reprehensible, let alone illegal. I just need you to recognise that there is a wider national security issue at stake here; and that you, like me, in the light of this, need to make an exceptional compromise to our normal procedures." This last comment, seeking to link them together in a matter of 'procedure' was at once, Seymour thought, a stroke of genius and the most complete load of bollocks he had ever heard, in a life time of bollocking.

Seymour knew that he would have his answer in less than a second. Either Reynolds exploded with outrage, probably storming out in the process, or Seymour had him. He was pleased to see that Reynolds sat, rooted to his chair, as a distraught look settled onto his now paling face. But Seymour could see, he could tell. Reynolds wasn't going to explode with righteous indignation, and so he had lost. Whether it was the 'stench of failure' the lack of access to a good career or wealth after he left the Prosecution Service, or having to explain to his wife that she would never become Lady Reynolds Seymour did not know, but some combination had skewered Reynolds. The rest was going to be easy.

Lost though he was, Reynolds wasn't ready to succumb directly to whatever Seymour wanted.

"What is this national security matter that apparently justifies such blackmail?" he asked.

"My government was attempting, in the interest of maintaining peace in Northern Ireland throughout the referendum process, to negotiate secretly with the IRA. Andrew Palmer was heavily involved in that. The negotiations went wrong, and Palmer was murdered, by the IRA. Palmer, for reasons that need not concern us, used a British woman, Katherine Kimball, as a means of contacting the IRA, but she was never more than that. However, the police have got it into their heads that she was complicit in Palmer's death; and have charged her with conspiracy to murder. They have a tape recording of her which, apparently is quite damning, but which she claims, maybe correctly, is faked. Beyond that there is only circumstantial evidence against her, but if the case goes to trial, everything I have just told you will come out. That cannot be allowed to happen. The fact that Her Majesty's Government had been in secret talks with the IRA, however well intentioned, would enflame Northern Ireland; and whoever lost the referendum would claim that its result had been invalidated. It is not fanciful to believe that it would reignite a civil war there and, quite possibly, bring down the government just when a forceful lead would be needed. So, I repeat, this cannot be allowed to happen. But the only way to stop it is if the case against Kimball is dropped. That is why I have been prepared to adopt such a brutal approach to your future. There is just so much more at stake. given, as I say, the evidence against Kimball is only circumstantial, dropping the case shouldn't create any glaring anomaly."

Reynolds's reply was, he himself recognised, completely irrelevant, but just filled in while he gave himself time to think.

"I know nothing of the case against this Kimball woman" he said.

"Of course you don't, yet" said Seymour. "I'm not familiar with the timescale of the procedures involved, but I imagine there will be a time lag before the papers are forwarded to you by the Met. I would have asked for an assurance that you would kill the case when it comes to you, but that would be quite pointless – I'd have no way of keeping you to it. But, as I have made as clear as possible, when the papers do reach you, you have a clear choice. One is the right one for the stability of the country and your future. The other will, I assure you, be a disaster for both."

Seymour very much would have wanted to hear Reynolds admit that he would do as asked, but knew better than to push that humiliation on him. It was enough to let him ponder the choice, or recognise that he really had no choice at all. When Reynolds made no reply, Seymour added "There is one subsidiary matter. Once the case is dropped, I need you to bring me the tape recording of the Kimball woman. I cannot afford to have that left loose, albeit mouldering way in your archives. I'm sure you can arrange that."

"That definitely won't be possible" said Reynolds. "Where we decide not to proceed, the material goes back to the police. They file it away, in case, at some later date they get new information which might lead them to re-open a case. So, as I say, that will not be possible."

"You seem to have difficulty understanding the priorities here" said Seymour. "I need the tape, so, if the file goes back to the police, the tape must unfortunately, disappear from it before it goes back to them. No doubt an embarrassment, maybe needing an internal inquiry, which will discover nothing, and life will move on. If you think that a missing tape can undermine what I have explained is at stake here, then you haven't really been listening. Don't let that become a fatal mistake."

Reynolds now descended into impotent rage. "You're just not fit for public office" he said "any public office, but especially not the one you hold. Your proposal is a perversion of the course of justice, nothing more or less. People have gone to prison for less, much less."

"No doubt" said Seymour in a deliberately casual manner. "But I am facing, I am trying to deal with the sort of national problem that ordinary crooks can't even imagine. So, let us have no more of this. I want the case dropped and the tape returned to me, That's it. Do it and life will be very pleasant for you. Cross me and…… it won't be." He glared at Reynolds, daring him to continue his opposition. But Reynolds had nothing more in his tank.

"How will I get the tape to you?" He asked, so quietly that Seymour almost didn't hear him.

"Once the case against Kimball is dropped, I will make a speech, praising your work in the battle against knife crime. When you have the tape, call my office just to say 'thank you – much appreciated". I will then arrange for someone to come to your office to collect it. Let's say his name will be a Mr. Jack Evans, due to see you on whatever pretext will satisfy your office staff. Is that clear?"

Reynolds stood, none too steadily, gave a perfunctory nod and turned to leave. But Seymour had not quite finished.

"We'll not meet again on this matter" said Seymour "but do not, for one moment think that there is any way forward other than the two futures I have outlined to you. If you persuade yourself that I would not go through with the consequences of a bad decision on your part, then you will, I assure you, regret it for the rest of your life. I need hardly add that, if a whiff of this discussion ever appeared, anywhere, anytime, then I would deny it completely and have you removed as unfit for your post. If anyone asks, this was a meeting so that I could inform myself on the problems of stemming the rising tide of knife crime in the Capital, the problems of securing successful convictions and so on." He paused, but it was clear that Reynolds still had no stomach for any sort of reply. Seeing this, Seymour decided that he had said enough, or all that he usefully could. "I think that that concludes what I wanted to say" he added.

Reynolds stared at Seymour, fury so obviously written across his face. But the consequences of his not acceding to Seymour's 'request' were already seared into his brain, not least because he *had* always seen his time as DPP as a stepping stone to greater things in public life. This had not, until this moment, included the possibility of membership of the House of Lords, always a gateway to the most attractive roles, but that now seemed very much on the cards. But then it struck him that, if he ditched the Kimball case – and it sounded like he could do that fairly easily – what assurance would he have that Seymour would make good on his promise of advancement. As he sat there, he realised that he had to pursue this point, but that, in doing so, he was clearly indicating that he was, in principle, ready to go along with Seymour; and part of him still wanted to resist this admission. In the end, though, he just couldn't leave without finding out what Seymour would say. The question, so damning once put, was easily formulated.

"What assurance could you possibly give me that you would keep to your side of the bargain" he asked. Your support for me would be some time after the Kimball case was kicked out."

"A very reasonable question" said Seymour. "There are two parts of my answer. First, why would I not? There is no cost to me in doing what I said I would do to assist your career; and the last thing I need in this convoluted situation is a mistreated and disgruntled public employee. Fulfilling my side of the bargain would, from my point of view, just be a painless closing off of the whole sorry mess. There is absolutely nothing to be gained by my backtracking on what I have promised. Second, I can assure you that I will, very definitely, keep to my side of the matter if you don't kill the Kimball case; and that is perhaps what you need to focus on, rather more than the alternative. There is no gamble involved here. No weighing up competing risks, probabilities of what might happen. The consequences of either decision are absolutely certain. So, as I say, I think that concludes our meeting."

Reynolds realised that he would get no more from Seymour – what more could he get? This was a deal that would never appear anywhere – as damning to Reynolds as it would be to Seymour if it ever did come out. As Reynolds got up to go, some element in his thinking told him that he would need to think this all through very carefully – he certainly would have time - but his inner core was somewhere else. He had, through no fault of his own, been put in an impossible position; and there was, he knew, only one way out. He would help preserve peace in Northern Ireland, and secure a rather rosy future for himself and his wife. Not so difficult really.

CHAPTER 59

For the next six weeks, Kate wore a locator tag on her leg, discreetly hidden under a pair of trousers, and reported once a day to the central police station in Oxford. She was required to make another court appearance, four weeks after the first one, but was simply bailed again to a still later date. Two days after that, DI Leyton asked to see her again at Charing Cross police station. A time was arranged which Irwin could also do. Once they were settled, in the same interview room as before, Leyton, this time with no other police officer present, announced that this meeting was not a formal interview; and he was not recording it.

"I wanted, first, to update you," he said. "We have reviewed all the evidence. The tape recording Palmer forced you to make provides a clear motive for wanting to see him dead. You went to his flat with him and a member of the IRA. He was shot dead; and you then headed off with the unknown member of the IRA, whom you refuse to identify. We consider that this is sufficient grounds for the charge of conspiracy to murder which we have made against you; and we now intend to proceed to trial. However, before we do, I wanted to explore with you, in the presence of your legal adviser, the possibility of an alternative. If you admit that you were present when Palmer was shot, tell us what happened, and provide the name of the IRA member with you, then we will drop the charge of conspiracy, and not use you as a witness in the case. We would charge you with obstructing the police, which will give some assurance to the IRA that we have not learnt anything from you; but will seek to ensure that you do not receive a custodial sentence. You will, essentially, be free of all this. That is my offer. I will leave you to discuss this with Sir Charles. Let the officer outside know when you are ready to respond." With that, he got up and left the room.

Kate was completely taken aback by this proposal, one she had not, at any point anticipated. Irwin said that he was also somewhat surprised, even though such deals were not that unusual, where the police wanted to leapfrog more minor players in a crime to get at the key perpetrators.

"Where has that come from?" she asked. Irwin said that Leyton was, very clearly desperate to locate Kate's mystery companion on the day of Palmer's death and, quite probably, far from confident that the charge against Kate would stick in court. So, the offer was a way of solving both problems simultaneously.

"How do I respond?" asked Kate. She already felt an acute tension between the prospect of getting out from under the appalling strain she felt, and the prospect of providing the name of Declan O'Connell to the police. This was not because of any great liking for, or loyalty to O'Connell, but the feeling that, if she did so, she would not in fact be free of the tide of events into which she had been dragged, not now, not ever. Fortunately for Kate, Irwin resolved her dilemma.

"Don't touch it" he said, referring to Leyton's offer. "I'm very confident that we can get the conspiracy charge dropped. So, you don't need to risk the wrath of the IRA. It won't necessarily be quick but if you just hang in there, this will all go away. If they ever catch your erstwhile collaborator, it will be without your help."

"Well, that's is very re-assuring" said Kate, "but how confident can you be? Leyton seemed very sure of himself in terms of pressing ahead with the charge if I don't agree to his proposal."

"You will just have to trust me on this" replied Irwin. "This case is never going to make it to court. The evidence is simply not that strong, and the DPP will not want to risk a failed prosecution. I can't guarantee that they won't, out of pique as much as anything else, bring in a charge of obstructing the police, but I think it unlikely; and that would be no worse than what Leyton is offering you. So, as I say, just walk away. Leyton won't like it. He'll probably add whatever other threats he thinks he can get away with in front of me, but just don't engage with him. Can you do that?"

Kate did not have to reflect for long to decide that she could. It was partly the fact of Irwin being a leading barrister, with the reputational impact that carried, somewhat the quiet confidence in his manner, but also that following his advice removed the uncertainty as to what to do that otherwise was gnawing away at her. He was offering a clear way forward, and Kate, carrying weeks of stress, was very much disposed to take on board any such suggestion. She managed a rare smile. "Oh yes" she said. "I can do that. You've been a godsend to me in this nightmare. I'm very happy to be guided by you. And Leyton won't bully me if you are there to ensure proper procedure. So, let's tell him we are ready."

Once DI Leyton was back with them, he immediately asked if she had made a decision on what he had put to him. He was about to add that he hoped she had seen the good sense of what he proposed, but Kate cut in before he could do so.

"I can't agree to any such arrangement" she said. "I don't want to face a trial, but I at no point conspired in Palmer's death, and I have sufficient faith in our justice system that no jury could, therefore, find, 'beyond reasonable doubt' that I did so." She was aware that this sounded rather supercilious but, for this particular moment, this did not in the least bother her.

Leyton looked every bit as aggrieved as he felt. He turned to Irwin. "Do you think Miss Kimball is fully aware of the seriousness of what she is saying? Of the opportunity that she is rejecting?" Irwin barely nodded.

"She is, yes" was all he said.

"So be it" said Leyton, in a deliberately menacing tone. "Do not ever, if things develop rather differently to the way you anticipate, claim that I did not offer you an easy way out, Miss Kimball. That's all. For now" he added.

As Kate and Irwin left the building, Leyton focused his mind on the problem. He was certainly not going to give up on getting Kimball to co-operate, far from. Perhaps her smug assumption of a 'fair trial' might weaken somewhat as reality hit. So, the imperative, from his point of view, was to bring on the trial as quicky as possible. There would then be time to reiterate the offer – procedurally more awkward but by no means off limits. No time like the present, he thought, and went straight back to the large, open plan office where his team worked. Calling them together, he explained that he wanted to prioritise and accelerate the work on the Palmer murder case, for delivery to the CPS that week at the latest. No-one actually questioned this, but Leyton could sense that they were somewhat surprised.

"Too much pressure from above" he said, in a formulaic explanation that all of them would immediately understand. "The case is too high profile. The wish is that we finish our work on this before some high-minded politician or self-appointed commentator decides to complain; and then we're seen as just responding to criticism. Not good optics. We need to be on the front foot so, go to it please." Detective Inspector Leyton had no idea that he was playing straight into the hands of Sir

Charles Irwin, nor that the impact on 'Miss Kimball' would be the very opposite of what he intended.

The files prepared by the Met - both electronic and a hardcopy paper version - including a Statement of Case, transcripts of all the interviews, together with the evidence amassed – photos from CCTV and, with the paperwork in a box file, the tape recording of Kate from two years earlier – were duly sent to the Crown Prosecution Service three days later. Reynolds, following his bruising session with the Prime minister, had thought to ask that the files, as soon as they came in, should be shown to him; but then rejected this idea. He did not want to do anything out of the ordinary in relation to the Kimball case; and knew that, in a case such as this, given its seriousness and certainty to attract much media attention, the file would in any event be delivered to him for his approval to go ahead, rather than be signed off by his deputy or, for minor cases, a Division Head. It was therefore another ten days before the file came across to him, together with his own Staff Team's assessment of the case and their recommendation. Reynolds had hoped that this might be a recommendation not to proceed, which would have made his life very much easier; but he had recognised that this was relatively unlikely, and so it proved to be. The essence of their view was that, by Kimball's own admission, Palmer had double-crossed the IRA and, as a result, most members of its Army Council had disappeared. This would have created a massive sense of betrayal and grievance, on the part of a well-established terrorist organisation. But, notwithstanding this, and again by her own admission, the defendant had acted to bring a senior member of that Army Council into contact with Palmer, and had seen his Private Protection Officer removed from the scene. The notion that she nonetheless had no knowledge or expectation of violence towards Palmer strained credulity too far; and anticipation of it would have been quite acceptable to her, given the way in which Palmer had utilised the tape recording of her, irrespective of whether it was genuine or false, as the defendant claimed. That the meeting might well end in Palmer's murder should and, indeed, would have been obvious. Therefore, this set of circumstances, the staff paper concluded, fully justified a charge of conspiracy to murder.

Reynolds was not far short of devastated by this assessment. He had genuinely imagined that the case would be more nuanced, maybe even some pros and cons of proceeding, in which case the intervention he knew he had to make would have been, if not easy, at least no more disruptive than previous disagreements on the wisdom of pursuing a case had sometimes been. But it was now clear that he would have to come up with a much more detailed set of reasons not to proceed; and that would involve time, effort and a whole heap of stress. If he could not do it convincingly, then his staff would be bound to start asking questions, even if only in their minds, as to what was going on; and if there were the slightest whiff of political pressure, then he would be finished. The only small shaft of light was the prospect that no-one would anticipate political pressure *not* to pursue the case, given that a senior government official had been murdered, but that was no great consolation.

The first step, he clearly saw, was not to rush matters. That really would set alarm bells ringing. And so he sat on the case for two weeks – quite a long time, but by no means unprecedented – not enough to raise any suspicion of unusual handling. He was aware, though it was of no great concern to him, that Katherine Kimball would be anxiously awaiting his decision; he was well aware of the Prime minister's concern over the national security issue involved; and he was overwhelmingly aware of the consequences for his future of how he proceeded. What he was not aware of – indeed could have no inkling of – was the monumental long-term consequences for the British economy, the standard of living of its population, the peace process in Northern Ireland, the future of the present government and Seymour's place in history; and that all hung, suspended by a thread, on his decision. Even this was an incomplete roll call of those with an abiding interest in the outcome, whether they knew it or not. Sir Charles Irwin waited to know if his strategy for defending Kate had worked; Declan O'Connell awaited news, any news at all, of the fate of his comrades in arms; and Preston's EnergiCorp stood poised to make one of the biggest killings in UK corporate history, provided the referendum vote went the right way. All these participants, in the intersecting geological, political, corporate, criminal and terrorist worlds, and all the issues that mattered to them, hovered around Reynolds as he sought to square, first, his conscience and, second, his staff in the matter of the Crown versus Katherine Kimball.

CHAPTER 60

As the Leave and Remain campaigns in the Northern Ireland Referendum cranked themselves up into full flow, Reynolds, utterly unaware of the link between this activity and the problem with which he was wrestling, prepared his position. He had initially thought to meet his staff team to deliver his verdict on a Friday afternoon, when everyone was likely to be tired and wanting to get away; but past experience had taught him this was unwise. Tiredness led to irritability, cussedness, and more emotional responses, which became quite unpredictable. A better bet was first thing Monday morning when he would be fully fired up from his weekend preparation on the case, and his staff would not be fully in gear. At least, that was his hope.

Having called them in, he launched into his prepared speech.

"I should start" he said "by saying that I have no problem with this file. It's a very solid piece of analysis and, in many key respects, persuasive. In fact, by last Friday, I was ready to sign off on it – a few small amendments but nothing major. But, over the week-end, I have started to have misgivings. My starting point is the obvious one, that this is going to be very high profile, and we simply cannot risk failure to convict. To put it more bluntly than I should, or would ever admit to, I would rather say that the Met has not provided convincing enough evidence than proceed and risk a 'not guilty' verdict. So, I went back over the case with the mindset of whether there are any even slight weaknesses that a defence QC could exploit to a 'not beyond reasonable doubt' status. And from that perspective, I can, unfortunately, see three. First, that Kimball must have foreseen the potential for harm to befall Palmer is, I think, rock solid. But that doesn't constitute foreseeing his murder. Whoever was with her may have had no more than the intention of forcing information out of Palmer, maybe causing him bodily harm in the process. If so, even though it led to murder, it will be hard to substantiate that Kimball could foresee that, in which case a 'conspiracy to murder' charge would fail."

Reynolds could tell, from both their faces and their body language that this was not going down well with his staff team, but that was, he knew, inevitable. Rather than let them interject, he hurried straight on.

"Second, there is no actual evidence that Kimball entered Palmer's flat. She almost certainly did, but she has not admitted it, and we have no-one who saw her enter. Now, that doesn't, of course, mean that she was not part of a conspiracy to murder Palmer – she could have been a designated look-out while the murder was committed – but I can easily see a jury giving her the benefit of the doubt if we can't place her in Palmer's flat. It's just too circumstantial." The facial expressions and body language remained worrying, but Reynolds noticed that at least they hadn't got worse. No one was squirming with irritation, or even anxious to cut in on his monologue. He pressed on.

"The third problem is this. The tape recording of Kimball clearly gives her a motive to threaten, maybe even murder Palmer. But, Palmer's ownership of the tape can also be used by the defence to explain why, irrespective of whether it is genuine or false, Kimball was forced to be a completely unwilling intermediary between Palmer and the IRA, with no role, or any wish to be involved in the substance of the issue between Palmer and the IRA. She brought them together, she didn't go in the flat and she had no idea what was going to happen. I don't really believe any of that, but I can't see how a defence along those lines, no doubt skilfully presented, could easily be defeated. In a much less high-profile case, I'd take the risk – we have to sometimes – but there is just too much at stake here. So, my view is that we leave it as an open file, and tell the Met we will proceed if they can come up with evidence to break down at least two of those three points. I know they won't be happy, but I don't think that they can regard that as unreasonable."

He paused, tempted to think that now was the moment of truth, yet he knew it wasn't. It was a moment fuelled by deceit and corruption; and whatever was now said would not, in the end make any difference to his decision, only how much loss of face and trust it engendered. Looking at his team of five, he invited his deputy, Martin Hawkins to comment, not only because he was the most senior of the others present but because Reynolds knew him to be a rather cautious soul; and if, as a result, he didn't seek to shoot down Reynolds' pitch, then he would be half way to gaining their acceptance, however grudging it might be. He was not disappointed.

"I can't say that I'm happy with this" said Hawkins. "I wasn't involved in the file's recommendation – though like you I thought it quite resilient – and I don't think we should be too persuaded by what a clever defence lawyer might do – that's an occupational risk. But giving the Met more time to pursue the case might be wise, especially if we can focus them onto the three specific areas of concern, and be clear that we are quite prepared to run a risk in relation to any one of them, just not all three."

David Percival, the head of the team that had put the file together, pulled a long face, but recognised that the moment for a full-scale attack on what Reynolds had presented was already past. "I can't say I'm happy either" he echoed Hawkins. "I think our case is strong; we always have to take some risk; and whatever we say to the Met, I think our service will be castigated publicly if we do not design to take the case. Even if we lose, we will have been seen to be doing what we can to enforce the law, in relation to one of the most serious crimes on the Statute Book. So, I really think we should proceed." None of his more junior colleagues spoke, but two of the three, with different degrees of animation, nodded their support. However, that didn't matter to Reynolds. It wasn't a matter of voting. He had the split of views that he wanted, that he needed, over which he could preside.

"I don't really disagree much with that" he said, in conciliatory, if quite misleading fashion. "It is, very much, a judgement call but, for the reasons I've given, I'm going to err on the side of caution. I can't say that I know it's the right decision, but I think it is, for the moment at least, the one that is in the best interests of the principles that we serve." Even the reason he had given – playing it safe – hardly fitted under this rather pompous conclusion, but it was meant to be a sign-off for the discussion, and the file team could read the runes well enough. The meeting broke up, and Reynolds, for the first time since he had been summoned to see Seymour, began, little by little, to relax. It had all gone rather better than he had anticipated.

While Percival set about notifying the Met of the DPP's decision, the box file on Kate, together with the tape recording, was returned to the Crown Prosecution Service archives in the building's basement. Reynolds was clear in his mind that he would take no immediate action on retrieving the tape; and, in any event, Seymour had yet to make his speech about knife crime. Meantime, apparently unrelated, but in fact inextricably linked, the referendum campaign gathered momentum,

Victor O'Connell and his men spent boring day after boring day in east Cumbria, and Kate tried, if not to forget then certainly to ignore, as far as she could, that she was facing trial and, potentially, a long prison sentence.

The Met were, predictably, furious when they heard that the DPP had decided not to proceed with the case, or at least not for the moment. The only very slight silver lining was the prospect that, if they could somehow tie Kimball in a little more tightly to Palmer's murder – and Detective Inspector Leyton was determined that was possible - then they could still go after her. It was nonetheless very depressing when, at Kate's next court appearance, the lawyer acting for the prosecution announced that the Crown Prosecution Service had decided to defer the case pending further inquiries. This came as no great surprise to Irwin, who had been confident that Seymour knew only too well where his best interests lay, but for Kate it was an overwhelming surprise and, if possible, an even more overwhelming relief. She barely heard the magistrate comment that the case was deferred rather than dropped, and wouldn't have cared much if she had taken it in. As she re-joined Irwin and Paul she could manage little more than that she couldn't believe it. As they went for a coffee, Irwin explained that the DPP must have decided that the evidence was, as Irwin had always thought, too circumstantial; and didn't want to risk failure in a high-profile case. Of his own role in the matter he made no mention.

Reynolds allowed ten days to pass before he asked his p.a. to pick up the Kimball box file from the archives. He would have preferred that she did not know that he had wanted to see it, but it would have been much too suspicious if he had gone down to collect it himself and, in any event, a member of the archives team would have to be approached. Having got possession of it, it lay, along with some other files on which he was working, on his desk. So far, nothing out of the ordinary. He then waited for the Prime Minister's speech.

Seymour had decided that three weeks was quite time enough for Reynolds to make his preparations; and duly took the opportunity of a pre-arranged speech to a group of party constituency agents to dwell on the scourge of knife crime, primarily in the capital, of the great efforts he recognised that police forces were putting into combatting it, and his approval of the prioritisation that he understood the Director of Public

Prosecutions was putting into this troubling issue. He concluded with vague promises of more resources.

Reynolds, sitting in his office the next day, reading the speech and the media coverage of it found himself weighing up the good publicity against what he was about to do. In any normal time, the risks inherent in the criminal action he was planning would, if his heart didn't give up through the shear stress of it, completely obliterate any one-day boost to the CPS's reputation. But Reynolds was now so far into Seymour's trap, had taken its enormity to bed with him every night for weeks, that arranging for a small tape recording to go missing seemed increasingly minor; and the good publicity was just a hint of what Seymour had promised would follow through in time to bolster the life and times of, in due course, Lord and Lady Reynolds.

Given what depended on it, far more than Reynolds could ever imagine, the act itself was remarkably trivial. He simply took the cassette and put it in his pocket, just before leaving for the night. Once home he hid it in clear sight, adding it to several dozen other old cassettes that he had on a shelf in his main living room. The next morning, back in the office, he tied up the small cord on the box file, gave it to his p.a. and asked her to take it back to the archives. His chest spent the morning pounding rather too heavily, in case whoever was on duty there queried the contents of the file; but the chances were that it would not be the same person from whom he had obtained the file; and even if it was, he would not notice any small difference in weight from a file he had given out three weeks earlier. His p.a. made no mention of the file again; and by lunchtime he felt he was more or less in the clear. Shortly before leaving the office, he dictated a short note, addressed to the Prime Minister but directed via an adviser at No. 10, thanking him for his supportive words, which were, of course, much appreciated.

The next step in the elaborate charade being played out was Seymour's. Reynolds clearly had the tape, and was ready to hand it over; but there was no way that Seymour, whose every waking moment was organised and scripted, could get anyone on either his political or civil service staff, to pick up the tape or, indeed, have any contact with the CPS. But he had thought this problem through, and knew he had an answer. He called in Amanda Belling, who had first put him and Sir Charles Irwin in touch.

"Amanda" he said "could you get in touch with that Irwin chap I saw a few weeks ago? I promised I'd try and put him in contact with someone who could help him on a mini research project he's working on. Tell him that his colleague Jack, that's Jack Evans, can pick up the data – he knows where to go – they'll leave it at the front desk. All okay?" Amanda nodded, made a brief note, saw nothing odd, and they moved effortlessly onto further business.

On receiving an email from Belling with this information, Irwin had no difficulty in decoding it. The tape would clearly be at the front desk of the Crown Prosecution Service's office awaiting collection by a Mr. Jack Evans. Irwin's only problem was whom to recruit as the subsequently untraceable Mr. Evans – he was far too well known in such circles to collect it himself; and he did not want to run any risks from asking anyone in his chambers to act for him. But he instinctively knew the solution. He rang Kate that evening and, somewhat to her surprise, asked to speak to Paul Emmerson. Irwin then asked if Paul could find time the next day to get to Central London, call in at the CPS office, give his name as Jack Evans, and pick up a package that would be waiting for him at the front desk. Paul was about to say that it would be a little difficult to get away from various commitments at such short notice; but when Irwin told him what the package would contain, he immediately agreed.

"Let me know when you have got it" said Irwin "and then Kate, you and I need to talk." That didn't sound all that re-assuring to Emmerson; and the sense that they were in the final straight which Irwin's request had engendered started to dissipate rather too quickly. He decided that further discussion could wait.

"Will do" he said. "I'll call you tomorrow night." The call completed, Paul turned to Kate and, to her immense relief, explained that, by tomorrow, they should have the second and only other copy of the incriminating tape that had hung over her head for the previous two years.

"We can destroy them both" said Paul "and I think you will be well and truly free of Palmer, the O'Connells, the pack of them."

"But how did Charles manage to fix for the return on the second tape?" asked Kate. "Maybe he had to offer something in return, something to do with my case?"

"He did say that we needed to talk, once I had the tape" said Paul, "which is slightly alarming, but I'm sure he will be doing everything in your best interests, so let's not worry unless we have something concrete to worry about." On that only slightly re-assuring note, they headed for bed.

CHAPTER 61

Given the anxiety, indeed absolute dread that the existence of the second tape had occasioned in Kate, its recovery was a massive anti-climax. Paul took the train to London, a taxi to the offices of the Crown Prosecution Service, gave his name as Jack Evans at the desk, and said there should be a package waiting for him to collect. He was asked to sign for it, but no identification was requested; and a minute after entering the office, he was back out in the street, with the package – a small, padded envelope – in his hand. Once he was a hundred metres away, he opened the package and there, in his hand, was a small cassette tape. He had no means of verifying that it was the one they wanted, but he had little doubt that it was. There would be no rational explanation for the charade that this would all have been if it was not what it was supposed to be.

He rang Kate to confirm that he had the tape; and then, as he had pre-arranged with Irwin, headed off to his chambers. Irwin did not actually have a cassette player; but had not attempted to get one. Instead, he took Paul round to the sort of perk that only a very distinguished barrister gets in central London, namely his own parking space. They both got into Irwin's great pride and joy, a magnificent and immaculate 22 year old Jaguar Sovereign, old enough still to have a cassette player in its console. A few seconds were enough to establish that they indeed had the all-important second copy.

"Leave it with me" said Irwin. "I will ensure that, by tonight, it will have ceased to exist. Tell Kate it is now time to get rid of the one she is holding. I'm sure I don't need to tell either of you, but don't just chuck it out with the rubbish. Break it up, get the tape out, cut it up into small sections and then either burn it – if it will burn – or sprinkle it into the general waste section of your local recycling centre. Or anything that ensures destruction."

"All fine" said Paul, as they headed back to Irwin's chambers "but you said you needed to talk, which sounds like we are not quite at the end of things here?" Irwin made no immediate reply, as they reached his room. He organised coffee for them but, even after his assistant had left, he seemed reluctant to explain. Eventually, he tapped the desk in front of him, as if signalling that he had made up his mind.

"It's like this" he started. "There are two aspects of this that together have been worrying me, a lot. The first is that the stakes must be very high indeed. What Palmer did, what he has done – an all-out attack on the leadership of the IRA, weaker though they now are – implies very high stakes indeed. Palmer may not have reckoned on being murdered, but he would have known that, if his plans ever came to light, he'd be facing many years in prison; but he still went ahead. Is keeping Northern Ireland in the UK really *that* important, to him? There must be more to it than that. This leads onto the second point – Seymour must, he just absolutely must, have known what Palmer was doing and, if not approved, at least acquiesced in it. The stakes, whatever they are, have got to be highly political. Palmer was a functionary – a very high-class one of course – but a functionary nonetheless, not a political animal, not someone with a political agenda worth sacrificing himself for. So, I conclude that Seymour knows all, and this is a very high stakes game he is playing. And if that is correct, then it is vital, absolutely vital, that what is going on does not, now or ever, become public knowledge." Suddenly, ominously, Paul saw where Irwin was headed.

Irwin plunged on. "There are three possible threats to Seymour. The first is the IRA, but they would be laughed out of court if they went public with what they know has happened. No one would believe that the British government would mount a military-style campaign against a largely quiescent IRA over the referendum; there would be not a shred of evidence to support any such allegation; and if anyone did believe them it would almost be worse given how completely they would have to admit they had been defeated. No, the IRA will never reveal any of this; it couldn't make it stick if they tried; and Seymour will know that. Second are the guys who carried out the kidnapping. We have no idea who they are – presumably mercenaries of some description – but, again, they are never going to say anything. They have been totally successful, they will have been paid handsomely, they have no motive to go public, and would only risk long periods of imprisonment if they did. So, they are even less likely than the IRA to say anything, and, again, Seymour will know this very well. He is almost home and dry" Irwin paused.

"Except for the third, the only remaining threat, and that's Kate. We don't know, but must presume, that Seymour knew about the role that Palmer got Kate to play in the whole exercise. If so, he will know that she knows the whole story. He may fathom that she has no great incentive to go public, but she is still potentially under the threat of a serious criminal charge and, either to manage that in some way in her favour, or even just by indiscretion, she clearly could be the cause of the whole plot unravelling in public. If the Press got even a hint of anything like the actual course of events, they wouldn't let up, not ever. So, my conclusion is that Kate is a serious threat to Seymour, or certainly that he will see her as such; and given what I take to be his track record in all of this, that leaves me very worried about Kate. To be very blunt, while no-one is going to be knocking down her front door carrying a gun, a hit-and-run accident, while she is walking to work or cycling round Oxford, is all too plausible a prospect. I don't like pointing this out, but it is better we address the issue than try to ignore it, or hope that I am just being melodramatic."

Emmerson was initially shocked into silence by this analysis from Irwin. He had, like Kate, so focused on getting her off the conspiracy charge, and then getting back the tape recording, that he had not thought beyond these two objectives, assuming, carelessly he could now see, that that would be the end of the matter. He stared at Irwin, feeling and looking both grim and despondent. Irwin looked back at him, equally grim. Eventually, Emmerson got his brain back in gear.

"Isn't that being too pessimistic" he said, not sounding that convincing even to himself. "I accept that we must presume Seymour knew what Palmer was doing, but if so, he was up against a long-standing terrorist organisation – for all we know he may have got the security services involved in some way; and, in any event, I can't really see our Prime Minister somehow setting up a fatal attack on anybody. Surely, to use your word, that is being melodramatic?

"I can't really disagree with that" replied Irwin, "but do you want to risk Kate's life on it? I'm willing to bet that if this story comes out, there will be an attempt to prosecute Seymour. It may or may not succeed, but either way it will be the end of his career, maybe his freedom; but no-one can prove anything, even give evidence against him, if Kate is out of the way. So, I think she is in danger. I really do."

Emmerson, now even more depressed, nodded silently. He wasn't, he thought, totally convinced, but he had to accept Irwin's point, that they couldn't ignore the risk. However, that just led to the obvious question.

"So, what can we do?" he asked.

"I have given some thought to that," said Irwin. "There is only one way I can see to safeguard her position. If Seymour knows that, if anything happens to Kate, then the details of what she knows will automatically be released to the press and the police, then I think she would be secure. So, we need, first, a clear written statement from her, sworn as an affidavit under oath; second a copy lodged with me, as her legal adviser; and, third, some way of letting Seymour know that if anything happens to Kate, I will release the document to the world. That should do it," he added with a slight smile. "No-one would attach much credence to the IRA revealing what happened, but I think they'd be happy to corroborate anything I released; and that certainly would be listened to. Seymour would be finished but, more important, he'd know that he'd be finished."

"Emmerson, visibly cheered, cut in. "The first two elements are straight-forward, but how are you going to convey this to Seymour without any of his entourage finding out – because if they did, that would undermine the whole purpose. We must, surely, assume that no-one in Number 10 other than Palmer was in on this project?"

"I've thought about that, too" was Irwin's even more encouraging reply. "Seymour sent me an apparently quite innocuous message, via one of his staff, that in fact, and quite unbeknown to his staff, enabled me to collect the tape from the CPS. What more natural than for me, via the same innocuous route, to thank him for his help, but phrased in such a way as to make our intention quite clear, at least to him. I've got a draft already." With that he recovered a sheet of paper from his desk. "See what you think."

Emmerson read what Irwin had written.

Many thanks for your help, Prime Minister. As a result, my colleague has concluded that this aspect of her work is complete; and her focus is now very much back on previous projects. She has, at the moment, some concerns about her health; but has copied all her research results to date to another team member, so that the path to publication can continue if she has to step down. Your support has been invaluable and will be properly recognised if the research work is deemed suitable for publication. I trust that is acceptable?

"Admirable, if I may say so," said Emmerson.

"Glad you like it" replied Irwin. I will just email it to Amanda Belling, to pass on to Seymour with his other papers. I've added the question at the end to lower the risk of her summarising the note for him, but I will call her and stress that I'd like Seymour to know about the publication plans; and I would like to be sure he is happy with them. If I don't get confirmation from him via Belling, I'll know to go back to him, but I think this will work."

"I have just one other question" said Emmerson. "Do we tell Kate about your concerns, and what you are doing to overcome them?"

"That must be a question for you" was Irwin's very immediate reply. I have no objection, but it is very much a question of her resilience versus what I suppose we could call her need-to-know. You will have to be the judge of that. You know her better than anyone else."

"You're right, of course" Emmerson acknowledged. "I'll give it some thought on the way home." He then thanked Irwin profusely for his help, thanks which Irwin shrugged aside; and Emmerson left. He really did think that the matter could now be laid to rest as far as Kate was concerned.

CHAPTER 62

Emmerson thought long and hard on the train back to Oxford as to how much, if at all, he should tell Kate as to Irwin's concern about hers safety; and how he proposed to handle it. Unusually for him, he was still undecided when he got back to his laboratory, and no further forward when he got back home, shortly after Kate herself arrived back from work. She was delighted that Paul had managed to get the second tape recording, retrieved the original from their bedroom and, together, over a celebratory glass of wine, they pulled the plastic cassette apart, extracted the tapes, cut them up into tiny pieces, immersed the pieces in water, and put the resulting soggy pulp in a plastic bag. Paul then took it outside, walked a couple of streets away and dropped the bag in a random rubbish bin belonging to a nearby small hotel. The pleasure of finally removing one major threat to Kate had offset the feeling that this was all rather too much destruction. But he still didn't know what to say about the other one, about Seymour.

In the event, he needn't have been so anxious. When he returned, stating that the tapes were well and truly gone, Kate merely nodded, a little distractedly.

"But it isn't over, is it?" she said, rather disconsolately. Paul knew better than to deny it.

"No, it isn't" he said. "But if you are worried about Seymour gunning for you, I have some good news." Kate's response was an interrogatory look, but with a heavy dose of doubt in it. "Irwin had the same worry" Paul continued. "But he has sent a message to Seymour, via one of his aides, innocuous enough to anyone other than Seymour , but he will know its true meaning, which is that if anything, anything at all, were to happen to you, then a full written statement of everything you know will be released, by Irwin, to the press; and Seymour can see how long his career, or even his freedom, would survive that. So, Seymour has every incentive just to let sleeping dogs lie. Irwin is awaiting an equally innocuous but quite clear reply to him. He will let us know when he gets it."

Kate couldn't immediately walk away from the fears that she had been nursing, but as Paul explained the nature of Irwin's email to Amanda Belling – he couldn't fully recall the exact wording – Kate finally began to relax. Paul built on this by recalling the reasons Irwin had given for why no-one else was going to constitute a threat to Seymour; and by the time she went to bed, she was more cheerful than she had felt for a very long time.

Irwin rang Kate at work three days later, to say merely that he had had the reply he wanted and, half joking, half serious, wishing her all the best in the future. He did not give any details of what Seymour had said by way of reply, but she was quite happy to leave its content and interpretation to Irwin. The reply, from Amanda Belling had, in fact, been very short indeed.

The PM has asked me to thank you for your note. He takes your point and is in full agreement. With best wishes. Amanda Belling

Kate phoned Paul to let him know; and the matter seemed sufficiently behind them for them to touch on arrangements for paying Sir Charles for his time and extraordinarily helpful intervention, quite unaware of the ruinous impact Irwin's gambit had had on the probity and integrity of one of the most senior figures in the Whitehall galaxy, and the risk that the Director of Public Prosecutions was now running if the absence of the tape in the CPS archives should ever come to light. But he was just one more person with no incentive to reveal what he knew.

The next six weeks saw the working out of Palmer's various strategems and, had he survived, he would have been delighted with them. The PR firm, Peyton Brown, under the very effective guiding hand of Stephen Peyton had initiated a tsunami of briefings, interviews, analyses and the like demonstrating how much less economic support Dublin could or would give to Northern Ireland if it left the UK for Eire, matched only by various announcements, by Seymour and some of his ministers, as to the investment the Government would make, in infrastructure projects, science parks, support for innovation, even a free port if the future of Northern Ireland within the UK was assured. In addition, two senior members of the Dublin government, who had not survived Stephen Peyton's deep research, were singled out for a very public defenestration, one for financial irregularities, the other for sexual harassment, despite a strong Catholic-based pro-family stance in public. And then there was a third, unplanned but not unexpected factor. A freight train heading from Belfast to Dublin was deliberately derailed.

The rear railway wagon was then firebombed. Only the driver was hurt, and he not seriously.

Protestant paramilitaries claimed responsibility, and pointed out that, if the Province 'succumbed' to Dublin, there would be many more such incidents, but on passenger trains, on buses, cars and trucks, indefinitely, until Dublin had had enough. For reasons that no one outside the IRA, other than Prime Minister Seymour knew, the IRA did not retaliate. Though Palmer was dead, he had somehow conveyed to the men holding Victor O'Connell and his compatriots that they should not be released before Declan O'Connell shot him. The IRA had no way of knowing whether Palmer's threat to murder his hostages, one by one, if the IRA started their own bombing campaign, still applied, but were not remotely minded to take the risk. Instead, they attempted to turn the threat to their advantage, saying that they had, many years before, agreed a peace deal for Northern Ireland, were not going to backtrack on that, abhorred the work of protestant terrorists, and invited the public not to be swayed by such tactics. They island's long-term destiny was clear, and now was the opportunity to embrace it peacefully.

No one would ever know what did or did not sway the public amongst these competing influences, but the referendum result was crystal clear. By a majority of 56% to 44% the Province voted to stay part of the United Kingdom, not a huge margin but enough to put beyond doubt the people's will.

For nearly all those who were affected by the result, it was something of an anti-climax, a re-assertion of business – both government business and private business – as normal. A number of precautionary steps that had been taken in case of a leave vote were wound down but they were, in truth, rather inadequate precautions anyway. The stream of opinion polls had strongly indicated the likelihood of no change, undermining any momentum towards unification activities with the Republic that might otherwise have developed.

But for three groups of individuals – all of them far from the public eye – the impact was considerably more dramatic. The most immediate of these impacts occurred in a remote and little-known corner of East Cumbria. The day after the referendum result had been announced, General Sykes instructed Alastair Ferguson to head up to the property where his men had been carefully guarding Victor O'Connell and his comrades in arms. Taking a large van with him he rendezvoused with his men and explained how they would bring the 'preventative detention' they had been operating to an end. He then summoned Victor O'Connell to the only gate in the fences surrounding the motor caravans that had been the Irishmen's home for several months. Each 'intern' should arrive at the gate five minutes apart, after which they would be handcuffed and escorted to the van waiting outside. There, each would be handcuffed to a side bar in the van. Once all were aboard, they would be driven to freedom, though where exactly this was he did not, at this stage, reveal.

There was, in these arrangements, no possibility that the IRA members, resilient and troublesome as they would undoubtedly be if given the chance, could deviate from what Ferguson had planned; and the prospect of freedom, after months of utterly tiresome inactivity, in any event sapped any desire to protest. . Once they were all hooked up in the van, Ferguson and two of his men got into the driving cab, while two more, well-armed, rode in the back but at some distance from the O'Connells and their men. They then drove a tortuously indirect route, using minor roads and avoiding all motorways, from the now abandoned site in Cumbria to a spot two miles short of the Heysham terminal for ferries to Northern Ireland. Satisfied that the van's passengers could have no sensible idea as to where they had come from, Ferguson drove the van down a short track into a wood which they had identified a long time before, and then released the Irishmen, one by one, insisting, at the point of their guns, that they lie face down on the ground. If any of those on the ground started to have a concern that this might not end with their freedom but with their execution, they did not show it.

Once they had all been released, Ferguson told them it was a two-mile walk to the ferry terminal, where they could all head for home. As much a reflection of organisational efficiency as any concern for his erstwhile captives, Ferguson checked that they had sufficient means of payment on them from when they had been seized to be able to buy tickets, and then, with his men aboard, simply drove off. He reported back to Sykes that all was well; by the end of the day, the O'Connells and their men were all back in their homes. Celebration was out of the question, given the rather humiliating defeat they had suffered, both militarily and, now, politically; but there was, nonetheless, considerable relief that they were back, alive, able to re-group, and no less committed to their cause than they had ever been. Sykes' operation was now at a very successful end; the O'Connells just lived to fight another day.

The second, only slightly more public impact, concerned Anthony Preston and EnergiCorp. True to his understanding with Seymour, Preston had ensured that the development of the gas field in the Irish Sea had been very slow, and only in the central channel that would have remained international waters whatever the outcome of the referendum. The Financial Times and some business sections of the UK Press had noted the beginnings of new gas fracking operations in the Irish Sea, but the general view, much encouraged by both official and leaked 'information sources' from EnergiCorp was that this was unlikely to be much more than a marginal extension of the UK's energy resources going forward. At the same time, EnergiCorp put in rather generous bids for the exploration and development rights for areas of the Irish Sea to the West of their current operations. As far as anyone outside EnergiCorp knew, none had yet detected commercially viable volumes of gas, and none had been extracted.

Now that the referendum result was in, Preston gave out new instructions. Over the next year, exploration of the western side of the Irish Sea, across all the sites they had acquired, would be completed. Construction of the infrastructure necessary for the fracking, extraction and delivery of the gas to the English mainland would be initiated. However, in line with his agreement with Seymour, no gas from any site within 12 miles of the Irish coast would be processed for another year. Only then would the extent of the gas field be revealed, and then only gradually. Preston was as aware as Seymour that none of this would prevent siren voices calling for a re-run of the referendum, once the economic consequences were fully appreciated; but Seymour's clear statement that it was a once-and-for-all decision, the size of the majority for remaining as part of the UK, and the mere passage of time between the referendum and full realisation of the extent of the bonanza that would eventually come on stream were all key elements in Seymour's calculation – that he could hold off another referendum for at least a decade, if not longer; and that was all he needed for the transformation of the UK economy and, with it, a securing of his position as the UK's most successful Prime Minster of recent times.

There was, however, a fourth factor in Seymour's calculation, which involved the other only partly visible impact of the referendum result. Seymour arranged to meet his Chancellor, David Flemming, the day after the result. Flemming needed no elaboration of the opportunity that he, as the ultimate controller of the country's fiscal policy, had just been handed.

"We are planning to take up to a year, if we can" said Seymour, "for the whole story to come out. but you already have some approximate figures from Preston. You can make sure that his company makes a fortune from the drilling rights, and can start to allow for the tax bonanza that is going to result over the next few years, and more. In due course, we will need a special committee but, for the moment, the distribution of the benefits between lower taxation and higher spending, and the spending priorities to be adopted will be for just you and me David – no-one else at all. I hope that is absolutely clear? Your next budget will, inevitably, appear to the uninformed far too cavalier with the government's deficit, given that you will not for the moment be able to set out the forecast extra tax revenues you know are coming, but that will all be lost in history by the time of the next election which, for the first time for a long, long time, I'm beginning to feel confident we will win. Three years of a declining tax burden, and lots more money for health, education, defence, crime prevention, and everyone's pet projects to boot will do the trick – because it always has."

"I'll no doubt get a lot of stick from my team" replied Flemming "but leave that with me. I can tough that out, and if anyone gives me a really hard time, then I will simply replace them, with more junior but ambitious individuals who will happily go along with me if it sits alongside career promotion. Twelve months from now it won't be a problem." He paused. "I wonder, will you be a first?"

"A first what?" asked Seymour, aware that he was being set up for a clever reply.

"It is said that all Prime Ministerships end in failure or defeat" said Flemming "and history tends to support that. Maybe you'll be the first to go out on a high at a time of your own choosing."

"If so" said Seymour "I won't forget that I owe it all to Andrew Palmer. I'm really sorry he is not here to witness the result of all his endeavours. I know he was a scheming monster, but he was our scheming monster. Maybe his great legacy will be that I don't need someone like that anymore?"

"A step too far" replied Flemming. "We will always need such people, to try to exert some consistency, some pulling of threads together, out of what otherwise is just the random and uncontrollable chaos that is Western liberal democracy, and to employ methods, where necessary, that we mere politicians cannot afford to embrace. Palmer's epitaph is just that he was so much better at it than most."

CHAPTER 63

Kate knew nothing of Seymour's satisfaction with the outcome of Palmer's plans, of Flemming's preparations for a popular budget, nor of Preston's plans for EnergiCorp. She was, in fact, completely unaware of the pivotal role she had unwittingly played in the transformed prospects for the UK economy and the economic well-being of its inhabitants. She did, however, wonder at some length, and discussed with Paul at even greater length, the fate of the O'Connells, and the men she had briefly seen in Northern Ireland before Palmer's paramilitary types had intervened, and she had been forcefully removed from the scene by Declan O'Connell. They presumed that the Irishmen were all still alive though, given what little they knew, that was by no means certain; but eventually recognised that speculation was a waste of time. The more important story was that Kate, finally, felt free of the events that had enveloped her. She was free of Palmer; the incriminating tapes he had held were destroyed; she had no further connections with the IRA; and Irwin had safeguarded her from any potentially harmful intervention from Seymour. Given the multitude of considerably worse outcomes that could have arisen from the appalling circumstances she had found herself in - including the tape-based prosecution for assisting the IRA's murder of Seymour's predecessor, summary execution by the IRA, and prosecution for being an accessory to Palmer's murder - the resolution that had now emerged, and the degree of tranquillity which it generated as Kate sought to re-establish her career in publishing, were more welcome than she could readily put into words. She would come to look back on this as rather happy interlude, because it was not to last.

Eleven days after the referendum result was announced, eleven days in which the matter very rapidly fell out of the news, and with another rather satisfactory day behind her at the University's Press, Kate was on foot, strolling along one of the many leafy back streets between the Woodstock and Banbury Roads of North Oxford, heading for the flat and pleasantly contemplating what she and Paul might have for dinner that evening. As she made her way home, on the left-hand pavement, a car pulled up just in front of her. A man got out of the front passenger seat and, to Kate's shock and astonishment, she saw that it was Declan O'Connell.

"Hello, Kate" he said, in a confident voice, accompanied by what, in other circumstances, might have been thought a welcoming smile. Kate, stunned, stood rooted to the spot.

"I didn't expect to see you again" she said, quietly, her mind furiously trying to process what Declan O'Connell's appearance here could mean. The options, though still unformed in her mind, turned more stark as she realised that someone else had got out of the driver's seat and walked round behind her. She turned to see that it was Vincent O'Connell. Well, that at least answered one question – the men so abruptly bundled off and away from the meeting she had herself set up in Northern Ireland had clearly survived. Vincent smiled at her as well, but said nothing.

"What do you want?" was Kate's next attempt to appear unphased, even if it was eminently predictable.

"Not to worry" said Declan. "Victor would like to have a wee chat with you, that's all."

"Where is he?" asked Kate.

"In the back of the car" said Declan. He'd much appreciate it if you joined him there." As he spoke, Vincent opened the rear door of the car.

Kate remained motionless. Two contradictory thoughts reverberated around her brain, one being that she felt much more comfortable if she had to talk to Victor O'Connell than either of his two sons. Both of them, unlike Victor, had at some point decided that she should be killed. That didn't make Victor safe territory, but it was better than nothing. On the other hand, she knew as certainly as she had ever known anything, that she did not want to get in the car, that it would not, in any shape or form, be a life-enhancing move.

She vaguely remembered reading somewhere that, although in normal life, honesty is not always the best policy, when dealing with traumatic circumstances it usually is.

"I don't want to" she said and, when this was met by silence, she repeated "I really don't want to, I can't."

The silence that followed this was somewhat shorter.

"I'm sorry" said Vincent O'Connell, "but it isn't a request. We need to talk to you and we need to do so now. But, I can assure you that you will not be in any danger. Now, please, do get in the car."

"And if I don't?" asked Kate, aware that this was only a pointless delaying of the inevitable.

Vincent merely looked at her and shook his head, rather sadly. He knew, and Kate knew, and Vincent knew that Kate knew, that no words were necessary. She was getting in the car, one way or another; and there really was nothing that she could do to prevent it. Kate did look up briefly to see if there was anyone near who might come to her aid if she started to scream; but there was no-one and, even if there had been, the O'Connells would have had her in the car and driven away long before anyone could intervene. In what could have been construed as a delirious moment, Kate imagined the shock that a good Samaritan would have had, to find themselves in sleepy, leafy north Oxford, pitched against the three main figures in the IRA's Army Council. With only Vincent's assurance that she would not be harmed to console her, Kate got in the car, to find herself sat next to Victor O'Connell.

"My apologies, Kate" said Victor, in a slightly sad tone, as the car drove off. "We do not intend to delay you long, I assure you." While offering a modicum of comfort to Kate, it did little to turn down, still less switch off, the alarm bells deafening her – why were the O'Connells here, what could they possibly want? The only clear thought in her head was that, whatever it was, it was not going to be welcome news. She slipped easily into displacement activity.

"What happened to you?" she asked. "Where have you been?"

"Palmer's mercenaries have been holding nine of us in the outbuildings of a farm, somewhere in the north of England is as much as I know. They would have included Declan if he hadn't been late for the meeting with Palmer. Declan has told me what happened to you and him – very distressing I imagine – and then your arrest, but I understand that you are now out of that particular wood; and we were all released as soon as the referendum result was announced. So, here we all are" he concluded somewhat elliptically.

"So we are" said Kate, whose degree of control over her thoughts and options, severely dented by the arrival of the O'Connells in Oxford, was beginning to recover. "But why? You are all free, the charges against me have been dropped, the referendum is over, what more is there to say?"

"Quite a lot, as it happens" replied O'Connell. "We have done a little ferreting, with a few well placed politicos, some sympathetic journalists, even, I have to confess some rather disreputable investigators; and it is clear that getting us out of the picture was just part of a much wider plot – frankly, a conspiracy – orchestrated by Palmer, to ensure that the referendum was lost. Well, Palmer has had his just desserts and, in passing, I infer from the lack of anyone banging on our door that you at no point mentioned Declan when you were arrested in connection with Palmer's death. For that, many thanks. But – and this is the nub of the issue – I do not for one moment believe that Palmer plotted and planned this all by himself. Why would he? There is no question in my mind that Seymour knew about this; and approved it before Palmer went ahead. There will not, of course, be a single item on paper or in any computer file to substantiate this. The whole operation will have been totally deniable on Seymour's part. But, nonetheless, he will have been the person authorising it; and that is not something we can allow him to get away with."

So, there it was, thought Kate. The words she had, at some half-conscious level, been dreading since the O'Connell's car had drawn alongside her. The O'Connells were after Seymour, and they weren't telling Kate just for fun.

O'Connell fell silent, content to let that thought sink in. Kate also remained silent, knowing that her next words could be rather crucial to her future. She decided to go for, if not the moral high ground, then at least higher practical ground.

"What can you do?" she asked. "You will never get the referendum result reversed, or not for a very long time; and after what the IRA did to Gerrard, you will never get near enough to Seymour to do him any harm. And anyway" she decided to add for good measure "why bother? Northern Ireland has settled down to a very comfortable existence. There is no great appetite to change its constitutional position, nowhere near a majority for changing it. Why not just let the population enjoy their release from all the previous violence?"

"All true" was O'Connell's somewhat surprising reply. "But it is important – it will be important – that Northern Ireland knows how the British government deceived it, manipulated it. The present constitutional settlement is not set in stone; and there will, one day, be another referendum - maybe sooner than you think if what Seymour did comes out – and that will all be conditioned by the knowledge of how the Brits treated the people of Northern Ireland. So, what happened has to come out."

With that phrase, Kate knew she was lost, so completely that she didn't need – couldn't bear – to ask how they planned to achieve that. With the IRA both clearly too committed and too reviled in the UK – on both counts its credibility would be very poor – and with Palmer dead, that left only one available source of information as to what had actually happened; and so now she knew beyond doubt why the O'Connells had picked her up. The only possible consolation, which quickly coursed through her mind, was that if she was their only route to damaging Seymour, then they would not want to harm her.

"Victor, please, stop the car" she said. "Let me out. I can't help you – you must know that. I'm a publishing agent, I'm nobody. I don't know about Palmer's other machinations; and if I so much as mention you, to anyone, the Crown Prosecution Service will get back to me faster than a bullet. I couldn't help you, even if I wanted to. Please, just let it go. Just let me go."

"I'm sorry, Kate" said O'Connell "But I can't. We can't. First of all, you are definitely not no-one in all this. It is public knowledge that you knew Palmer, that you were with him shortly before his death, may even have been implicated in it. So, what you have to say will certainly have credibility. We can arrange, through various sources, to release information pointing to the other aspects of Palmer's whole operation; and, as for the prospect of you being prosecuted for Palmer's murder, we wouldn't expect you to say anything that implicates you any more than at present, which has clearly not been enough to charge you. This is something you can do, something only you can do, something you have to do" he added, for the first time more menacingly.

Whether it was the shock of that final phrase, or something else, Kate didn't know, but she suddenly had an inspirational moment. There was something that the O'Connells didn't know.

"They have a copy of the tape" she said. "The Police got hold of it; and they will have sent it to the Crown Prosecution Service. It's completely fabricated – you know it is - but it ties me into you during Gerrard's assassination. Anything I say will just be dismissed as more IRA-generated lies, not to mention putting me right back in the firing line for Palmer's murder." If Kate had hoped this would close the door on O'Connell's proposal, even before he had outlined what it was, she would be very disappointed.

"If they have the tape and still dropped the charges, then you have nothing to worry about" said O'Connell. "As for your credibility, I'm sure you can make people believe you, enough anyway to put Seymour on a hook from which he won't be able to wriggle. Anyway, you are, if you will excuse me putting it this way, all we have got, Kate; and together I think we can make this work." Kate had no idea what that 'together' might mean; but was far from giving up.

"Victor, this just won't work. It can't" she said. "What's supposed to happen? I wander into a police station, or maybe a newspaper editor's office and say 'Hello, I'm the woman recently charged with conspiracy to murder the Prime Minister's Press Officer, but I'm now free to tell you that the PM is a highly corrupt bastard who should be hounded from office. Happy to write it all out. They'd just push me out the door, if they didn't ring for medical assistance."

"Kate" said O'Connell, in a more forthright manner than he had, up to that point, deployed, "You may not be happy with the situation, but do not make the mistake of thinking that I or my two sons are stupid. Nothing like that is going to happen. Nor should you make the mistake of thinking that we are here to ask for your assistance. My talking to you now is simply to give you advance warning of what is going to happen, and therefore a chance for you to prepare for it. We will shortly be letting a number of media sources know, in outline at least, what happened, what Palmer did. Speculation will start to appear, from anonymous sources, that the referendum was stolen, and stolen by corrupt and illegal means. We have one or two sympathetic journalists who will follow up on the story, but we won't need them. It will be a gift for any journalist looking for a career-making scoop. They will, of course, be looking for further information, for corroboration and, somehow, your name will float to the surface as someone who can provide that. So, you won't need to 'wander' into any police station. The media will be beating a path to your door. And then one of two things will happen." He paused, deliberately, for effect. The critical point of their meeting had arrived.

"The one I recommend is that you simply explain what Palmer did, how he used you, employed mercenaries and illegally seized and detained people at gunpoint. You might add that he said Seymour knew about it, which would be helpful but isn't really necessary – no-one will believe otherwise. The alternative is that, mysteriously, the gun used to kill Palmer will surface; and it has your fingerprints on it. I know it also has Declan's, but they don't know who he is. They have nothing to match it with, whereas yours will match. You could give them Declan's name, but I can assure you he will be long gone, and that will do nothing to reduce your involvement in Palmer's murder. Believe me when I say that I really do not want to go down this route, but we will have Seymour, by any means possible; and at the moment, you are our way in to him."

Since getting in the car, Kate had been grasping at anything that would reduce her fear that the ride was not going to end well; but she now saw that it had all been in vain. In a few sentences, Victor O'Connell had crystallised her very worst fear, that she would become the epicentre of a political maelstrom, not to mention a criminal conspiracy and murder investigation. With it came the realisation that she had no more defences or cards to play.

"Declan got rid of the gun" said Kate, "along with a lot of other stuff from Palmer's flat. He dumped it in the sea on the ferry home."

"Slight correction" repaid O'Connell "he *said* he would do that; but, on reflection, he felt that a number of the things he took might one day be useful – Palmer's little black book and phone, and his pistol. I really do assure you, Kate, that we do not want the weapon re-surfacing; but if that threat is the only way to convey our determination to get to Seymour, then so be it."

Kate was, if possible, even more shocked by this turn of events than anything that had gone before; and thought to say that she just didn't believe O'Connell. But that, she could see was a totally blind alley – she could never, she would never, rely on that possibility; and so had no answer.

"Please, Victor, don't do this." She whispered. "I helped you before with Gerrard; I helped you get to Palmer; and I never gave them Declan's name. Isn't that worth something?"

"It's worth a lot" said O'Connell. "Which is why, when the world has caught up with Seymour, we will ensure that Palmer's death is solely at our door, not yours. Once everyone knows what he did, we won't mind claiming responsibility for his death; noting that you were nothing more than a very temporary pawn in the process by which Palmer got to us. You will finally be free of any police investigation; and all this will be behind you for ever. This doesn't affect the choice which you have to make, but I hope it will convince you that it is the best one to make."

Kate desperately tried to engage with this latest proclamation from O'Connell. Could it work? Would these bloody Irish terrorists keep to their word on this? Why would they; and what exactly would be involved in offering up Seymour to a predatory world of, first, journalists, then politicians and probably, then the police and the courts. The only certain things, she realised, was that she couldn't deal with this here and now. It was all just too overwhelming and, anyway, O'Connell had said that they weren't asking for co-operation, or wanting any reply from her. They were planning to drop her into the nightmare of a public scandal and, while she could not see any way out of it, at least she didn't have to commit herself now, before she could even begin to think out the options – if there were any – or their consequences. So suddenly it was clear, that she had to talk to Paul; and she would have to talk to Sir Charles Irwin again. He had been remarkably helpful and innovative in the past. Maybe he could be the same again? Buoyed by this thought, she sought to regain some ground and presence in what had been a dreadfully one-way conversation so far.

"It's what you Irish are famous for, isn't it?" she said, deliberately obtuse. "You are just locked in the past. You can only look back and fight yesterday's battles. Not a thought for what might be best for the people of Northern Ireland going forward. Whatever 'success' you might have with Seymour will not enhance your cause one bit, not one bit" she repeated.

"Bravely spoken" replied O'Connell with a slight smile; but we can't – no-one can - just ignore decades of discrimination, of second-class citizenship, of religious and political intolerance, and more. But now is not the time for this. I've tried to explain what will happen shortly; and I hope you respond wisely."

"I need to get home" said Kate, as brusquely as she could muster. Please drop me off, now. I'll find my own way home." Only at this point did she actually look out of the window; and realised that they had been driving round local Oxford roads, so that she was, in fact, quite near home.

"We'll take you back" said O'Connell, in a tone that brooked no argument. Now that their conversation was over, Kate just wanted to get away, from O'Connell, his two sons, from the whole mess they had created for her; but was too emotionally exhausted to argue. They travelled in stony silence, neither aware of anything they could say that would enhance their respective positions; and Kate was just desperate to get home, to pause, to collect her thoughts, Vincent O'Connell brought the car to a halt at the end of Kate's road. She got out, without a word but Victor had a parting shot.

"You may not like it" he said "but the fact is that our interests coincide, again, not for long maybe, but they do. Don't …." But Kate slammed the door; and didn't hear the end of the sentence. She needed advice, but from Paul and Irwin. She had had quite enough input from the O'Connells.

CHAPTER 64

Paul had not yet returned from his laboratory, which allowed Kate to try to process what O'Connell had said, aided by a glass of wine to steady her nerves. By the time he did arrive, she had got no further than deciding that she would have to talk to Irwin, but that, at least to some extent, was a calming step forward. Paul was shocked to see the state she was in, not least because she was normally so completely in control of herself, her thoughts, her emotions and her surroundings. All this had clearly taken a heavy knock and, as Kate explained, he realised just how much trouble she was in. Several things were very clear when she had finished telling him what had transpired. The O'Connells would leak against Palmer and, by implication, Seymour. They would leak Kate's name; and she would come under horrendous pressure to reveal what she knew of Palmer's activities. If she did, it would probably contribute to a major scandal that would certainly bring Seymour down, and maybe his government, with unknown consequences for her own position. But if she didn't then O'Connell had made it very clear that they would provide all the evidence necessary for her prosecution to be re-instigated, with little hope, she thought, of her escaping a long prison sentence. The only solution appeared, once again, to be that she must disappear completely and for ever, which was not much better a solution than complete fantasy.

Paul, as she had known and expected, was a comforting influence. He agreed that they must speak to Irwin, as soon as possible, emphasised that the only consideration was what would get Kate out from under such an intolerable situation; and if that meant disaster for Seymour, then so be it. The situation was not of her making; and she owed no one anything; and it was for the world to decide how much, if anything, Seymour knew of Palmer's activities. Kate had no knowledge of that, and need express no opinion on it. While Kate was not yet ready to sign up to this, by the time they went to bed it had become, in some ill-defined way, the default option if Irwin couldn't come up with something better.

Kate managed to get hold of Irwin on the phone the next morning, said, without giving any details, that there had been developments, that she was potentially in serious trouble; and could she and Paul meet him later that day. After a day in which she found it almost impossible to concentrate on any of her various projects at work, she and Paul duly arrived at Irwin's chambers at six pm. that evening. It took Kate only a few minutes to describe the events of the evening before and what O'Connell had said. She concluded by laying out what seemed to be the only two possible outcomes, both of them disastrous.

Irwin had not risen to the pre-eminent position he held in the legal profession by being precipitate. There was a long silence as he digested what Kate had said; and both Kate and Paul were sensible enough to keep quiet while he reflected on the matter.

"The first question" he eventually said "is whether there is anything that we can say or do, or even threaten, that might cause the O'Connells to back off. The obvious one is to say that you would reveal who killed Palmer but, from what you say, that prospect doesn't really seem to be much of a deterrent; and it would put you back in jeopardy, just when you have extricated yourself from it. So, is there anything else?"

Kate had to admit that she could think of nothing, no leverage that she could exert, to divert the O'Connells from their chosen course of action.

"Then I think there is only one way forward" said Irwin. "We must see how the leaks develop. Only then can we develop the best response. Unfortunately, I assured the PM that you would not be undermining his position, but circumstances have changed. We must, as a consequence, adjust our strategy."

"Will you give him any warning of that?" asked Paul. "Maybe give him a chance to get his retaliation in first, if he can think how to."

"Sadly, no" was Irwin's emphatic reply. "If he has advance warning that Kate may be part of a public attack on him, then she becomes very vulnerable again. We do not want to risk that. Once your evidence is out there, then you are safe, Kate. There would be nothing to gain from….. ensuring your silence; and any such move would have his fingerprints all over it. So, no, we say nothing until we say it in public. Seymour must then take his chances. It will no doubt be tough going for a while, but you should be safe from the O'Connells, and I have a feeling, when this all blows up, that both the Press and the police will be aiming at much bigger fish than you. We will need to monitor and manage the process as best we can, but I think we can make you a nine-day wonder – maybe less – in the turmoil that Seymour will face. Does that sound, if not persuasive, then at any rate the least bad alternative available?"

Not for the first time since she had been dragged into the world of the IRA, Kate reflected that, however bad a prospect was, it was somehow better than indecision, and the uncertainty it generated.

"There isn't really any other option is there?" she asked. She looked at Paul and Irwin, and both quietly shook their heads. Kate rather assumed that that was as far as they could go, but was quickly disabused of this notion.

"Now, " Irwin said, "we must prepare you for action." He acknowledged Kate's puzzled look with a smile. "It's clear how the O'Connells are planning to play this and, fortunately, I have had some experience of dealing with cases that revolve around a fair degree of publicity. So, this is how you need to prepare. My guess is that the first you will hear is a journalist doorstepping you, saying they are planning to publish some horror story about you, probably the next day, and do you have any comments. The main point to understand is that, whatever you say, of substance, or even of no substance, like 'no comment', it will be twisted in any way they can to harm you. The only way to avoid this is to be inaccessible to them. So, you need to move out – is there a trustworthy friend you can stay with, Kate? You can easily avoid them at work, and I'd recommend that Paul takes you to work each day – any arrangements such that they can't get to you. Then, if and when you have to say something, it will be on your terms, not theirs. Is that all okay?"

Kate nodded. "I'm sure I can go and stay with Sarah again in Marston" she said but if I remain unavailable, won't that just look as guilty as hell?"

"You won't remain unavailable" said Irwin, but we can see how things develop before we make a move. I'll be on hand throughout."

It was just words, but Kate found them of some comfort. They agreed that Paul would stay at their flat, as that was where they were likely to get whatever forewarning might be available. Irwin reiterated that even Paul must say nothing to the press; and on that note, the meeting finally ended. Kate felt totally drained, but to some extent re-assured by the support – clearly well-informed support – that she was getting from Irwin.

The next day, Kate moved in with Sarah, her oldest and most loyal friend throughout all the troubles she had encountered in the past. This gave Kate some sense that she had not totally lost control of her own fate; but the succeeding days were nonetheless almost as anxious for Kate as when she had been facing the prospect of prosecution; casting a pall of gloom over everything and making it very hard indeed to concentrate on anything useful at work. Paul, as ever, provided support, not least in ferrying her to and from work every day; but they both knew that it was she, and she alone, whom the O'Connells were going to throw into battle.

The nightmare they had been dreading began at six pm the following Saturday. Paul was just tying up some work in the flat before heading off to Sarah's for the evening when the doorbell rang. On answering the door, two men confronted Paul, one very much to the fore. He looked very far from good news, quite tall, with a rather muscular build, and in rather non-descript clothing under a leather jacket.

"My name is Bob Conlon" he said in a clipped and rather determined tone. "I'm a free lance journalist and, along with my colleague here, Tony Levett, I am the author of an in-depth piece that the Sunday Times will be running tomorrow. It concerns the Northern Ireland Referendum and, as it refers to Kate Kimball, I was hoping that she would like to offer some comment that we could include. I can quickly summarise what it says for her."

Never, thought Paul, has 'forewarned means forearmed' been more amply justified.

"She is not here" he said. "I'm sorry" and made to close the door. Conlon put his foot forward to stop Paul closing it.

"Can you tell me how to contact her?" he said, his tone no less peremptory than before. Conlon was clearly a man with a powerful, somewhat intimidating physique. But then history is littered with examples of the extent to which right and, indeed, righteous indignation can match and triumph over might.

"Remove you foot, or I will do it for you" said Paul. The tone was casual, but the look in his eye rather more brutal. Conlon eased back, but only slightly.

"I only want to ask her for her comment" he said, a touch more lamely than before. "It will be in her own interest to give us her side of the story." Paul made no reply, but took out his phone and punched in three numbers.

"Police" he said in answer to what appeared to be a question down the line; and then, before Conlon had fully absorbed this "a journalist called Bob Conlon has broken into my flat and is threatening my partner. Please get someone here as fast as you can" which he followed by his address. "He has someone with him ……." But before he could complete the sentence, someone with somewhat more sense of the risks involved pulled on Conlon's shoulder.

"Let's go" he said. "Now." Conlon was not the sort to take defeat lightly; he shot Paul a look of pure venom as he finally backed away. Cliche as he knew it to be, he could not stop himself.

"You will live to regret this" he sneered.

"No, I rather think *you* will" was Paul's retort, unwarranted he supposed, maybe meaningless, but from Conlon's departing "fuck off" it had clearly wound him up, which was remarkably satisfying in the circumstances. Almost as much as having dialled 888.

Paul ensured he wasn't followed before setting off to Marston to see Kate. He told her what had happened; and then they phoned Irwin, catching him at home on his mobile phone. They agreed to be in touch the next morning, to see what the forthcoming article would say, and what options they might have to address the situation. Paul and Sarah imagined that it would be a very tense night for Kate but, once again action, however unwelcome, seemed less stressful than uncertainty, and she found Paul's assurance that they would get through the current quagmire surprisingly comforting. 'I have faced worse' she thought. 'I'm not at fault, and I'll face down anyone who attempts to suggest otherwise'. On this rather sturdy basis, she spent a pleasant enough evening, followed by a much better night's sleep than she had had for some time.

CHAPTER 65

The 'article' in The Sunday Times was a three-page expose signposted by a front page headline article headed *Stolen Referendum*. From Kate's point of view it was just about as bad as it could be, not because of wild accusations or malign untruths but, quite the reverse, because it was a rather soberly researched piece which, in its references to Kate, was entirely accurate. Much of the article recorded, all based on 'authoritative sources', various ways in which Palmer had orchestrated not only the PR for the government in the referendum but provided misleading or simply false information; and then, far more damagingly, went on to describe how he had organised the illegal detention of what were described as 'leading members of the Unite Ireland Campaign – with no mention anywhere of the IRA – and that this had been facilitated by a British publisher, Kate Kimball, with historical links to supporters of a United Ireland. According to the article, she had not only acted as an intermediary between Palmer and various prominent supporters of the movement but had been the means by which an armed unit had found and seized them.

The article carefully avoided stating explicitly that she had knowingly been complicit in this, but the clear implication was that she had conspired with Palmer to achieve this outcome. Palmer's murder was described as a complete mystery, but no doubt in some way associated with his activity in seeking to destroy any possibility of a fair referendum vote. The 'seizure and detention of those opposed to the government' was then likened to the actions of the Fascists in Germany in the 30's, the Communists in Russia for much of the 20th century, and numerous other murderous regimes in Africa, Asia and South America. It concluded by posing the question as to who could possibly have the motive and the means – the authority – to sanction such heinous behaviour. The implied answer was obvious; and it was, without question, the preliminary to the biggest political scandal in the UK since the Profumo affair over fifty years previously, with very much the same capacity to bring down both the Prime Minister and the Government of the day.

Paul had spent the night with Kate at Sarah's house, and together, on speaker phone, they rang Irwin early Sunday morning. After agreeing that it was a very devastating piece of journalism, Kate asked Irwin the obvious question – what should they do?

"The short-term answer" said Irwin "is actually very simple. We do precisely nothing, except make sure that no-one can get to you. The key points are that you first facilitated contact with the so-called leaders of the Unite Ireland Campaign – that's a neat touch – but second, you thought you were assisting dialogue not setting up illegal 'seizure and detention'. However, you are never going to be able to explain this or get a fair hearing through the press, so we wait to see what more properly based type of investigation will emerge. That will be the time to speak, if at all. I say 'if at all' because it looks like they have what they call 'authoritative sources', but they are in fact anonymous sources – no doubt your IRA friends - and without hard evidence to back up the press investigation, they may find that, despite the scoop of the century, it will be difficult for them to get much further. Anyway, you must take leave from work; and under no circumstances use your mobile. We can talk on your friend's line. Paul, don't go back to your flat for a day or two, and then, sorry to say, make sure you are not followed when you do. If this sounds like a military operation, that is because that is exactly what dealing with the press requires, believe me."

This extended call to arms was followed by much more desultory speculation as to what might happen next but, with Irwin pointing out that this was all it was, they concluded the call, agreeing to speak again the next day.

Predictably, the first major response was from the twenty-four hour round of TV and Radio news programmes. By noon that Sunday there was virtually no other topic on the airwaves. Numerous politicians, journalists and other commentators, and a quickly rounded-up cross-section of *vox pop* gave their opinions in a relentless wave of commentary, none of it adding anything to what was known or, at least, asserted in the article that had triggered the media onslaught. Apart from saturating the airwaves, all it achieved was to confirm what must have been clear from the moment the Sunday Times hit the streets, namely that Prime Minister Seymour would need to make a statement, and sooner rather than later.

Seymour had been alerted to the article at 7.30 am that morning, considerably earlier than he was used to on a Sunday. Having been shown the article by his Principal Private Secretary, he immediately summoned his Chief of Staff in Number 10, Alastair Crowthorne, and his new Senior Press Officer, Colin Sharpe, who had moved across from the Treasury Press Office after Andrew Palmer's murder. Both were seasoned Whitehall warriors, known for not taking prisoners when it came to pushing through their master's bidding. Both were with the PM by 9 am and, even for such diehard individuals in the turbulent world of politics, somewhat aghast at the crisis that was clearly opening up before them.

While heading into Downing Street, Seymour had a decision to make – one that only he could make and one which would, almost certainly, determine much of what was likely to follow from the article in the coming days. Palmer and he had agreed that any involvement by Seymour had to be completely untraceable and deniable, a situation that was only reinforced by Palmer's untimely death. But now, he reflected, at least three other people knew much or all of what had occurred – the Director of the Crown Prosecution Service, Sir Charles Irwin, and the woman Irwin represented, whose name he had forgotten but was now there in black and white in the Sunday Times article, Kate Kimball. So, while he realised that he would be denying any knowledge, still less involvement in any aspect of what Palmer had instigated, there was the question - should he tell Crowthorne and Sharpe the truth? It was obviously sensible for as few people as possible to know the truth; and he had already digested that none of the three individuals who already knew the truth would have the slightest incentive to reveal it; but Crowthorne and Sharpe were, he knew, intensely loyal, and he needed all the wise council he could muster, to get him through a crisis so potentially far reaching that it could utterly destroy not only his position and his government - just as the economic benefits he had so cleverly secured were beginning to appear - not only his place in history, but, quite possibly his freedom. He resolved to take them fully into his confidence.

Once Crowthorne and Sharpe had arrived, looking quite as disgruntled as Seymour felt, and with coffee served, Seymour paused, deliberately. He needed his next words to be taken very seriously indeed.

"Before I fill you in on the background" he said "I need to ask you both whether you are fully prepared to help me, to back me, whatever it takes and whatever the consequences. Normally, knowing you both, I would take this for granted, but this time it might involve lying to the police, perjury, prosecution, certainly the end of your careers in Whitehall; and I won't risk any of that unless you are both clear about the risks, which will start the moment this meeting proceeds, and are ready to accept them. I shall fully understand if not and, if so, will not continue with the meeting, with, genuinely, no hard feelings. This is just too big not to have a clear understanding amongst us from the start."

Crowthorne and Sharpe both looked at each other, initially expressionless. Then Crowthorne smiled at Seymour

"Provided, once I'm banged up in my little cell" he mused, "I have exclusive rights to write the book, then I for one am on board." He turned to Sharpe.

"If, Prime Minister" Sharpe said "you think I'm going to turn down being at the epicentre of the biggest political scandal of a lifetime, then you are about to be surprised. I'm in, and bugger the consequences."

Seymour was normally so far from being an emotional man that many around him suspected he might be slightly autistic. They were wrong, but how he conducted himself meant that they weren't entirely unjustified in this view. But now, faced with a degree of selfless loyalty, from two people whose skill, experience and support he very desperately needed, he was, for a moment, visibly moved.

"I can't tell you how much that means to me" he said. The tone was flat, as ever unemotional, but the fact that he had uttered such words indicated how grateful and relieved he was. "So, to business."

He proceeded to tell them the whole saga of the last year. He had meant to keep the briefing succinct, but it took him nearly half an hour to bring the other two fully up to speed. He explained the attempt to import Russian gas despite the embargo, how the Russians had totally fooled him, the dire political consequences he then faced; and then the lifeline, the solution to all his problems, or so it appeared, when vast quantities of fracking gas were discovered in the Irish Sea. And then the bombshell that the huge economic bonanza would end up accruing to Northern Ireland, which would then have every incentive to leave the UK to become part of a United Ireland, after that Northern Ireland would become one of the richest areas in Europe, indeed the world, compared to the infinitely smaller benefit that would accrue to the province if still part of the UK.

He then explained Palmer's irrefutable logic, that they would have to get the referendum that many were calling for in Northern Ireland out of the way first; and then outlined the measures that Palmer identified as necessary to ensure a Remain vote. An essential part of this was neutralising any attempt by the IRA to coerce, threaten or terrify the population away from simply embracing the status quo - the known and now peaceful world that had emerged since the Good Friday agreement. For the IRA there could now be a peaceful unification, secured democratically, but a new reign of terror would be threatened if the opportunity were to be ducked; and Palmer had seen that that risk had to be neutralised. Seymour touched on how Palmer had got to the IRA leadership via the British woman named in the Sunday Times article, the completely erroneous tale that he had fed the Irish, and the taking of of the IRA men he had then engineered, Everything had gone according to plan, the referendum won, the gas starting to flow. Palmer had paid with his life, supposedly by person or persons unknown, but clearly a revenge killing by the IRA; and he had had to intervene to stop the CPS from prosecuting the woman involved, to avoid any risk of the matter coming out in court. This confession was the only information that caused a raised eyebrow from Crowthorne; both he and Sharpe wondered how Seymour had successfully got to a formidably independent DPP. Now the IRA – for there was no doubt in Seymour's mind that they were the source of the morning's article – were out to get him. He concluded by asking whether, before they discussed what to do, either of them had any questions so far.

It was Crowthorne who asked the obvious one. "How many people know of your involvement in Palmer's actions?"

"No-one knows for sure, now that Palmer is dead" replied Seymour. "but there are four who may have been told, or strongly suspect it. There is the woman, Kimball – I just don't know how much Palmer told her – and her legal counsel, Sir Charles Irwin. Then there is the DPP. I told him that it was all an issue of national security, but once he has read the article he will no doubt be able to put two and two together. And then, of course, the IRA. However, the first three have good reasons to keep very quiet about what they know or suspect; and without any corroboration, the IRA will have no credibility at all. I'm inclined to deny any knowledge whatsoever of what Palmer got up to; and let the press hounds do their worst. What do you think?"

It was Sharpe who replied. "Before we assess that, can we just go over the whole story again, step by step? Only I have an instinct that there might be a better way, but we must be clear that no gremlins are lurking in the detail. Sorry to ask, but it will be worth it." And so Seymour went over the events again, in much greater detail this time – every meeting, every conversation he could remember, every nuance. Sharpe checked that Preston, the CEO of EnergiCorp knew only about the gas field, not Palmer's strategy for winning the referendum; and that he was committed to continuing with only a very slow build-up of delivery from the Irish Sea. When Seymour had finished for a second time, he looked at Sharpe, expectantly. "Well, what is your thinking?" he asked.

"I'd rather we could reflect overnight, but we clearly don't have that luxury" said Sharpe. "But I'd counsel against an outright, overall denial of any knowledge, not so much because it is a hostage to fortune, though it is, but because the Opposition, any opponents elsewhere and, above all the Press, will just refuse to believe you; and will make an all too credible case that only a political idiot would accept that Palmer acted entirely on his own, with no support to cover his back. It will just be your word against the story. Everyone loves a scandal; and there is only a big political scandal if you were in on this, so that is what people will want to believe."

"I see that" intervened Seymour "but how can I avoid it?"

"We need, first, to complicate the story and, second, give you a role, the more heroic the better, around which loyalist support can congregate. And I think there may be a way." With both Seymour and Crowthorne hovering on every word, Sharpe then outlined how he thought the matter might be steered to a successful conclusion. When it was clear that all three were agreed, he suggested that he announce that the PM would make a statement at 5 pm, with the three of them meeting again that afternoon to go over the draft speech that he would in the meantime prepare. As the meeting broke up, Seymour reflected that his decision to take Crowthorne and Sharpe fully into his confidence had undoubtedly proved the right one.

CHAPTER 66

At 5 pm, Seymour appeared at the door of Number 10 Downing Street and walked across to a lectern set up in the street. Facing him were well over one hundred of the world's press, jostling amongst themselves with microphones and cameras, trying not to trip over cables or, indeed, each other. Seymour paused at the lectern, took out a sheet of paper with his prepared text, and waited for the hubbub that his appearance had triggered to die away. He moved straight into the sober, dignified but powerful tone of speech which he had always been good at summoning up when required.

"I have been shocked beyond measure" he intoned "as no doubt everyone here has been, by the allegations of impropriety and illegality that appeared in this morning's Sunday Times. The allegations of wrong-doing are, at this stage, only that - allegations - but if they turn out to be even half true, they represent a devastating attack on our democracy, the proper conduct of government, and the accountability of our public officials. It is a particularly grief to me that the allegations should concern Andrew Palmer, not just because he is, sadly, no longer alive to respond to these allegations but because I valued him as both an able public servant and a friend for many years. At the same time, any inclination that I may have had to dismiss the allegations as purely fanciful must be tempered by the fact that he was, very recently, murdered, by as yet an unknown assassin. This must reinforce the suspicion that some element of criminal behaviour has, indeed occurred.

To that end I have, earlier today, sought assurances from the head of the Metropolitan Police Force, Sir Colin Duggan, that these allegations will be investigated as quickly and as thoroughly as possible; and he has let me know that he has already appointed senior officers to commence this from tomorrow morning. I very much hope that this will clear Andrew Palmer of any wrong-doing; but if he, or indeed anyone else is found to have been complicit in illegal activity, then I trust the full force of the law will be applied.

I will refrain from taking questions at the moment, as it is my clear duty to report first to the House. This I will do tomorrow afternoon. Thank you." As a predictable thunderclap of noise emanated from the assembled crowd, the combination of a hundred pointless questions,

Seymour calmy turned and walked back into Number 10, where Crowthorne and Sharpe immediately joined him.

"Excellent" said Sharpe, with Crowthorne nodding fulsome agreement.

"Your words" said Seymour "so thank you for that."

"The brilliance was in what it didn't put into words" said Crowthorne. "Not the slightest hint that you could be involved in any way – just a non-issue. It won't stop speculation of course, but it will put the opposition on the back foot; and if tomorrow's statement to the House goes as well, we may be in sight of sunny uplands by tomorrow night."

"Let's not get ahead of ourselves" cautioned Seymour "but, yes, this has got us moving in the right direction. Let's review your draft for tomorrow; then we can maybe get a reasonably early night."

The Monday morning press, TV and radio coverage focused heavily on what Seymour had said the night before, because that was the only new news they had to go on. The news coverage itself remained fairly factual, with numerous excerpts from Seymour's delivery. Commentators were asked the number one question – could the Prime Minister himself have been in any way involved – but, given what Seymour had said, the responses were fairly muted, mainly hovering around 'we will have to wait and see'. There was speculation about the Sunday Times's sources, but the paper was never going to release this commercially invaluable information; no one could find the elusive Kate Kimball. All in all, Seymour and his advisers felt that they had prepared the ground for Seymour's statement to the House as well as they could.

At 3 pm precisely, Seymour walked into the Chamber of the House of Commons; and the Speaker announced "The Prime Minister." On many occasions in the past this would have led to almighty cheers, boos, or roars of rage according to political taste but today the stakes were just too high for such tomfoolery. The House went deathly quiet.

"Mr. Speaker" said Seymour, "I wish to make a statement to the House concerning the allegations that appeared in yesterday's Sunday Times. As Honourable Members will know, there has been considerable pressure from certain quarters, over a number of years, for a referendum on whether Northern Ireland should remain part of the United Kingdom, or leave and unite with the Republic of Ireland. The position of Her Majesty's Government has always been that this is a matter for the people of Northern Ireland to decide, which clearly implies a need at some point to hold a referendum on the issue. There is no obvious or easy way to determine when might be an appropriate time to conduct such a referendum, but I confess to the House that when I took office, I did not see this as a particularly urgent problem. However, the House will also know that it has been a major objective of this administration to bring about a much fairer distribution of the wealth and economic activity of the United Kingdom, which for too long as been too heavily concentrated in London and the South-East; and as one element of this, this Government's future economic policy has involved major investment and other forms of expenditure in Northern Ireland, in new businesses, major innovation projects, a very substantial infrastructure programme, funding for various forms of training and re-training and more. I did not believe that it would be right or fair to the people of the United Kingdom if this major strain on the country's finances were to go ahead, only to see the benefits lost, completely lost, through Northern Ireland's subsequent departure from the UK. That is why I decided that the referendum had to be held sooner rather than later.

"However, both I and the government I lead deeply believed, and continue to believe, that the interests of both the people of Northern Ireland and the population of the UK are best served by the province remaining part of the United Kingdom. Therefore, once the referendum had been called, I instructed Andrew Palmer, my Senior Press Officer, to mount as effective a media campaign as he could devise to explain the benefits of remaining in the United Kingdom; and this he did. In pursuing this campaign, I know of no action by him that would constitute illegal or, indeed even inappropriate behaviour; but that will be for the police investigation, now under way, to determine.

"I now come to the heart of the matter. Early on in the referendum campaign, I received information from intelligence sources that the IRA, a largely dormant organisation in recent years, was planning to take whatever action it could to bring about a Leave majority, thereby achieving, through democratic means, the single objective it had sought unsuccessfully to achieve in nearly a century of terrorist activity. To that end, so I was informed, it was planning to instigate a bombing campaign, against random targets in the Province, with the threat that these would be a prelude to a return of the so-called 'Troubles' which had deprived Northern Ireland of any peace or security for several decades. By this means they hoped to 'persuade' – I prefer to use the word 'terrorise' - a population that had become used to a new peace and prosperity, to accept a United Ireland. Given that opinion polls indicated that the vote might be quite close, it would require only a small percentage to be thus influenced for the IRA to achieve its aim.

"I trust I will have the unanimous support of the House when I say that this quite appalling threat to distort and usurp the freely expressed democratic will of the people of Northern Ireland was not something I could accept or idly ignore. But I hope the House will also understand the dilemma of how to proceed, given that no act of terrorism had actually occurred at that point." Seymour paused. Sharpe had advised him that this was the critical moment. If there was some shuffling of feet, small hints of restlessness on the crowded benches in front, and behind him, then he would struggle to win the day. But if the serried ranks of MPs were still, alert and attentive, then Seymour would have the measure of them; and if he did, then he could go on to execute a manoeuvre which would see him home and dry. He looked up and saw no sign of movement.

"I discussed the matter with senior staff and with Andrew Palmer. He said that he thought he had a means by which secretly to contact the Army Council of the IRA; and that we might use that conduit to send a message – that they could of course campaign peacefully for a United Ireland, but if there were any terrorist activity by them then I would immediately suspend the referendum; and the opportunity for Northern Ireland to leave the UK, at least for the foreseeable future, would be lost. This strategy appears to have been successful. I have no evidence or reason to believe that Andrew Palmer went any further than this, but that is for the police investigation to ascertain. All I will say today is that, to the extent that the source of the allegations is, directly or indirectly, the IRA, then I hope the investigation will recognise the extent to which both their plans and the referendum failed.

"Let me conclude. I realise that, as Prime minister, my engaging, albeit at a distance, in secret negotiations with a terrorist organisation, could be subject to criticism, which is why, when I have finished speaking, I will call for a Vote of Confidence in my actions. Those who feel that they cannot condone my actions must vote against and, should they be in the majority, I will resign my office forthwith. For my part, I believe what I did preserved peace, democratic control and proper government; and I invite all who agree with me to support me in that vote." With that final flourish, he sat back in his seat.

No-one, not even those most opposed to Seymour, could deny that it was a *tour de force*. Seymour's side of the House broke into applause, restrained given such a weighty matter, but applause nonetheless. The Opposition benches were largely silent, though a small number were seen to nod a degree of approval. Not a single person present doubted that Seymour would win the Confidence Vote and resoundingly so. Most important of all, as Sharpe had so clearly seen as he drafted Seymour's way forward, the context and content had made it very difficult for anyone to pose the direct question as to whether Seymour had in any way been involved in the illegal detention of senior members of the IRA. He had, almost in passing, declared not; he had made it clear that that was for the police investigation, not political debate in the House and, for good measure had painted the IRA as a dangerous and defeated terror group, for which therefore any sympathy was going to border on non-existent. There was clearly much more to come in the media in the coming days but, almost certainly, the one threat to Seymour, that he had authorised or condoned illegal activity had no longer, to use a journalist's familiar phrase 'got legs'.

In the subsequent debate, despite a few spirited attempts, no-one came close to laying a blow on the Prime Minister; and the vote saw over 400 supporting him, against only 55 against, the rest, mainly Her Majesty's Opposition abstaining, a result that Sharpe predicted would not cause any great grief to the man in the street next day. All in all, he reckoned, a very successful day, plucked from, if not the jaws of defeat, then certainly from a very unpromising start to the week. The question was, could it last?

CHAPTER 67

Sir Colin Duggan, an unobtrusive but well-respected head of the Met, was not one to let the grass grow under his feet. By mid-morning on the following day, he had appointed Detective Chief Superintendent Harry Penfold, one of the most experienced and most respected senior officers in the force to lead the inquiry into the Sunday Times allegations. Duggan made it clear that Penfold could take on board anyone else he wanted in addition to his usual team. Even after only the briefest acquaintance with the case, Penfold identified that there were precisely two officers he wanted to join him, DI Leyton and DS Cooper, who had handled the interrogation of the woman identified in the article and suspected of being involved in some way in the murder of Andrew Palmer. Having made arrangements to recruit them to his team, he then set up a meeting later that day, at which they could brief his team on that previous investigation. He then set in motion his two other key lines of inquiry: the source of the revelations in the newspaper article, and Kate Kimball.

That afternoon, DI Leyton addressed Penfold and his team. He explained that he had led the so far unsuccessful investigation into the shooting dead of Andrew Palmer at his home. There was little doubt that the IRA had carried this out; and if the allegations that had now surfaced were accurate, they provided a clear motive for the shooting. Kate Kimball, the woman named in the allegations had, by her own admission, put Palmer in touch with leaders of the IRA Army council; and had originally been charged with conspiracy to murder. However, she claimed that she had been forced - in practice, blackmailed – into providing this link, presumably by Palmer, had no knowledge of any plan to murder him and no involvement in his murder. CCTV showed that she had certainly been with Palmer and persons unknown the day he died, but there was no evidence that she had actually been present when Palmer was shot; and the CPS had declined to prosecute without further evidence. Whether, if the allegation of illegal detention was correct, she had any knowledge of it was unknown, but was clearly a main source of inquiry.

Penfold thanked Leyton for his summary. One of his officers then said they had been unable to contact Kimball at either her home or office. Nor was her long-term partner, a Professor Paul Emmerson, at their home, but they had got through to him by phone at his place of work, a laboratory at Oxford University; and stressed that he should arrange for Kimball to be interviewed about the Sunday Times article as soon as possible. He had, apparently, been non-committal. This was followed by another of Penfold's officers, who said they had interviewed the two journalists responsible for the article that afternoon. They said that they had permission to reveal that their source was an Irish freelance journalist based in Dublin by the name of Patrick Reilly, but it was unclear to what extent he would reveal his own sources. The officer concerned was currently seeking his whereabouts but, as Reilly had allowed his name to be mentioned, it was thought that this was unlikely to be a problem.

Penfold was reasonably happy with what looked to be rapid progress, and invited any comments, suggestions, or questions. One immediately loomed larger than any other. A DS near the back of the team voiced it, very succinctly.

"How did Palmer blackmail Kimball?" she asked. Leyton replied.

"He had a tape recording of tapped phone calls indicating that she was involved with terrorist operations by the IRA. We recovered it from a safe deposit box Palmer owned. Kimball says that it is a complete fabrication, designed to keep her quiet, which it might or might not be, but the decision of the CPS to drop the case made any further investigation rather a waste of time."

"I think this latest development rather changes things" said Penfold. "Let's get the tape and see if the techie team can offer any advice on its validity. Soon as possible. We probably won't make much progress until we have interviewed Kimball; I'd like to know more about the tape before we do. Okay? Once we have heard from her and Reilly, we should be able to determine the best way forward." On this slightly uplifting note, the meeting broke up.

The next day, Irwin having been alerted by Paul that the police wanted to interview Kate, he arranged to meet her, in a pub restaurant in a village near Reading, well away from any prying eyes in either Oxford or around his chambers. He made it clear that Kate would have to talk to the police, but he would brief her very thoroughly on what to say; and he would be with her throughout to help her stay on message. While that was some comfort to Kate, she went straight to the fear that had kept her awake the previous night, ever since she heard what Seymour had said to the House of Commons.

"What Seymour said is quite untrue" she said. "I know it is untrue; and the police are going to ask me about it. what can I say?"

"I have given that considerable thought" replied Irwin. "We need to think much more broadly but, to deal with that issue first – and I agree it is the central one – I have a suggestion. There will be all sorts of questions about how you came to be helping Palmer, which we will come to; but when they ask you what you know of *why* Palmer wanted to contact the IRA, you can say that he wasn't very clear, which is true, but you gathered it was to try to stop them from interfering in the referendum process. This is absolutely true, so you can say it with full force and credibility – that will come through – but it is also entirely consistent with what Seymour said yesterday. You can respond to any attempt to get further details out of you by saying that Palmer did not explain any more to you – why would he – and once you had put them in touch, your role was over."

Kate could immediately see the attraction of this line. Not just that she was not perjuring herself to the police, but that, as Irwin had implied, she would be much more convincing telling a truth than feeding blatant lies to the police.

"What about the seizure of O'Connell and his men?" she asked.

"You said that, once you had hooked Palmer's man up to the IRA, they escorted you from the room" said Irwin. "Isn't that correct?" Kate nodded. "Well then, just tell then that."

They discussed a whole range of questions that might be put to her, and possible answers that avoided the dreaded 'no comment' but, with the two main ones dealt with, the only other potential problem was the blackmail – how was it that Palmer could force her into a role she clearly did not wish to play. On this, Irwin's answer was as before. The tape looked damming, but was a complete forgery. Despite having a copy, the CPS declined to prosecute Kate for lack of compelling evidence; and that, as far as Kate was concerned, was the end of the matter. Nothing more to say. It remained only to agree a time for them to attend Charing Cross police station. Where the matter might end up as far as Seymour was concerned remained uncertain, but Irwin, and Kate, lived in hopes that, after the unavoidable interview, her position would be clear and, more important, cease to be a topic of interest to either the police or the press.

While this was going on over lunch near Reading, DI Leyton was having a very worrying discussion with an officer of the Crown Prosecution Service. He had requested the file on Kate, plus the tape recording of her, supposedly, consorting with the IRA. The hapless officer explained that although the file was on its way, electronic and hard copy, they were having difficulty tracing the tape. They would, of course, keep looking, but had already examined anywhere that it could conceivably have been deposited, with no success. A furious Leyton said that Sir Colin, as head of the Met, would like to hear directly from the DPP as soon as possible on what would appear to be an extremely serious issue; and slammed down the phone. He knew that Kate claimed it to be a forgery, and he knew that the CPS wouldn't run with it; but it was, to his mind, leverage – a threat he could credibly hold over Kimball's head – and now it looked like the CPS had screwed up, royally. He doubted there was much, if anything, he could do about it; and he would still give Kimball a hard time, to get what he could from her, but it was looking like he had lost a significant weapon in his fight to get to the bottom of the whole thing; and that made him very angry indeed.

The next day, Leyton, together with Penfold, for whom this was a key element in the investigation, sat down in an interview room in Charing Cross police station with Kate and Irwin. The atmosphere, unsurprisingly, was tense.

Irwin immediately went into battle. "I should say that my client is here voluntarily, in the hope that she can help with your investigation. She is not, as far as I know, in any way a suspect in relation to the allegations that have been made and which you are investigating. If at any point it appears to me that that is no longer the case, I will advise my client to cease cooperation, and will request time alone with my client as to how that situation should be addressed. I hope that is clear and understood?"

On top of the continuing lack of any information from the CPS as to the whereabouts of the missing tape, this did not do much for Leyton's peace of mind, but he could see that he had no choice but to accept the terms Irwin had laid down. He looked at Penfold for some indication of his response, but the only reaction - a slight nod – confirmed that judgement.

From then on, the interview went very much as Irwin had foreseen, or perhaps 'stage managed' was a better description. Kate repeated that she had only helped Palmer because he threatened her with a forged tape recording. She said that his intention, in trying to contact the IRA, was to persuade them not to start a terror campaign around the referendum; and that once she had put Palmer's representative in touch with the IRA in Northern Ireland she had been, rather abruptly, escorted from the proceedings. Even as she was speaking, she noted how much easier it was to tell the truth – not having to keep reminding yourself, as with lying, of the story you were trying to tell; and, as Irwin had predicted, it came across with a credibility, even an authority, that made it difficult for Leyton or Penfold to challenge. Kate made no mention of what had happened either shortly before or after she left the meeting, in Northern Ireland, but neither Penfold nor Leyton knew enough or thought it through enough to ask about either. And without the tape, there was no mileage in harping on about Kimball's reasons for helping Palmer. By the end of the interview, any plans either policeman might have had for treating Kate as more than a witness had evaporated; and in her evidence there was nothing to support the allegations that had been made against Palmer. Nor was there anything to cast doubt on what the PM had said, however much the press was darkly speculating on the point.

In sharp contrast to Penfold and Leyton, Kate and Irwin left the interview feeling both satisfied and vindicated in their approach. The police might not be happy, but it wasn't clear that there was much further they could go as far as Kate was concerned; and Irwin would find ways of letting that information percolate into the continuing press coverage. Could Kate, once again, start to feel that she was out of the limelight and out of danger? Even Irwin, ever cautious, thought, after the interview, that maybe that was the case. Unfortunately, he was not aware that someone, a person not given to great bouts of anger, was currently very cross indeed; and was about to propel Kate into a new situation, one that in her worst dreams, she could not have foreseen.

CHAPTER 68

Sir Colin Duggan, head of the Metropolitan Police Force, had handled the impossibly difficult post with, it was widely recognised, more skill and aplomb than most. After a rough childhood in Leeds, in a rather dysfunctional family, he had joined the police force straight from school, at the trainee level but, by dint of determination and a remarkable knack for catching criminals, had risen through the detective ranks to become a Chief Constable at the age of forty-two. He had then shown equal skill in tackling organised crime and terrorism; and it was a surprise to no-one when, four years later, he became head of the London Metropolitan Police Force. He was familiar with all aspects of crime prevention, known to be tough, but very level-headed and – important in the job – good at the public relations aspect. This morning, however, his calm demeanour was being severely tested.

Across the desk, Detective Superintendent Harry Penfold had just informed him that the Crown Prosecution Service had, unaccountably, lost the tape recording which purported to show that Katherine Kimball was, in some way, a tool of the IRA. While Duggan digested this information, Penfold added "We have said that you will wish to speak to the DPP."

"Damn right I will" replied Duggan. "Have they given any explanation?"

"No" said Penfold. "They say they are looking for it as a top priority, but I don't sense that they think they will find it."

"I don't think they will either" mused Duggan. "Nothing like this has ever happened before, has it? And now, a crucial piece of evidence goes missing on as high profile a case as you could imagine. I know one should always prefer the cock-up explanation over conspiracy, but not this time. This is deliberate."

Penfold concurred. "It certainly looks like it."

"Which will make my conversation with the DPP something of a challenge" Duggan added. "Still, we will come to that. Let's start by trying to deduce what may have happened. In whose interest is it that the tape disappears?"

Penfold knew his boss well enough to know that this was rhetorical, and remained silent.

"It's likely to have been in Palmer's interest" continued Duggan, "but he's dead. It's clearly in Kimball's interest, but unless she has a secret lover on the staff of the CPS, which is highly unlikely, I can't see how she could have had a hand in this; but you might want to check out her private life, Harry, discreetly. So, what about the Irish? If Kimball does work – or has worked – for them, and the tape is genuine, they might wish to cover that up, but how could they engineer it?"

Penfold decided he could now intervene. "Maybe an IRA sympathiser in the CPS? Or maybe someone the IRA could pressurise through some family connection back in Ireland?"

"That's somewhat more plausible, I suppose" said Duggan. "I could put that to the DPP, ask him to check his staff; but I doubt it will produce anything. And what if it isn't the Irish?"

The two men stared impassively at each other. The same thought was going through both their heads; and they both knew it. What if Kimball knew something damaging to a certain party, and that party wished to reduce or eliminate any pressure on Kimball to reveal what she knew. Because, if so, that certain party could really only be one person, Graham Seymour.

Penfold said nothing, but raised his eyebrows in a plainly interrogatively manner. Duggan too was silent, but gave a grimly determined nod.

"But how could Seymour engineer it?" asked Penfold. "The CPS is totally independent; and I don't see Daniel Reynolds as the sort of person to compromise on that."

"Nor I" said Duggan. "But, as far as I can see, there are just the four possibilities. A cock-up, which I simply don't believe; Kimball, the Irish or Seymour. I'd say each was only a ten percent chance, but they have to add up to a hundred, which is a right bugger. Any thoughts, Harry?"

Penfold did, indeed, have a thought. "Why don't you hold off the call to Reynolds, give them more time to check, so we will know for sure that the tape has gone AWOL – no more 'we're still looking' nonsense – meanwhile Leyton and I could go and interview the Irish journalist who gave the story to the Sunday Times hacks – see what he has to say. He won't provide his sources, but we know they will be members of a currently very disgruntled IRA; and he seems more than ready to be identified. We can see what light his true or false information might throw on the situation. It should give us some leads on Palmer's role, maybe on Kimball's and even, possibly, on Seymour's. We can go more or less immediately."

"Do it" replied Duggan. "Soon as you can. Then get back to me and we will see where we go from there."

As expected, it had proved very easy to track down Patrick Reilly and that same evening, Penfold and Leyton met him in a pub in Dublin. Both of them had, independently, formed a picture in their mind of what Reilly – a freelance Dublin journalist with clear IRA sympathies and a readiness to create the mother of all political scandals in London – would look like, comprising some combination of long hair, unshaven, aggressive, couldn't-care-less attire and a strong inclination towards alcohol. So, both were very surprised indeed to meet a polite, short-haired, bespectacled man in a jacket and tie, with a slightly shy manner. As for a predilection for alcohol, this stretched to one small beer in the hour-long meeting.

Though needless in the circumstances, Penfold explained that they were investigating the allegation that Palmer had engaged in an unauthorised and illegal semi-military operation against the IRA in an effort to prevent them disrupting or distorting the Northern Ireland referendum campaign, an allegation for which, as they understood it, Reilly was the source. If so, could he give them as much detail as possible and, if possible, any sort of evidence he had to corroborate the allegation.

Reilly paused before replying, taking a rare sip of his beer. "I will tell you what you want to know" he said "but before I do, two things need to be made clear. First, I will not, under any circumstances, be formally interviewed by the British police. If what I tell you is useful, and steers you in the right direction, then fine; but I will not be part of any formal investigation process. Second, I need your assurance now, which I will record" – he pointed to a small recording device which he had placed on the table between them – "that in any report you make, I will be referred to only as a 'journalistic source' or some such phrase, but with no mention of my name. I realise that many people will deduce that I am that 'journalistic source' but, in the absence of my name I can, if I so wish, deny my involvement without undermining your report. Are these terms acceptable? I hope so, because, without them, this meeting is over."

This was clearly Penfold's call; and he did not seek to duck it. "Agreed" was all he said.

"Both conditions?" asked Reilly

"Both conditions, yes" Penfold confirmed. "So, tell us what you know and, as far as you can, how you know it."

Reilly, who had been fully briefed by the O'Connells, proceeded to lay out, briefly, but with no important detail missing, what had happened in the months before the referendum. Kate Kimball had turned up out of the blue, with a message for the leadership of the IRA Army Council, that Andrew Palmer, Graham Seymour's Chief Press Officer, wished to send a representative to discuss, in total secrecy, a potential coalescence of their interests about the referendum on the future of Northern Ireland. The essence of Palmer's line was that the Prime Minister and several other senior politicians in the UK government were no longer prepared to pour large amounts of public expenditure into the province, given that at some point, sooner or later, it was likely to leave the UK, so best for it to go now – no great loss for the rest of the UK. The discussion with Palmer's representative would revolve around how best to work, secretly but harmoniously, to achieve what, for once, was a shared objective.

Totally gripped, Penfold nonetheless could not stop himself from intervening. "Can I just check, this was all from Kimball, her message, not someone from the government, or Palmer's office maybe, whom she had taken to meet the Army Council?"

"Correct" said Reilly. "She had come alone, and was fully briefed."

Both Penfold and Leyton were dumfounded. This put a very different complexion on Kimball's role, not to mention her future.

"Okay" said Penfold, "what happened next?"

"The IRA agreed to meet" said Reilly, "and made arrangement for Kimball to bring over Palmer's representative. They made very detailed plans to ensure that the meeting place would be secret; and that Kimball and her associate could not be followed. But in this they failed, because no sooner were Kimball and Palmer's man in the same room but a battalion of armed men rushed in and seized the Irish, took them away in handcuffs and didn't release them until after the referendum. The whole thing had been a stitch up, designed to eliminate any IRA threat to the referendum. They are all back home now, embarrassed beyond measure by their failure, but wanting the truth of the British government's illegal actions out in the open."

What they had just heard was not that different from what had been in the Sunday Times article. But both Penfold and Leyton were still rather stunned by the enormity of it, what apparently had happened to silence and incapacitate the IRA. Both men identified quite quickly the two main questions that need to be asked, but it was Penfold who put them.

"Did Kimball know that the whole thing was false, a stitch-up? Was she part of Palmer's underlying purpose?"

"I don't think so" said Reilly. My sources say that she looked stunned, absolutely stunned, when the cavalry turned up, and was quickly escorted from the scene. And why would Palmer tell her his true intentions? She was bound to be much more believable when she made contact if she believed his cover story. So, no, I don't think she knew. She was fooled as much as anyone."

"But she did see what happened, that the IRA people were forcibly seized?"

"Oh, yes" said Reilly. "That is why she was so shocked."

Penfold looked across at Leyton. How much more disinformation, or outrageous omission, on the part of Kate Kimball would they discover? She might be innocent of Palmer's deeper ploy, but hers was not the harmless 'meeter and greeter' role that she had indicated when interviewed. They were both looking forward to interviewing her again.

"My other question is this" said Penfold. "Is there anything to support, or even just indicate, that any member of the government in London – by that I mean anyone outside Palmer's Press office – knew, approved of or authorised Palmer's plan?"

All three men recognised that they had come to the pivotal point in the conversation. The references to 'any member of the government' or to 'the Press office' were transparently redundant. They all knew – it was Palmer, or it was Seymour and Palmer; and rather a lot hung on which.

Reilly took another sip of his beer. "As I understand it, there is no hard evidence that Seymour knew what was planned. But, two things. First, would Palmer, however loyal a Press Officer, really carry out such a project with no backing from Seymour. What would he have to gain? He'd certainly have a lot to lose, more, as it turns out than he could have imagined. And, second, his plans involved a full-scale armed assault – I'm told they might have been as many as twenty involved – plus what must have been a very sophisticated surveillance system to track Kimball – and then the resources to keep eight men locked up for several months. The total cost must have been very substantial – into the millions I would think – and where would Palmer dig up that kind of money, for a clandestine operation? It really doesn't make sense. You might ask where Seymour could find that kind of money – clearly not from any legitimate, or even secret, public purse. But history is littered with examples of wealthy, less than fastidious backers of politicians, who quietly finance them in return for favours, economic or political. I can't see any other credible source. Can you?"

Neither Penfold nor Leyton replied, but that was as good as a 'yes'; and shortly after that the meeting ended. "Do remember my conditions" was Reilly's parting shot as they left the pub. Penfold merely raised his hand in acknowledgment but it was enough; the two policemen headed off back to Dublin airport, anxious to pass on what they had learnt as soon as possible.

CHAPTER 69

Back at New Scotland Yard, Penfold and Leyton had an urgent meeting with Sir Colin, filling him in with what Reilly had told them, and the terms on which he had provided the information. Penfold acknowledged that the whole story could be, as he termed it, utter bullshit, but he, and Leyton, were inclined to believe what they had been told. The lack of any real action by the IRA in the run up to the referendum was entirely consistent with them having been decapitated as an organisation; and Seymour himself had admitted that he and Palmer wanted to neutralise them during the process. All that was really in doubt was, first, precisely what part Kate Kimball had played, which wasn't, in the totality of the situation, that important an issue; and second, was Seymour involved, which was a whole lot more important.

Duggan thanked them for what had clearly been a useful trip to Dublin—time to offer words of wisdom.

"One or more people are yanking my chain" he said, in a phrase which was a throwback to his upbringing in Yorkshire, "and I very much do not like that. I don't know if it is the IRA, or bloody Miss Kimball, or the DPP or the PM, or all of them for all I know at the moment, but I'm not having it. The trouble is, we won't get anything on the record from Reilly; I've no doubt that Kimball will continue to protest her innocence, and I have no way of disproving it; I can't exactly mount a police inquiry into the workings of the Crown Prosecution Service; and I really don't have enough to swoop into Number 10 with a charge sheet against the PM. The simple answer would be to conclude that it was all down to Palmer, aided by a gullible but essentially innocent Kimball; but I can't do that. Someone is protecting Kimball, and that must be because of what she knows. What is it she knows that is so dangerous, and to whom? The only answer I can come up with, if Reilly is right, is that Seymour's explanation to the House of what he was trying to do by contacting the IRA is, to borrow you phrase, Harry, utter bullshit. Kimball knows it; and Seymour is desperate to stop her revealing this, or to put it more specifically, being forced to reveal it. That must be why the tape has disappeared, though how Seymour managed to achieve that remains unclear. Am I making sense?"

"Totally" said Penfold. "Reilly said that there was no solid proof that Seymour was behind Palmer's plans, but he gave some very cogent reasons why, in his view, it had to be Seymour. Palmer didn't have enough incentive, nor the resources. But if we are clear that Seymour is involved, how do we proceed? Unless we are absolutely certain of a conviction, and that's fantasy land, an attempt by the Met to arrest the PM would probably end up destroying us as an organisation, not to mention that, for all we know, the DPP, who would have to bring the prosecution, may be in Seymour's pocket."

"All true" said Duggen, almost to himself. Then, more forcefully, "so, let's interview Kimball again; and I will talk to the DPP. Then let's see what options, if any, we have." It was not exactly a strategy, even a road map, but it was the best any of them could come up with.

Two days later, Kate, accompanied by Sir Charles, once again found herself in front of Leyton and, this time Penfold. Irwin again kicked off by announcing his client's willingness to help, as a witness, but that would change if she was treated as a potential suspect. Rather to his surprise, Penfold responded saying that Irwin's intervention was helpful, because Mis Kimball was, indeed, now being interviewed as a suspect, more specifically as an accomplice in the illegal detention of a number of Irish citizens, orchestrated by the now deceased Andrew Palmer. On hearing this, Irwin requested time alone with his client, a request to which Penfold agreed.

Once alone, Kate asked Irwin what she should now do, or not do.

"Two things" said Irwin. "Stick to your line that you were coerced into helping Palmer set up a meeting, nothing more; and that you have had no involvement of any kind in any illegal detention. If they press further and you feel uncomfortable, fall back on 'no comment'; but avoid it for as long as you can. It will only encourage them to think that they are onto something. Okay?"

Kate was far from 'okay' but it would have to do; and they regrouped with Penfold and Leyton. As he had led before, they had agreed that Leyton would lead the questioning.

"I don' propose to go back in great detail over what you said in your previous interview" he said, dangerously calm Kate thought, "but you said that you were merely a go-between, someone who could arrange for Palmer, or at least a representative of Palmer's to meet up with the IRA Army Council. Is that correct?"

Kate nodded. "And" Leyton continued, "you had no knowledge of any illegal action intended against them?" Kate nodded again.

"But" said Leyton, "we have it on very good authority that you were fully cognisant of the deal that Andrew Palmer was seeking to achieve, a key link in the process, and at least a witness, perhaps a participant, in the abduction of eight Irishmen who had arrived for the meeting, a meeting that you had yourself set up. Is that not true, Miss Kimball?" The addition of her name at the end of this charge, though easily dismissed as unnecessary, was a ploy by Leyton to emphasise that he was pinning her down, pinning guilt on her; and Kate felt the intimidation, just as Leyton had intended.

Kate's instinct was to look to Irwin for advice but, perhaps for the first time since the whole ghastly mess had started, she found herself thinking clearly, logically, and swiftly enough to inform her response. Palmer was dead. The mercenaries she had inadvertently led to the O'Connells would never have said anything, even supposing anyone could find them. So, the only possible source of Leyton's information was the O'Connells, via the journalist they had clearly recruited; and that was never going to stand up in any court of law. She didn't need Irwin.

"Of course I was 'cognisant' of the deal" she said, with dismissive venom. "I contacted the Army Council with a message that Palmer wanted to talk to them. What did you expect me to say when they asked why? Oh, sorry, can't tell you that. I told them what Palmer told me to tell them, that he wanted to discuss the position of the IRA in the referendum period. They are not stupid. They recognised that Palmer would be, in some way, wanting to stop them taking terrorist action; and they agreed to meet his representative to find out what might be on offer in return. Correct me if I am wrong, but I don't think that infringes any law?"

Leyton and, indeed, Penfold, were somewhat taken aback by this rather more spirited reply than they had anticipated; and Irwin was most impressed. But Penfold was not about to give up.

"And what was on offer in return?" he asked. Irwin was about to intervene – this was the pivotal question, on which Seymour's credibility could depend – but Kate was now firing on all cylinders.

"That was a matter for him, for Palmer that is, not me. I'm not a politician. I negotiate book deals with authors, not constitutional matters with terrorists." She was about to add more, but felt she had said enough to deflect any immediate danger. To her relief, Penfold clearly, though less enthusiastically, took the same view. He changed tack.

"But you knew the men at the meeting were, in fact, seized, bundled off to an unknown destination, and subsequently kept in captivity for some months. You were there when they were abducted, you saw what happened." Much as he wished to avoid it, he could not keep an element of triumphalism from his voice.

"Says who?" was Kate's short but devastating reply. The silence that followed was as good a moment as she had experienced in a long time.

"We have our sources" was the best that Penfold could come up. He recognised, every bit as much as Kate, how pathetic this sounded.

"Well, you don't need anything from me then, do you?" was Kate's final hammer blow on the subject.

"We would like to know your side of the story" was Penfold's desperate attempt to hang onto the interview, but to no avail.

"I don't have anything more to say on the subject" said Kate. "Do you have any other questions?"

Irwin would have clapped if it hadn't been totally inappropriate; and without a single 'no comment'. He was, as he would tell Kate later, much impressed. But they weren't entirely out of the woods yet.

"I do have one other question" said Penfold. "We are taking another look at the tape recording that you have said was the reason that you agreed to help Palmer, one that you say is a forgery, correct?"

Kate, and Irwin, were both mentally thrown backwards by this. How could it be true, given that the tape, both copies, had been retrieved and destroyed. Kate, feeling somewhat ebullient immediately prior to the question, was now lost for words. Instinctively she glanced at Irwin, who gave such an imperceptible shake of his head that Kate wasn't even sure he had done so.

"That is correct" said Kate. "It is a forgery. I was forced to record it, by Palmer.

"This was to buy your silence on previous activities carried out by Palmer?" asked Penfold. Kate nodded. "And how did he force you?"

"He had me locked up; no-one knew where I was being held; and he threatened that I would disappear, or worse, if I did not make the recording. I have said all this before."

"True" said Penfold. He now wanted to end the interview as soon as possible, because, quite unexpectedly, he had struck gold. "I won't detain you any longer. You are free to go."

As Kate and Irwin, heading back to Irwin's chambers, and Penfold and Leyton, heading back to New Scotland Yard, each reviewed the interview, they all experienced a very strange sensation. It was clear to all of them that, on the surface, it had been very satisfactory from Kate's point of view; and very unproductive from the point of view of the police investigation – they had nothing more they could use than before – but it was Kate and Irwin who were perplexed, in fact quite worried, and Penfold and Leyton who were feeling almost jubilant.

"Did you see that?" asked Penfold. "Did you see it? That reference to the tape absolutely threw them. It was a fraction of a second before she recovered, but what you said really shocked them and why is that? I'll tell you why. It's because they know the tape's gone. Or at least they think they know that it's gone. And that tells us that we are not dealing with the little miss innocent she claims to be. Someone is protecting her, and she knows it. Forget cock-up. This is conspiracy, pure and simple. Let's go see the boss."

Duggan, when he heard the news, was both surprised and yet not surprised, because he had not for one moment given any credence to the idea that the loss of the tape was just one almighty bureaucratic mistake. So, it was good to have that confirmed, but nonetheless astonishing in its implications. Someone was protecting Kimball. A secret lover in the CPS he discounted as totally fanciful. Which left…. Who? An Irish unification sympathiser in the CPS, but that meant Kimball must be more than just a go-between. So, at the least she was guilty of aiding and abetting a terrorist organisation, perverting the course of justice and, quite possibly Palmer's murder. Or, Palmer's backer in the government, which could only mean Seymour. And if he was protecting Kimball then, once again, she was up to her neck in whatever was ging on.

The problem, as Duggan Immediately knew, was that he had nowhere near enough to confront Seymour; and, just as bad, he had nothing with which to confront Kimball. Seymour would not provide anything, Kimball would not incriminate herself and, it was clear from what Penfold had reported, that she knew she had nothing to fear from IRA back chat. He would push Reynolds, maybe scare him if he could, but he doubted anything but bland assurances as to improving security arrangements would materialise. In short, he was the most powerful policeman in the land. He was fairly sure that the Prime Minister had been involved in completely illegal quasi-military action on home soil; and the world was waiting for an answer from him. But the witnesses he needed were, respectively, dead – Palmer; unknown – the men involved in the operation itself; not reliable, or even credible – the IRA: and a lone female civilian who had had some dealings with the IRA, extent uncertain, but was quite clearly savvy enough not to incriminate herself. Having elaborated the problem to himself in this way, something lurked at the back of his mind, as yet unformed, or at least as yet not conscious, as to how he might break through this problem; but it clearly wasn't yet ready to illuminate his thinking, and he knew from experience that the best thing was simply to forget about it for a while. It would emerge in its own good time. Meanwhile, he would call the DPP.

The moment his call went through to Daniel Reynolds, the DPP started to apologise. He was mortified that the tape that the Met had asked to be sent back to them was not in the file where it should be; he had instigated both an investigation and search, but as yet had had no success. He had himself listened to the tape on the 23rd September, his P.A had then returned the file to the CPS archive; and she was a completely trustworthy, long-standing member of the CPS, twenty-two years with them and seven as his P.A. Reliable, stable, happily married to a senior civil servant in HMRC, and evidently distressed that she was the last person to legitimately have had the file.

Paradoxically perhaps, Duggen found this little speech to be quite helpful, because it seemed to confirm that the file, or at least the tape within it, had not just been lost. It had, according to Reynolds, clearly gone back to the archive; and so, when Duggen finally was given an opportunity to cut in, he went straight to the point.

"How easy would it be for anyone in the CPS, without proper authority, to gain access to a file in the archive?" he asked. He had no way of knowing that this was a direction of the conversation with which Reynolds was entirely happy.

"In retrospect, I have to confess, too easy" said Reynolds. "Anyone wanting to enter needs authorisation, which is always checked, but once in, there isn't anything to stop someone accessing a different file to the one they have indicated they wish to see. That looks sloppy now – I see that – but we have never in all my time at the CPS, nor as far as I know, ever before, had such a problem. And short of locking every file, I'm not sure how we would address the problem."

"But you will have a record of everyone who, within a certain period accessed the archive?" asked Duggan.

"Absolutely" replied Reynolds, "and it is shorter than it might have been in that most access requirements are for documents that are in the equivalent electronic file, and therefore accessed on line; but we have done an initial check and there are still over twenty individuals who visited the physical archive between the date I sent it back and your request to see it again. You will probably want to do some sort of checking of them, but if one of them took the tape, I doubt they will have left any sort of incriminating trail for you to follow."

Duggen left that suggestion unanswered. "So, any of them could have walked out with the tape?"

"I'm afraid so" said Reynolds, "or they could just have put it in a different file. There are over one hundred thousand there, many of which will never be looked at again, and therefore virtually impossible to find. Either way, this is disastrous for the organisation, without precedent, and I can't apologise enough. Just how important is the tape? As you know, we didn't proceed because we had no evidence to counter the woman's statement that it was a forgery. Has that situation changed?"

"I can't really discuss that" said Duggan, "other than to say that we do have further information, which might mean we attach more importance to the tape than previously, whether a forgery or not. But I guess we will have to proceed without it."

There was a pause in the conversation, from Duggan's side because there wasn't really any more to say, but from Reynolds side because he was plucking up the nerve to ask what for him was the critical question. But there was nowhere else to go.

"Will the loss of the tape have to become public knowledge?" he asked. "I appreciate that this must be a matter for the Met alone – it would be quite improper for me to voice a view. It is more that forewarning would allow me to prepare for what would be a serious blow to our public reputation – possibly a resigning matter for me, sad to say – so any advance warning would be appreciated."

You will appreciate that I can't give any guarantee" said Duggan, "but it is a perfectly reasonable request, with which, if I can, I will comply." Reynolds thanked him, and the call ended.

Both men felt somewhat satisfied with the conversation, though for quite contrary reasons. Reynolds felt that despite deliberately putting himself to some extent in the firing line – he and his P.A. were the last legitimately to have hold of the file – Duggan showed no sign at all that he, Reynolds, could be a suspect. Implicitly accepting that the tape had not just been lost through some stupid mistake, but that it probably had been purloined, he also thought was not the re-action of a guilty man. So, there might be public ructions to come, though he didn't for one moment contemplate that he would actually need to resign, but there seemed negligible risk that the truth would ever emerge. The only people who knew what he had done were the PM and the man who had collected the tape; neither of them would ever reveal what they learned. So, all in all, a satisfactory conversation.

He would have been less pleased had he known Duggan's reaction, which rested on no fewer than four points arising from the conversation. First, even the DPP had ditched any notion of a cock-up. The tape had been stolen, full stop. Second, Duggan would, indeed, identify and research everyone who had had access to the archive in the relevant time period – his team were, unsurprisingly, very good at that sort of operation – but he was willing to bet quite a lot that there would be no links to Kimball and no links to the Irish, for the simple reason that any culprit would know that any such connection would, almost certainly, run them to ground. Third, it wasn't just that, logically, this just left the DPP himself, nor even that Duggan now knew that it could easily have been the DPP himself who took the tape, before he sent the file back to the archive, but Duggan's antenna – such a critical factor in his rise to the pre-eminent position he now held – that told him Reynolds was playing him along, providing information and creating a context for their discussion which manifestly precluded – or supposedly so – any suggestion that the DPP could be involved. Duggan had seen it so often before – thieves who admitted they were near a crime scene but were, of course, innocent, even murderers who admitted to hating the victim, but quite innocent – and now, many years on, he could just tell when something similar was happening. And he was sure it had just happened again.

Plus, fourth, most important of all, he was now convinced that he knew who was protecting Kimball. The IRA could, he supposed, have threatened Reynolds, but he was sure that Reynolds would in that case have sought support and protection. No, it had to be Seymour. He didn't know how Seymour had got to Reynolds, nor did he particularly care; and in truth he wasn't that much concerned with whether or how Reynolds' actions might come to light. The key thing was that he now felt he knew who was pulling the strings, pulling his chain. The only question was how he would now proceed.

CHAPTER 70

Duggan decided that he would refrain from sharing his deductions with Penfold. Until he had decided how to handle Reynolds, he felt it was best to keep the matter to himself. What he wanted to discuss was his next step, but some little voice told him to sleep on it for a night, let his brain restore its full powers, and reveal to him the solution he knew was in there somewhere. He was not disappointed. He woke at seven the following day, and the key element of the answer he craved just popped up, almost gift-wrapped, he thought. He reviewed it, over and over in fact as he shared his breakfast with his wife, who merely thought him rather more taciturn than usual at that time of the day; and then set off to do battle, in a more underhand way than was usual for him, but he had total confidence that the circumstances warranted it.

Once in his office he summoned Penfold and Leyton. Rather than state categorically that he was persuaded Seymour was involved, he softened this to saying that he very much feared that might be so, in which case the problem was how to proceed. But overnight he had decided on a course of action. Curiously, perhaps, it did not involve the Met, at least, not officially, but it was the best hope of getting to the bottom of the matter. The key observation, the aspect of the situation from which all else would follow, was that, while they had interviewed Kimball four times, no-one outside the Met, other than Kimball and her lawyer, knew what she was saying. If Seymour was, as Duggan strongly suspected, the architect of what happened, then he would be praying that Kimball said nothing, or at least nothing verifiable, to incriminate him. The IRA, on the other hand would be wanting her fully to back up the story they had released to the Press via Patrick Reilly, which was clearly intended to destroy Seymour. So far, Kimball had chartered a rather ambiguous course between the two, though overall rather more favourable to Seymour; but this she could do because it was all in interviews with the Met and in connection with her own involvement. What if she had to go public, without the protection of secrecy she had to date enjoyed?

"My guess" he said, " is that if she really, genuinely knows or believes that this was all Palmer, not Seymour, she will say so – she just isn't going to tell a pack of lies that she knows will bring down a PM, maybe the government, and she wouldn't be at all convincing if she tried; but, if she knows the IRA are correct, then I think she will rightly be terrified that if she lies to save Seymour – and why would she do that - she will be the IRA's number one target, for just as long as it takes for them to find her at an unguarded moment. In short, I think we will get the truth." He was going to ask them what they thought, but he was, by now, totally committed in his mind to the way forward that he had come up with; and it was too late for anyone to stop him now.

Penfold nodded. "Very persuasive, boss" he said. "Works for me. The only question is how you're going to get her out in the open, to go public. There's no incentive for her to talk to the Press. I bet she just wants the whole thing to die, at least as far as she is concerned, as quickly as possible.

"You're right" said Duggan, "so, no, not the Press. I have another strategy, which he proceeded to lay before his two detectives. Though novel, they immediately saw how it could and would work and, having confirmed that to Duggan, the meeting broke up, leaving the head of the Met to embark on probably the most audacious operation that he or any of his predecessors had ever embarked on.

One man would be critical to the operation, and Duggan needed to contact him in complete secrecy. That man was, that morning, quite unsuspecting of what was about to come his way, sitting at his desk in Portcullis House, overlooking Westminster Bridge. His name was Barry Brotherton MP, an opposition member for a safe Midlands constituency; and generally regarded as a moderate, a safe pair of hands, but not necessarily a high flyer, neither while in opposition nor, should they come to power in a general election, in any future government.

A great deal of the work of the House of Commons is done in Commons Committees, with MPs from all parties sitting on each of them. Similarly, much of the work of the House of Lords is conducted in multi-party committees. A rare exception is the JSC, the Joint Security Committee which, as its name implies, is a joint committee of the two houses, tasked with looking at national security matters. It can choose its own topics, construct its own agendas, sit in public or, if security issues require it, behind closed doors. The seriousness of its remit, and the somewhat restraining hand of the Lords' members on the rather more argumentative Commons members means that it was one of the least fractious and, therefore, most influential of all Parliamentary committees.

It was Brotherton's good or bad fortune – that was still to be decided – that he was Chairman of the JSC.

Duggan proceeded very cautiously. He first established Brotherton's routine and, from this, when he would be at home in his constituency. He then arranged for his tennis partner, a management consultant with one of the major accountancy firms, a long-standing friend but with no connection to the Met or, indeed, any police organisation, to call on Brotherton late the next Saturday afternoon. His message was simple. The Head of the Met would like to consult Brotherton, in his capacity as Chairman of the JSC, on a matter of national importance but in complete secrecy. With apologies for the cloak and dagger aspect, could Brotherton and Sir Colin both separately drive to a remote spot of Brotherton's choosing, outside his constituency, at a convenient time, for an entirely off-the-record conversation. The matter, he added was an entirely legitimate one that fell completely within the remit of the committee which Brotherton chaired. The matter was of some urgency, so that if the following day was possible, Duggan would make sure to fit in with Brotherton's schedule.

Duggan had not the slightest doubt that, unless he was wall-to-wall booked up for the Sunday, which was unlikely, Brotherton would meet him the next day - few individuals, and still fewer politicians would be able to restrain their curiosity enough to turn down such a proposal; and he was not disappointed. At 4 pm the following day, two cars, almost simultaneously, drew up and parked in a parking bay off the A513, north of Tamworth, designed mainly for walkers intent on a circular walk through the countryside east of the main road, but at that time of the day in early October, quite deserted.

The two men shook hands; and Duggan pitched right in. "I apologise for the somewhat melodramatic arrangements to meet" he said. "It is simply that, after we have talked, it will be entirely for you, exercising your complete independence as Chairman of the JSC, to decide what, if anything to do; and I did not want to take any risk whatsoever that that independence of action might, quite unfairly, be questioned by anyone as a result of us accidently being seen together. Neither of us is unknown to the media."

"You are too polite, Sir Colin" cut in Brotherton. "You are certainly a very recognisable figure. Outside my constituency – and maybe even inside it – I, sadly, am wholly unknown to the world outside Westminster. But I take your point." He smiled. "So, how can I help you? You will not be surprised to know that I am immensely intrigued."

"I imagine that you will be equally unsurprised" said Duggan, "that it concerns the Met's investigation into the allegation against Andrew Palmer, and maybe others, that he mounted an illegal military operation in Northern Ireland during the referendum campaign."

Brotherton smiled again, and nodded. "I did suspect as much" he said. "Do go on."

"Entirely between ourselves – I assume that is accepted?" Brotherton nodded agreement, "the information we have strongly indicates that such illegal activity did occur, that Andrew Palmer was instrumental in carrying out, but that he almost certainly had backing – financial and political – for the operation. I won't waste our time by being coy – if Palmer did have that backing, it would almost certainly have come from the Prime Minister. Nothing remotely on file, of course, no paper trial and, indeed, no money trail, but nonetheless, almost certainly Seymour. However, our Irish sources will be torn apart in court as entirely self-serving; and I certainly do not have enough concrete evidence to charge Seymour. The only reason that that is not the end of the matter is that I have one witness, the woman referred to in the Sunday Times article, Katherine Kimball. Just what her role was is not clear, but as she is potentially vulnerable to the Met bringing charges against her, I cannot get her full co-operation." He paused, to let Brotherton digest all this.

"Therefore" he continued, "later this week, I will issue a report that confirms the illegal action, and Palmer's responsibility for it. I have to confess that this decision is made much easier by the fact that Palmer is dead, so that no prosecution will follow from it. But my report will also indicate our assessment that Palmer could not have instigated such an operation alone; but must have had assistance from person or persons unknown. We will deploy some wording that, while stating that the Met will carry on with its inquiries, will indicate to the intelligent reader that we have little confidence in making any further headway. Our meeting here today is, first, to give you advance notice of this intention; and, second, to ask whether, once our report is issued, your committee might take it upon itself to investigate. It will be obvious to everyone that the matter is highly politically charged; military intervention against the IRA clearly involves national security, which is the committee's remit; and the Met's report, unfortunately will leave people wanting – in some cases, demanding – that the matter does not end there. As I said at the beginning, this is obviously – it can only be – a question for you to decide; but I hope you will understand why I am keen for you to pursue the matter."

Brotherton took a deep, almost theatrical breath. He wanted to appear thoughtful, grave even. Within Westminster he was someone of no little importance, who had dealt with a number of significant and controversial issues. He knew that he should take time to consider the pros and cons of what Duggan had proposed; and he would, indeed, say that he would reflect over night and get back to Duggan in the morning. But he also knew, as well as he perhaps had ever known anything, that he would get his committee onto the matter just as soon as the Met's report was issued. It would put his committee, and him as its chairman, at the heart of the biggest political scandal for a generation; and it might well result in a discredited government, a general election and his own party's return to power, after so many years in the opposition wilderness. Brotherton couldn't believe his good fortune.

"If you do go ahead" added Duggan – though he recognised every bit as much as Brotherton that there was no 'if' involved, "I have one other request. Could you please hold your hearings in public?" I realise that you have the power to go into secret session, and that this is sometimes necessary: but, subject to your own assessment, while there may be significant issues of political embarrassment involved, there is, I suggest, no threat to national security from full transparency – we have no reason to think, for example, that the security services are in any way involved."

"I take your point" said Brotherton. "You will have to leave that with me."

"Of course" said Duggan. Neither of them gave even the lightest glimmer of what they both knew – that Brotherton was as likely to dismiss the public and the cameras from his hearings as turn up naked for them.

CHAPTER 71

Two days later, Duggan called a press conference to release what he described as 'an interim report' which spelt out exactly what he had described to Brotherton. In a short speech, he summarised the main points, that the Met believed a serious crime, as alleged in the Sunday Times, had been committed, that Andrew Palmer had been involved in the execution of that crime, and that it was likely that he had had assistance in mounting the operation. He, Duggan, was not in a position to speculate on whom that might involve; that the Met would continue to investigate but, with Palmer being deceased, no easy leads currently presented themselves for fully resolving the facts of the matter. He declined to take questions, which was just as well, because several reporters, almost simultaneously shouted out 'is the Prime Minister a suspect?' That this was clearly one interpretation would, by some long way, be the main item of news, for the rest of the day and for some time to come.

Later that day, Brotherton consulted the members of his committee by email, saying that he proposed to have the situation considered by them, as a matter of national importance and some urgency. He invited comments, but his wording clearly brooked no opposition and, by the next morning, his staff had set up a planning session for the committee the next day. By the week-end, which in the nature of these things was unprecedently fast, Brotherton had established a set of dates for the committee to have an initial meeting, and to take evidence from Patrick Reilly. He contacted 10 Downing Street, to say that the committee would wish to hear from the PM any elaboration he could give on what he had said to the House of Commons; and, having asked Duggan how best to contact Katherine Kimball, contacted Sir Charles Irwin to say that the committee would wish to interview her. Duggan could not honestly say that his job gave him many moments of sheer delight, but this, undoubtedly, was one such.

The following week, Patrick Reilly duly appeared in front of the committee of twelve. He had insisted to Penfold that he not be named by the police, nor formally interviewed by them, but the Sunday Times had named him; and he was not about to pass up the chance to describe the iniquity of the British government in its own back yard. Brotherton was slightly anxious that, in front of the press and the live camera recording, the session might fall a little flat, because Reilly had already divulged what he had to say to the two journalists who had written the newspaper article. But all such fears were allayed when Reilly described the message that Kimball had brought from Palmer, that sections of the British government, including the Prime Minister secretly wished to see Northern Ireland leave the UK and become part of a United Ireland, so as not to have to expend substantial quantities of public money on an area that would probably leave anyway, sometime soon. This was so explosive that few of the reporters who dashed outside to make report stopped to think that this might be a complete fabrication on Palmer's part, designed to construct the appearance of common ground with the IRA but not, in fact, a remotely accurate description of the PM's thinking or, indeed, anyone else's in the government.

Once the committee had given this part of Reilly's evidence a thorough going over, Brotherton steered them onto the other element that could play to the advantage of its investigation – what roll did he understand Katherine Kimball had played? Was she a party to Palmer's line, whether it be a deception or not; and did she know that the plan all along had been to seize and thereby neutralise the IRA's senior commanders?

When Penfold has asked him this, he had repeated what the O'Connells had told him, that she had seemed stunned by the development, as much fooled by Palmer as the IRA themselves. Since then he had checked back with the O'Connells – was that the story they wished him to maintain, or was there any mileage in suggesting Kimball was more involved, perhaps much more involved, than she was letting on. The O'Connells had discussed this at some length, but concluded Reilly should stick to the same story. It was partly that they thought Kate would be more credible if she was seen more as Palmer's victim than his accomplice; but also that they had decided on the stick they would be applying, and Reilly's account could be seen as a little bit of carrot to go with it.

So, in reply, Reilly confirmed that he had been told, by people present at the tme, that Miss Kimball had seemed shaken by the arrival of a military force; and had been forcibly escort from the scene forthwith. She was, therefore, in his view, a clear party to Palmer's deception strategy, but unlikely to have known his true purpose.

Any doubts that Graham Seymour might have had about turning up to the committee were banished when he saw the TV coverage that evening, heard the radio coverage and, the next morning read the press coverage. Acreages of coverage but all essentially asking one question – did he know, was he involved, did he authorise the action? That could not be left unanswered.

The following day, with standing room only, he walked into the committee room with his Chief of Staff, sat down in front of the horseshoe table from which the committee operated and stated, in a manner that let everyone know he was not happy to be there, that he had made a very full statement to the House of Commons, so there was no need for any opening statement from him, but that he would be happy to answer any questions the committee might have for him.

Brotherton was not perhaps the highest of high flyers, but he was intelligent, subtle, and not about to enter a head-to-head clash with Seymour that he had little chance of winning. So, a straightforward questioning of the integrity of the MP's statement to the House, much as some hothead MPs in his own party might like that, was not going to be his strategy.

"Prime Minister," he said in a slightly deferential tone, reflecting seriousness of purpose rather than any element of actual deference, "I must first thank you for attending the committee today. I appreciate that this will be a distraction from your work in Number 10, but hope you will in turn appreciate that you may be able to help us in our deliberations, on what is a matter of great national importance and interest." Once this preliminary, designed to set a more harmonious atmosphere, was over, Brotherton turned to the substantive matter before them.

"You will have seen the Metropolitan Police Interim Report, suggesting that a serious crime, an illegal military action, was carried out; and that the former Government Press Chief, Andrew Palmer was involved in this." It did not go unnoticed that he had refrained from referring to Palmer as 'your' former press officer. "You explained in you statement to the House that you had asked Palmer to use whatever contacts he had to let the IRA know you would cancel the referendum if they embarked on a terror campaign." He left a moment for Seymour to confirm this, but he sat, rather grim faced and impassive.

"Patrick Reilly, whose evidence to us you will have seen, says that the IRA were told a quite different story by Palmer or, more accurately, were sent a quite different message by him. So my question is why do you think Palmer went so off track? I presume your instructions to him were quite clear?"

Only a very junior or a very naïve person watching would have not understood Brotherton's plan of attack. He was, at least for the moment, not remotely seeming to question Seymour's honesty to the House, or the integrity of his efforts to protect the referendum process. But, at the same time, he was publicly forcing the PM to face the fact that his statement to the House was being publicly challenged. The tension in the room as everyone waited to see how Seymour would deal with this was positively electric.

Seymour had not made it to the top of the greasy pole of politics without being a very agile operator; and he had had time to prepare for what was always going to be a very obvious sort of question from the Committee.

"Chairman," he said, in one word instilling a slightly calmer atmosphere, "it will be no surprise to you, or to your committee, that I have in the last week or so repeatedly asked myself that very question. Andrew Palmer, with whom I worked for many years, and therefore knew well, was, first of all, extremely loyal. He knew what I was seeking to achieve, and his sense of loyalty meant he very much did not want to let me down. Second, he was a very 'can-do' character, if I may use that term. He had an enviable and justified reputation for 'getting things done' – a reputation he valued and, to be quite frank, played up to. And third, he did not like or readily accept defeat, not at all. So, in answer to your question, I believe that in some way or the other, the IRA refused to play ball, perhaps – though this is pure speculation on my part – believing that I was not serious, or could not be trusted by them. At which point Andrew's loyalty, determination and refusal to let the IRA off the hook led him to formulate a much more clandestine plan to neutralise them. The three characteristics I have mentioned – his loyalty, his 'can-do' spirit and his refusal to accept defeat - are, to my mind, all very creditable – very much why he was in the position he held long before I entered Number 10; but on this occasion, tragically, they led him astray. If he were still with us, I have no doubt he would face prosecution, but I would have happily been a character witness for him."

It was, as every member of the Committee recognised, a consummate performance. It was measured, in its own way loyal; it purported to explain the inconsistency between his statement to the House and what the Committee had heard from Reilly and, most important of all, did not go anywhere the notion that he, Seymour, could in any way be party to illegal action. But he was not out of the wood yet, not by any means. The Committee still had two missiles to fire, one pyrotechnic but, ultimately, unlikely to shake Seymour. The other was more prosaic, but with the capacity to inflict real damage.

The Committee, in its preparation, had decided that, however 'disrespectful' it might seem, the question on everyone's lips – was the PM complicit – had to be asked, but to avoid any notion of party politicking, it should be someone from the PM's own party who should put the question. Brotherton nodded to the member who had been volunteered, a woman who would be a whole lot better known by the evening than at any time so far in her life.

"Notwithstanding those attributes" she said, disarmingly, Andrew Palmer was a Civil Servant, a powerful and, it would seem very effective one, but not a politician. I do not think I am alone on this committee in thinking that, if as you say, the original strategy had failed in some way, he wouldn't want, wouldn't seek, indeed wouldn't need, some form of authorisation - some clear backing - to embark on what seems to have been a quite extraordinary departure from the original plan. Surely, Prime Minister, he must have contacted you before embarking on the action we have heard about, must have had some green light from you to proceed?"

So there it finally was, out in the open, in the presentable but less than thrilling location of a committee room in the House of Commons, the question that had absorbed every news channel for nearly a week. Was the PM complicit?

"I only wish Andrew had contacted me," Seymour replied. "Had he done so, I could have made it clear, beyond any shred of doubt, that any plan to pursue what apparently transpired would be absolutely out of the question. How or why would I have said differently? I guess we might have discussed other possible ways forward, but I can assure the committee that any such options would have been fully within the realms of the legal. Why didn't Andrew contact me? I think the answer will be evident to you all. He knew me well enough to know that I would have immediately shut down any such suggestion and so, as I say, out of loyalty and determination, he took it upon himself to proceed. The best of intentions, but a mistake of truly epic proportion."

Brotherton was neither surprised nor daunted by this reply. What else could the PM say, what else could they expect? It might be true; and if it wasn't there would not be any sort of electronic or paper trail to confirm it, of that he was quite sure. They had had to ask the question – no doubt about that – but it was never going to produce a confession. Their remaining question might stir things up more. Brotherton nodded to another committee member, a long-standing member of the House of Lords.

"Accepting what you say," he opened, "I'm puzzled, truly puzzled, by one aspect of what happened. If we are to believe the evidence presented previously, Palmer's Plan B, if I may use that for shorthand, involved a significant military operation, the seizure of a very well-established terrorist group, and their detention over a considerable period of time. I do not doubt, from what you have said that Palmer's organising abilities would be up to it, but where on earth would he have got the resources - the men, the equipment, the money – to carry out such an operation. He was, after all, just your press officer."

The switch to Palmer being described as Seymour's man, in this context, was quite deliberate, no doubt in part reflecting that being a member of the House of Lords gives one the freedom from influence to be as awkward as one wants. Only someone wo knew Seymour very well, and who was watching him very closely, would have noticed that, for the first time since he had entered the room, Seymour was slightly uneasy.

"I confess that I do not know the answer to that question" said Seymour, "but – and here I can only once again speculate – there would have been private sector organisations which would have had a commercial interest in Northern Ireland remaining part of the United Kingdom. And there are, I have no doubt, ex-military personnel who, in 'the Troubles' fought in support of retaining the province in the UK - no doubt some who lost comrades in that war. It would not surprise me for one moment if, via Andrew's extraordinary network of contacts, he was able to tap into the money and men for such an operation. May I add that, if there is lurking in your question the idea that I might have in some way found or sanctioned the use of such resources, I reject it out of hand; and your committee is most welcome to conduct whatever investigation it wishes into the allocation of any and every last penny of public expenditure. I will personally deal with anyone who might seek to obstruct you in that."

A number of observers noted, as did Seymour, that this was the only point in the whole hearing at which he became mildly aggressive in manner, taking the battle to the committee, so to speak but, slightly paradoxically, the only time when he seemed at all on the defensive and, as a result, rather weaker than he had hoped. But, it was enough. He had not slipped up. He had produced solid replies to all the committee's questions, delivered in a resilient manner. There was, he felt sure, no basis for any sort of conclusion, or even suggestion, that he had been a guilty party. Once the committee had reported he could, he was very hopeful, return to normal life, or as normal as it ever was for a Prime Minister, with an economic boom to come and the political benefits that would naturally follow.

CHAPTER 72

The committee had previously accepted Brotherton's proposal that they meet in private after the Hearing with Seymour, to consider what they had learnt, and how best to proceed. But they were all aware that there was not a lot new to discuss. Seymour had said very much what they anticipated he would say, with some aplomb and a number of powerful flourishes, but nothing startling; and nothing that gave the committee any clear inferences, still less conclusions. They therefore quite quickly agreed that they should move forward to a hearing with Katherine Kimball who from the committee's perspective remained something of a mystery, to see what she might be able tell them. Whether it would be definitive was doubtful, but she had clearly been in a central role in what Palmer had organised, so she might, just might, lift the committee towards some sort of conclusion.

Brotherton, immediately the Committee's way forward had been agreed, had got the Committee Secretary to contact Sir Charles to say that they would want Kimball to attend a Hearing. Irwin had been non-committal, saying merely that he would pass that on to his client; and when he, Kate and Paul met up, raised the question of whether she should agree to attend or not.

"Do I have any choice?" asked Kate, assuming that a Parliamentary Committee was not unlike a police interview, just with politicians not the police.

"It's a grey area" said Irwin. "Virtually everyone 'invited' does turn up, but it's not clear that the committees actually have any legal power to compel attendance; and there have been a few high-profile cases of people refusing to appear. So, yes, you do have a choice; but my strong recommendation would be to attend, for two reasons. The first is that a refusal to attend, whatever reason you give, will be seen and taken as evidence that you have something to hide. Whatever further action the police may or may not take, you will have the – I'm sorry to be blunt – the stigma of guilt, that you really were to some extent in bed with the IRA. And second, more generally, you must want all this to end, to just go away, to let you get back to and on with your life, with Paul, and as a publisher. I can't by any means guarantee that it will all end if you attend the Hearing, but I can absolutely guarantee that it won't go away if you don't. Interviewing you, finding out what you did or did not know, or do, will become the major scoop that dozens of journalists will want to pursue. So, best to say everything you possibly can say, in public, to the committee; and then they might leave you alone – though there is obviously a good book for you to publish" he added with a broad grin.

Kate saw this for the good advice it was but, in any event, the decision was made for her later that same day when she got back to her flat. Pushed through the letter box was a hand-delivered brown envelope. Inside there was just one sheet of paper, a photograph, of a gun, of what she immediately recognised as the gun that Declan O'Connell had used to shoot Palmer, the gun with her fingerprints on it which Declan had failed to dispose of. There was no text – the message was abundantly clear. The O'Connells were looking for validation, a validation that only Kate could provide.

Thus it was that the day after the hearing with Seymour, twenty-four hours in which for the most part Seymour had had fairly good media coverage of his testimony, Kate, accompanied by Irwin, entered the Committee Room. Her initial instinct had been to put on a bit of a show, partly to boost her confidence, partly to show that she was not going to be intimidated by the no doubt illustrious members of the committee, nor the reporters and others packing the room. Her highest heels she had thought, to make her one of the tallest people in the room, a very stylish suit, her very best professional look. But Irwin had cautioned against.

"You are a member of the public who has, through great misfortune, been dragged into something way beyond your experience or your control. You are an innocent party, just doing what you can to serve justice. Make them feel a little sorry for you. If you will allow me to advise, I suggest a smart but otherwise as unprepossessing outfit as you have, low heels, hair pinned up rather than flowing locks, do you see what I mean?" She had, and so it was, to the extent that someone with her natural presence could manage it, a rather colourless, even slightly dowdy Kate who was ushered in to face the committee. Some introductory pleasantries over, Brotherton pitched in.

"Could you please let the Committee know how you came to know Andrew Palmer; and then what part you played in his approach to the IRA Army Council during the Northern Ireland referendum campaign?"

Just as many actors say that all their pre-performance nerves disappear the moment they walk on stage, so Kate felt, for the first time in ages, a huge release of tension. She was not, she thought, under threat from this committee; she was not guilty of any crime; and she was being given the opportunity finally to put her story to the world. She would answer their questions and then, as Irwin had mooted, she would go back to living the life she wanted. She was highly adept at making business presentations. This would be the presentation to beat all the others.

The first two rules of any public speaking she knew were, first, get their undivided attention by initially saying nothing. It always worked. Second, your first sentence must absolutely grab them, if possible, startle them, make then gasp if you can. Because if you can do that, you are in command, and that is where Kate was determined to be.

She paused for several highly pregnant seconds. Then she was into battle. "I 'came to know' Andrew Palmer as you put it in your question, when he had me forcibly seized and imprisoned two years ago." Another pause, to let that sink in. "What I am about to tell you is now in the public domain, and so you may well be familiar with it, but it is important background to your investigation. My partner, Paul Emmerson, a Professor of Engineering at Oxford University discovered that there had been, many years before, an IRA attack on Sellafield Nuclear power station. The attack failed, but the previous Prime Minister, Alan Gerrard, had, when in an earlier much more junior government position, covered up the attack and had the IRA unit that carried out the attack liquidated. Professor Emmerson was illegally detained, in order to keep all this secret but, with the assistance of some current members of the IRA, whom I contacted to help me, I discovered the truth and made arrangements to have Professor Emmerson, released. Unfortunately, Andrew Palmer, then working for Alan Gerrard, seized me instead, to ensure that Professor Emmerson would remain silent; and then, under extreme threat, forced me to make a forged tape recording, that purported to be tapped phone conversations in which I plotted terrorist acts with the IRA. That secured, Palmer released me.

"I had not expected, and certainly hoped never to hear from him again. But he contacted me shortly before the referendum campaign to say that he wished to contact the IRA's current commanders. He said that that wouldn't be possible unless the first contact was from someone that they would be prepared to trust; and because I had helped expose what happened to their earlier members, they would, despite my being British, listen to me. As you may imagine, I wanted no part of this, but he still had the tape, and so I complied. That is how I 'came to know' Andrew Palmer."

"Thank you for frankness," said Brotherton, "and my apologies if this is at all stressful for you to recount. We just need to understand how you came to be involved in the matter we are investigating; and I think we are now clear on that?" He looked round the committee to see if any questions arose from what Kate had said so far, but there were none.

"What did Palmer ask, or should I say, force you to do?"

"He assured me that it was simple, quick and legal, but something only I could do, because of my previous contact with the IRA. I was to go to Northern Ireland, make contact, say that Palmer wanted to send a representative to talk to them and, if they agreed, I would return to Northern Ireland with his representative. After making that introduction, I could then leave; and Palmer would hand over the tape recording to me."

"So, you agreed to do this for him?" said Brotherton.

"Yes" said Kate. "I had little, no, I had no choice really. It sounded, as he had said, simple, quick and legal; and it held out the promise that I would be free from his control for good. So, yes, I agreed to it."

"Did you have any suspicion, any inkling, that Palmer was, in fact, planning to seize and detain the IRA personnel attending the meeting, the moment his representative arrived?"

"Absolutely not" replied Kate. "I was shocked out of my mind, in fact I was terrified that I was going to be detained or even murdered, until I was firmly escorted out and told to make my way home as best I could."

"But how could you not have known?" asked one of the committee members. We understand that a substantial body of armed men were involved; and they can only have been there if either you told them the meeting place or they followed you there. If so, surely you couldn't have failed to notice that?"

"I certainly didn't tell anyone" said Kate. "I'd never seen them before. I can only assume they had discreet surveillance on me, relaying my movements to the unit that seized the IRA team. The fact is that I was tricked by Palmer every bit as much as the IRA. I have several times thought how stupid I was, how gullible, and yet, I do not see how, for one moment, I could have foreseen what Palmer was actually planning."

No-one on the committee seemed inclined to pursue that aspect further; and so, with the tension in the room steadily rising, Brotherton turned to the crux of the matter.

"When your IRA contact asked you, as they must have done, what Palmer wanted to discuss, what were you supposed to tell them? What message were you to deliver?"

Kate had no hesitation in replying. "Palmer said that the Government was resigned to losing Northern Ireland, in which case the sooner the better, before the British government poured ever more money into the province. The referendum was a chance to do it quickly and peacefully; and he didn't want to risk terrorist action by the IRA disrupting and maybe derailing a Leave majority."

"You will, I assume, be aware" said Brotherton, with icy calm, "that the Prime Minister's recollection is different. He said that the project he agreed with Palmer was to threaten to cancel the referendum if the IRA started a bombing campaign. Was that any part of Palmer's briefing to you?"

As Irwin commented later, the cliché about being able to hear a pin drop in the absolute silence that followed this question was completely inappropriate – you could, he said, have heard a feather drop. It was as if no-one was even breathing, so acute was the tension. But Kate was now, finally, in command of the situation.

"No" she said in a clear and authoritative voice. "That was no part of the message."

Brotherton deliberately let this answer hang in the air. He wished to appear a scrupulously fair chairman but, if the Prime Minister had lied to the Committee, had lied to the House. He was in serious, perhaps terminal, trouble, and it was no part of Brotherton, as an opposition MP, to come to his aid.

The MPs on the Committee from the PM's party were fully aware of what Brotherton was doing, and one of them, Christopher Wallace, MP, decided that it was necessary to intervene.

"But, Miss Kimball" he said "we have heard that Palmer may have taken it upon himself to pursue the line you have described, as part of a plan to disable the IRA, only because the Prime Minister's intended strategy failed to work. Does not that readily reconcile what you have told us with what we have heard from the Prime minster?"

It is commonplace that time, or at least the perception of time, is highly elastic. Enjoyable times can flash by; dramatic moments hang on and on and on. For Kate, the few seconds before she replied were as if time had stopped altogether, as she suddenly realised that she knew everything. She knew exactly what had happened and she didn't have to rely on people choosing to believe her. The weeks and weeks of stress, the threats to her life to her freedom, almost to her sanity were, finally, at an end. And she also realised what the Committee, those present, those watching on TV, the press other media and ultimately the world would shortly realise; that through a maze of interlocking circumstances a reasonably successful but otherwise unremarkable publisher from Oxford could bring down the most powerful politician in the land, perhaps even his government. Furthermore, because she now knew that not just Palmer but Seymour had been instrumental in the terrifying ordeal she had endured in recent months, she would have no compunction in doing so.

The pause had been long enough that Wallace, sensing that Kate's hesitation might indicate that she was on shaky ground, repeated his question, this time more forcefully. "Doesn't what the Prime Minster said reconcile his actions with what you have told us?"

Kate was now ready to answer. Her four-word answer would, in time, come to be seen as a pivotal moment in modern British history. "No" she said. "It does not."

There was a series of gasps from several people in the room, and a flurry of whispers as those present sought to absorb this entirely unexpected reply. The disruption was sufficient that Brotherton had to ask for people to remain quiet, while they all waited for him to put the obvious question, namely why she believed this or how she thought she knew. But Brotherton decided, on the spur of the moment, on a more aggressive approach.

"Are you saying that the Prime Minister lied to this Committee, Mis Kimball?"

"That is for you to decide" said Kate, now rather more in command of the proceedings than Brotherton. So Brotherton had no option but to ask the obvious question.

"Why do you claim that the Prime Minister's evidence cannot be reconciled with what you say happened?"

Kate was tempted to say that the answer was both simple and obvious, but thought this might not endear her to the committee. So she launched straight into what was now crystal clear to her.

"Palmer had no way of contacting the IRA himself. That's why he dragooned me into making contact. When I first met them, the message that Palmer had given me to pass on was the one I have already described – to set up a meeting to discuss a mutual interest in Northern Ireland seceding from the UK. This couldn't have been a fallback plan if a threat to cancel the referendum had failed, because it was, through me, Palmer's first contact with the IRA." She paused, to let this sink in. For the first time, at least some of those present began to wonder whether Seymour would emerge unscathed from the affair.

Wallace moved into fully protective mode. "Could not Palmer have decided that the Prime Minister's approach was very likely to fail; and so took it upon himself, out of misplaced loyalty, to pursue his own strategy?"

"That, again, is for the committee to determine" said Kate, her authority and presence now dominating the room. "But you will need to ask why Palmer would embark on an expensive, dangerous and totally illegal operation that could put him in prison for many years, without at least trying the very simple operation that the Prime Minister had apparently asked him to carry out." She did not emphasise 'apparently' but her inclusion of the word cut through an atmosphere already taught to breaking point like a knife. And she wasn't finished. "I say 'very simple'. If the message was the threat to cancel the referendum, then Palmer could have told me to say that on my first trip. If he had got a negative answer, then, yes, he could have embarked on a plan B, but only because he would by then know that he needed one." She paused, quite deliberately, for effect. "However, that is not what happened" she added, her tone both sombre and definitive. Irwin sat beside her and was not alone in seeing that Kate was now almost playing with the committee. In a move imperceptible to anyone else, his hand just brushed her arm as he moved to adjust his tie; but Kate registered the caution Irwin was communicating, and said no more.

Brotherton was, inside, delighted. His committee was centre stage in investigating the biggest scandal in decades; and it increasingly looked as if the Prime Minister might not survive it. He would be severely damaged if he did limp on and, either way, the likelihood of an election defeat sometime soon had just increased massively. He did not think the situation could improve, so prepared to wind up the session.

"Thank you, Miss Kimball" he said. "As you say, it will be for the committee to consider what has emerged in our hearings. "Does any member of the committee have any final questions?"

"I do have one more" said Wallace, fighting to salvage anything he could, and not entirely clear where his question was heading. "If sending a clear message to the IRA - that in the event of terrorist acts by them, the referendum would be cancelled – would have been such a, as you say, very simple strategy, why do you suppose it was, according to you, not even tried?" His emphasis on 'according to you' was as unsubtle as Kate's approach moments before.

"It is clear" said Kate, "from the scale and enormity of the operation that Palmer carried out, that whoever instigated it was determined, at all costs, to hold the referendum and secure a Remain majority vote. Why that should be is for you, as politicians, but, if so, it would rule out any strategy that contemplated cancelling the referendum, wouldn't it?"

It passed through Irwin's mind that Kate was wasted in publishing. With instincts like this she could have been a top QC. The little question, tacked on at the end of her supposition, with little or no prospect of being answered, represented as close to total victory as he had seen in any courtroom battle.

Even had he had more time, Wallace was not remotely prepared to respond, but Brotherton gave him no opportunity. After repeating his thanks to Kate, he closed the hearing. As he did so, an unprecedented scene of chaos erupted, as numerous media members fought to get to Kate, trying to get a microphone in front of her, asking questions, one on top of another or asking for an interview. Irwin offered some bodily protection, as best he could, but also caught Brotherton's eye and held out a pleading hand. Brotherton immediately got the Secretary of the committee and two security guards who had watched the proceedings from the door to step in and start clearing people away from where Kate sat, silent and motionless.

As the crowd reluctantly edged, or were edged, away, Paul, who had been in the audience forced his way to Kate's side. Irwin, on her other side, leaned in close to her.

"That was, if I may say so, bloody brilliant" he said "Absolutely amazing. But, you are now the hottest property in the twenty-four-hour news round; and we must carefully manage the fall-out.

CHAPTER 73

Kate, Paul and Sir Charles waited while the room slowly cleared. The committee members waited to begin a private session but before that, Barry Brotherton came round to join Kate and the others.

"Thank you" he said to Kate, "that can't have been easy, but it has certainly helped the committee." Now beginning to feel slightly disorientated as she thought back over what she had said, Kate made no reply. Irwin acknowledged the thanks and said they would be on their way as soon as the scrum which he knew was assembling outside had dissipated.

"I can help" there said Brotherton. "A member of my staff will guide you through the corridors over to the House of Lords entrance. If you leave there, I doubt there will be many members of the press there; and even if there is, if you go first and get a taxi, it is a very short step from that entrance to the road. You should be fine."

And so it transpired; and after a cross between a debriefing and a celebration at Irwin's chambers, Paul and Kate headed off, unrecognized and unknown, back to Oxford. They had agreed with Irwin that Kate would stay at Sarah's house, with Paul ferrying Kate to work, dropping her well inside the precincts of the Oxford University Press's impressive grounds; and picking her up in the evening. With mail and phone calls screened, and a lot of emails deleted, Kate managed to remain unobtainable but still able to get back to her work, meeting authors, arranging editing, organising printing and all the million other jobs that went into successful publication of the sort of books the OUP Press aimed to bring to the world. Slowly but surely, her life began to return to normal.

The same very definitely could not be said for Graham Seymour. On advice from his Press Office, he made no statement nor gave any interview, on the Palmer affair or on anything else, knowing that any interviewer worth his or her salt, whatever the pretext of the interview, would quickly home in on the only political topic of interest to them or, it had to be said to the population at large. But in the absence of anything from Seymour, speculation that he would be forced to resign grew by the day.

A President or Prime Minister of virtually any other democratic regime – not to mention undemocratic ones – can, if he or she so wishes, disappear from view if that is thought to be the least bad strategy in difficult times. One thing stops that in the United Kingdom, namely PMQs – Prime Minister's Questions – the once-a-week battle in the House of Commons between an Opposition, out to find as many embarrassing questions as possible, and a Prime Minister equally determined to fend them off and, if possible, score some resounding points of their own. Only a very small percentage of the population ever watches these skirmishes, but if one side or the other gains some sort of ascendency over time, this creeps into the general consciousness and can be a significant factor in determining the outcome of elections. Against this background, failure by the PM to turn up would represent a major loss of nerve, a blatant confession of something to hide; and so Seymour had to face the music.

That Her Majesty's Opposition would be at his throat went without saying, but Seymour had a clear majority and could – however unpleasant it might be – see them off. The question, the only question, was whether he could hold onto his own side. He had no strategy other than to reiterate what he had told the House before, that he had not known about, still less authorised any illegal activity by Palmer. That might be enough for those who hadn't followed the JSC hearings too closely, but it might well not work with those who had tracked the wretched Kimball woman's evidence closely; and on such an incendiary issue, that could well be enough in his party to sink him. The utter frustration was that he had himself connived at eliminating the tape recording that could so easily have been used to discredit her, in order that none of Palmer's actions would come out in court; but out they had nonetheless come; and now he had lost that potentially winning card.

The next PMQs, in the end turned out to be rather a damp squid, for two reasons. The Leader of the Labour Opposition, Ccolin Williams, had recognised that, only by winning over enough Conservatives in a Vote of Confidence could they bring Seymour down; and a full-scale assault on him might well drive a number of them, however reluctantly, to support him. So Williams tried for a loftier approach, formulating his questions in terms of how could the Prime Minister expect to retain the trust of the House and of the nation, so necessary for effective government, in the light of the events in which he had been involved. This judicious wording was designed to implicate Seymour whatever he might say about the extent of his knowledge of Palmer's action.

The second reason the occasion fell flatter than anticipated was Seymour's insistence, not that he was blameless, but that the House should wait to see the JSC's Report. The implication was that Seymour believed it would exonerate him which, though he had only slender hopes of this, at least kept him afloat for the moment; and he had allies on the JSC. How loyal they could or would be remained to be seen.

Four days later, days in which any and every media outlet speculated endlessly and pointlessly on what the JSC would say; and what it might mean for Seymour, the JSC Report was published. There was much to ponder in it, but one sentence sealed Seymour's fate. After a detailed description of the events as described by Patrick Reilly and by Kate, the Report went on to say

While we do not totally discount the possibility that the operation was designed to deter IRA terrorist action by the threat of cancelling the referendum, the Committee does not see how this is consistent with the testimony it received concerning the contact made with the IRA or their subsequent seizure and detention.

This sentence would later find its way into Civil Service training manuals as a masterpiece of how to handle difficult situations. It made no mention of the Prime Minister; it held out at least a possibility that his statements to the Committee and the House were accurate; it referred to 'testimony' rather than 'evidence' to indicate that the committee was not totally credulous; and did not, in any formal sense, pass judgement as between what Reilly and Kate had said on the one hand, and what Seymour had said on the other. And yet, no-on reading it could be under the slightest illusion that it signified, beyond doubt, that the Committee simply did not accept the Prime Minister's version of events. The meaning between the words was crystal clear. Truly it was a death sentence.

Having given its damming conclusion in so many words, the report did not need to dwell on the consequences of its conclusion, but they were equally clear to everyone. If the PM's story did not stand, then Kate's did; and as no one believed that Palmer could have mounted the operation she had described without the political backing – and associated resources – that only Seymour could have provided, then he must have had some involvement in what transpired.

Straight after publication of the report, Seymour tried to get back on the front foot by himself calling for a Vote of Confidence in the House, not remotely confident that he could win it, but knowing it was unavoidable and, if so, better instigated by him rather than the Leader of the Opposition. But this did nothing to save him. The reiteration of his previous stance fell on deaf ears; and he had no coherent response to the line that the Committee had taken. Loyalty was enough to keep just over half his party behind him, but abstentions and a small but significant number of his own back benchers voting against him left him over forty votes adrift; and he resigned that evening.

The Press, TV and Radio and social media were immediately dominated by four issues: who would succeed Seymour; would there be a general election; would Seymour be prosecuted; and who exactly was the woman who had been mainly responsible for bringing Seymour down. Kate, however, took great pains to remain completely incommunicado, with Paul referring all inquiries to Irwin who, in turn, stonewalled everyone. This did not prevent all sorts of speculative stories to emerge but, without support, they eventually began to die away, increasingly replaced by the other three topics. But then the issue of prosecution also died away, once the head of the Met had announced that it was not taking its inquiries any further. This caused a media storm, but Duggan had always known that there was never going to be enough solid evidence to get a conviction – that was, after all, why he had initiated, or at least encouraged, action by the JSC as being the most effective way to see some measure of justice done.

Three candidates put themselves forward to succeed Seymour, but the Chancellor, David Flemming, was in pole position from the start. But what absolutely clinched his election was the remaining question – would there be a general election once the new Prime Mister was in place. The pressure for one was immense, because the prospect of having a PM without the legitimacy of their having won a general election bore down heavily on the candidates and the party. As a result, both of Flemming's contestants had decided that they must hold out the prospect of a general election soon after they were appointed; but Flemming was the one man in the government who knew the huge benefit of waiting, of not giving into any such demands for another 12 to 18 month, by which time the benefits of the economic strategy he was following, based on what he knew about the Irish Sea development – benefits to the public finances, to public spending, lower taxation, higher living standards and the country's economic growth – would be clear for all to see, and an election winner. So Flemming launched on a whirlwind of private meetings with the party's backbenchers, explaining as far as he dare that this was the way to many more years in power, whereas an early election in the wake of the Seymour scandal would probably result in defeat. Entirely predictably, this strategy won the day; and three weeks later David Flemming moved into Number 10. All he now needed was a Chancellor of the Exchequer who would grasp and pursue the strategy that the Irish gas fields would finance while, for political reasons, keeping that development slow and low key for as long as possible. Palmer in his time had loyally served Alan Gerrard, but failed to prevent his assassination. He had loyally served Graham Seymour, but had failed to prevent his elimination from the political scene in disgrace. The one true beneficiary of his machinations had been Flemming, a man he barely knew and for whom he had never worked.

As all this developed, so interest in Kate declined, to her great relief, her life, at work and with Paul gradually returned to normal, though one thing still nagged at her. However, this was resolved one evening, a week after Seymour resigned. She and Paul had gone out for dinner and, on returning to their flat, found a small but quite heavy package had been hand delivered, addressed to Kate. She opened it to find a gun, the gun that Declan O'Connell had used to kill Palmer but which she had also handled. With the gun was – a duster. With just a touch of humour, the O'Connells had fulfilled their pledge to remove this potentially very incriminating piece of evidence, in the only way in which Kate could be certain that they had done so, by sending the weapon to her, for her to dust off the finger prints but, so much more reliably, dispose of it as she thought fit, never to be seen again.

"Where do you think we should dump it?" she asked Paul.

"In the sea" said Paul. "I think we could do with a week-end away." Kate smiled her agreement and, the following week-end after a pleasant stay in the Grand Hotel in Swanage, they rented a small pleasure boat and, when around a quarter of a mile out on a calm sea, they dropped the gun overboard.

"Do you think that you could now concentrate on publishing high-quality books?" asked Paul, "and retire from terrorism, murder and dangerous political intrigue?"

"I thought I'd done that two years ago" said Kate, "until bloody Andrew Palmer walked back into my life. But he's gone now, so I hereby retire from all that."

"Let's hope the world understands that this time" said Paul, no longer jocular.

"Maybe I should have hung on to the gun" mused Kate, not clear even to herself how serious she was.

"You'll be fine." said Paul. "Armed or not, you've been more than a match for some of the most dangerous men of modern times. No-one's going to trouble you from now on."

"I hope you're right" Kate replied. "I do hope you're right."

EPILOGUE

Eighteen months later David Flemming won a comfortable majority for another five years in government. No-one was in any doubt that the major factor in this had been the steady improvement over the intervening period, resulting from a modestly expansionary budget shortly after Flemming came to power, followed by an undisguised 'give-away' budget one year later. Every politician, every economic analyst, in fact most members of the public could see this for what it was – a quite shameless attempt to sway the electorate to vote for Flemming; but this did not prevent it from succeeding, any the less than such a strategy had succeeded on numerous occasions before, in the UK and throughout the world's democracies.

Bu there were other factors at play. Increased tax revenues from the development of the Irish Sea meant that, despite increased government spending and lower income tax, the government's public finances nonetheless improved; and this increasingly built up a reputation for financial responsibility and economic competence which was hard for her Majesty's Opposition actually to oppose; and was almost as significant a contribution to Flemming's victory as any actual increase in living standards.

Flemming's overwhelming pre-occupation in the eighteen months since he had taken over was, first, to disguise for as long as possible the role of the Irish Sea gas field in the economic recovery over which he was presiding; and second, once it could no longer be kept hidden from either industry analysts or economists and other commentators on the government's finances, to obfuscate the position, not just for as long as possible but, he thought, with some help and a fair wind, indefinitely.

In both of these quests, Anthony Preston, CEO of EnergiCorp was, albeit for quite self-serving reasons, very helpfully on board. He ensured first that the field was developed at least as slowly as he had promised to Seymour; explored areas for which his company had licences to the east as well as the west of what would have been the demarcation line between the offshore rights of an independent Northern Ireland and Great Britain; and, via the network of interlocking pipelines across the whole field covered by EnergiCorp's licences, which included the bulk of those to the west, concealed from everyone except the company's own employees – and only a select few of them – that the gas was increasingly flowing from the western licence areas. It was over a year before it started to become clear, first to analysts and then more widely, that this was the case. But by then the Irish gas field had come to occupy a standing not unlike that which North Sea oil had been accorded previously for over thirty years, that is to say an energy resource for the United Kingdom as a whole, however much it might be the case that an independent Scotland could and no doubt would claim the lion's share of that resource. This perception was greatly helped by two things, the first being that by then the referendum and, indeed the whole scandal surrounding Gerald Seymour, was well over year in the past; and memories are, in the political arena, notoriously short. A few journalists could not resist pointing out the implications for the gas field and its benefits had the referendum gone the other way, but this occasioned little response, and most of that was to suggest that it would have been quite unfair to have allowed the economic benefits of an area which had been part of the United Kingdom for centuries to then accrue to one tiny part of its population.

The second hugely supporting factor was Flemming's strategy of pouring vast resources into Northern Ireland. Hospitals, schools, the province's energy infrastructure, roads, transport and a range of services associated with them were all given major financial infusions. The sums were modest in relation to the tax revenues now beginning to be generated from the Irish Sea gas field, but they shifted employment and living standards in the province to a new level, so there was little if any sense of Westminster cheating the region, or unfairly discriminating against it. Its economic well-being, its stability and security, and its confidence in the ongoing peace process had never been stronger.

Given all this, no-one - greatly to both Flemming's and Preston's relief - suggested that Seymour could somehow have known about how the gas field would develop; and his conduct at the time of the referendum remained lost in the past, of no significance eighteen months later. No-one that is except Kate who, as news of the development of the gas field emerged in the media, began to realise that she was staring at the missing link, the reason Seymour had been so determined, at whatever risk, to hold the referendum when he did, and make sure of the referendum result. Whether the plan was his or Palmer's she didn't know, and it didn't make a whole lot of difference. Seymour, she reasoned, could not threaten to cancel the referendum because he had to see it completed before knowledge of the economic bonanza sitting off the east coast of the province became known. There was no solid evidence, but she felt increasingly certain that Seymour had known what was coming; and that explained his actions. As Paul agreed, this was not something they would point out to the world any time soon.

Three weeks after the election, Kate received a rather grand looking envelope, with an even more grand invitation card inside, informing her that the CEO of EnergiCorp, Anthony Preston requested the pleasure of her company, plus guest, at a reception to celebrate the 40th anniversary of the founding of the company. Preston was, in fact, celebrating a year of bumper profits and the election of a government that was generally friendly towards business and one with which he had an undisclosed but particularly beneficial relationship. However, neither of these were appropriate matters to celebrate in public, so he fastened to the company's timely anniversary. His invitation to Kate had no ulterior motive. He was just curious to meet the woman who had played a not insignificant part in the Irish Sea saga. Kate, equally, was somewhat intrigued by the invitation from a man she had never met, heading a company with which she had never come across, but which, she knew from her brief reading of the papers, was at the centre of the Irish sea gas field development.

The reception was held in the foyer of EnergiCorp's headquarters in the City, near Canary Wharf. Its advantage was that it was quite large enough to accommodate the nearly three hundred invited guests. Its disadvantage - a degree of business-like austereness – was completely overcome by the importation of extensive greenery and a host of grand pictures of various rigs and ships which the company had owned and deployed over the years, together with a monumentally grand buffet, limitless champagne and a very superior waiter and waitress serving staff, all wafted by unobtrusive but melodious new age music from a top-notch audio system. As a wit said in Kate and Paul's hearing "this is either a hugely successful business or it is about to go under" but neither he nor Paul or Kate had much doubt as to which it was.

Preston did not go so far as to line himself and his wife up as a formal welcoming pair, but he made sure that they remained close enough to the entrance for him to be able to see each new arrival, and excuse himself from each conversation in order to meet the more important guests as they appeared at the doorway, primarily politicians and major industrialists, though also a few better known figures from the arts world to add a touch of glamour. Kate, though she fitted none of these categories, was very much on his list.

As she and Paul arrived, Preston, with his wife at his side, moved to introduce themselves.

"I'm delighted that you were able to come" he said, shaking both Kate and Paul's hand. He introduced his wife; and Kate remarked what a splendid occasion it clearly was. Preston accepted the compliment, remarking that the company was in good shape after forty exciting years in business.

"I understand that this last year has been another good year for you." Said Kate.

"It has indeed" replied Preston. "We explore and develop oil and gas fields all over the world. Some go well, some, sad to say, do not – that's the nature of the business – but the Irish Sea field has been a great success. I'm just sorry our mutual acquaintance did not feel he could attend." He noticed the look of incomprehension on Kate's face. "Graham Seymour I mean. This all started while he was in office; and I had hoped he might join us."

So, Kate registered, Seymour and Preston had been 'acquaintances'; suddenly it all clicked, the last piece of the jigsaw that confirmed her suspicions about Seymour; it very much looked like Preston might be part of the conspiracy.

"I have to correct you" said Kate, as politely as she could, "but he and I were never acquaintances. In fact, we never met."

"Oh" said Preston. "My apologies. I clearly wasn't following events back then as closely as I should have done." He was about to go on, but Kate decided this was her only chance to confirm her suspicions.

"You were no doubt very busy" said Kate with a disarming smile. "When did you first strike gas in the Irish Sea?"

The slightly shocked silence before Preston replied told Kate all she needed to know. But if confirmation needed, his reply supplied it.

"Oh, its very difficult to say with this technology," he said. "You are for ever exploring, analysing the geology, getting small amounts of shale that don't amount to much and then, bit by bit, you piece together a picture; and then dribbles of gas, that might or might not become commercially viable amounts start to appear. It's a process rather than any Eureka moment. That's fine in a novel, but the reality isn't like that."

Kate knew, beyond doubt, that he was lying – too wordy, some overtone in the delivery – that he was, therefore, covering up; and she knew why that was. Not something she could pursue, not here, not in public, not ever, but there was satisfaction in knowing that she had been right in her speculation about Seymour. Time to move on. She did not know – there was no way she could have known – that just across the room, not twenty feet from where she stood, Ray Simpson, the man in charge the day the EnergiCorp drilling rig struck oil, the one man who could – but never would – disclose that date, was enjoying a celebratory glass of champagne. She couldn't change the subject completely, but to get away from Seymour's or Preston's or, for that matter, her own activities eighteen months previously, "Was the development particularly difficult?" she asked.

"Technologically it was quite challenging" said Preston, "and there is always a host of competitors breathing down your back; but we pulled through quite well" conscious that both statements were less true of the Irish Sea development than almost any he had undertaken with EnergiCorp, but Kate was not to know that. "'Pulling through quite well' seems something of an understatement" said Paul, with a slight movement of his hand to indicate the very extravagant reception now in full swing. "I sense that you have seen off most of the opposition" he added with a smile.

"I guess you're right" acknowledged Preston. "We faced some tough competition, but we have achieved a notable victory; and, as they say, 'to the victor the spoils'."

"I know one Victor for whom that hasn't worked" said Kate, slightly mysteriously.

"Who is that?" asked Preston.

"Oh, just someone I knew a while ago." Said Kate. "Just someone I once knew."

Printed in Great Britain
by Amazon